THE SECOND WOMAN

THE SECOND WOMAN

A Seamus Moynihan Novel

MARK SULLIVAN

For Linda Chester and Joanna Pulcini,
extraordinary friends and agents.

And Cain went out from the presence of the LORD, and dwelt in the land of Nod, on the east of Eden. And Cain knew his wife...

—GENESIS, 4:16–17

CONTENTS

PROLOGUE

*T*he naked man on the bed was dying and he had no idea why.

Moonlight filtered through sheer curtains billowing before a window next to the bed. He smelled the ocean, moaned, and tried to string together thoughts. But there was neither logic nor pattern to the things that flitted through his brain now: the canopy of a lone tree silhouetted in a garden at twilight; the assured, fluid rustle of an invisible animal moving through tall grass; the rubbery tart taste of green apple; the musky redolence that hung in the air after sex. Questions came to him like raindrops: What is my name? How did I get here? What is the fire that has replaced my blood?

He asked himself all these things and could not come up with a single coherent answer; in the last hour his consciousness had been reduced to sensory fragments. No past. No future. Just terrifying blips of the now.

He was aware, for example, that his vision kept blurring yellow, then clearing and blurring again as if he had been cast adrift in a small boat in a sea storm, pelted in the eyes with salt water, able only to see the horizon when he crested the waves. His teeth chattered. His fingers, toes, and scalp prickled and stung. His left thigh and right armpit felt swollen, hollow and tight, throbbing so he swore his skin might burst. Deep in his ears, his own erratic heartbeat backfired.

He lost the instinct to respire. It happened in an instant. Now every breath was cruel labor, a forced expansion of the chest, a deep drawing to fill the lungs. An excruciating pressure built in his skull directly behind his eyes. Scream, *he thought.* Scream and someone will hear you and come to help.

But he managed only an impotent blatting noise. He felt his heart stall, cough, then throttle up again, like an ill-tuned engine choking on stale diesel.

Water, *he thought.* Need water. *He wanted to bring his hands to his mouth, so they might somehow move his tongue aside to let him swallow, but he could not; his wrists seemed anchored above and behind his head. His legs would not move, either.*

For a moment he faded. Then a tremendous cinching occurred inside his rib cage, and he flailed back toward the shore of consciousness. Breathe. Breathe.

His vision was almost gone. Everything in the room, the bed, the ceiling, the curtains, the moonlight, seemed to submerge into a brackish yellow liquid.

Then he was aware of a presence in the liquid with him, a shadowed form that swam his way. The shadow seemed tapered, cowled, vaguely sexual. He caught the scent of caves and rotted logs emanating from somewhere within the form. That and a dry clattering noise.

"Help me," he managed to whisper.

The shadow arched and rose over him. A voice came to him as if through yards and yards of water: "I am helping you: Mark the sixteens…"

The voice continued on, but the man took no heed of the confusing words. He was intent on a sudden weight against his chest, cool, slick, and writhing and the voice in the liquid became a chant heard at a distance.

Something cut jaggedly into the side of his throat. Fluid fire poured into him. He convulsed and fought for air even as his mind seized on a final vision: Heat lightning flashed in a night sky. Cicadas called. Owls screeched. Low, menacing clouds appeared on the horizon and he waited for them on a cliff in a forest of scrub oak, pine, and kudzu. The raindrops became bigger, darker, then turned to sleet. The pattern of the frozen rain became a whirlpool that spun him, then knocked him from his cliff perch, and he fell in spirals into black liquid depths.

ONE

Thirty hours later, at seven forty-five in the morning, clouds the hue of Tahitian pearls rolled in off the Pacific, pushed by a chill, relentless wind that trod down the waves, gnawed the cliffs, and prowled inland. These were unusually harsh conditions for mid-April in a place that rarely sees a bad day weatherwise. But on this Saturday April Fool's morning in La Jolla, California, it was cold. Indeed, if you asked Mary Aboubacar, a chambermaid recently immigrated from Kenya, the air was downright frigid.

Mary shivered, took her eyes off the churning ocean far below, and turned her back to the wind. A tall woman, late twenties, with skin like whipped mocha, she clutched her sweater at the lapels, hoisted a bucket containing her cleaning gear, then hurried along a walkway that curved through the lush courtyard of an apartment complex, aptly, if dully, named Sea View Villas. The facility catered to white-collar workers who toiled on a contract basis for the vibrant San Diego biotechnology industry and rented month-to-month for $1,800 to $2,200. Laundry and maid service, $400 extra.

Mary's supervisor had called at six A.M. to tell her the regular Saturday maid was ill. She was on double overtime, seven units to clean.

She bent her head into the wind. The cement path looped back toward the ocean and building five, a three-story structure that reminded her of one of the embassies in Nairobi. Whitewashed stucco walls, carved wooden doors, and a tiled roof the color of red clay in the highlands where she'd grown up.

Mary set the bucket down at the bottom of the staircase and stood aside as a man rushed down the last flight. Sea View residents all seemed to look alike: young, rich, in such a hurry, and they stayed so little time that she'd long since abandoned her early habit of greeting them. Still, she noticed as he passed that he was white and that she had never seen him before. And she had the impression he was agitated. He lugged a burgundy leather suitcase and soon disappeared toward the parking lot.

Massaging her lower back, Mary lifted the bucket again and climbed three flights of stairs to her first unit. She stopped at the door, rang the bell, waited a minute, then rang again. When no one answered, she unlocked the door and pushed it open a few inches. "Maid service," she called out in her singsong voice. "Anybody home?"

Mary pushed the door wide open. Hesitating, she stepped inside, flipped on the lights, and took in the particulars of the large outer room in a single glance. This was a Gold Level apartment—the views, furniture upgrades. Sliding glass doors led to a balcony overlooking the ocean. Bone curtains, drawn. Off-white carpet. Glass coffee table, tan leather sofa, and love seat arranged before an entertainment center. Beyond a bar-height counter lay a small kitchen, appliances in stainless steel.

The place looked like it had just been cleaned. No newspapers strewn about. No dishes in the sink. Carpet vacuumed. The faint smell of bleach in the air.

From her pocket, Mary pulled out a piece of paper and checked what she'd scrawled there—*building five, unit nine*—against the numbers on the outer door. She shrugged and smiled at her good fortune. She could claim the unit as done without having to work a lick.

Ready to leave and go have a couple of smokes in her secret place out on the cliff, she thought to at least check the rest of the apartment. Down the hall, past a framed photograph of the outer Coronado Islands at sunset, the young maid frowned at red candle wax in the carpet right in front of the closed door to the bedroom. A stench reached her and she paused, thinking that the current resident—she didn't even know his name—had been using the bathroom when she'd rung the bell and called out.

She knocked. "Hello?" Hearing nothing, she twisted the handle, then pushed at the door, and felt a strong wind coming through the bedroom window. Mary took one look inside the bedroom and jumped back in abject terror.

"Ebola!" she screamed, racing down the hallway. "Ebola!"

Two

Some sixteen miles away on a field of dreams in North Park, a considerably less tony part of San Diego, Jimmy Moynihan was experiencing his first crucifixion.

It was the bottom of the first and he'd given up three hits, walked two, and was now behind three-and-oh on the best hitter in the league, a brute named Rafael Quintana, who, at twelve years old, had the first shade of a mustache on his upper lip and sported shoulders that suggested his old man had been force-feeding him testosterone-producing supplements.

"C'mon, Jimbo, fire one by him," I called from a fence along the right-field line. "Gimme a strike, here."

Jimmy didn't look my way from behind his wire-rimmed glasses. He seemed somewhere else, playing with the ball behind his back. Unsure of himself. A bad thing for a pitcher. Like myself at age ten, he's a tall, skinny kid with freckles, thick dark hair and a mouth full of braces. And, like myself, he was blessed early on with deceptive arm strength and fluid coordination. But as I've learned over the years, there are days you've got control and days you don't, and so far that dank morning my one and only offspring looked like he never did.

He went into his windup. I lobbed a silent prayer to the god of Little League, then shuddered at a sinker that did not sink. Jimmy delivered a deli sandwich, middle of the plate, thigh-high. Rafael pulverized it. Three runs scored. And I felt like the guy Paul Newman kicks in the balls in *Butch Cassidy and the Sundance Kid*.

I suppose I expected tears from Jimmy. That's usually what happens when young kids get hammered. But his eyes flared up with rage and he began kicking at the mound.

"What do you think?" asked Don Stetson, my assistant coach, a fit little dude who worships me because once upon a time, many, many moons ago, I actually pitched in the major leagues. Even if it was only for nineteen games.

"I think we ought to check Rafael's birth certificate, see if he's old enough to down a few Coronas with us after the game. Maybe throw in a blood test or two."

"C'mon, Shay," Don pleaded. "We're getting crushed here."

"I know. Shit, I hate this part," I replied, stepping onto the field to yell, "Time."

I walked across the infield toward Jimmy, who was doing his best to dig an irrigation ditch on the mound. He would not look at me.

"Buncha balls been heading that a way," I said, nodding at the left-field fence.

"I'm fine, everyone and everything's fine," Jimmy replied. "Leave me in."

"Getting shelled happens to everyone sooner or later."

"Not to you."

"You got a lot to learn about your old man."

"Mom says that all the time."

"Savvy woman, your mom."

"She isn't trying to be nice."

"Imagine that," I said. "Look, send the Lawton kid in and take his place in right field. Do me proud out there, okay? Never quit, right?"

He looked up at me and replied with sarcasm, "Never quit. Right, Dad. I'll remember that." Then he slapped the ball in my hand, turned, and stormed toward left. I watched him go a moment, then shook my head and started back to the dugout, wondering why boys have to begin learning about the harshness of life after only a decade on earth.

My ex-wife, Fay, watched me from the bleachers. Even in cutoff shorts and an old sweatshirt, she looked stunning. Her sun-streaked crimson hair fell in chaos about her shoulders, framing freckled cheeks, an aquiline nose, and lips half twisted up in bemusement, half down in despair, as if she alone appreciated the irony of life's cruel jokes. But it was the opal eyes that got me—that always got me—eyes laced with clouds, able to look right through me. Half our problem.

I caught her attention and shrugged. She did not smile, but arched her eyebrows and turned to talk with her latest beau. This one, Walter Patterson, liked to garden, bake bread, drum, go to poetry slams, and take long walks on the beach—all this when he wasn't toiling as chief resident of emergency medicine at the UCSD Medical Center, the largest hospital in the county.

Walter had regular hours, never missed an appointment, never broke a promise, never screwed around, never sabotaged, and let Fay control the boundaries of their relationship. Probably his main attraction, I thought, turning back to the game.

Luckily, the Lawton kid got us out of the inning. Soon enough we had two on in the second, with no outs and Jimmy on deck. The beeper on my hip lit off.

"Son of a bitch," I said, seeing the number. I got my cell phone and walked around the back of the dugout. "This better be good. My kid's up next."

"Sorry, Sergeant," replied the silky voice of Lieutenant Anna Cleary, the watch commander. "We've got a body. County is hauling moon suits to the scene."

"Moon suits?"

"Patrol says there could be a biohazard. Rogers doesn't want to take any chances. Neither does the medical examiner."

"Wonderful."

"Thought I'd make your day."

8

"You're always kind to the downtrodden, Anna," I said.

"Only to you, Shay," she replied.

"Address?"

"Sea View Villas, La Jolla."

"Death among the brilliant, the superrich, and the fleeting doyens of DNA," I said, then hung up and came back around the dugout to find Jimmy at the plate. As he dug in he looked up at me with those please-don't-go eyes I've learned to live with the past five years. I lifted my badge from its lanyard around my neck. At the sight of it, his expression moved toward anger again, then he turned his attention from me, the weight of the world in his bat, a weight somehow connected to the shoveled-out feeling that always spreads through my gut whenever I have to leave him like this.

THREE

Twenty minutes later, I pulled into Sea View Villas and parked my 1967 metallic-green Corvette, about the only thing in my life I've managed to maintain in mint condition. I almost never drive the old muscle car when I'm on rotation. The department gives me an unmarked Plymouth sedan for my excursions into the dark side of San Diego. But Jimmy loves the Monster, and it was my turn that morning to drive him to his game. Giving him a ride in an old Corvette is the least I can do for him, considering.

Mist and fog hung thick over the parking lot when I climbed out. And the air was heavy with the scent of the sea as I walked toward the uniformed patrol officers standing at the rear doors to a white van belonging to the San Diego County Hazardous Materials Response team. The flashing cruiser lights caught the fog in a weird blue strobe effect and I stopped, stricken with the image of a much younger Seamus Michael Moynihan, twenty-one to be exact, clicking on spikes down a shadowed tunnel tainted with sweat, glory, and soon-to-be shattered dreams.

These flashbacks to an earlier me had been happening with increasing and frustrating regularity the few months prior to Mary Aboubacar's discovery of the body: I would encounter the apparatus of death investigations and my mind would spin back to a youthful me walking down that tunnel toward brilliant sunlight and a roaring crowd.

I stop just shy of the light, look at my glove, and think I'm going to puke. Then the gathered voices of the park become irresistibly deafening, like sirens that draw me out into the light and the storied confines of Fenway.

During warm-ups I don't let myself look at the crowd. I stay focused on my catcher, on his mitt, on the shimmering grass, on the moist, red clay between us. And every once in a while, between pitches, I allow myself a glance at that wall rising impossibly high out there in left. Then the national anthem ends and I take the mound, oblivious to the fact that this will be my last outing as a major leaguer.

Between each pitch of my final warm-up, I finally allow myself to look across the third-base line into the stands. At first the crowd appears as a blur composed of thousands of bits of moving, screaming color, an impressionist painting come to life.

Then individual faces leap out at me, all female. The redhead near the corner of the backstop winks. I swear I know her. The brunette three rows behind the Yankees dugout raises her beer and I'm unsure.

The blonde beyond third base holds up a hotel room key, but I turn away, startled: *I do know her.*

The umpire yells, "Play ball!" Just before the batter steps into the box, I take one last look at the crowd, way out past the blonde, deep into the grand-stands that abut the Green Monster. A man stands there. He's rawboned, wears a blue polo shirt, and sports a startling shock of red hair. For a second I'm befuddled. He looks just like my dad. And it's like my whole past and future is contained in this one moment. *This one moment.*

I blink, shake my head, and he's gone. A ghost. A specter that haunts me to this day. Everything else changes, but these things never do. The constants of my life: baseball, women, and death.

Chill rain spit out of the fog, shaking me from my memories. I ran the rest of the way to the HazMat van. And soon a tech was helping me into one of those suits you might see on the swank set at Chernobyl. We had no idea if it was Ebola, but we weren't taking any chances.

As I tightened the pants' waist, the patrolmen gath-ered at the rear of the van stood aside for a swarthy man wearing a blue Homicide windbreaker. Detective Rikko Varjjan was in his early forties, an even six feet tall, two hundred hard pounds, with close-cropped salt-and-pepper hair and a diamond in his left ear.

"How we doing?" I asked.

"Missy, she talks to the super," Rikko grunted in the thickly accented English of an Israeli.

"Jorge's with the maid. Me? Praying for suicide, what else?"

"Detective Varjjan, you never give up on the possibility of suicide, do you?" snorted Dr. Marshall Solomon, the San Diego County medical examiner, who stood beside me, being strapped into his own biohazard suit.

Rikko's face clouded. "You call suicide, I go home, see my babies' ballet recital. I try not to miss those things because some fool decides death is better than life."

I smiled. Rikko's always coming up with stuff like that. His father was a Hungarian Jew who survived Treblinka, then emigrated to Israel, where he married an American visiting from San Diego. Like all Israeli youth do, he had served in the military. Rikko had been a commando patrolling the streets of Jerusalem during the *intifada* of the late 1980's. Afterward he went to work for the Jerusalem Police Department, eventually becoming a top homicide detective in the holy city.

Seven years ago, while working a case that brought him to San Diego, Rikko met me, and through me he met my sister, and they fell in love. He was bitter about life in Israel and applied for work with the San Diego PD. With his dual citizenship and remarkable background, he was soon hired. His strong-arm tactics make some higher-ups queasy. But he's extremely effective. He's also funny and my best friend.

Ordinarily, Rikko is pretty much unflappable. But right then, standing at the rear of the van, a look of anxiousness crossed his face. "Doc, you seen this Ebola before?"

Solomon, an angular man with a silver goatee, shook his head. "But we had a case of hantavirus, a distant relative of Ebola, out in East County a few years back. Autopsy was a nightmare. State health insisted we build a sealed container to perform it in."

I cringed and asked the biohazards tech to put more duct tape on my wrists as a stocky Asian woman hustled through the rain toward us, carrying a Starbucks cup and a slim white notebook.

"Got a preliminary ID on the victim, Sarge," she said.

"Gimme."

"Morgan Cook, Jr.," she began. "Biotech researcher for Double Helix, Inc. Been here three months on and off. Married. Kids. House up north of L.A. Normally goes home on weekends. The super says he has no complaints against him. Kept to himself."

"The maid sure about Ebola?" Rikko demanded.

Solomon's face screwed up. "Sure she's sure," he snapped. "She's got a Ph.D. in cleanology and that gives her the ability to diagnose one of the world's rarest and deadliest viruses."

"I don't know, Doc," Missy said, waving the notebook at him. "She says she worked as a nurse's aide at a hospital in Nairobi and saw bodies like that before."

Even buffered by the department issue raincoat, Missy Pan looked like an athlete. In college, she was second team all-American field hockey midfielder. She has the most powerful legs and the broadest shoulders of any woman I've ever known. No matter what she does to soften her big frame, it is there—this coiled power in her carriage that always makes me think of her as a not-so-hidden dragon with fierce determination, a contagious laugh, and the ability to work twenty-four hours straight and never yawn. Not once.

Solomon scowled at her. "We'll check it out for ourselves, thank you, Detective."

I said, "Anyone know what Cook was working on at that biotech firm? Maybe a virus we should know about?"

"I'll get on that," Missy promised. She turned and marched off toward her car.

Rikko looked after her through the steady rain toward the yellow barrier tape on the staircase of building five. "Think there's any way you can commit suicide by Ebola?"

"Bet it happens all the time," I replied. "In Mombasa."

Four

"One small step for Moynihan," I said, pushing open the apartment door, still ajar after Mary Aboubacar's flight.

"One giant leap for America's finest PD," Dr. Solomon chortled in return, his transmission crackly and hollow. We carried cameras, mine a Polaroid, his a Nikon.

At an ordinary death scene, Solomon and I would have been accompanied by a team of evidence experts. But this was so far from common we had decided to make a preliminary visit to evaluate what precautions we should take if Cook had in fact died of Ebola. I reached the doorway to the bedroom. Rain poured in the open window, slanting through the room. Water puddled on the carpet and peppered the mirror on the far wall. The body was on the bed.

"Christ almighty," I muttered.

As a cop I had seen the gamut: decomposing corpses, floaters, the worst gunshots and multiple stabbings you could imagine. But I had never seen anything like this and it triggered in me a rolling vertigo I had first experienced at age ten, a sensation of being Tilt-A-Whirled, a feeling that once experienced you never, ever forget.

"Christ almighty is right," Solomon said. "Shoot him *in situ* before we go in."

I nodded, swallowed, called up the professional numbness necessary to deal with the situation, then flipped on the weak ceiling light over the bed and fumbled with the Polaroid. I squeezed off ten pictures while Solomon shot with the Nikon.

"As usual the light is horrible, but I think that should cover us," I said, then pointed across the room to the window. "I'm gonna get that shut."

"Don't get near anything sharp that could cut your suit," Solomon cautioned. "The latest research suggests Ebola's not airborne. But let's not take any chances."

"Believe me, Doc, I'm not making any big moves here."

The flooring was crème carpet and crunched against the sole of the booties that covered my sneakers. I moved past a pine armoire, a blue suitcase, and a matching computer satchel before stepping gingerly through the puddled water to the double-hung window and pressing it closed. I turned, peering through the hood visor at a sopping, low pine credenza below a fogged and dripping mirror. A man's toiletry kit and its partially spilled and rain-soaked contents covered the chest: Gillette shaving gel, Rogaine, Dial deodorant, Southern Nights men's cologne, and an open box of Sheik condoms.

The bedsteads to either side of the wrought-iron four-poster matched the armoire and the credenza and were topped with lamps that echoed the rusty accents on the entire set. It could have been one of those soft-lensed scenes in the Pottery Barn catalog.

Except for the corpse.

He lay spread-eagle and nude, facing upright in the middle of the bed. The mauve top sheet, white cotton blanket, and comforter were kicked back below his feet. He had the shaggy, sun-bleached hair of a surfer. His head was arched backward, his torso canted to the left, as if he had shifted against agony in his last moments. His skin was mottled black, grotesquely swollen, the distension and bruising most pronounced along his right thigh and left arm, so inflated they looked like charred quarter kegs of beer. Where the swelling was worst, the skin appeared beaded, as if decorated with scores of ruby rhinestones, most the size of dimes, but some the size of dollar pieces. At least a dozen of the beads had burst. Blood and fluid had run from the sores and dried on his arms and legs in mosaics of pale crimson watercolor. Tears of dried blood showed on his cheeks. Dried blood caked the oval of his slack mouth, like lipstick applied by an Alzheimer's patient. A dirty copper rivulet twisted across the white sheets from high between his legs.

On the stand to the right of the bed lay a wallet and a framed picture lying facedown. I set the camera on the floor, turned the frame over, and saw a handsome man in his mid-thirties with a surfer's hairdo and a rugged, muscular build. He sat on a rock, flanked by a pretty, plump blond woman and two young children, one boy, one girl. They all wore khaki shorts and blue polo shirts. A posed professional family portrait.

I set it down and reached for the wallet. The gloves of the bio-hazard suit were cumbersome and the wallet's contents dumped on the floor: credit cards, business cards, membership in the Texas A&M Alumni Association, and a California driver's license, all in the same name.

"Morgan Cook, Jr., what the hell happened to you?" I muttered into the mike.

Solomon, on the other side of the corpse, now looked up at me. His voice came crackling over my earphones. "Good question."

"Ms. Africa's off base with her diagnosis?"

"He's bled at the major orifices, consistent with Ebola. The discoloration and obliteration of the vascular system too. And victims of Ebola and its associated viruses often display bulla—these bubbles and beads here on the skin. He's been dead awhile, probably more than a day, so some of what we're seeing is putrefaction. But what doesn't jibe with Ebola is the right leg, left arm, and the head and neck."

"Okay?" I said.

"If it was Ebola, why would these appendages present such gross edema in relation to the rest of the body?" Solomon pondered aloud. "Why wouldn't the entire body be uniformly distorted? And look at the left wrist and right ankle."

I had to shift to see exactly what he was talking about. Then I made it out: Both joints looked like the pinch points of hourglasses, and the color of the skin there was the blackest and shiniest on the body. "What the hell caused that?" I asked.

Solomon pointed to the right wrist and then the left ankle, the ones that were not as swollen, black, and shiny. "Same thing that caused the three uninterrupted striations around these other joints."

"Ropes."

"As restraints," Solomon said.

Then the medical examiner leaned over to bring the face of his visor close to the blood blisters and open sores on the corpse's neck. After a moment's study he stood and tore off the hood. "Can't see for shit with this damn thing on," he said.

I looked at him like he was nuts. *"Doc, you're exposing yourself—"*

"It's not Ebola, Shay," he said grimly. "This man died of envenomation."

"Envenawhat?"

"Snakebite."

"Snakebite did all this?"

Solomon nodded. "Certain kinds of venom destroys flesh and the vascular systems, much like Ebola. And it can create exactly these kind of blood blisters and swelling over time. But I've never seen anyone get hit this bad. From the looks of it, Cook was probably bitten multiple times. We'll have to go over his body with magnification to find the fang marks."

I looked from the rope abrasions to the drum-like swellings on Cook's body and felt myself take another ride on the mental Tilt-A-Whirl. "What kind of twisted bastard gets someone naked, ties them up, then releases a snake on their body?"

"You're the homicide genius of San Diego, my friend. You tell me."

FIVE

The san diego police Department investigates death differently than most metropolitan law enforcement agencies. As evidenced ad nauseam in movies and television series, unexplained bodies with temperatures of less than ninety degrees in Los Angeles, Chicago, and New York are handled by detectives working in pairs. Not so here beside Mexico and the fair Pacific. We work in teams: four detectives plus a sergeant.

The system works. San Diego boasts the highest clearance rate of any homicide department in the country. For three years running my team—Rikko Varjjan, Missy Pan, Jorge Zapata, and Freddie Burnette—posted the highest clearance rate of any in the homicide division. Why? Because we were an experiment that worked.

The idea, which was largely an extrapolation of modern community-based policing theories, was to put together a homicide squad that better reflected the cultural melting pot that is San Diego. The approach met great resistance at first, and in some quarters still does. But because my team can slip inside the various civilizations of the city, our solve rate remained unparalleled for nearly thirty-six months.

Four weeks before Cook's body was discovered, however, Freddie Burnette, one of my best detectives, blitzed her knee chasing a suspect. Shorthanded since she'd gone on medical leave, I'd been working open cases as well as attending to my administrative duties. Our clearance rate was down and I was feeling the pressure from on high, specifically from Lieutenant Aaron Fraiser, my boss. And, indeed, not five minutes after Solomon and I exited the apartment, Lieutenant Fraiser came striding up the path. He's a pink-skinned, slope-shouldered, shaved-headed, large-lobed ex-Marine who's never particularly cared for me, because, among other things, he suspects quite correctly that I'm responsible for his departmental nickname: The Prick with Ears. He looked ticked, an expression that deepened when he saw me, Rikko, and Missy standing there.

"Great, the PCPD is on the case," he grumbled. "What's the story?"

I laid it out for him. He listened, grimacing. "Who's principal?" Principal death-scene investigator is a rotational assignment. The job requires the administration of all evidence at a murder scene. The principal is also charged with running the "murder book"—the evidential story of the slaying that the district attorney's office will ultimately rely upon to present its case in court. Ordinarily supervising sergeants do not act as principals, but given our shorthanded situation, I was not about to stuff the duty down someone else's throat. "Yours truly."

Fraiser's ears flattened against the side of his head. "God help us."

"Your confidence in me is, as always, overwhelming."

The Prick went half-lidded, then marched off to make sure the Sea View Villas perimeter was secure. As luck would have it, the clouds opened wide right then and full sails of rain billowed across the courtyard. Fraiser was drenched in five seconds. Life is beautiful like that from time to time.

Over the next six and a half hours, the criminalists collected evidence. As principal investigator, I focused on keeping a catalog of what they were finding, which wasn't much at first. The furniture, countertops, and glassware in the kitchen had all been wiped clean. So had the doorknobs, interior and exterior. Dr no had been dumped into the drains of the bathroom sink and tub, then flushed out.

The only solid prints, besides Mary Aboubacar's, were on the lamp on the bedstead, on the bars of the headboard, and on the cologne bottle next to the toiletry kit. We had better luck gathering fibers and hairs on the rugs, upholstery, and floors. Indeed, too much luck: Despite the fact that Sea View Villas had a policy of steam cleaning at each tenant turnover, thirteen different hair samples were discovered on the carpet in the bedroom, in the bathroom, and buried in the rug fibers in the hallway and the living/dining area. In a closet off the kitchen, we found an electric broom and bagged the contents for lab analysis. In Cook's toiletry kit, we noted a vial of Wellbutrin, an antianxiety drug.

Then, under clothes in the suitcase, Rikko turned up an interesting twist: the current volume of *Ménage,* a pornographic magazine dedicated to two-on-one sex. There were graphic photo spreads throughout of both varieties of the fetish: two men servicing one woman, and two women with one man. Hidden behind the entertainment center was a DVD disc dedicated to the same turn-on.

"Mr. Cook had a secret life," Rikko said, waving the disc at me.

"Imagine that," I said.

On the posts of the wrought-iron bed, the techs found green nylon fibers, the sort woven together to create parachute cord. On the railings of the headboard there were clusters of prints as if they had been grabbed at from many angles. The sheets showed specks of abraded bloody skin, dried seminal fluid, vaginal discharge, and a lubricant like K-Y jelly. Oddly, we were able to come up with only blond hairs, head and pubic, in the bedroom. In the folds of the blanket, however, we at last stumbled on evidence to corroborate Solomon's belief that Cook died of snakebite: two ragged pieces of skin, one about the size of a thumbnail, the other triangular and larger.

"Rattler?" Rikko asked, holding up the evidence bag to a light in the living room as Solomon helped wheel Cook's body from the apartment on a gurney.

"Assume so," I said, looking out the window. "We'll have to find someone who knows how to identify these things. I can just hear the defense attorney tearing us apart for not knowing exactly what kind of snake the skin came from."

Missy entered. "Just talked to Alfred Woolsley CEO of Double Helix, Inc."

"Uh-huh?"

She took a belt of her latte, then went on. "He hired Cook away from Biogen four months ago to lead research into a promising new treatment for renal failure. Cook and his wife, Sophia, wanted their kids to finish out the school year before making the move from Westlake Village. Cook lived here and made the five-hour commute north every other weekend. Woolsley described Cook as a hardworking scientist: driven, brilliant, moody at times, a man who spent his free time training for mini-triathlons. He said Cook left work Thursday at noon to prepare to put his home on the market. Cook's secretary said he had a meeting set for two P.M. on Friday with a Sotheby's Realty agent."

"You call the agent?" Rikko grunted.

"Way ahead of you," she said. "Cook didn't show, never called to cancel."

I frowned. "So we've got almost seventy-two hours unaccounted for between his time of departure from Double Helix and the discovery of his corpse."

"Correct," Missy said. "And his wife said she hadn't heard from him since Wednesday morning. She's down at a resort in Los Cabos, vacationing with her kids and in-laws. I called from Double Helix."

"How'd she take it?" I asked.

"Devastated," Missy said, sobering. "She'll be on the first plane north."

Jorge Zapata entered the apartment carrying a police artist's sketch. He'd spent the morning working with Mary Aboubacar to come up with a drawing of the man she'd seen leaving building five: big-jawed, narrow-nosed, with irises riding high in his sockets, lips thin and drawn, brown hair slicked back.

"You shown this door to door yet?" I asked.

"Whole place," Jorge said, shaking his head. "Maid's the only one who saw him."

Jorge is thirty-two, five ten, with thick, curly black hair, a single weird eyebrow that stretches like a woolly caterpillar from one side of his face to the other, and a lithe body from years of cross-country running. He's a rising star in the department, made detective in the minimum seven years of duty, and an expert with computers.

"Walk the perimeter outside the tape," I said. "Record all license plate numbers and watch for this guy among the lookie-Lous. Don't talk to the reporters."

"Right," Jorge said, then zipped up his rain jacket and headed back outside.

It was nearly three-thirty in the afternoon by then and the storm was easing. Far out on the ocean a shaft of sunlight bore down on arched, ivory-tipped swells that put me in mind of so many teeth gnashing. I glanced again at the sketch. The face was drawn, with tense cheek muscles, furrowed brows, and stretched lips. For an instant I flashed on the image of a wet dock at night and a man crouching behind wooden crates. For that instant the crouching man bore the face of the man in this sketch, the man Mary Aboubacar saw.

I looked up from the drawing, slightly flushed, feeling agitated. An evidence tech was striding down the bedroom hallway toward me, a stricken expression on her face.

"Sergeant, I ... uh," she stammered. "I decided to run luminol over all the surfaces in the bedroom and ... I guess all that rain must have been preventing us from seeing it at first. You better come take a look at this."

Luminol is a chemical that reacts with the iron in hemoglobin to cause a blue glowing effect called chemiluminescence. We use it to find blood, even the smallest trace.

I shook off the image of the man on the dock and hurried after the criminologist. I halted in the bedroom doorway, stunned to see great, glowing swirls that the chemical had raised on the mirror, and within the swirls nine blurry words:

Joy unspeakable to be holding death in your hands.

SIX

It was after seven P.M. by the time I finished writing up my initial report, put it on Lieutenant Fraiser's desk, and trudged to my parking spot in the lot outside downtown headquarters. I climbed into the Green Monster, turned the ignition, and took solace in the awesome rumble of its 427-cubic-inch engine.

A breeze had picked up, drying the pavement by the time I accelerated up the ramp to the 163, a freeway that runs a winding course through the bottom of a steep-sided canyon. I rolled down the window and stomped on the gas, letting the old Corvette's four hundred horses press me back into the leather bucket seats while the cool night air whipped around me, swirling away the awful image of Morgan Cook and the bloody message the killer had left on the mirror.

I've had the Green Monster since the day I signed with the Boston Red Sox, end of my sophomore year at Stanford. Other guys bought spanking-new Porsches or BMWs with their signing bonuses. But growing up back in Roslindale, then a blue-collar neighborhood of greater Boston, there was a plumber down the street who had a cherry-condition lacquer-black '67 Vette with chrome sidepipes. From the rear, it looked like the head of a dragonfly. From the front, it was angular and menacing, like its namesake, the stingray. I loved to ride my bike down the street and just look at the '67 whenever the plumber would bring it out into his driveway for a tune-up or to wax it on a sunny summer day. All I wanted was a ride, but I never had the courage to ask.

Then one day, out of the blue, the plumber pulled into our driveway, knocked on the door, and asked my mom if it would be all right if he took me for a ride. I guess he'd heard that my dad had been killed the night before, but he never mentioned it. I strapped myself into the passenger seat. He took us out on I-93, heading south along the coast through Dorchester toward Quincy. The windows were down and we were pushing ninety. The salt air of the Atlantic whipped all around me, stung my eyes, and swirled away the gut-wrenching vision of my mother sobbing her soul out at the kitchen table.

Even now, nearly twenty eight years later, a ride in my '67 can help keep the things I see as a cop from eating at me. And by the time I reached Interstate 8, the main east-west corridor in San Diego, I was feeling a little better about life.

A more normal Saturday night for me would have required a race north to Del Mar, where a funky little bar attracts a crowd of smart, beautiful women to its unplugged rock-'n'-roll series. But something about the shitty tenor of the day checked my appetite for companionship, and I found myself just wanting to drive. I made a grand loop through Mission Valley back toward downtown and eventually up onto the arched bridge that links the mainland to Coronado Island. Coming off the bridge, I navigated through the backstreets toward the island's west side.

Thirty years ago, Coronado was a sleepy, conservative place populated by U.S. Navy brass. Today the island is San Diego's silk-stocking suburb, a chunk of real estate as pricey as any in California. Shacks fetch more than a million bucks, then are torn down and replaced with starter castles for the rich-and-think-they're-famous.

Six blocks north of the Hotel Del Coronado, I found the correct side street and parked the Monster under palms that crowded a high stucco wall. Above the wall, in the light thrown by the street lamp, the weathered shake shingles and gables of the house appeared. A red plank door hung inside wild roses that clung to the archway that defined a gate. For a long moment I sat there, looking at the door as if it defined a lifetime.

Then I climbed out and opened the gate. The yard was dominated by a pool Fay had installed the year before. Beyond it stood a small greenhouse. There were more orchids than I remembered, at least three hundred different plants by then, many of them flowering in pots set about the pool.

Through the sliding glass door I could see Jimmy sitting on the floor, still in his baseball pants, watching Nickelodeon. Fay washed dishes in the kitchen. She'd changed into overalls that somehow made her look better than ever.

I rapped on the glass nearest Jimmy. His mother saw me and scowled. Jimmy looked up, hesitated, then brightened and ran to the door. "Hey, Dad," he said.

"Hey, Jimbo," I said, giving him a hug. "How'd the rest of the game go?"

"Rained out in the fourth," he said. "But I got a double. Are all the rods ready for tomorrow? How's your case?"

I winced. "My case is nasty, sport. So no fishing trip tomorrow."

"What?" he asked, the disappointment palpable in his voice.

"We're shorthanded these days and this is one of the worst I've ever seen."

Even as he nodded, Jimmy's eyes drifted from me, his face molding into an expression I'd always thought was Fay's sole possession: a rubber mask of skepticism and confusion. "What about next Sunday?" he asked. "If you solve the case, I mean."

"Next Sunday it is," I promised.

Behind me, my ex cleared her throat. "Can I talk to you outside, please?"

I popped Jimmy lightly in the shoulder. "I'll be at all your practices this week."

"Sure," Jimmy said, forcing a smile on his face before returning to his cartoons. Fay led me outside and closed the glass door. The perfume of orchids was thick in the still air. She rubbed the back of her hand against her forehead, a sure sign she was about to preach a litany of my shortcomings.

"I'd appreciate it if you called ahead to say you were stopping by," she began. "If I wanted to be a jerk, I could enforce the custody agreement to a tee. But I don't, so I'd appreciate the civility of a phone call before you arrive. Even amoebas have cells, Shay."

"Yeah. Sorry. Walter here?"

"That's none of your business. And that's the second time in a row you've stood your son up on a fishing trip."

The anger that pulsed through me was immediately doused with regret and guilt.

"Can't be helped. The victim was slain nightmare fashion. He's about my age. I feel personal with this one."

Fay studied me with those all-knowing cloudy opal eyes. "You always make it so personal when you're dealing with a corpse, Shay. How come you can't feel the same about the living? You see that boy in there? He's yours, but you don't put him first. He looks up to you and too often you're not seeing him looking. Pretty soon he's going to start looking past you."

"That what you did?"

Fay got a pained, ironic smile on her face. "No, that's what you did to me."

We stood there not saying anything, feeling the weight of the years we'd spent together hanging between us like a shifting, liquid weight. I got suddenly weary.

"Look, can we save this for another time? I got a medical question. For Walter."

"And what am I?"

"Not looking for a neonatal expert, sweetness. I need his expertise."

Fay considered me a moment. "You'll play nice?"

"Don't I always?"

"No," she said, then shrugged and turned toward the house. "Wait here."

She soon returned followed by a wiry, bearded man in a tan sweat suit and Birkenstock sandals. When he saw me standing in the open doorway, his hands flexed to fists, opened, and flexed again. "Fay says you need my help?"

"Yeah, Walt, you see many snakebites? In the ER, I mean."

Walter knows I know he hates being called Walt and he grimaced, but replied, "We get our share. People exploring the canyons, mostly out in east county. Past few have been transients and itinerant agricultural workers. Why?"

"Working a case involving death by snakebite. How many you see a year?"

"Fifteen, maybe twenty. Rarely fatal if we see them within the first hour or two. The antivenin serums are quite effective. We use CroFab, the new synthetic."

"Bad way to go if you don't get the serum?"

"There a good way?" Walter sniffed.

"Guess not," I said. "But that doesn't answer the question."

Walter's hands stopped flexing. "Patients who've been bitten describe it as excruciatingly painful. In the advanced stages of envenomization they say you forget who you are, what you are, even that a snake bit you. You know you are dying, but you don't know why. It's brutal, physically and psychologically."

"Why psychologically?"

Walter had the upper hand now and knew it. His voice took on the inflection of a medical resident lecturing an intern.

"There's the initial shock of being bitten, of course, which generates its own terror and adrenaline surge—essential to control if you're going to survive," he said. "Countering that need is the fact that you know you've been bitten and you know you've got a limited time in which to live. There would have to be a period of extreme torment before the reasoning faculties became too clouded to function properly. It's one thing to die, Moynihan. It's another thing to know it quite clearly, especially when it comes from the mouth of something so archetypically evil."

SEVEN

A half hour later, I parked the Green Monster in a garage on Shelter Island, about ten miles north of Coronado, then walked toward the marina where I live. Gravel crackled under my shoes. The sweet scents of wisteria mingled in the salt air. My thoughts were on Walter's take on death by snakebite.

Archetypically evil. Much as I hated to admit it, Fay's boyfriend was right: Cook's murder was cold, calculated, and designed to induce abject terror into his very soul. I was dealing with a torture killing as sadistic as any I'd encountered.

I unlocked the gate to the marina and went toward the docks and out across the wooden planking to Z-30, the last slip in the westernmost row of slips, the berth closest to where the harbor becomes the breakwater and beyond it the open sea. My home is a forty-two-foot light ocean vessel, a flybridge cruiser with a three-hundred-mile range. She boasts twin 530-horsepower Cat diesels, capable of powering her along at thirty-one knots. Satellite communications system, Loran, Sonar, GPS, and a computer in the cockpit. Full marlin setup, including fighting chair on the aft deck. She's sleek, with an aerodynamic hull and superstructure.

My late ex-father-in-law, Harry Gordon, spent two years designing the boat and overseeing its construction. Harry made a nice little bundle providing seed money to start-ups in the field of handheld communications, a staple of the San Diego economy. The marlin boat was to be Harry's final payoff, the big pat on the back for a life well done. But a week before she was to be christened, he had a heart attack and died. He hadn't yet named his vessel.

Fay and I were separated at the time. Her mom got the house with the view up on Mount Soledad and most of Harry's money. Fay got the boat and enough cash that she doesn't have to work, though she still does, as a doctor in the preemie ward at the UCSD medical center. California is a fifty-fifty-split state. Shortly before our divorce became final, we decided Jimmy should stay in the only home he'd ever known. Fay offered me Harry's boat. I refused. But she insisted that she could not afford the upkeep, yet wanted the vessel to remain in the family. Besides, it would be a familiar place for Jimmy to visit.

Five years ago, the night our divorce became final, I lay below deck on my nameless boat, drinking my fifth brew of the night and watching a *National Geographic* special on the Tuareg people of Niger. The Tuareg rode camels in long caravans out over the sea of sand, hauling salt from mines in the farthest reaches of the Sahara Desert. They wore shiny indigo turbans that blued their smooth brown skin. They squatted on their haunches around sparking campfires, drinking tea and singing in strange trilling voices that raised the hair on the back of my neck. I had no idea what the words meant, but the narrator said their song described the pain of a life without attachment.

I stumbled to the refrigerator, got the champagne, went out into the night, and broke the bottle over the bow, christening my new home the *Nomad's Chant.*

I keyed my code into the *Chant's* security system, then boarded the aft deck and entered the cabin. Flipping the lights on in the galley, I got a Fat Tire Amber from the fridge, then went forward through the small salon to the cockpit. I checked the computer for any diagnostic alerts, then shut down the security system and went below deck.

My stateroom is ample, with a king-size sleigh-style bed and wood paneling crafted in Brazil. Tax returns were stacked atop the drop-down desk. Piles of novels and biographies stood inside open cabinets. Empty CD cases lay on the stereo. There was a smell in the air that surprised me. It was the first tinge of an odor I had encountered in a dozen dark apartments before—the bitter, alkaline scent of the aging male living alone.

Before I could drop fully into melancholy, I put on a sweatshirt and padded down the hall past the stateroom Jimmy uses when he sleeps over. My old

Red Sox jersey, number 67, hangs in a frame on the wall above his bed. The sheets were still rumpled and I almost went in to straighten them, but decided to leave them that way as I often do when I know he won't be around for a while. I finished the beer, got another—my limit—then sat at the table off the galley with a yellow legal pad before me.

Joy unspeakable to be holding death in your hands.

You spend your early years as an athlete and you learn to play to your strengths. My fastball topped out in the mid-nineties. My curve and change-up were solid. But that was the extent of my repertoire. My sinker and slider came and went. I never got the hang of a splitter. But what I lacked in technical versatility, I made up for with raw strength and an ability to get in the heads of the batters facing me, to understand their desires, then select the exact pitch in my arsenal that exploited those hungers.

I do the same as a homicide detective. There are others in the unit, Jorge and Missy, for example, better at gathering evidence and chasing down leads. Rikko is gifted at sweating a suspect. He uses a patented guerrilla-on-peyote act that scares the living shit out of them. My forte is analysis: taking the pieces of the puzzle as they come, using my imagination to arrange them into the landscape of what must have occurred.

Joy unspeakable to be holding death in your hands.

The words provoked the disturbing vision of a snake arching its belly across outstretched palms. The head glided toward a naked Morgan Cook, frantic in his restraints. The thin-lipped man in the police artist sketch turned rapturous. His hands quivered ever so slightly when the viper bit.

A pressure built inside my head as the vision unfolded. My temples throbbed. My mind flashed again on that image of a rain-soaked dock at night and the man hiding in the shadows behind the empty crates, clutching a shotgun. My heart beat hard, my throat constricted, and I had a panicked need for fresh air.

I grabbed the beer, went up on the bridge, and stood there calming myself down, telling myself these flashbacks were nothing. After many minutes I felt calm enough to sit down in the captain's chair, gazing into the darkness, listening to the faint break of the ocean and the distant blare of the Point Loma foghorn. A ship passed on its way out to sea and I watched it go with the unsteady feeling that I, too, was embarking on a voyage into the unknown.

EIGHT

When you are on call as a death investigator, you rarely sleep soundly. Even when you have the next day off, there's this net of anticipation that prevents you from falling into the deep unconscious you need to filter out the things you see. You're constantly rolling over, shaking, sweating, jerking alert, sure that the phone has rung and they're calling you again, that there's been a gangbanger found stabbed in an alley downtown, a little girl raped and dumped in a canyon in Burlingame, a drunk drowned and washed ashore in Pacific Beach, a jumper hanging from the bay bridge, or a little old lady with her head half blown off sitting on her back porch in Mira Mesa.

But that night, for the first time in nearly a month, the phone did not ring and I slept the deep sleep of the emotionally exhausted. Just after dawn, I dreamed of double green doors that became a turquoise ocean wave arching high over a reef. I lay on a towel on a white sand beach. Suddenly, I caught sight of a black shape in the wave, a shape that I first interpreted as a seal, then recognized as a human body bejeweled by blood blisters and blackened by fire.

I jerked awake sweating and looked around. It was day, but in my mind's eye all I could see was that body in the wave. I forced myself up and looked out the porthole. The sun shone in a sapphire sky. I knew I'd have to go into the office at some point, but it was Sunday and I had been working straight for nearly fourteen days.

So, swim trunks in hand, I drove the unmarked up to the La Jolla Cove. Three times a week I go there to swim the open water course. Six miles of ocean thrashing every seven days keeps my torso trim and my bad arm limber.

I got back to the boat around nine A.M., beat from fighting chop but determined to tear into all the chores I'd been neglecting: vacuuming the *Chant*'s interior, washing her windows, and mopping her deck. Afterward, I got out my portable drill to tighten up the railings and cleats loosened during winter storms.

As I worked I thought about the ways the killer could have gotten Cook tied up. The first scenario had Cook not knowing the killer. He was surprised and forced at gunpoint to strip and lie on the bed before the snake was laid on him. Or Cook knew the killer, who confronted him, then forced him to strip and lay on the bed. The third and most disturbing premise was that Cook knew the killer and was willingly tied up before the snake was brought out—that what might have started as Cook living out some sexual fantasy went deadly wrong.

"Well, well, if it isn't Sergeant Moynihan up and at it on a Sunday morning. And what's this—without female companionship?"

"Imagine that," I said, turning.

Brett Tarentino leaned on the railing of the *Hard News,* the thirty-six-foot cabin cruiser in the slip next to mine. He carried a mug of steaming coffee and wore dark sunglasses, black wind pants, and a matching T-shirt that strained against a gym-crafted chest. Tarentino's five years younger than me, smart, well-read, and very ambitious. He used to work as an investigative reporter at *The San Diego Union-Tribune,* the largest daily in the city. Now he has his own muckracking column in the *San Diego Daily News,* an upstart, well-financed tabloid that paid him a small fortune to jump ship.

"Not losing your touch, are you?" he asked, sipping on the coffee. "We've got to keep the hound reputation up at this end of the marina."

"Uh-huh. And what about your date?"

He smiled. "Left before dawn."

"Well, good for you," I said, wanting to get back to my work.

But Tarentino went on: "You know I've been giving you a lot of thought lately."

"Have you, now?"

"That's right," Brett replied. 'This newspaper gig's getting old. I'm considering a career change. Mystery writer."

I crossed my arms. 'And because of that you've been giving me a lot of thought?"

"Yeah. I'm thinking I'll pattern my detective hero after you."

"Not yourself? How unnarcissistic. What's gotten into you?"

He made a dismissive gesture. "Simply a recognition of the marketplace, Seamus. They won't buy a gay newspaper columnist action-hero detective no matter how macho he really is. So it's you, pal. Want to hear my deep, dark psychological read on your persona and so my protagonist? The thing that will really hook them in New York?"

I leaned back against the bridge, amused. "Wouldn't miss it."

"You're just like Kennedy, Beatty, Nicholson, and Clinton."

"Really?"

"Really," he went on. "Guys like you can't help it. It's part of your chemical wiring. The hetero satyr's genetic makeup. First thing you see in your mind's eye when you wake up in the morning is that furry little cleft. Last thing you see before you go to bed—same thing. Know what it's gonna read on your gravestone someday?"

"Tell me."

"*Seamus Moynihan. Fought Crime. Loved Pussy.*"

I couldn't help myself and roared with laughter. "And what about your gravestone? *Brett Tarentino. Tilted at Windmills. Chased cock?*"

"Something like that," he said, smiling.

"*Fought Crime. Loved Pussy.* You should make that the title."

"Probably sell millions in paperback," he agreed. Then his grin firmed and we weren't friends or neighbors anymore. He was a reporter. I was a cop. "You looked smashing in your Pillsbury Doughboy outfit on television last evening."

"*Seamus Moynihan. Fought Crime. Loved Fashion,*" I replied. "Doesn't have quite the same ring, does it?"

He ignored me and tugged off his sunglasses. "What did the killer write on the mirror? Something about 'joy,' I heard. And how clean was the apartment?"

I startled, then got angry. The reporters and television crews had been all over Sea View Villas once word got out that Cook had been killed by a snake. We gave them perfunctory information about the case but demanded everyone who'd been inside withhold the particulars, especially the message on the mirror and the fact that the place had been scoured. Someone had leaked. Not surprising, I suppose. Tarentino had contacts everywhere. At least his source hadn't given up the exact message.

I summoned control. "Don't know what you're talking about."

"Right," Tarentino said. "Then my two sources must be wrong."

'Two!" I said, unable to hold back my wrath. "You planning on reporting—"

My cell phone rang before I could finish. As I fished in my pockets for it, he grinned, leaned over, and picked up that morning's *Daily News*. The headline read:

HISS!
CLEAN FIEND USES SNAKE TO MURDER
MEDICAL RESEARCHER
PROFESSES 'JOY' IN MESSAGE TO COPS

"What the fuck," I snarled into the cell phone.

"Excuse me?" said Lieutenant Anna Cleary, the watch commander.

"Sorry, Anna," I said. "I just got an eyeful of this morning's paper."

"You and Cook's wife," she replied. "She called from the airport very upset. She'll be here in twenty minutes. Solomon called too. He wants to do the autopsy ASAP. The body's deteriorating."

NINE

At first glance, Sophia Cook seemed to be one of those Texas women Fay used to describe as having had Neiman Marcus injections. She wore dark sunglasses, a chic navy pantsuit, and gold at her neck, ears, and wrists. It was an outfit designed for a wealthy woman in her fifties, but it suited her. She had natural poise, and gave off the sense of being well bred, able to evoke grace amidst adversity. She was thinner than she'd appeared in the framed photograph we'd found on the bedstead next to her husband's body. But you could tell that the weight loss had not been deliberate. It was there in the sunken spots in her cheeks and between the worried knuckles, the impression that she'd been through an ordeal lately, an ordeal that had begun long before her husband's death.

Sophia Cook gestured at the bantam rooster of a man standing next to her in the lobby of downtown headquarters. "This is Morgan's father," she said in a genteel twang.

Morgan Cook, Sr., clad in black cowboy boots and pressed jeans, stood on his tiptoe to try to cut down

47

the size advantage I had over him. I'm six four, two fifteen. Cook was barely five seven, hundred and forty, early sixties, built all lean muscle and sinew. He had callused hands and a weather-tooled face. It turned out he had started out as a cement finisher in McAllen, Texas, then made a fortune transporting steel rebar from Galveston to the construction boom towns of Houston, Dallas, and Fort Worth. He was a self-made man used to giving orders and chafing under the queries of men he deemed his inferior. Men like me.

"I wanna see my boy," he said, not bothering to shake my hand. "Now."

"He's a good twenty minutes from here, sir, at the medical examiner's facility," I said. "If you and Mrs. Cook could answer some questions now, it'll save you some time."

"Got nothing but time," he said, spitting the words. "I done lost my boy."

Sophia Cook put a hand on his shoulder. "Sergeant Moynihan is just trying to help, M.C. No use making him our enemy."

She took off her sunglasses, revealing swollen, bloodshot eyes. "You'll have to excuse us for being a little on edge, Sergeant," she said. "We haven't slept since your call. And we've seen the newspapers. We'll answer your questions as best we can."

I got them visitors passes and led them to the elevator. When we reached the fourth floor, home to the San Diego PD Homicide Division, Detective Missy Pan was waiting. I'd called her in; she's good to have around when we interview family members.

We went into the conference room and shut the door. I steeled myself for the questions I was going to have to pose. It's strange, but when people ask about my pitching career, they almost always ask how I could possibly have taken the mound in front of 34,000 screaming fans. I tell them pitching in the major leagues was easy: When it was right, I was out of my mind, deaf and blind to the crowd, acting on instinct. Probing the deepest emotions of a victim's family, however, is much, much more difficult. It requires me to be outwardly cool. But inside I feel as burned, raw, violated, and angry as they do.

"I'm going to tell you what I tell every family of a murder victim," I said once we'd all taken seats. "I know how you feel right now."

"You couldn't possibly," M.C. snapped.

"No, sir, I can," I replied. "My dad was murdered when I was boy. They never caught his killer. That's part of why I do what I do. I promise you here and now that I will do everything in my power to find, arrest, and convict whoever committed this crime. I want you both to know that."

I paused, looked both of them in the eyes, and saw they believed me. I needed their faith. It was the same when I pitched. I always needed to see that the players backing me up believed. It was what gave me the strength to carry on when the bases were loaded and the count was full. It's what satisfies me most in life now: having the victims believe that I can be their avenging angel.

"Thank you," Sophia Cook said.

"Thank me when I catch whoever did this," I said, then paused. "Now, I'm going to ask you some questions that you're not going to like. But for me to do my job, to catch your husband's and your son's killer, I've got to ask. And you've got to be truthful."

M.C.'s expression tightened, but Sophia Cook just nodded and said, "Go ahead."

"We found an antianxiety prescription in his shaving kit."

"Yes. He'd seen a doctor," Sophia Cook said.

"What was he anxious about?" Missy asked.

"Life, I guess," she replied softly.

"Married life?" I asked.

M.C. said, "The marriage was fine."

I turned to the older man. "I'm not talking to you, Mr. Cook."

Sophia Cook put her hand on her father-in-law's forearm. "We had our troubles, like any couple married fourteen years," she said; then tears welled in her eyes. "But lately I think Morgan felt trapped. Men get like that after a while, don't they?"

"Sure they do, hon," her father-in-law agreed. "But the good ones like Morgan keep on keeping on despite them feelings."

Missy spoke up again. "How was your relationship sexually?"

"What kind of goddamned question is that?" M.C. demanded.

"A rotten but necessary one," Missy replied.

"People where I come from do not ask these things of strangers," he grumbled.

"They do when they have to," I said. "And if you continue to interrupt I'm going to have to ask you to leave."

Sophia Cook, meanwhile, bent forward at the waist, looking at her fingers, which were interlaced and moving against each other as if she were worrying prayer beads.

"We—I mean, Morgan—wasn't...happy...that way. At least lately."

Her father-in-law appeared stricken.

"How so?" Missy asked.

The widow still watched her hands. "It's not so easy to talk about."

"We found pornography at your husband's apartment," I said. "All of it was about group sex. Ménage à trois. Women and men."

M.C.'s turtle head strained out of his neck. He slammed his palms flat on the tabletop and jumped to his feet, sputtering in rage: "What the hell is this? What kind of *preevo* minds you people have? My boy? *My* boy? He was a fine man. Good father. Great scientist. Great athlete. Women and men? You're making out like he was a faggot. My boy was no faggot!"

"Mr. Cook!" I said, raising the cold, detached voice I've learned to summon in situations like this. "No one is making judgments here. The way your son was killed suggests sex was part of the equation. We have to know everything."

"He played corner back at A&M. Toughest SOB I ever saw," M.C. shot back.

Sophia Cook had not once raised her head to look at us.

"Mrs. Cook?" Missy said. "Please help us. It could be important."

Sophia Cook's shoulders and chin trembled when at last she looked up at Missy, then back at her father-in-law. "You didn't know him, M.C., not the real him."

For an instant her father-in-law looked ready to do battle with her, then he saw the agony in her face and the color went out of him. He got up and left the room.

She watched him go with a sad look of relief. "I wanted to tell someone," she said when the door shut. "But who could I tell? M.C. and Marlene were so proud of him. And the way I was raised, it was not the kind of thing you told other people."

Then she turned back to Missy and me, speaking in a voice that was barely audible. "We met in college and he was this brilliant student and big-time athlete. I loved him the moment we met. And he loved me too. We were such good, close friends from the get-go. And the sex"—she glanced at me and reddened—"well, it was incredible."

"Okay," I said. "What happened to change that?"

Her chin trembled. "Twenty years of hard work. Two kids. The weight I could never keep off. Let's say his interest in me waned. Unless…"

Her voice trailed off and she stared into her folded hands, her cheeks trembling.

"Unless what, Mrs. Cook?" Missy asked.

She looked up at us both, tears running down her cheeks. "This is all going to come out in court someday, isn't it? It would be so horrible for people to think of him and ... me ... that way."

"What way is that?" I asked, puzzled.

Sophia Cook shut her eyes and shuddered. "I was raised Southern Baptist, Sergeant Moynihan. One man. One woman. That's how God meant it to be."

"But he wanted more?" Missy pressed.

She nodded stiffly. "I don't know where it came from. This despicable hunger. One night a few years ago, Morgan asked me if I ever had thoughts of having sex with another man. It startled me, especially when he said it would excite him. First I sort of went along with it. A fantasy, you know? I've read that's okay to do. Just talk, right? And it helped our sex life for a while. Then that bored him, too, and he started bringing home the videos and make me watch while we were having sex. Before you know it, he was asking me to actually do it, you know, use one of those swingers hotlines to find another man. Or a woman. He said group sex was his fantasy. He wanted me to participate."

"Did you?" I asked.

She shook her head violently. "No! Call me a prude. Whatever. I just couldn't."

"And what did your husband do when you refused?" Missy asked.

She grinned pain at us. "He went looking to fulfill his desires by himself."

"How do you know that?" I asked.

She picked up a tissue and dabbed at her eyes. "I read somewhere about caches on computers, how there are records of the Internet sites you visit? So I learned how to figure out what sites he visited. I found some dedicated to swingers. There were E-mails, too, about various rendezvous."

"How many of these rendezvous do you figure he'd had?"

Sophia's posture spoke of tragedy. "Enough to kill him, I'd say, Sergeant."

TEN

Back before the world became a place ruled by semanticists, a medical examiner was a coroner and the medical examiner's offices a morgue. No matter what you call them or their place of work, there's always a smell that surrounds them, a smell that cannot be masked by powerful cleansers no matter how hard they try. The odor of morgues is the one thing about my job I never get used to: It always reminds me of red licorice and lavender.

Two days after my father died, the day after my virgin ride in a '67 Corvette, my mother put on a black dress and the freshwater pearls Dad had given her the Christmas before. Then she dressed me and my younger sister, Christina, in our church clothes. Accompanied by my Uncle Anthony, who had flown in from San Diego, we all trooped down to the Suffolk County Morgue. Uncle Anthony tried to convince my mom that it was not necessary for her to view the body. But my mother, Angelina Moynihan, was a stubborn, fiery, second-generation Sicilian who taught English composition with a velvet fist at Latin, the best school in Boston. She was not one to wait until the mortician had done his job. No one was going to keep her from seeing exactly what they had done to my father, her beloved James Michael Moynihan. We kids were brought along, I guess, to keep her on her feet once she'd seen the damage.

Back in the spring of 1976, the Southern Mortuary, the morgue for Boston, was a tall brick building near the Mattapan neighborhood. I had turned ten the week before and I remember holding my Uncle Anthony's meaty callused hand as we all trooped past City Hospital, around a corner, down two blocks, then up a cement front stoop toward a doorway topped by a window the shape of a half moon. A ruddy-faced Boston Police captain named Slattery met us in the dim hallway.

"You don't have to do this, Mrs. Moynihan," he said, taking her hand. "He's been identified from dental records."

"Been telling her that all morning," Uncle Anthony said.

"Let's go," my mother said firmly. And then she and the captain were gone through green metal double doors that swung after them, wafting toward us an odor I would come to know all too intimately.

Christina and I sat beside Uncle Anthony on a bench in the hallway. Anthony was my mother's brother, a stonemason like his father, a devout Roman Catholic and baseball fanatic like my dad. He gave us whips of red licorice to eat while we waited. I had recently been fitted with braces and had to chomp on the licorice in order not to get it caught in the hasps and wires that bound my teeth. I chomped and watched the green doors and the clock on the wall, wrestling with the unknowable, the image of my father dead somewhere on the other side. Late the night before I had heard my mother talking with Uncle Anthony. She said my dad had been blasted twice at close range with a shotgun, then his body doused with gasoline and torched.

The clock ticked in counterpoint to each crunch of my jaw. And every once in a while the green doors would open and shut with the same sort of rhythmic, creaking noise I'd heard the week before on my birthday when my dad had taken me to the amusement park at Nantasket Beach. It was the sound of the Tilt-A-Whirl. And with every moment of my mother gone behind the green doors, the feeling of being caged, rising, and spinning grew stronger and stronger, until I swore I could not breathe against the centrifugal force of her absence.

When at last my mom came back through the green doors, the spinning slowed and I knew she was different, that we were all different from the people we'd been when we'd passed inside the Southern Mortuary. Until that moment, despite the knowledge and the grave assurances, we had all clung to the thread of hope that somehow it was a case of mistaken identity, that a shotgun had not taken my father's life, that his body had not been burned, that some other man was lying back there on a cold steel table, that my dad was just away on the job but coming home to make us all laugh and feel safe again, to sit in his sleeveless T-shirt, smoke a Camel, drink a Miller High Life, play gin when Uncle Anthony came east to visit, dance with my mom in the kitchen, and take me to Fenway Park, where we'd sit in the grandstands and eat popcorn and watch Jim Rice play line drives off the left field wall forever and ever. Amen.

But my mom trudged wavering toward us and stopped, suddenly old, blinking in confusion at newly formed twitches about her eyes, twitches that have never fully eased to this day. She seemed befuddled by the fact that Christina and I had been eating red licorice whips while she viewed what remained of our father. For a moment I swore she would fall to the floor and never get up. But she steadied herself, then knelt in front of me. She smelled, as always, of lavender. Her big beautiful brown eyes welled with tears and she took my hands and squeezed them so tight I almost cried out.

"You make me a promise and you make it right now, Seamus Moynihan!" she yelled. "You promise me you'll never become a police officer!"

At first I was too stunned to say anything. Then everything I had been holding back for two days broke and I hugged her and sobbed, "I promise."

It would not be the first pact with a loved one I'd break in my life. Nor the last.

"I don't think I can do this," Sophia Cook said.

"Don't you fret, honey, M.C. will," her father-in-law said.

It was an hour later. We stood outside what passes for a morgue in San Diego—a low, tan, flat-roofed cinder-block building surrounded by chain-link fence amidst acres and acres of light industrial factories and warehouses that squat atop a hot, dusty mesa near the geographic center of the city.

I looked at Sophia Cook, flashed on the image of my mother at the morgue, and nodded. "I think that would be a good idea. Mrs. Cook, you can wait here."

Inside, Dr. Marshall Solomon waited. He shook M.C.'s hand, told him he was sorry for his loss, then led us through an office area where clerks manage the bureaucracy of death in America's sixth largest city. We went down a hall past Solomon's office and through a swinging door into the guts of the morgue. Immaculate lime-colored tile floors. Stainless-steel tables with built-in hoses and drains. Large oval halogen lights. Microphones hanging above the tables. Scales. Test tubes. Scalpels. Saws. The taste of red licorice. The smell of lavender. And on top of a gurney Solomon wheeled from a walk-in cooler, the body of Morgan Cook, Jr.

M.C. stood there ramrod stiff, looking down at the blackened thing that had been his son. His boy who led a secret life. "When can we have him for the funeral?"

Solomon said, "Day after tomorrow."

M.C. nodded absently, still gazing at the body; then he picked up his head and stared at me with eyes like water seeping over granite. "One thing about Morgan: He never gave up," he said, his voice quavering. "I want you to do the same. I want you to hunt this sick son of a bitch down, Sergeant Moynihan. I want you to hunt him until the end of time if you have to. You hear?"

The autopsy of Morgan Cook, Jr., took more than four hours to complete. Because the skin and muscle tissue was so necrotic and fissured along Cook's right thigh and left arm, it took Solomon a while to find the exact position of the bites. But as he had predicted, they were there, one set of fang slashes on his inner thigh, close to his testicles, a second where his biceps met his left elbow, and a third under the turn of his jaw.

There was other evidence of massive envenomation as well: Cook's brain was enlarged, his tongue was swollen nearly twice its normal size, and his heart was edemic and damaged. The lungs on a man Cook's size will ordinarily weigh between 250 and 300 grams each. But when we examined Cook's lobes, they were so filled with bloody fluid caused by the venom destroying his respiratory system that they weighed nearly 700 grams a piece. Based on the deterioration in the skin, the flesh, and the vascular system surrounding the fang slashes, Solomon determined that Cook took the first bite below his right elbow, the second near his testicles, and the final at the neck. The bites occurred at least an hour apart, perhaps more.

"Guy must have gone through hell," I said as Solomon examined Cook's mouth. "How long did the whole thing take?"

"Six, maybe seven hours."

"What kind of rattlesnake did this?"

"Does it matter?"

"Might in court. It is the murder weapon, after all."

Solomon shrugged. "We'll have to send the venom off for analysis. There's a lab at the University of Southern California that ... what the hell?"

"What?" I said, leaning over the body to get a closer look.

The medical examiner picked up a pair of tweezers and brought out a small green chunk of matter that had been caught under Cook's tongue. He sniffed it. "Apple. And there are other chunks stuck between his teeth. Probably last thing he ate."

Solomon placed the apple chunk in a plastic bag, then used tweezers to push Cook's tongue around again. He frowned and moved a large magnifying glass suspended on a spring-loaded metal arm over Cook's mouth. After a moment of study, he stood up and gestured at me. "Take a look at the gums and tongue. That's not from snakebite."

I leaned over and peered through the magnifying glass. Along Cook's gumline and the rims of his tongue the flesh appeared rippled, raw, and shiny, like a skinned knee. "What causes that?"

"Poison," Solomon said.

ELEVEN

I t was strychnine.

Sometime during the murder of Morgan Cook, the killer made him drink the active ingredient in rat poison. Lab results would eventually show a relatively small quantity of the chemical in his system, certainly not enough to kill a man as big, strong, and healthy as Cook had been.

It didn't make any sense to Solomon or me. Why use strychnine at all when you were introducing so much deadly venom into the bloodstream? I tossed and turned that night, trying to fit this new piece of jigsaw and others into the big puzzle. The bites took place about an hour apart. Did that mean that the snake had been on Cook the whole time and bitten him at random? Or was the snake brought to him at intervals and the bite positions intentional? Before dawn, I became convinced the use and removal of restraints, the pattern of the bites, the message of "joy unspeakable," and the prolonged suffering Cook had been forced to endure suggested that the killing was ritualistic. Which meant that it might have happened before and would surely happen again.

And so, shortly after sunrise that morning, I got up and called my sister.

Every Monday at eight A.M., the six sergeants and two lieutenants who oversee the SDPD homicide teams meet to discuss progress on active cases. Ordinarily the powwow is overseen by Captain Hugh Merriweather, a gruff walrus of a man with a gray mustache and more than thirty years of active duty. But as I stumbled into the conference room yawning and gulping down coffee, I was surprised to see Assistant Chief Helen Adler seated beside Merriweather and Lieutenant Fraiser.

Helen's a handsome African-American woman in her late forties. She has a law degree and was the first woman in the history of the force to be pro-moted to assistant chief. Despite the snide rumors, her singular achievement was the result not of affir-mative action but hard work, dedication, and the solving of a series of prostitute murders that rocked San Diego in the early nineties. She's tough, fair, and possesses a raucous laugh and a body to die for. She went through a rough divorce about six months after I did and one night after too many drinks we ended up in the forward stateroom of the *Nomad's Chant*. For a month we got together in secret, each of us using the other for much-needed healing. We went our own ways after that. It was an amicable but politically motivated breakup: A white male sergeant with little ambition to move higher up the chain of command having an affair with a black female captain with her eye on the top rung simply had no future.

"You seen this?" she said, tossing the morning *Daily News* across the table at me.

Below the fold was a follow-up story by Brett Tarentino. I scanned it, feeling sicker by the word. He'd gotten someone to leak him the fact that group-sex pornography was found at the crime scene. He'd tracked down Sophia Cook in the lobby of the Omni Hotel downtown to ask her about her husband's carnal predilections. We had assured her Morgan's secret life would remain secret for the time being. She felt betrayed and broke down sobbing. M.C. went stark raving mad, punched Tarentino, and had to be restrained.

"What can I say?" I shrugged, finishing the article. "He can be an asshole. Unfortunately, that's what makes him a good reporter."

"A reporter who lives on the boat next to you," Lieutenant Fraiser said.

"Your point?" I asked.

"You look like a leaker from here."

"You honestly think I'd leak that to Tarentino?"

Fraiser let loose with a snarfling laugh. "I think you'd do anything to get more publicity for yourself."

The Prick was one of those guys who almost never let loose a laugh of any kind, unless it was at my expense. Indeed, the hardest I'd ever seen him chuckle was the day he was promoted to lieutenant. We'd run competing homicide teams for nearly four years, and it galled him to no end that my team was better. He was one of those legwork-trumps-all detectives, no room spared for creative analysis. His forte: paperwork, time management, and obsession with departmentally proscribed procedure.

It was my conviction that his flintiness was due to the fact that he'd spent his Marine years laden under a fifty-pound pack, marching the dusty hills of Camp Pendleton in preparation for war, but never got his chance in combat: He'd been commissioned shortly after Grenada, was not called up for Panama, and found himself mustered out of the Marine Corps shortly before Desert Storm. My greatest fear was that one day he'd encounter a perp in military fatigues spouting Arabic and go Rambo.

In any case, when the position of homicide lieutenant opened up, Fraiser was able to convince our superiors that I was a flake with, admittedly, an aptitude for running investigations but clearly not leadership material, an opinion I have a tough time disputing. So The Prick became my boss and I've had to deal with his snide comments, snarfles, and personal attacks ever since.

But now I looked him square in the eye and said, "I don't see my name mentioned anywhere in there. You, on the other hand, are featured prominently in your denials."

Fraiser reddened and seemed on the verge of exploding, but Helen held up her hand. "The point is this case is going to be high-profile, Shay."

I sat down, ignoring Fraiser's glower. "I know. *The Daily*'s having circulation problems. They'll keep Tarentino on it full time. The television stations will follow."

"I want daily updates on my desk," Helen insisted. "Understood?"

I did understand. Chief Norman Strutt had recently announced that he was going to retire soon, and Helen Adler did not want any embarrassments to taint her chance to become the first black woman to run a major metropolitan law enforcement agency.

"You got it," I promised.

Merriweather tapped the newspaper. "Snakes and group sex. This some kind of new thing? You know, like the gays and gerbils a few years back?"

"That was an urban myth, Cap," I replied.

"Better ask your pal Tarentino to be sure of that," Fraiser sniped.

Before I could reply, there was a knock at the door and Dr. Christina Varjjan walked in. With her distracted expression, porcelain skin, long, curly red hair, and gray-linen sack dress, she looked like she had just wandered out of a Laura Ashley photo shoot. I am dark-featured like my mother. My baby sister got her Irish beauty from Dad.

Christina got Dad's built-in bullshit detector too. It's a trait she exploits to great effect in her work. For nearly a decade she has served as the chief psychiatric consultant to the San Diego District Attorney's Office. In that capacity she has interviewed thousands of criminals. The running joke is that that's the source of her attraction to

Rikko: By marrying him my sister could engage in a lifelong study of the soul of a gangster who's managed to stay just inside the law. Police agencies throughout Southern California use Christina to help profile criminals when the FBI's Behavioral Sciences Unit is too backed up to provide timely reports.

"What's she doing here?" Fraiser demanded.

"Nice to see you, too, Lieutenant," Christina said, taking a seat beside me. "Seamus thought I might help with the snake killer."

"There's no evidence of a series," Fraiser protested.

"What planet are you on?" I demanded. "The whole thing stinks of a ceremony."

"Shay's right," Christina said, looking all around the table. "Look at the message alone: *Joy unspeakable to be holding death in your hands.* This is an ecstatic experience for him. And he refers to 'your hands.' He wants you to identify with him in his ecstasy. My opinion, with this guy, it's only a matter of time."

Merriweather rubbed his thumbs across his temples. "How much time?"

My sister shrugged. "Depends on how long he's been doing it."

Assistant Chief Adler turned a pen over and over between her index finger and thumb. "Have you had a chance to look at the files, Dr. Varjjan?"

Christina nodded. "Cursory, but Shay has brought me up to speed."

"I'm sure you two have got him all figured out," Fraiser said, rolling his eyes.

"Hardly," Christina said. "But I think we can make a few suppositions."

"Go ahead, Dr. Moynihan," Adler said.

Christina sat forward in her chair. "Your killer is mostly likely male, white, late twenties to early forties, highly intelligent, organized. He may have been traumatized as a child, most likely in a sexual manner, perhaps even with snakes."

"You're saying one guy?" I interrupted. "Morgan had a taste for couples. And we found vaginal fluids at the scene."

She nodded. "I figure her for gone at the time of the killing. But if she was there, she was under the killer's control. It's his desire, not hers."

"How do you know that?" Adler demanded.

"Numbers," Christina replied. "For whatever complex reasons, women do not manifest their frustrations and emotional injuries in the same aggressive ways as men. They do not become predators as men do, and they do not take out emotional and sexual rage on strangers. By definition, this is sexist, but by definition, men are the problem. Indeed, there's been only one confirmed ritualistic woman killer—Aileen Wuornos. So we assume a man is behind this. Perhaps he's using the woman as a lure. But ultimately this is his game."

Adler set her pen down and studied my sister. "And what is his game?"

"That's the key, isn't it?" Christina replied, throwing up her hands. "But I can't give you that yet, because I don't know. What I do know is that there was no sign of struggle on Cook's body other than the rope burns and the snakebites. Because of that I'd say it's likely that you're looking for an extrovert who has the ability to put people, especially men, at ease."

"How the hell do you know that?" Captain Merriweather demanded.

Christina smiled serenely. "Because when it comes to sex, heterosexual male humans are territorial animals. In the presence of a receptive female, even though there's this swinging thing going on, there would undoubtedly be awkwardness. But again, no sign of struggle on Cook. So our killer is such a good actor, like Ted Bundy, that he doesn't let Cook see the sexual rage building in him."

Fraiser snorted. "What's this territorial mumbo jumbo? They could have shoved a gun in his face and told Cook to get on the bed or die."

Christina shook her head. "Too easy. Sexual predators as a group feel they are superior to other humans. Selecting Cook and manipulating him into position would be something he'd take pleasure from. He would want that phase of the ceremony to be difficult just so he could prove it could be done."

Adler asked. "Why Cook?"

Christina sat back, pressing her fingers together in a prayer pose. "That's tougher to explain. But let's focus on the sexual angle. Cook likes group sex.

That's the lure. For reasons unknown, that's probably what enrages your killer. Why? Perhaps because Cook is an adulterer. Or maybe it's just that Cook is a victim of lust and the killer can't stand those feelings in himself."

"Very titillating and intellectual," Fraiser said sarcastically. "Now can we get to some real police work here? None of this is gonna help catch this guy."

"Let's hear the doctor out, Lieutenant," Adler snapped. "What else?"

Christina sat forward. "Look at how the snake is being used, Chief. Bites at timed intervals. Your killer isn't just interested in being a scourge, wiping away those cursed by whatever affliction he finds damnable: He's interested in keeping his victims alive for a while. So here the snake is being used not only as an instrument of death but, as Seamus pointed out to me, of torture. Extrapolate that and he's a sadist, someone who derives joy unspeakable from the pain Cook must have suffered. It's a horrific, deadly mix."

"What do you suggest we do, Dr. Moynihan?" Adler asked.

"Only thing you can do," Christina said, looking at me. "Catch him before he can kill again."

TWELVE

The haute decor of the San Diego Homicide Division offices could have been lifted straight out of any insurance adjusters' pied-a-terre in Omaha. Sectional dividers constructed of gray metal frames and bland gray fabric walls cut up much of the fourth floor of downtown headquarters into a series of large cubicles filled with simple metal desks and filing cabinets. Each of the six death-investigation teams has its own cramped enclosure.

After the meeting adjourned, I pinned the artist's sketch of the man Mary Aboubacar had seen leaving Sea View Villas above my desk next to Jimmy's Little League photograph, then briefed the team on what we'd learned from Sophia Cook, the autopsy, and my sister.

"So where do we go from here, boss?" Jorge asked.

"You're going to scour Cook's laptop," I said. "See if you can find any date books or references to the chat rooms his wife said he frequented."

"I'll take it up to the FBI's forensic computer lab this morning," he promised.

71

"And prepare a ViCAP alert. Send it state and national."

ViCAP stands for Violent Criminal Apprehension Program. It is a computer network that links almost every law enforcement agency in the country. We often use it to see if signature criminal actions—in this case, committing a homicide with ropes and a snake— match other killings in some distant city or state.

"I'm on it," Jorge promised again.

"Fine. We need to talk to someone who knows poisonous snakes and can give us a positive ID on the skin we found."

Missy set her morning latte on her desk. "The zoo," she said. 'They've got a snake house there run by the star of *Cold Blooded!*"

"I see that clown on cable," Rikko said, stuffing the last of a Danish into his mouth. "How do you say this? Fifty cents short of a buck? Always sticking his face right in front of cobras and alligators and say- ing, 'Crikey, he's a nasty one.' "

Missy scowled at Rikko. "I think he's kinda cute. Then again, I'm a sucker for those Australian accents."

"Get us a meeting with Mr. Crikey," I said. "And, Rikko, after you finish up your paperwork, go back up to Double Helix. Talk with Cook's coworkers. See if they know more about his private shenanigans than his boss did."

The San Diego Zoo houses one of the most exten- sive collections of animals, reptiles, and birds in the world. It is renowned for its sensitive and intelligent approach to the manner in which they are exhibited. The Klauber-Shaw Reptile House is a case in point. At first glance it looks like a tidy stucco bungalow surrounded by a veranda. Then you notice the large glass enclosures set into the veranda's inner wall. Inside them on this early afternoon, boa constrictors and pythons hung from tree limbs. An anaconda basked in a large pool. A giant Komodo dragon prowled an open air enclosure.

It was early afternoon when Missy and I maneuvered through dozens of kids who ran from tank to tank shrieking with fascination and fear. We rang a bell outside a large tan metal door, which was answered by a very attractive woman in her early thirties, sleek and nearly six feet tall. Her posture was that of a dancer's, and you knew immediately that she was comfortable with her size and looks. Her hair was a dark brunette cut fashionably short. In addition to the ubiquitous uniform of the zoo— khaki blouse, shorts, and hiking boots—she wore beaded earrings and a matching necklace but no makeup. Her brown eyes were almond-shaped and set off by naturally thick lashes. Her rose lips were full, her cheekbones smoothly arched as if they'd been wind-carved. Her nose was a bit on the generous size, but to my mind that only served to spice her overall appearance with a sense of the exotic. A badge pinned to her shirt said, DR. JAN HOOD, ASSISTANT DIRECTOR OF HERPETOLOGY.

Usually my size and looks have an effect on women, but Hood barely noticed.

"Can I help you?" she asked.

We identified ourselves, showed her our badges, and said we were looking for Nick Foster.

She rolled her eyebrows and attempted a smile. "You and everybody else. Well, c'mon, he's about to do his show. I'm sure he'll talk to you afterwards."

We followed Dr. Hood across a cement walkway to a large, steep-sided amphitheater. At the bottom lay a pool and, beyond it, a stage and curtained backdrop. 'They do the seal show here too," Dr. Hood informed us. "Go on, sit down. If anything, Nick can be fun to watch. Nice meeting you both."

Much to my dismay, she walked away without so much as another glance at me. Missy and I found seats along with five hundred others. Young and middle-aged women filled the front six rows. Soon the crowd began to clap, stomp their feet, and call for the show to begin. The speakers began booming out the heart-pounding theme music from *Cold Blooded!*—the highest-rated nature show in the history of cable television. The stage curtains pulled back several feet to reveal a lone woven basket and, behind it, a large projection screen. As the music built to a crescendo, the image of a king cobra appeared on the screen. The cobra stirred and rose out of coil, swayed, and flared its hood, the eyes like tiny polished stones, tongue lashing the air.

"Check it out," Missy said, pointing to the stage, where the actual cobra was rising from its basket.

Women in the front rows screamed. Kids all around us either threw themselves into their mothers' arms or strained to get a better look. Then the curtains drew back and the star of *Cold Blooded!* himself bounded out onto the stage, his microphone attached to a headset.

Nick Foster was a craggily handsome man with shoulder-length sun-streaked brown hair and biceps that strained against a short-sleeve safari-style shirt open to the navel. The crowd went wild, and to my surprise Missy clapped vigorously right along with them. He waited until the applause died down, then stalked the snake.

The man was a master entertainer. With little preamble he was giving the audience what it had come to see—someone who'd try to tempt death. Tense silence fell over the amphitheater, broken only by the soft cries of a child. Foster stopped his stalk, looked out into the audience, located the crying child, and put a finger to his lips. The little girl stopped crying, nodded, and sat up in her mother's lap.

Foster grinned, gave her the thumbs-up, waited until gentle laughter died, then eased into a stance that reminded me of a figure skater preparing for a series of dangerous leaps. He side-slipped toward the snake, which was still paying attention to those frightened women in the front row; it did not notice Foster until he was within five feet.

The snake twisted its head and glared right at Foster. Then it dropped out of its upright position, swirled within its coil, and rose again to face him, swaying with a backward arch. Foster crouched before the serpent, his weight on the balls of his feet, his mouth agape as if he did not know whether he'd survive his predicament.

"Spitters," he warned into his microphone. "These nasty blokes like to spit you in the eye before they go in for the kill. Blind you, ladies and gentlemen, boys and girls. Watch him. Watch him, folks."

This patter had no sooner left his mouth when the snake reared back, opened its mouth to reveal two scythelike fangs, and then snapped its head forward. A thin comet of fluid flashed through the air right at Foster.

But the director of herpetology was already in motion, his head and right shoulder turning down and away from the cobra's spit, flipping his entire body at an angle toward the snake. The venom struck harmlessly across his upper back. Foster rolled out of the maneuver, ending up with his legs splayed to either side of the basket, his nose inches from the snake's open mouth. The cobra made to rear back and strike again and the crowd gasped as one.

Foster moved so fast you weren't sure what you'd seen. One instant the snake was lunging forward; the next, he had the cobra throttled, his hand wrapped under its gaping jaw.

There was a moment of dramatic pause filled with appreciative howls from the audience, then Foster rolled backward and to his feet, the cobra held high overhead, the serpent's mouth open and angry, its body whipping and wrapping around his forearm.

"Welcome to *Cold Blooded!*" Foster roared.

The amphitheater erupted. Missy leaped to her feet, cheering lustily, then turned to me. "Isn't he just like Indiana Jones?"

I chortled at one of my toughest detectives acting like a groupie before Mick Jagger, but the sound choked off in my throat. Dr. Hood strode onto the stage carrying a black metal box. Foster turned and held out the snake toward her. She cringed but opened the box. He laughed. "Everyone who watches the show regularly knows Janice Hood's one of the world's experts on reptiles. Especially chameleons. But the venomous snakes make her nervous."

Hood made a show of laughing at herself. "C'mon, Nick, they make everyone with half a brain nervous."

"Everyone with half a brain 'cept me," Foster said, leering at the women in the front row.

Thirteen

The rest of the show was geared toward education. Foster and Hood interwove biology, conservation, and gripping anecdotes to present an admirable profile of the cobra as one of the most dangerous serpents on earth.

Afterward we returned to the reptile house and rang the bell again. An intern answered this time and led us into a large rectangular room with cement floors. It was hot and humid inside. There was an acrid scent to the air that reminded me of animal urine, though more primal. The intern led us past screened cages holding snakes and a large, upright glass-fronted refrigerator. A sign taped to the glass door read ANTIVENIN. On each shelf inside were little white boxes labeled with names like PUFF ADDER, GABOON VIPER, TAIPAN, and MAMBA. We passed into an atrium of sorts and then to a door marked NICK.

We knocked and from the other side heard Foster bellow in his distinctly Australian accent: "Yeah, c'mon in!"

I twisted the doorknob and entered a crowded office dominated by a massive oak desk and framed photographs of Foster with celebrities and politicians. Mr. Cold Blooded stood behind the desk. Up close, he had an almost simian build, with a gorilla's forearms and hands. A cigarette smoldered between stubby, powerful fingers. A plume of blue smoke swirled up around his face, even craggier than it appeared under the stage lights. A telephone headset had replaced his show microphone. He was nodding into it even as his beefy paw clasped mine and he squinted in happy appraisal of Missy.

"G'day, mate," he said in a rough burr. "G'day, miss. Sit down. Be right with you."

Missy looked at him with complete adoration. He winked at her as she plopped in a wooden chair in front of the desk I bent over and lifted the various zoological journals on my chair and set them on the floor. Foster gave me a hearty thumbs-up before his brows knitted together and he crushed the cigarette into an ashtray.

"Don't give me that shit, Richard!" he growled. "I got a goddamned eleven share in prime time, first for an animal show in the history of cable. Now you barneys up there in New York better come up with more cash or we'll take *Cold Blooded!* to Discovery or Geographic or one of the goddamned networks!"

He listened a second, then stabbed the air with a finger. "You don't think so, eh? Well, let me tell you, mate, ABC is already talking to my agent about putting together a string of hour-long specials, full funding, whatever I want, the way they used to do with Jacques fucking Cousteau. So let's get this nailed down or I'll stick our deal on the barbie and broil it. We clear on that, Richard?"

Foster listened, then nodded vigorously. "Now you're talking, mate," he said. "Keep me updated."

He ripped off the headphones, threw them on the desk, and plucked up a pack of Marlboros. "Sorry 'bout that. Them New York boys take the position that they're responsible for the success of *Cold Blooded!*, rather than yours truly." He winked again. "Got it all wrong, don't they?"

Missy blinked, then forced a grin. "I love your show. I watch it every week."

'Always appreciate the fans," he said. "Now, how can old Nick Foster help?"

From my shirt pocket I drew the plastic evidence bag containing the two pieces of skin we'd found in Cook's bedclothes. "We were hoping you might be able to tell us what kind of snake these came from."

Foster scrunched up his eyebrows, then reached over, took the bag, and held it to the light. He studied it a moment, then tugged his telephone headset back on and punched in a number on the console. "Janice? You busy? Yeah, well, drop the chameleon and get over to my office."

He snatched off the headset a second time. "I'm best at identifying them on the belly, but to be honest, when there's just pieces of 'em like this, Janice is better at identification than I am."

A minute later Hood barged in and began barking at him, "I've got two weeks to finish this project and you know it!"

"Dr. Janice Hood," Foster said to us, with no trace of warmth.

Hood stopped, her mouth open, then she looked at us chagrined. "Sorry, Officers, I forgot you were here."

"Coppers here need our help, Janice," Foster said, enjoying her predicament. He handed her the bag. "Any idea what kind of snake this skin came off of?"

Hood took the bag and held it up to the light. A flicker of confusion passed through her face, then she said, "Do you have a magnifying glass?"

Foster rummaged through a drawer and handed her one with a brass handle. She flipped the bag over and studied it again. "Two different snakes," she said at last. "Square piece is from a *Crotalid*, a rattler. Triangular piece is from a *Dendroaspis*. A mamba."

"Really?" Foster replied, suddenly interested. "Black or green?"

"Green, I think, but you won't know for sure unless you do a DNA analysis," she said. "Same thing with the rattler."

"Two snakes?" I said, puzzled. "You sure?"

"Positive," she said. "The mambas all have these same striations, like the narrow leaves of a creeping vine."

"What's a mamba look like?" Missy asked.

"Like that nasty bastard right there," Foster said, pointing at a framed poster.

The poster showed Foster in that same semicrouched stance we'd seen him exhibit onstage. His attention was focused on an enraged black snake that he grasped a good foot below the tail. The serpent was writhing back on itself, jaws flung wide, orange pallet showing against prominent fangs. Above the dramatic action shot, which struck me as having been dreamed up by a designer of romance novel covers, the headline screamed: NICK FOSTER IS COLD BLOODED!

Foster came out from behind the desk toward the poster, a palpable excitement building in his voice. "Mamba's one of the deadliest snakes on earth. Scourge of Africa. This one lived in the forests of Tanzania near the border with Kenya. Rumored to have killed six people in one village. They heard yours truly was in the area, collecting samples, and asked me to come catch him. Big bugger. He's out there in one of the tanks right now."

Foster was like a kid in his revelry, and I realized that in addition to his outdoorsy looks, his unbridled enthusiasm for what most people found unnerving was part of his success: Like Missy, his fans adored the fact that he was unabashedly in love with danger.

"Does someone bitten by a mamba end up looking like someone who died of Ebola?" I asked.

"Now I get it," Foster said, snapping his fingers. "This is that story in the papers."

"That's right," Missy said. 'The victim's body was blackened and covered with blood blisters. Is that what happens after several mamba bites?"

Foster thought, then shook his head. "Can't say I've ever seen anyone suffered a mamba bite. Puff adders. Brown snake. Cobra once. But no mambas. You, Janice?"

She shook her head. "But my basic understanding is that mamba venom is composed of neurotoxins: It attacks the central nervous system. *Crotalid* or rattler venom goes after the respiratory and circulatory organs. That seems more likely to create blood blisters. But again, this isn't my area."

"Could we see him anyway?" I asked. "The mamba, I mean."

Foster's expression mutated into a frown and he checked his watch. "Sorry, mate, but I'm due for a conference call," he said. "Janice, show them the mamba, help them with their other questions."

For a moment Dr. Hood didn't say anything; then she smiled and shook her head incredulously. "That's what I've always loved about you, Nick. Always so gracious."

FOURTEEN

The mamba lay in a tank in a hidden hallway behind the public displays. He was nearly five feet long and his skin was so shiny it looked varnished, more olive brown than black along the top of his body. His fish-scale underbelly was pearl white, a coloration that extended across the sides of his temples, giving his unblinking ebony eyes a mesmerizing quality. His head was roughly the shape of a sea horse's, only thicker and wider. The upper part of his torso was up and weaving back and forth across the glass.

"Felt us walking toward him," Dr. Hood said. "Snakes feel by vibration. These guys are real territorial. Very aggressive."

"Deadly, huh?" Missy said.

The herpetologist nodded. "*Dendroaspis polylepis* can bring down a water buffalo. In parts of southern Africa, they're known as the Shadow of Death. Very fast. Completely unafraid of man."

"Who has access to the snakes here?" I asked.

"Just about everyone who works in the department," she replied. "There are eleven of us. Not to mention the various security personnel. But let me assure you, it would be impossible to get a snake in and out of here without someone noticing."

"And no rattlesnakes or mambas have been moved in or out lately?"

"Not to my knowledge," she replied.

"So if the snake didn't come from here ... could an ordinary citizen get hold of one of these things?" I asked. "I mean, someone not like you or your Mr. Foster."

Her face screwed in annoyance. "Get one thing straight: He's not my Mr. Foster."

"I admit he's not the guy you see on television," Missy said. "But you aren't exactly in like with him, are you?"

"The amphibious Fabio?" she replied, amused. "No, Detective, I'm not."

"Can I ask why?" I said.

She threw up her hands. "Shall I count the ways?"

Foster, she said, grew up in a family that owned a snake show in the bush south of Cairns, Australia, arguably the poisonous reptile capital of the world. From an early age he showed a talent for handling snakes: king browns, adders, and, the deadliest of all, the taipan. Foster was shrewd, if anything, and understood that people are innately enthralled by someone unafraid of snakes. He figured if he could bring his skills to the attention of a wider audience, he might make a name for himself. Foster bought a video camera and began shooting footage of himself playing chicken with poisonous reptiles in the outback. Australian television ate it up.

"A few years ago one of the bigwigs here at the San Diego Zoo saw Nick on television down under and came up with the idea of using him as a marketing tool," she went on, bitterness creeping into her voice. "They brought him up here, gave him the title of director of herpetology, and helped underwrite the first season of *Cold Blooded!* The rest, as they say, is history. I have a Ph.D. from the University of Florida. I've been published in every major zoological journal. Still, according to the powers that be here, the most important part of my job is to make sure what he says onstage is scientifically sound, then play his girl Friday in his shows."

"Sounds like a crappy situation," I said.

"And getting crappier by the minute."

"Back to my original question: How does someone—not a professional zoologist, like yourself, or a showman, like Foster—get hold of a mamba or a rattlesnake?"

Dr. Hood thought a moment, then said, "Rattlesnake? Just go catch one in the desert. Mamba? I suppose you could apply for an import permit with U.S. Fish and Wildlife. That would be the legal way. But we're sixteen miles from the border. There's a black market here, I'm sure. Even for hot herps."

" 'Hot herps'?"

"Venomous reptiles," Hood replied. "Go to any local pet store that sells exotics. I'm sure they would know someone who collects them. Or go on the Web: You'll find all sorts of discussion groups and sites dedicated to the underworld of people who trade and keep them. I'd bet there are scores of collectors right here in Southern California."

"Scores?" Missy groaned.

"If not hundreds."

"Don't you have to be specially trained to handle these things?" I asked.

"If you don't want to die, Sergeant, but no one said you had to have a brain to own a poisonous snake. Just money."

The mamba dropped into a coil; its beady eyes watched us.

Missy said, "You'd have to tick one of these things off to get them to strike, wouldn't you?"

"Not necessarily," she said. "That's why most of us treat them with the utmost respect. I'm no expert handler like Nick, but the more I watch him work around these creatures, the more they frighten me."

"Why?" I asked.

"They're unpredictable," Dr. Hood said.

Then she eased her hand toward the tank as if to touch the mamba. The snake exploded out of itself, its body unwrapping like a rope after a grappling hook. The mouth flared. A clacking noise filled the hallway. The snake retreated. She drew her hand away from the enclosure, revealing two thin streams of yellow venom dripping down the glass.

FIFTEEN

"That thing wanted to kill her, Rikko," I said. "Glass wasn't there, she woulda been toast."

"Hate snakes," he announced. "One of the bastards almost got me a couple of years ago when I was taking a hike with Christina out in the desert near Borrego Springs. Never rattled, that one. Just flung itself at me. Big." He made a fist. "Like this one here."

"What'd you do?"

"Shot him. Nine millimeter. Five times."

"That's illegal, isn't it?"

"Deport me."

It was nearly five. I'd dropped Missy off downtown and picked up Rikko. We were on our way to the Yellowtail, a notorious pickup joint in Mission Beach. During my absence, Rikko had gotten a printout of Cook's Visa card. The genetic researcher had been at the nightclub the previous Thursday, the evening after he'd disappeared, and we wanted to know who he'd been with.

Rikko's conversations with the members of Cook's staff, meanwhile, had reinforced his reputation as a driven commercial scientist. None of the women or men who worked for Cook on the renal research project reported him making any kind of sexual comment at all, much less an overt proposal.

"This guy Cook put different parts of his life in boxes," Rikko said as we pulled off the Sea World exit. "Must have been one lonely guy."

"She was a babe, by the way."

"Who? The snake?"

"No, you Middle Eastern fool. The lizard lady."

"Really? How much babe was this one?"

"Seven point two on the Richter scale."

"Drop bridges. Bring down apartment buildings. Impressive."

Ten minutes later, we pulled up outside the Yellow Tail, an aging building just off the boardwalk. Before Rikko could get out, I said, "You ever have nightmares or flashbacks? About the bad stuff you saw back in Israel?"

Rikko hardened. "Sometimes."

"What do you do about them?"

He looked out the windshield. "Pray to God to wash them from my head. The things that can't be washed, I paint over by looking at my babies sleeping. What else can you do about these things?"

Then he turned his great head and trained his slate-colored eyes on me. "You okay, my friend?"

"Just been having some bad dreams about my father lately."

"Christina, she worries about you these days. She says you are not yourself the last few times she sees you."

"Yeah. What do you think?"

"You do seem more in the dreamland than usual."

"Springtime, Rikko," I said. "I get like this when life begins its ritual unfolding."

Rikko cocked his eyebrow. " 'Ritual unfolding'? What, you put the shit on me?"

"No, just a little poetry in the language."

Rikko waved his hand dismissively. "Christina says you are a professional at using the language to put the attention off you."

"Christina should mind her own business. No offense."

"None taken," he said, opening his door. "She can be a pain, always wanting to know how you feel, trying to explain you to you. But she's a good woman."

"That she is."

"But these dreams get worse, you two should talk."

I did not reply, but headed toward the Yellow Tail. In my early years on the force, after my baseball career and before Fay, the nightclub had been one of my late-night haunts. Stepping inside nearly eleven years after my last visit, however, put a more severe damper on my mood than my conversation with Rikko. The parquet floor was chipped, the paint dull; the windows needed washing. The posters were new—athletes and Hollywood stars—but the clientele were still all lonely losers looking for love.

A redhead in her late twenties with a bored expression, too much makeup, and a sleeveless jumpsuit in a zebra motif crossed the dining area toward us. The pale gray name-tag said CAMILLE.

She said, "Two? For dinner?"

"Our stomachs are too weak for this experience," Rikko said, showing her his badge. "I call earlier, about talking to the staff?"

Her expression turned stony. "Evening shift's just coming on."

"How about you, Camille?" I asked. "You work last Thursday?"

"Yeah," she said, chomping on gum, looking up at me. "So?"

Rikko produced a head-shot photograph of Cook and the artist's sketch of the man Mary Aboubacar had seen leaving Sea View Villas. "You have seen these guys?"

Camille looked at the drawing and shook her head. Then she took the photograph and studied it a moment. "This one, maybe. Why?"

"He got dead," I said. "We're trying to figure out how."

"Oh," she said, her plucked brows knitting. Then she tapped the photograph with a fingernail so long it defied structural analysis. "Yeah, I think I saw him. Good-looking guy, for his age. Kinda like you, Sergeant."

"He leave with anyone?" I asked, ignoring the come-on.

"Got me." Camille shrugged. "Thursday, the place gets pretty packed. This guy ate at the bar. Talk to Stan over there."

Rikko looked down the bar at a scrawny man with a heavy-metal hairdo arranging beer mugs, then shot me a wolfish grin. "Stanley Galusha. I know this guy."

The bartender remembered Rikko as well. As soon as he noticed the Israeli stalking toward him, a lunatic intensity screwed into his face, Galusha's own face flooded with terror and he bolted.

Rikko vaulted the bar and tore after him down a narrow hallway. In the military my brother-in-law studied Krav Maga, the Israeli military hand-to-hand fighting system. Since then he has practiced Aikido, a Japanese grappling art based on using your opponent's weight and force against himself.

He caught Galusha by the collar three feet shy of the back door. He pivoted on one foot, spinning his other leg behind him. The twisting action unbalanced the bartender, who cartwheeled through the door backward and sprawled in the gravel beside a Dumpster. By the time I arrived on the scene, Rikko was doing his best to swab the wax out of the bartender's left ear with the muzzle of his Beretta.

"Give me the reason, Stanley," Rikko growled. "Just the one fucking reason."

"I'm clean, Varjjan," Galusha moaned. "I swear."

Rikko looked up at me. "He is clean and yet he runs from us, Shay."

"Doesn't make sense, does it?" I said, squatting down next to them.

"He scares me," Galusha cried at me, walleyed as a spooked horse.

"Detective Varjjan scares everyone," I agreed. "But they don't all run."

"What would you do if the guy who put you in a hospital for two weeks came creeping toward you with that same twisted fuck look on his face?"

"You put him in a hospital, Rikko?"

"I should have put him in a hole," he replied, pressing the gun tighter into Galusha's ear. "I run into this guy on an investigation first year here, before I joined your team. Stanley was a pimp, were you not, Stanley? An angry pimp who liked to take out his issues of the inner child on runaway young girls. One of them, a young Vietnamese, ended up with two busted arms and a hysterectomy. I don't know, Shay. This just made me mad and nothing but busted bones would do, you know?"

"I could see that," I replied.

"I went through an anger management program in the joint," Galusha whined. "I'm a new man."

Rikko jerked the bartender to his feet. Galusha was blubbering, sure that his face was about to become goulash. I shoved the picture of Cook at him. "Seen this guy?"

Galusha wiped his sleeve across his face, then looked at the photo a moment.

"Sure. Last week sometime. Drank Cuervo neat, ate sirloin, worked the floor."

"He meets someone?" Rikko asked.

"Whole slew of chicks. Busy boy."

"There is one in particular, yes?"

"Nah, Varjjan, he worked the field inside."

"So no one special?" I said.

"Like I said, not inside," he replied, his attention shifting to me.

I saw where he was going and looked around. "What about outside?"

"Must have been like midnight," Galusha replied, turning and pointing toward the parking lot. "City ordinance, no smoking inside, so I was out here having a butt. Usually I go down on the boardwalk for my break, but it was drizzling and misty that night and I stayed here under the eaves."

"And what do you see?" Rikko demanded.

"This one," he said, nervously pointing at Cook's photograph. "I know it was him 'cause of that blond hair. Anyway, he's about halfway across the lot, talking to some dude with his back to me. Couldn't see his face. But he was wearing a baggy trench coat, greenish-brown, and a matching hat, floppy."

"Floppy?" I said.

"You know, not a baseball cap—more like you see guys wear fishing."

"This him?" I asked, holding up the artist's sketch.

Galusha shook his head. "Like I said, I only saw him from behind and across car hoods. But he had short dark hair like this guy. And he was definitely taller than Cook, maybe by a couple of inches."

"Heavy, light, black, white, what?" Rikko said.

"Definitely white or maybe Mexican, but not black. Weight?" He shrugged. "Seemed to fill out the trench coat."

"Any way it could have been a woman?" I asked, thinking about my sister's theory of the killer using a lure.

"Maybe," he said, then the bartender's face pinched. "Nah, he moved like a guy. Athletic-like."

"Okay," I said. "What happened?"

"They talked," Stan said. "Blond guy seemed pretty happy to see trench coat. And they left."

"Together?" Rikko asked.

Galusha shrugged. "Don't know about that. Saw 'em walking toward the far end of the lot; then it was time to get back to work until last call."

"You didn't see them leave in a car?"

"Nope. I was inside by then."

Rikko and I peppered questions at Galusha, the busboys, and the waitresses for another half hour, but got no more real information. No one had seen the trench-coated man inside the Yellow Tail. It was nearly six and I was due at Jimmy's practice in forty minutes. We were climbing back into the unmarked when my cell phone rang.

"Moynihan."

"Hey boss," Jorge said. "Been working on Cook's computer hard drive all day and I got something you're gonna want to see ASAP."

I looked at my watch. "This worth missing Jimmy's practice?"

"Afraid so," Jorge said.

Sixteen

Ever since computers became part of daily life in the mid-eighties, they have become a powerful tool in the fight against crime. Computers have become our personal file cabinets, electronic data lockers where people store the minutiae of their lives, both public and private. The difference between a lockable file cabinet and a computer, however, is that you can easily shred or burn paper. Electronic files are not so easily destroyed. A skilled technician can detect the echoes of deleted files on hard drives.

Jorge Zapata majored in computer science with a minor in law enforcement at Cal State Fullerton. Since early that morning, he had been at the FBI's Forensic Computer Lab off I-15, poring over the data shadows in Cook's laptop.

Jorge said that Cook's personal files turned out to be much as his wife had described them: chat room correspondence, E-mails, and the coded directions to various Internet sites, including several swinger directories.

"Okay," Rikko said. "She was right. He broadens his horizons. So what?"

"It's more than that," Jorge said.

"A lot more," Missy said, excitement palpable in her face.

We were gathered around the computer that sits on Jorge's desk. Jorge sat at the keyboard. He typed in several commands and chat-room dialog appeared on the screen.

"Cook uses the handle Hunter," Jorge said. "There are others in on the discussion, but the interaction you want to focus on is between Hunter and this guy here, the one who calls himself Seeker."

"Wait until you get toward the end," Missy said. "You're not gonna believe it."

I stared at the screen as Jorge scrolled downward.

>*Seeker: You still hot after last week?*
>*Hunter: Sweating. Hard.*
>*Seeker: We'd like another ren-*
>*dezvous if you're game?*
>*Hunter: I'm more than game.*
>*Seeker: Do you still have our toys?*
>*Hunter: All here. Awaiting your*
>*arrival. How is our friend?*
>*Seeker: She's salivating at the thought of*
>*you and your big bad python of love.*
>*Hunter: Thursday? My place?*
>*Seeker: Thursday it is. Same time?*
>*Hunter: The door will be open.*
>*Seeker: We can't wait.*

"Jesus," I said. "When did this conver—uh, chat take place?"

Jorge looked up at me with a satisfied grin. "Week ago today. Two days before Cook disappears."

I reread the dialog. "I want to talk with Seeker and his friend."

"How do you know there's a friend?" Rikko grunted.

"Keeps referring to a 'we.' And then a 'she.' The lure."

"For sure," Jorge nodded. "But Seeker's an anonymous handle. We won't get to him or his lady friend unless we crack the electronic security system guarding the company that hosts this chat room."

"Find out where the swinger's service is located," Missy offered. "Subpoena their records. Get them to break the fire wall."

"Already tracked the service," Jorge said. "Part of this big Internet sex network out of Reno. Guaranteed they'll fight to hide the Seeker's identity on jurisdiction and First Amendment grounds. Could take weeks."

"I got a better idea," I said. "I say Mr. Seeker and his gal pal are locals. They live here in Southern Cal. I say we pay a visit to this chat room and lay an ambush for them."

Not surprisingly, Lieutenant Fraiser was not enamored of the idea of his homicide detectives posting lascivious thoughts on a computer bulletin board. But once Captain Merriweather read the transcript of the dialog between Cook and Seeker, we were given the go-ahead.

We decided to monitor the chat room in shifts, from ten in the morning until midnight. The idea was for each of my detectives to establish distinct handles and identities, each with a specific set of sexual proclivities. We figured that if we cast the net wide, we might raise Seeker quicker and arrange a meeting.

Jorge's handle was Wrangler, a male in his late thirties looking to experiment outside the confines of his marriage. Rikko represented himself as Randy Man, newly divorced, trolling for a willing couple to party with, no strings attached. I figured because Cook had advertised on the Web for female-female-male encounters as well as male-male-female, we'd run one of the fake handles as a woman. At first Missy balked at the idea of posing as Ms. Lover, a single late-twenties swinger into spicing up her life by engaging in ménage à trois with male-female couples. But when I told her my pose would be Anaconda, a superbly endowed professional male with an interest in aggressive role-playing, she reluctantly agreed.

It was dark by the time I headed toward Shelter Island. I tried to call Jimmy at Fay's, to assure him that, no matter what, I would be there for his game the next evening. But no one answered my call.

Aboard the *Chant*, I got a beer and went up on the flying bridge again. Out beyond the buoys that define the marina, the city lights threw shadows across the harbor. I looked into the shadows as if they were inkblots and I found myself thinking about the conversation I'd had with Rikko.

Sadly, I realized I was more likely to bare my soul to an expatriate Israeli I've known less than seven years than to any of the women in my life. Christina. My mom. Fay. The women in bars. The women at work. The ones who'd invited me into their bed. The ones I invited into mine. The truth was, I loved the company of women, and not just for their bodies. They seem infinitely powerful, yet terribly fragile. Fascinating mysteries all.

But for reasons that frankly baffled me, I had to admit that, approaching the age of thirty-eight, I was able to get only so close to women before I put up a wall and drove them away. Sitting there, listening to reggae, I felt suddenly agitated by these thoughts and the image they kept provoking: the agony on my mother's face as the priest blessed my father's casket. I had been unable to look at that face twenty-eight years ago. I was unable to think about it now.

I went to the railing to clear my head. Leaning over to look into the rippling black water, taking deep breaths, I told myself it was no good to dwell in the past. To get my mind off these things, I forced myself to begin imagining Morgan Cook's killer. It's something I often do. It helps me to have a fix on him as the investigation goes forward.

Standing there, looking at the black channel water, I rendered the killer as the man in the trench coat Cook met outside the Yellow Tail, a man I gave thin lips and gray irises riding high in his head, a man who called himself Seeker. He was backlit by the neon sign outside the nightclub, the contours of his exact shape obscured by the late hour, the mist, the coat, and the floppy hat. From inside his sleeve a serpent's head appeared, arched, and swayed in the pale light like a cobra emerging from a basket.

Then, despite every effort to keep this image dominant in my thoughts, the form of the trench-coated man and his snake mutated into a broad-backed figure crouched in shadows behind crates on the South Boston waterfront in the darkest hours before dawn.

It is two o'clock in the morning. The docks are empty and silent, except for the breeze, the lapping of harbor water against the piers, and the slap of my father's shoes against the wet planks. My dad looks around expectantly. A faceless man emerges from behind the crates. But my dad does not hesitate. He goes toward him. He gets so close that the man can shoot him twice with a shotgun. Then the man pours gas on my dad's body and lights it, sending my life up in flames.

SEVENTEEN

Tuesday began with a four-hour on-line session as Anaconda that left me feeling as if I needed a second shower. I received quite a few come-ons, some of them shocking in their complexity, but none from Seeker.

The rest of the day I caught up on paperwork, wrote a memo for Assistant Chief Adler, put together the murder book, and organized a chart to track the flow of the investigation. I managed to get away in time to coach practice. Jimmy seemed happy I was there, but when I asked him if he wanted to get a pizza, he said he had homework.

Wednesday, Rikko and I passed the early afternoon and late evening at the Yellow Tail, trying to find a regular who might have seen Morgan Cook with the man in the olive trench coat and floppy hat. But no one we talked with remembered seeing Cook or his companion the night he disappeared.

The early lab results came in Thursday morning. The semen on Cook's bed was identified as belonging to a person with blood type O. Cook was an O. Unfortunately, a lot of people are type O. The vaginal secretions indicated a blood type of O-negative, rarer, but not that scarce in the general population.

The lubricant on the sheets was identified as Sensicare, an item available at most drugstores. The wax in the carpet was from a scented candle designed to increase sensual awareness and sold at twenty locations throughout the county. The apple found in Cook's mouth was identified as a Granny Smith, a green tart variety used in pies.

In addition to the low dose of strychnine, the lab found Cook had a blood alcohol level of .16 at the time of death. Twice the legal limit. They had also found traces of a substance they could not identify. Solomon said the matter appeared organic, not synthesized, and bore a chemical resemblance to mild sedatives such as belladonna.

The medical examiner concluded that the strychnine, the booze, and the mysterious soporific might have been enough to keep Cook in a bewildered enough state to get him tied to the bed before the snake came out.

The vacuum cleaner bag revealed more hairs, which the lab said came from as many as seventeen different people. Jorge had the unenviable task of running down the former tenants of the apartment as well as maids, custodial workers, and contractors who'd happened to be inside Cook's place in the past year. He asked for hair samples so we might do comparisons.

On Friday, Missy and I met with agents of the U.S. Fish and Wildlife Service, who allowed us to download the names of people who applied for permits to import venomous snakes in the entire Southwest region during the past five years. In the California-Nevada-Arizona area alone, 318 such applications had been made. The reasons given for importation were myriad, from zoos to wild animal farms to medical researchers to a company that milked snake venom, then injected it into horses to manufacture antivenin.

Jorge stayed late, feeding the names and organizations into our computer, while I went off to coach Jimmy's game. When I got there he was already out on the field. He looked wrung out and wouldn't talk to me. But his foul mood did not affect his playing. His first at bat, he ripped a triple to right. Walter and Fay came into the bleachers just after the hit. His mom saw him on third and came straight to the dugout.

"You're letting him play?"

"Sure, why not?"

Her face twisted in anger. "He didn't tell you? He was supposed to tell you."

"Tell me what?"

She held out her palms. "Okay, let's play his game. We'll talk afterwards."

She stormed back to Walter, who had his nose buried in a journal dedicated to Polynesian drums. Stetson's kid knocked Jimmy in on a bloop single. I almost said something to him, then decided to let it all wait until the game was over. Jimmy went four for five, including a home run.

Afterward, he ran off toward Walter's Suburban before I could grab him. Fay found me in the parking lot. "He slugged a kid at school."

"Slugged a kid?" I said, setting the bat bag down. "For what?"

"It doesn't really matter, does it? His teacher says he's got a lot of anger."

"He doesn't have a lot of anger. He's just a kid. A good kid. The other guy must have provoked him. He has the right to defend himself. It's just playground stuff."

Fay crossed her arms, shaking her head. "Principal says Jimmy was the aggressor. For some reason he's hurting these days, Shay; he won't talk about it and he's acting out. Think of the way he behaved the other night on the mound."

I glanced over at Jimmy, who was watching us. "He's just competitive. It's okay to get steamed when you screw up, you know. How do you know he isn't pissed that Walter's basically living with you."

"He likes Walter."

"Yeah, Walter's crazy about him."

"Walter spends more time with him than you do," she replied evenly. "Jimmy got suspended for two days. This is serious, Shay. You need to be there Wednesday morning, nine A.M. Meeting with his teacher, the guidance counselor, and the principal."

"This case, I can't—"

She poked me in the chest. "Be there, or so help me, Shay—"

I held up my hands. "Okay, okay. I surrender. I'll be there."

"Now, no dodging because disciplining him makes you feel bad. I need you not to be his fishing buddy here or his coach. I want you to be his dad. I need you to talk to him. I'm not getting through at all. He says he hates me."

I nodded, feeling worse than I had yanking him off the mound when he got shelled. Jimmy saw his mom's signal and came trudging toward me with his head down. About ten feet from me, he stopped and said, "You mad?"

"Damn straight I'm mad," I snapped. "I'd known about this, you wouldn't have played tonight. You're suspended from the team for the next two games."

"Suspended?" he shouted. "No, you can't do that!"

"Hell I can't," I said. "Get over here. Now."

Jimmy glared at me, then lowered his head, came forward four steps, and stopped, staring at my shoes, his hands gathered into fists. I plucked his cap off his head and held him by his chin. "You gonna tell me what happened?"

He looked up at me, his eyes flaring, "Tino was being an asshole, so I hit him."

"Nice language. Way to control yourself too. Haven't I told you being a good athlete is about keeping your act together?"

He pulled away, shaking his head. "What do you care, Dad? Unless it's your job or baseball or fishing, you don't see anything."

I got down on one knee. "What don't I see, Jimbo?"

He looked at me, then looked away, his chin trembling. Then he suddenly burst into tears. "Everything ending."

"What are you talking about?"

He pointed his finger at me, sobbing. "You'll see. It's all ending. And you just go on as if nothing matters. The way you always do!" He turned before I could grab him, then sprinted back toward the car, dodging by his mother.

"Jimmy!" I yelled after him. "Jimmy!"

But he never looked back.

EIGHTEEN

"*Judgment is here again,*" *the voice said.* "*Second trial.*"
The naked man lying on the bed was drenched in fever sweat. His elbow burned and pounded. Drool oozed from around the apple jammed in his mouth. His eyes were closed. He was barely conscious, but he tried to follow the voice, this evil voice that spoke of sex and salvation.

"*Are you as worthy as Saint Paul, Matthew?*"

He could not help it. Even though the naked man knew the voice was death, he felt he had to turn toward it, as if it were some siren that sang of flesh, God, and damnation.

Lust. Pure and unbridled. Isn't that what he had wanted? Isn't that what had been offered? Isn't that what he'd deserved after so many years of loneliness and denial? It had all been so primal and carnal and he'd loved every minute until it had gone to black and this new voice had come to him. This voice of Judgment speaking through a snake.

"*Matthew? You're not answering me.*"

The voice is between my legs now, *Matthew* thought. Between my legs!

In a panic that cut through his stupor, Matthew jammed his chin to his sweating chest and forced his eyes wide open. Judgment was right there above and between his legs, twisting and hissing in the air, held just out of striking range by the hands of a tormentor hidden in shadow.

Matthew looked into the serpent's graveyard eyes, saw its intent, and screamed against the apple: "Naauugh! Nauuggh!" He jerked his hips back and tore his head side to side as the hands lowered the snake into range.

It coiled to strike and the voice demanded, "Are you right with the Lord, Matthew?"

NINETEEN

On saturday we ran the names of the individuals and organizations that had requested snake import permits through our own criminal intelligence databases as well as state and regional police files. Results of nearly two days of work: not one match.

"Surprise, surprise, Seeker doesn't do things the legal way," Missy said.

"Still no hits off ViCAP?" I asked Jorge.

"Nada."

It was mid-afternoon. I was discouraged at our progress. Other than a vague description of the man in the long green coat at the Yellow Tail, Mary Aboubacar's police artist sketch, and the cryptic message on the mirror, we had no going leads.

"Let's pack it in for a needed day off," I said. "We're back at it bright and early Monday. I'm gonna take Jimbo fishing, see if I can get him to open up."

"Still no luck, huh?" Rikko asked.

"Fay says he's just sitting in his room, brooding."

Missy started grabbing her things. "Sorry I can't stick around to dissect your fragmented family, but

I got a date. You know how tough it is to get a date with shoulders like these?"

"I got a date too," Jorge said, getting up from his computer and winking at me and Rikko. "The blonde with the tits in patrol out in the Heights."

Missy elbowed him in the stomach. "Have respect, huh?"

Jorge doubled over and groaned, "What?!"

The phone rang. Laughing, I picked it up. "Moynihan."

"Sounds like you're having fun up there on a late Saturday afternoon," said Lieutenant Anna Cleary, the watch commander.

"Just getting started I hope. You free tonight?"

"Working. As you're going to be. Hate to ruin your evening, Shay, but we've got another one: black, blistered, and tied to a bed."

As the gull flies, Matthew Haines did not live far from my slip on Shelter Island, one, maybe two miles west in the community of Point Loma. His home, a yellow, three-bedroom Craftsman, was completely shielded from the quiet street and from the neighbors by a hedge of wild roses. Technically, Haines was employed as a systems technician for The Pantheon Group, a military contractor with corporate offices in Newport Beach. But he was assigned full time to the San Diego Naval Submarine Base, where he worked on sonar equipment.

Haines was a shy, balding, pudgy thirty-five-year-old who worked eight to four-thirty, Monday through

Friday, then went home and fixed up his home, the first he had ever owned. To cover his mortgage, he rented rooms to two junior submarine officers who spent most of their time away from San Diego. One of the roommates, Ensign Chuck Larsen, was currently on duty in the Philippines. The other, Lieutenant Commander Donald Aiken, returned early that afternoon from a three-week training course in Virginia to find the front door wide open and his landlord naked and tied to his bed.

"Been dead at least fifteen hours," said Dr. Marshall Solomon when I arrived on the porch. "Snakebites near his crotch, at his elbow, and along the jawline. And the killer left you another message."

"Everyone nonessential, out!" I yelled at the patrol officers milling about.

"What about us?" Missy asked.

"Rikko with me. You and Jorge organize the patrolmen, start canvassing the neighborhood. Somebody had to have seen or heard something."

Solomon gestured Rikko and me toward a hallway that exited off a kitchen in the shambles of remodeling. The passage smelled of new paint. The beige pile carpet appeared recently laid. There were two small bedrooms and a bathroom off the main hallway. The door to the master bedroom had been sanded but not yet stained.

The room beyond was filled with a hodgepodge of furniture that all looked like it had been purchased at yard sales, then refinished. In the corner, under a bank of halogen warming lights, were two fifty-gallon terrariums set on a wooden stand. Inside the first tank, clinging to a piece of bleached driftwood, was a reptile that looked like a smaller version of an iguana. Inside the second terrarium, a snake with an ink-black snout coiled on tan gravel. A mask of coral orange encircled its eyes. The pattern—coral orange and ebony—repeated itself the length of the serpent's body.

The remodeler himself lay on a wrought-iron bed in the same spread-eagle position in which we'd found Morgan Cook. This time the restraints had been left in place: simple white nylon cord about a quarter inch in diameter, the kind you might find in any hardware store, but now stained rust red from the abrasions about Haines's wrists and ankles. His eyes were stretched wide and dull against the puffiness of his face. His head and body twisted away from us, as if he'd been struggling to get away from something right up to the moment of death. A green apple jutted from his mouth. Mingling with the smell of death, there was a strange fruity scent I did not recognize.

Haines's skin exhibited the same sort of splotchy red fluids we'd seen on Cook. His left arm and thigh were inflated as well. But the rest of the body did not look quite the same. Part of it, according to Solomon, was that Haines did not have Cook's powerful physique. Rather, the sonar technician had a bell-shaped torso and a tire of flab about his abdomen, which affected the blackening of his body, making it more erratic than uniform. And streaks of a white substance had been painted along his inner thighs and through his pubic hair up to his lower abdomen.

On the far side of the bed was an open closet door. A mirror hung on the door. Words had been written there in Haines's own blood: *Acts 28:5–6.*

The room sawed and spun as it always does when I confront violent, inexplicable death. But this was different, accompanied by a seasick yawning in my stomach.

"Amen killer," I said.

"This is the shit," Rikko agreed.

Amen killers—what my sister calls murderers who act out of bizarre interpretations of God's will—are among the most dangerous. Because they believe they are anointed by a higher power, they rarely stop until they're caught. *Acts 28:5–6* was obviously a reference to the Book of Acts in the Bible.

"This isn't just about sex anymore," I said. "It's about religion too. Let's get Christina back right away."

"I'll call her," Rikko said. "See if she can get your mother to baby-sit."

Two crime scene technicians appeared in the doorway. "I want you guys to inhale this place," I said. "He made a mistake in here. I can feel it. Find his error."

But Haines's bedroom was almost as evidence-free as Cook's. The floor had been vacuumed. The dirt bag was missing from the Hoover we found on the back porch. The furniture had been dusted.

The bathroom counters wiped down. The white streaks about Haines's crotch turned out to be Clorox, which Solomon interpreted as an effort to blitz whatever DNA evidence had been left after sex. They also found semen on the inside of Haines's thigh, but no vaginal fluids.

"There has to be more evidence," I said. "Fibers, fingerprints. Something."

Jorge stuck his head in the room. "We've talked with all the immediate neighbors, boss," he said. "No one heard a thing. Other than a lot of hammering and sawing, the guy was quiet as a Buddhist monk. Most of them didn't even know who he was. But one of the roommates is here. Outside on the porch. A JAG's with him."

Twenty

Lieutenant commander donald aiken sat on the porch swing. He stared down into the Styrofoam cup of 7-Eleven coffee he held between his knees, a trim man in his early thirties with acne scars high on his cheeks. The JAG officer, a stout woman, pug-faced, early forties, stood next to him. Both wore khaki uniforms.

"Commander Betty Riggs," she said after I identified myself. "You're in charge, Sergeant?"

"For the time being," I said. "What's the lieutenant need a military attorney for?"

"Protocol," she replied. "We counsel all officers to contact the judge advocate general's office if they have any contact with civilian police. Don't worry, the lieutenant wishes to speak freely."

"Speak away, then," I said, turning to him.

"I'd been out at sea, came back after a month, and Matt was just lying there like that," he began, his head shaking side to side. "Can't believe it. He was a weird duck, but, you know...but never in a million years do you think this kind of thing could happen."

"Whaddaya mean, 'weird duck'?"

Aiken shrugged. "You know, one of those guys who's not one of the guys. Didn't like sports. Didn't go to parties. Worked on his house, whiz on computers, loved *Star Trek*, had a lizard for a pet."

"What about sex?" I asked.

Aiken rolled his jaw. "That's a whole different take," he replied. "Far as I know, Matt was a virgin. He was raised a strict Catholic back in Illinois, Champagne-Urbana, I think. He was always saying he didn't believe in premarital sex."

"He was thirty-six and still saving himself?"

"Amazing, huh? But I think it drove him nuts, because, like I said, he was a weird duck. Women weren't exactly lining up for him. Larsen and I got him drunk one night before we shipped out..." Aiken stopped to look at Commander Riggs, then shrugged and went on: "Sorry, Commander, but we told him it was abnormal for a guy his age not to be getting laid regularly and we said we'd bring in an escort so he could get his rocks off. On us."

Riggs raised an eyebrow but said nothing.

"He go for it?"

Aiken shook his head. "Thought he was gonna. Larsen was picking up the phone. Then he, Matt, got all red-faced and called off the dogs."

"Sure he wasn't gay?"

"I thought about that a couple of times," Aiken replied. "I don't think so. I mean, he read *Playboy* and seemed interested in the pictures. But who knows what goes on in people's brains? I mean,

Jesus, did you see what he looked like in there? He had to have gotten himself into a dark place to die like that."

I nodded. "What about the snake in the terrarium in his room?"

"That's new," he said. "Since I've been gone, anyway."

"We done?" Commander Briggs asked.

"For the time being," I replied. "You sticking around San Diego, Lieutenant?"

Aiken nodded. "Not due to ship out again for at least three months."

"Tell us if you're going to leave earlier," I said.

Briggs and Aiken left the porch. Twilight had come, turning Haines's yard a fiery purple. The first moths of the season fluttered in that eerie light. Beyond the hedge, voices murmured. And beyond the voices, San Diego churned along, oblivious to the horror that would greet them in their Sunday paper. I flashed on myself as a young boy, looking at the front page of *The Boston Globe* and the headline that described my father's murder. I did not understand much of the article, only that his captain called my father a hero. To this day I distrust the word *hero*. Too often it's used to describe someone who died and left a young family behind.

Lieutenant Fraiser hustled up the driveway, followed by Captain Merriweather and Assistant Chief Helen Adler.

"Same MO?" Merriweather asked. He was dressed like he'd been called off the golf course:

lime-green pants, matching shirt, and a blue cotton sweater.

"It's a match except for what's written on the mirror in there," I said, then gave them the Book of Acts angle.

"What's the citation mean?"

"Christina's looking it up and is on her way," I said.

Fraiser scowled. "Who gave you authorization to bring in an outside consultant? That decision has to occur at a level far above sergeant."

I said nothing but looked at Adler.

The assistant chief glanced at Fraiser, then back at me. "She's in. I want this guy caught and fast." Then she took a step closer to me. "But know this, Sergeant: The fire under your feet just caught wind. Everyone—the lieutenant, the captain, me, the chief, the mayor, the papers, the television stations, everyone who could make your life hell—is going to be watching over your shoulder. I know. I've been there."

"I can handle it," I assured her. "We'll work this day and night, but I'm going to need help: at least two more detectives."

"We can't go pulling detectives off of other teams," Fraiser protested. "Everyone's swamped as it is."

"You want this case solved, Chief, give me the men to do it," I said.

"When's Burnette back on the job?" Merriweather asked.

"Monday morning," I said. "But she's still in rehab on her knee. She's not going to be much use to us in the field."

"Put her to work on the phones, then," Adler said. "Best I can do for now."

The assistant chief and Merriweather went inside, leaving me on the porch with Fraiser, who waited until they were out of earshot to say: "Get one thing straight, hotshot: I'm watching you. Step out of line once, leave one thread of evidence hanging, sneeze the wrong way, Moynihan, and I'll get you busted back to patrol." I looked down on Fraiser's shiny dome and forced a smile. "Bet you say that to all the boys, Lieutenant."

TWENTY-ONE

Christina arrived at haines's house shortly past nine dressed in jeans, running shoes, and a hooded gray UC Berkeley sweatshirt. Her wavy red hair was pulled back in a ponytail and I flashed on her at seven years old, sitting in a little black dress in a church pew next to my mother while eight uniformed officers carried Dad's coffin to the hearse. We had both been watching our mom, who seemed on the verge of collapse, then dropped our eyes to each other. Christina looked at me in a way that told me we were all lost.

Thanks for coming down," I said, after the two uniformed officers guarding the driveway let her through. "The girls okay?"

"With Mom," she said, kissing Rikko on the cheek.

"You look like hell," she said as we started down the driveway.

"And you look like a young coed, but I know you're the mother of two with a thriving medical practice," I replied. "How *do* you do it, Sis?"

"See there," she said to Rikko. "Always trying to divert the attention from Shay." Then she turned back to me. "I hear you've been having flashbacks about Dad."

"Thanks, pal," I said, stopping to glare at Rikko. "Look, Chrissy, it's no big deal."

"I disagree," she said, watching me levelly. "To my knowledge you've never spoken with a mental health professional about Dad's murder. That's not healthy, Shay."

"Excellent diagnosis, Ms. Freud," I said, starting toward the house again. "But I honestly have no time for this now. I got Jimmy slugging kids and Fay blaming me and a lieutenant who's gunning for my badge and two guys killed with snakes, for Christ's sake. I have no time for a shrink session!"

She grabbed me by the arm, glanced back at the two uniformed officers, who'd turned at my raised voice, then whispered urgently: "Rikko's concerned. I'm concerned. Mom's concerned. You've been under a lot of stress lately. That can bring up stuff, like these flashbacks. You are not alone in this, Shay. You weren't the only one affected by his murder. I spent a lot of time in counseling because of it."

"I know that," I snapped. "Look, Sis, no offense, but I'm perfectly aware of the bottom line his death has had on me and on you. I want to put that nameless man on the dock and every other faceless bastard like him in the death chamber. You want to understand what drove the guy to the dock in the first place."

Our eyes locked in an understanding that can only be shared by siblings scarred by murder. "So we can catch him before he kills again," she said.

I smiled. "Exactly. So let's leave the past where it belongs and catch this guy. Okay?"

Her eyes studied me a moment. "Okay, Shay," she said. "Your call."

Once we were inside the house, the matter was dropped and Christina was all professional. After her initial shock at the condition of the corpse, she came in close while Solomon pointed out the position and order of the bite wounds: pocket of the right elbow; inner left thigh, just below the scrotum; high in the neck, below the turn of the jaw.

Then she went to the foot of the bed, looking all around her, lingering on the bloody biblical citation before announcing: "Artist."

"What artist?" Rikko asked.

She stuffed her hands in the pocket of her sweatshirt. "Many of these repeat killers like to take souvenirs of their grisly deeds," she began. "A popular keepsake is a Polaroid photograph of the scene. A lot of them do that. There's even a convincing theory that Jack the Ripper was a painter who later rendered depictions of women in the exact body positions of the prostitutes he butchered. The point is, Polaroids or paintings, these guys were acting journalistically: preserving an image of their carnage.

"But this guy is different, very different," she went on. "He's not acting the journalist here, taking candid pictures after the fact. He's posing his canvas up front."

I looked at Haines's body and around the room. "Run that by me again," I said.

Christina gestured toward the ropes, the bed, the bloody mirror, and the bites. "They're exactly the same," she said. "It's not enough that he kills these men. It's the way he does it. The ropes, the bed, the position of the bites—they all mean something to him, the way they would an artist posing a still life. It's very personal. It strikes me as less a ritual than a reenactment."

"So he's done it before?" I asked.

"Or seen someone do something like it before. I'd bet on it, Shay. The specifics are too striking."

"What about the message?" Rikko asked. "That's different."

"So is the bleach on the groin," I noted.

"Variations on a theme," she replied. "Think of him as an artist again, creating one massive work out of individual panels. Each murder, each panel of his painting, contains these constants: the naked man, the ropes, the suggestion of sadomasochism, the snakebite marks. But serial murders are often a progression. In each panel and each murder there'll be variations he adds or deletes to suit his fancy."

"But he's the only one who understands the iconography here," said Solomon, who'd been standing quietly in the doorway.

"And the ultimate meaning of his work," she agreed.

"So there's no way he stops after two," Rikko said.

"Not a chance," she replied. "He's killing at roughly one-week intervals already. More often than not, the time gaps between these sort of killings get shorter and shorter with every murder."

"What about the Book of Acts?" I asked. "You get the citation?"

"Out of Dad's old King James Bible," she said, tugged a piece of paper out of her back pocket. "The verses cited and the ones just before it refer to the years after Christ's death, when Saint Paul went forth to spread the Gospel and was shipwrecked among savages and attacked by a snake hiding in a stack of driftwood: *'And Paul shook off the beast into the fire, and felt no harm. Howbeit they looked when he should have swollen, or fallen down dead suddenly: but after they had looked a great while, and saw no harm come to him, they changed their minds and said he was a god.'*"

"He thinks he's God?" Rikko asked.

"Well, he certainly identifies with Saint Paul, who was not bitten, while his victim is bitten repeatedly," Christina said. "But honestly, I'm a bit out of my league here. I suggest you find an expert who might be better able to explain the passage's significance.

"It's probably important and you should pursue that line of inquiry," she went on, looking from Solomon to Rikko to me. "But I still think that the key is to think of this as a reenactment. You figure out where this scene came from and you'll have your man."

TWENTY-TWO

As helen adler predicted, by the time we left the Haines crime scene, the fire was gathering wind. The local stations all led their late Saturday newscasts with footage of the body bag being taken from the sonar technician's home.

I got back to the *Nomad's Chant* well after midnight, having put in a ninety-hour work week, and fell asleep facedown on my bed without taking my clothes off. The phone jangled me awake at 7:30 A.M.

"Moynihan."

"Dad?"

"Jimbo. Hey, what's up?"

"When are you coming to get me to go fishing?"

Before I could come to enough to answer, call-waiting clicked. I told Jimmy to hold on, then pressed Flash. "Moynihan."

"*Have you seen the Daily News this morning?*" Helen Adler shouted in my ear.

I rolled on my back, feeling like a spike was being driven into my head. "Why?"

"Go get it. *Now,*" she growled. "I'll wait on the line."

"Uh ... okay," I said, then struggled off the bed, hitting Flash again. "Jimmy?"

"When are you coming to pick me up?" he demanded again.

Stumbling up the stairs to the main deck, I put one hand to my head. "We may have to postpone our trip, pal," I said. "We got another body last night and my boss is on the warpath."

There was a long silence, then Jimmy snarled: "You're just like Mom. You just don't care about any of it."

"Jimbo," I said, stepping out into the brilliant sunlight, squinting, looking groggily for the paper. "I'm in a vise here, and you're not helping me out by—"

"No!" he shouted. "You're not helping me. Or anyone! Either of you."

The line went dead.

"Shit, Jimbo, goddamn it," I said, feeling ticked and tired and guilty, feelings that gave way to a gallows trap door dropping through my stomach. *The Sunday Daily News* lay facing me near the gangway. Brett Tarentino's column was bannered across the top:

SNAKE CHARMER STRIKES AGAIN
Left Biblical Citation
Police Probe Gay Angle

"What the fuck is this!" I raged, snatching up the paper.

After identifying Haines as a naval contract worker and the second victim of what Tarentino was calling the Snake Charmer, the story went on to quote an "unnamed source close to the investigation" as saying the killer "left a biblical citation from late in the New Testament on a mirror at the scene."

The story then introduced Lieutenant Donald Aiken as Haines's roommate. Aiken told Tarentino we'd asked him all sorts of questions about the victim's sexuality, including the possibility that he was gay.

Out of that single innocuous question, the story went on to raise vague parallels between the current slayings and those perpetrated by Andrew Cunanan, the gay gigolo from San Diego who murdered five men, including fashion designer Versace, several years back. Tarentino pointed out that both of the Snake Charmer's victims were men, then restated the fact we'd questioned Aiken about Haines's possible gay sex life, then baldly asserted that Cook's interest in group sex, especially with two men, could be construed as "at the very least bisexual if not outright homosexual longing."

The piece concluded with Tarentino warning the city's gay population that "a Bible-toting serial killer may be targeting you for death."

I punched flash again. "Chief?"

"I'm still here," she seethed. "You've read it?"

"Trash journalism and I had nothing to do with it," I began. "Tarentino was paging me all last night, but I never returned his calls—never even spoke with him. I did ask Aiken whether Haines was gay, but only because it seemed logical, given that he was thirty-six and had never slept with a woman. The rest Tarentino wove out of whole cloth."

"Let me tell you something, Sergeant: The mayor's been getting a steady stream of calls for the last hour and a half from leaders of the gay community," she said. "Which means I've been getting the mayor's calls."

"I hear you and I understand," I replied, "but I had nothing to do with this."

"Is this a gay serial killer?" she demanded.

"No," I said again. "We have no evidence of that at all. This is complete bullshit. I'm going to talk with Tarentino. Now. Get him to retract it."

I hung up before she could say anything, then stormed down the gangway, across the dock, and up onto Tarentino's boat. I pounded on the door. No one answered and I pounded again. I heard footsteps and a twenty-something bare-chested Latino with frosted spiked hair yanked open the door and glared at me. "What's your problem, man?"

"Where's Tarentino?"

He puffed up his chest. "What business that of yours, big man? Chaco here now."

I stared at him incredulously. "I am not a former lover, you macho moron. I'm a homicide detective and—"

"It's okay, Chaco, the sergeant is an old and dear friend," Tarentino called as he climbed the stairs from below deck, wearing sandals and blue surf trunks. A gold cross hung between his pecs. The columnist had a day's growth of beard on his chin and looked like he'd slept less than I had. An unlit cigarette dangled from his lip.

He plucked a pair of sunglasses from a galley table strewn with newspapers, shoved them on, and squeezed by Chaco out into the sunshine, groaning: "It's too early for a Sunday wake-up. To what do I owe the honor? My column, I'm guessing."

"That piece of trash has lit fires all over town," I said. "One of them under the mayor's ass."

Tarentino crossed his arms, his face darkening. "Trash? Is that what you call it when I write the truth, that gay men are being killed? As usual, the homophobia of the average policeman rears its head."

"We don't know that they're being killed because they're gay!"

"You don't know that they aren't," he retorted. "And I for once am not about to sit around waiting for a third man to be venomed to death before I report a lead the police are obviously following."

"It was a routine question because Haines was a virgin," I said. "And drawing parallels between what's going on here and Andrew Cunanan is complete crap."

"I don't think so," he retorted. "This could be a gay man, just like Cunanan, victimizing men on the verge of fleeing the closet."

"Brett, that's the problem with you reporters: Your minds aren't open enough to see any possibility except those ingrained by your prejudices—in this case, your gayness. We think it's a couple killing these guys. A man and a woman: the man, the predator; the woman, the lure."

"Possible," Tarentino allowed. "But unlikely. They'd both have to be monsters, and monsters rarely travel in pairs."

"Fine, Brett, I'll give you the benefit of the doubt. Know any violent queers who keep poisonous snakes?"

"Just one," he replied, a knowing sneer forming on his face.

"And who might that be?"

Tarentino looked over at his lover boy lounging against the hull. "Tell him what you told me the other night, Chaco."

The young Hispanic looked puzzled, then realized what Tarentino was talking about, brightened, and looked at me slyly. "Nick Foster. He tie me up once. Got really angry."

TWENTY-THREE

"Not a chance," missy Pan grumbled Monday morning, shaking her head. "I've got a built-in flame detector and Foster did not register."

"Your meter must be on the fritz," I replied, pulling Mary Aboubacar's artist sketch off the cubicle wall above my desk. I looked at it, then shrugged. "It's possible. Foster's got the jaw and the buff upper body. Anyway, this Chaco character says no doubt *Cold Blooded!* boy is bisexual. Says if you think women get swoony over a craggy guy wrestling gators, you should see the swish boys wilt when he makes a late-night entrance in the bars up in Hillcrest. Says he's got a penchant for rough trade too."

Rikko sat on the edge of his desk, drinking coffee. "What is this 'rough trade'?"

"Into ropes, chains, and leather."

"Oh, that," Rikko said.

"S and M dominator?" asked the intense African-American woman sitting across from me, her left leg in a brace and resting on a crutch laid against the desk.

"Certainly the picture Chaco paints, Freddie."

"We're just one step from saying he could have laid a rattlesnake on Cook's and Haines's bodies, aren't we?" she pressed.

"Not quite," I smiled.

Detective Freddie Burnette is one of my favorite people. She grew up in Watts and got a track scholarship to UCLA, where she majored in criminal science and accounting. She's the quickest study I know, street-wise, opinionated, and rugged: five foot five, 142 pounds of quick-twitch muscle. She can run the hundred in under eleven seconds. Or could, anyway. In early March, Freddie blew out her right knee during the takedown of an Amerasian gangbanger named Fatty Wu Marshall.

Fatty Wu was one of the meanest bastards in Southern California, a majordomo in the methamphetamine trade who coldly executed two of his top lieutenants when they had the temerity to challenge his authority. When we went to arrest Fatty Wu, he bailed out the back window of his girlfriend's crib and hightailed it into a construction site. Freddie went right out the window after him and chased him into the shell of an apartment building.

He waited in the shadows for Freddie and managed to hit her knee with a crowbar, causing a meniscus tear and a complete severing of the anterior cruciate ligament. When he attempted to do something similar to her skull, Freddie responded by putting four nine-millimeter holes in his chest. As I said, one of my favorite people.

Now she looked at me expectantly and said, "Well, shouldn't we at least bring Foster in for questioning?"

"Not until we get more," I said. "On paper we have nothing to link him to either Cook or Haines. And no motive. Or maybe we're not seeing it." I picked up the murder book and tossed it to Freddie. "Find something we missed and we'll bring him in."

Missy threw up her hands. "At least Foster's something, Boss. I mean we got less evidence out of Haines than we did at Cook's."

"Less in volume, maybe," I snapped. "But this morning's report is that the techs found two straight brown hairs on the headboard side of the mattress. I told you Seeker would make a mistake. By the way, who's on deviate detail today?"

Jorge raised his hand. "I'm up ten to two."

Missy got a foul look about her. "I'm two to four."

"All right, you two go wallow in the world of swingers, and Rikko and I'll—"

The phone on my desk rang. I picked up. "Homicide."

A woman's voice, thick southern accent: "I'm looking for Sergeant Moynihan."

"Speaking."

"The Sergeant Moynihan working the killing of those men with the snake?"

"The same. How can I help you?"

"My name is Susan Dahoney, Assistant Professor Susan Dahoney of the Department of Religious

Studies at San Diego State. Perhaps you've heard about my recently published book—"

"Is there a point to this call?" I asked impatiently. "I've got a lot on my plate."

She hesitated, cleared her throat, then forged on. "And I'm sorry for intruding on your time, but I read in the paper yesterday that there was a biblical citation the killer—"

"We're neither confirming nor denying that."

"Well, Sergeant, I might help explain it," she said. "To help you understand the killer's mind, I mean."

I hesitated, then said, "Can I put you on hold a second, Professor...?"

"Dahoney," she drawled. "Susan Dahoney. And of course."

I punched the Hold button, then turned toward Rikko and Jorge. "Check out a Susan Dahoney. Bible expert at SDSU. Wants to help us with the Haines citation. Do it quick. I'll stay on the line."

Both detectives understood immediately. These kinds of calls can be legitimate. Some are cranks. And every once in a while, especially when the case involves a serial killer, the perpetrators or their kin will try to insinuate themselves into the investigation. For that reason alone, we like to know to whom we're talking.

I punched the Hold button. "Sorry about that, Professor Dahoney."

"Not a problem," she replied agreeably.

"Anyway Professor, we have professionals who assist us in our psychological profiles, and we don't make it a practice to reveal the details of our investigations."

"Oh, I'm sure you don't," she said. "But as I said, I'm an expert on the Bible, Sergeant. Well, more a Bible sleuth, actually. I might be able to offer you some insight your professionals can't. And I'd be glad to come by your office."

She was being so insistent, my hidden agenda alarm started to ring. I glanced over my shoulder. Jorge held a finger in the air, phone pressed to his ear.

"Can I put you on hold one more time?" I said, not waiting for a reply, then stabbed the button and looked expectantly toward Jorge, who was just setting his phone down.

"She's for real," he said. "Hired in January on the basis of a book she wrote about the second woman in the Bible, or something like that. This is her first teaching position. But she's supposedly real smart. Real ambitious."

"Reason enough to talk with her, see what her angle is," I said, punching the Hold button a fourth time. "Professor, how about we come to your place?"

TWENTY-FOUR

The sun had a razor's glint to it when Rikko and I left downtown headquarters. That's the thing about San Diego: Three hundred days a year the weather's fine, so fine that it tends to overshadow everything that's sketchy about the city—the crime, the near-strangulation traffic, the unbridled development. San Diegans know they live on the edge of chaos, but don't care because it's chaos under sapphire skies, chaos at seventy-seven degrees, chaos by the beach with low relative humidity.

Forty-five minutes and eighteen tortured miles of east-bound traffic later, we arrived at San Diego State. The university occupies some 220 acres of prime real estate atop a bluff south of Interstate 8. The buildings are mostly cast cement and overlook quadrangles of lush green grass bisected by cement walkways, accented by clusters of palms, and populated by the American male fantasy come to life: tribes of nubile Southern California coeds.

Rikko and I hiked north through campus toward Crowley Hall, the building that houses the Department of Religious Studies, then climbed to the fourth floor where the office of Susan Dahoney, Ph.D., occupied the southeast corner. The upper panel of the oak door to her office was smoked glass.

Affixed to the glass was a book jacket dominated by a photograph of an ancient terra-cotta bas-relief of a nude woman sitting within the crotch of a tree trunk. A dragon lay beneath the woman's feet. A bird perched atop her head. The title, *The Second Woman,* ran above the photograph, Susan Dahoney's byline below.

I gave the glass a sharp rap.

Inside, a chair screeched, then sandals slapped across the floor and the door was flung back to reveal a flushed, beaming, gorgeous woman in her late twenties. She wore a shift of primitive fabric hand-dyed in a gold and indigo print. Her brunette hair had been given henna highlights, cut shoulder length, then feathered around a face that reminded me of a young Elizabeth Taylor.

She beamed at Rikko, then stuck out both hands, grabbed one of his, and began pumping it like a politician working a Fourth of July parade. "Susan Dahoney, Ph.D.," she said with Dixie gentility.

"Rikko Varjjan, Detective," he said, smiling wryly.

"The pleasure's all mine," Dahoney said, affecting delight to know him.

She turned to me, glanced at my left hand as if looking for a wedding ring, then grinned and took a step closer. She was a tall, fine-boned woman with large, startling blue movie-star eyes and a way of insisting her femininity on you by invading your personal space. And she wore a wonderfully subtle perfume.

"My," she drawled, "but you're a big one, aren't you, Sergeant Moynihan?"

Feeling slightly intoxicated, I smiled despite myself. Usually my job brings me in contact with the dregs of society, and here in the last week or so I'd been talking with a series of beautiful women. "Been that way since I was a boy," I said.

"I'll bet you were," she purred, sinewing one arm inside my elbow, guiding me into her office, calling over her shoulder, "C'mon, Detective Varjjan, I won't bite."

Her office was small and designed similarly to one on the other side of campus my mother had once occupied as an English composition instructor. The furniture was institutional. A horseman's waxed cotton duster hung off a coatrack in the corner. There were the books you'd expect, of course, most of them focused on various aspects of the Bible. But where the open walls of my mother's office had been covered with framed diplomas and pictures of our family, Dahoney had turned much of her space into a gallery of photographs of primitive artwork, many of them variations on the iconography present on the jacket cover affixed to her office door.

In some pieces, the nude woman was unabashedly sexual, flanked by owls, wearing a headdress of coils. In one she squatted on the backs of lions sporting wings, her knees wide to show her vulva. There were several in which the nude woman stood on an ocean shore, surrounded by threatening black figures. One small painting in particular caught my eye: The style was Old Master, with the nude woman rendered half voluptuous female, half serpent, her tail coiled about a tree trunk.

"Who's she?" I asked.

"Why the subject of my book, of course," Dahoney said, breaking the hold on my elbow to walk to a tidy pine desk and pick up two hard copies of *The Second Woman*. She handed us each one. "They're signed," she said.

"Thanks," I said, taking the book and looking at it. She had not received the bland academic publishing treatment I expected. Instead the book had been packaged as popular history. And her author's photo seemed designed to affect glamorous intrigue; in it she wore a black leather jacket, collar turned up, and a white blouse arranged to show a hint of cleavage. Her hair was perfectly messy.

"As I told you on the phone," she was saying, "I'm something of an accomplished detective myself. I mean, there it is, in your hands, gentlemen: the solution to the greatest unsolved mystery in the history of the Judeo-Christian world."

Rikko peered at the book. "That so?"

"Very much so," she said, gesturing us into two ladder-back chairs.

"So what is this great mystery?" Rikko grunted, sitting.

"Who was Cain's wife?" she said, circling her desk. She saw our confusion, bit her lip, and grinned.

Then she sat down and leaned toward us. "We know, or we think we know, who the first woman on earth was, at least according to the King James Version of the Bible."

"Eve," I said.

"The common supposition," she allowed. "And we know that after Adam and Eve were thrown out of Paradise, Eve bore two sons, Cain and Abel. Cain was a farmer. Abel was a shepherd. Cain grew jealous of Abel, because he seemed in God's favor. Cain slew his brother. For being the first murderer, God banished Cain and he ended up living east of Eden in the land of Nod."

"The Land of Nod?" I said, frowning. "I thought that was kids' bedtime stuff."

She shook her head. "Nod is Old Testament stuff, the book of Genesis stuff. The reason it's become synonymous with sleep, Sergeant, is that Nod can be interpreted as exile, a land of restless wandering. In a sense, the place of dreams or nightmares."

"But what about Cain's wife?" Rikko said.

"Give me time, Detective Varjjan," she gently chided. "Now, according to the King James Version, in the land of Nod, Cain met his wife, knew her, and she conceived and bore Enoch and so that the line of Adam went on. At no point, however, is Cain's wife ever named. We don't know who she was or where she came from. If you look at the world the way a lot of the folks back home did, Adam and Eve were made by God and placed here on earth. They had two sons, one of whom

142

was killed. The disgraced survivor got a wife, the second woman mentioned in the Bible. But here's the mystery: Who was she? Where did she come from?

"You see what a mess this creates now?" she asked, then pressed on before Rikko and I could reply. "Skeptics of creationism argue that for Cain to have found a wife, there must have been other people on earth who were not descendents of Adam and Eve.

"Defenders of the Bible as a true history of mankind," she went on, "need to be able to show that all human beings are descendants of one man and one woman, as only those who are such descendants can be saved from original sin by baptism. Unfortunately, that would mean that Cain had to have married one of the sisters that many early Christian writers say Adam and Eve bore. And that brings us to incest, one of the greatest taboos in the Bible. So, you see, the creationists are trapped too. They can't tell you who Cain's wife was, either. It becomes quite a loaded scenario, doesn't it?"

Before we could answer, she continued, gesturing at the book: The second woman, as I call her, has been the subject of great debate through the ages. She was used as a kind of silent witness at the Scopes Monkey Trial. Clarence Darrow, representing the evolutionists, questioned creationist witnesses about her at length in an effort to discredit the idea of Adam and Eve as the parents of mankind. Oh, it's all in the book. Read it."

"I will," I said. "But I get the feeling you have another theory about who the second woman was, right?"

There was a sudden fiery quality to Dahoney's gaze as she nodded and waved a finger at us. "You see, I've always believed—as an academic sleuth, if you will—that you have to keep asking questions, pushing deeper, finding original sources. So I went back and read ancient creation tales in the Jewish Talmud and in what are known as the Gnostic Gospels, lost writings that never made their way into the male-skewed King James version of the story of creation."

"So you are the feminist Bible expert," Rikko said.

"In a way, I suppose," Dahoney agreed. "According to the King James Bible, God created Adam first, then took one of his ribs to create Eve. Woman comes from man, according to this version of the creation tale. But the Gnostic writings suggest that God first created a hermaphroditic creature, half man, half woman, joined at the back: Adam and Lilith, not Adam and Eve. God separated Adam and Lilith and left them to prosper in Eden. Only Adam tried to subjugate Lilith by demanding she adopt the missionary position during intimate relations. Lilith saw herself as an equal and refused unless she was allowed in turn to mount Adam from above. Adam said no.

"Lilith left the Garden of Eden of her own accord," Dahoney went on, now swept up in the telling of her yarn, "and she went to live in exile near the Red Sea. When Adam protested to God, God sent his messengers to bring Lilith back. They found her living and engaging with demons in all manner of sensual pursuits. She refused to return to Paradise and live under Adam's command. So God created Eve and she bore Adam his sons. In the writings of the Gnostics I think I found my answer to the world's oldest mystery: When Cain was banished east of Eden, Lilith tired of the demons, left the Red Sea, went to Nod, found the second breaker of God's laws, and became his wife. That's the thesis of my book."

I nodded. "Very interesting."

"But not why we are here," Rikko said, setting the book in his lap.

"True enough," she said, resting back in her chair. "Now, how can I help? Was there or was there not a biblical citation where that poor man's body was found?"

I hesitated a moment, listening to my instincts, then decided to proceed.

"There was a New Testament citation," I said. "But before we discuss the details, I need you to swear not to relate our conversation to anyone else. Especially the media."

She paused, stiffened a beat, then nodded and made a zipping gesture across her mouth. "My lips are sealed, Sergeant. I just want to help."

For the next twenty minutes Rikko and I laid out the germane facts of the case and concluded with the two messages left on the mirror.

When we finished, she sat a moment, then shook her head. "This first one, *'Joy unspeakable to be holding death in your hands,'* is not from the Bible," she said. "Or at least I don't recollect it. I can run it through the computer concordances later if you like."

"Concordances?" Rikko said. "What is this?"

"Computer banks where I can word search through vast theological tracts like the Bible, the Talmud, and the Koran. I used them constantly to write my book."

"That would be helpful," I said. "What about the second message?"

"Book of Acts, chapter twenty-eight, verses five to six," Dahoney mumbled, turning to a leather-bound Bible on her desk.

She found the citation quickly and read the verses out loud: " *'And Paul shook off the beast into the fire, and felt no harm. Howbeit they looked when he should have become swollen, or fallen down dead suddenly; but after they had looked a great while and saw no harm come to him, they changed their minds and said he was a god.'* "

Raising her head, she tapped a finger on the open Bible. "The Book of Acts is essentially a history of the early Christian Church," she said. "It records what Jesus's disciples did in the years immediately after he was crucified. Luke, who wrote chapter twenty-eight of Acts, traveled extensively with the apostle Paul, the first real missionary. You see, before Saint Paul, the Christian faith was spread randomly, almost by accident, one person happening upon the story of Jesus and then another. Then Saint Peter, living at Antioch at the time, decided that the formal propagation and dissemination of the Gospel would be a deliberate policy of the young Church. So Peter sent Paul out on a series of missionary journeys throughout the Middle East, Asia, and Eastern Europe."

Dahoney got up and began pacing as she spoke. "Paul's calling was to convert Gentiles and Jews to the belief that Jesus was the Messiah foretold in the Old Testament. For his preaching he was stoned, beaten, and jailed. The first three of his missionary journeys were taken voluntarily. Paul's fourth missionary journey, which chapter twenty-eight of the Book of Acts describes, was involuntary. Paul was arrested for sedition and put aboard a ship to be brought to Rome to stand trial before Caesar. During the trip, in the year 59, if I remember correctly, Paul, Luke, and their Roman guards were shipwrecked on what is now the island of Malta. As the citation indicates, Paul was bitten by an adder, but did not suffer any consequences. As a result of that miracle, the people of Malta all became Christians."

I nodded. "So what does this say about our killer?"

Dahoney thought about it a moment. "Well, of course, I'm looking at this from a historical and textual perspective."

"We take any perspective right now," Rikko said.

She nodded. "I suppose you could speculate that your killer looks at himself as a missionary, spreading his own warped version of the word of God. Or as an exile, shipwrecked among barbarians. Or as a prisoner, for that matter."

"Or all three," I said.

"Yes, I suppose," she replied.

"We have reason to believe that Cook was into group sex, with the remote possibility that he might have been a closet bisexual or gay," I said. "Does that alter your interpretation any?"

The professor thought about that. "I suppose if your killer identifies with Saint Paul, as he seems to, he sees himself as someone anointed by God to do his bidding, and so unconstrained by the weaknesses of mere mortals. Homosexuality? Perhaps. The venom of a snake? Certainly. Perhaps he's also saying that if his victims were in God's favor—if they weren't into group sex or homosexuality, or whatever he sees as their weaknesses—then they, too, would be like Saint Paul: able to shake off the snake poison."

Rikko nodded. "I could see that."

"We found apples at both scenes," I said. "I'm thinking snake and forbidden fruit. Adam and Eve."

"Sure," she said. 'Throughout the Bible the serpent is the symbol of evil in the form of temptation. In my book you'll find pictures of Lilith in which she wears a headdress of snakes. Fruit, on the other hand, is the symbol of knowledge. The snake coaxes Eve to eat the forbidden fruit against God's will. Evil begets knowledge and—" Dahoney stopped and shook her head. "Maybe I'm reaching here."

"We're all reaching here," I said. "What are you thinking?"

Her right hand quivered ever so slightly. "If the remote possibility is true and these killings are both linked to the victim's sexual longings, then the symbolism of this suggests that the killer does equate the forbidden fruit with knowledge, in this case sexual knowledge, in the biblical sense: taboo sexual knowledge. He sees the snake not only as evil but also as a symbol of the phallus."

Rikko said, "You mean this guy thinks he killed Cook and Haines with his penis?"

Dahoney grimaced. "That's one way to put it, Detective."

"Oh, man," I said. "This guy's got issues."

TWENTY-FIVE

It was nearly three by the time we got back to head-quarters. Rikko left immediately for the District Attorney's Office to talk with prosecutors preparing for a trial involving a third-grader kidnapped from her schoolyard, then raped and slain, the year before. Rikko had worked the case like a dog and caught the perpetrator, the school gym teacher, who had a secret history of child abuse in Louisiana.

I tossed Professor Susan Dahoney's book on my desk. Jorge was working at his computer. Missy was on-line doing deviate detail, glowering at the screen. Freddie had left to talk with Officer Affairs about her insurance coverage.

"I scanned Haines's computer with software the FBI shared with me," Jorge said.

"Anything?" I said.

"No evidence that he spent time in bisexual or gay chat rooms."

"See. Tarentino's reaching."

"No evidence Haines spent any time in swinger chat rooms, either," Jorge countered. "He did, how-ever, make regular visits to Web sites dedicated to reptiles. In several there were references made to the trade and care of hot herps."

He held up a color picture of a coiled snake.

"Same one in Haines's terrarium," I said.

"Arizona coral. He's got a bunch of hits on the species. There may be more on the computer, but I have to go back up to the FBI computer lab to get it."

"I think that's a good way to spend the rest of the day," I said.

"On my way," Jorge said, placing Haines's laptop in a plastic evidence bag.

I sat down, glanced up at Jimmy's photograph, and almost called, then realized he wasn't yet out of school for the day. I pulled out my yellow legal pad and began doodling, playing with what Professor Dahoney had said about the Book of Acts, along with Chaco's assertions that Foster was into violent sex, including ropes. I couldn't make any of it fit together in a meaningful way.

Then again, there were all sorts of things about these two cases that did not fit. Other than the manner in which both men were killed, there'd been no overlap in their lives that we could find. No mention of the Yellow Tail or any other notorious San Diego nightspot in Haines's credit-card statements. Nor did we find any evidence linking Cook to an interest in reptiles.

Haines, on the other hand, had a file an inch thick on the lizard, a bearded dragon he'd bought nearly two years before from a store on Sports Arena Boulevard that specialized in exotic pets.

I got the file from a stack on my desk and went through it. On at least four dozen occasions since buying the lizard, Haines had purchased supplies at the same pet store, including a new terrarium less than ten days before his murder. I made a note to pay the store a visit, one lead in a growing list to be run down.

A pang of hunger shot through my stomach and I turned around to Missy, who was now hunched over her keyboard, typing furiously.

"You want get something to eat?" I said to her back. "Or are you too busy cooking up twisted sexual bait that might lure Seeker to our hook?"

Missy stiffened, reddened, and took her time pivoting toward me.

I laughed. "You were cooking up something twisted, weren't you?"

She reddened more, crossed her arms, and threw out her chin. "As a matter of fact, yes. My grandfather used to take me fishing when I was a little girl. He said to catch the biggest fish, you sometimes had to put out the nastiest stuff you could imagine."

"What kind of chum did you just throw in the ocean?"

She hesitated, then twisted her lips and said, "Ms. Lover is extremely hot for a three-way this coming weekend; dull, uncreative minds need not reply."

"Whoa," I said. "Maybe I should reply to that one."

"Dull, uncreative minds need not reply," Missy said again.

"Hardee-har. Any responses so far?"

"Been slow," Missy said, twisting in her chair back toward the screen. "Monday afternoons don't seem to be big with swingers, but I figure, what with the bait, maybe—"

She stopped, staring hard at the computer. "He answered me! He's on! We got him!"

I jumped out of my seat and looked at the screen over her shoulder.

»Seeker: Your proposal is intriguing, Ms. Lover. We are an adventurous San Diego County couple, late thirties, very attractive, fit, intelligent, financially secure. Interested?

"What do I say?" Missy asked.

I hunched over her shoulder. "Play hard to get."

»Ms. Lover: I asked for an indication of spark and creativity, not a resume.

We watched the screen for almost a minute with no reply, and I thought Missy had gone too far. Then a new message blipped up.

»Seeker: Tough grrrrl. We like that. But my lady and I hope you have a soft side, Ms. Lover. As far as our sexual flash and inventiveness are concerned, we have no peers. In all manner of role-playing we are experienced artists. And you?

"Artist," I said, thinking about Christina's appraisal of the murder scenes.

"How do I answer that?" Missy asked, chewing her lip.

"We've got to work this like a seduction," I said. "Only I've never had to seduce a man before."

"It's not just him, it's his partner," Missy said. "Besides, I'm not too bad at this myself."

"No, I guess not," I said, patting her on the shoulder. "We just don't want to seem too eager here. He's got to be nervous after Haines. Christ, that was only three days ago. So why's he responding—and to you, a woman?"

"Maybe he's changing the gender of his victims," Missy said, shrugging. "Maybe his motivation is androgynous. Maybe it applies to any person seeking deviate sex."

"I don't know—maybe, maybe," I said. "Let's sit here another couple of minutes, make him think you're not going to reply. That'll raise his level of anticipation. Then we need you to give him something to think about. Something to really whet his appetite."

Missy made a puffing noise and her knees started to jiggle.

After three minutes had passed, I asked, "You got an idea?"

"Yeah," she admitted. "But I'm kind of embarrassed to write it down."

"No one's gonna know but you and me."

"Gimme a break. This is gonna come out in court and you know it."

"You want to catch this guy?"

Missy did not reply, but bent over the keyboard.

»Ms. Lover: I have a Ph.D. in the Oriental arts of pleasure, hetero and Sapphic.

"Jesus, Missy, you're making me break out in a cold sweat."

"Told you it was embarrassing."

"No, no, it's really good."

"Unless he doesn't like Asians."

"No way," I assured her. "All men fantasize about Asian women. All men fantasize about lesbians. You're giving him a twofer. How could he not go for it?"

Missy twisted in her chair, her eyebrows raised almost to her hairline. "Excuse me?"

"There, see!" I said, pointing over her shoulder at the screen.

»Seeker: Asiatic bisexual? Now we are very, very intrigued. Might we see a nude photograph of you?

"Nude photograph?" Missy cried. "You never said anything about neggid pics!"

"Never thought about it," I shot back. "It's not like I'm experienced in the world of bisexual swinging, Ms. Lover."

"Well, neither am I! What do I say?"

"End of discussion: You say yes."

She walked away from the computer terminal, shaking her head and hands. "I am not posing naked and shipping my picture over the Internet. Next thing I know, it would be on the hard drive of every weirdo in the country—or at least every weirdo in the department. I'd never live it down."

"You don't have to pose nude," I assured her. "We'll have the computer geeks downstairs graft your face onto a picture we'll rip off from some men's magazine. In the meantime, get back on-line, ask them to send you photographs in return."

Missy looked at me with great skepticism. "This is getting strange, Boss."

"Believe me, you're doing it for Sophia Cook and Haines's mother."

Missy grumbled, but sat and typed her reply to Seeker, indicating that she'd send a photograph only if he and his partner did the same. There was a five-minute delay, then Seeker responded in the affirmative, but indicated that the photos should not be posted on the bulletin board but sent to secure E-mail boxes that were part of the swinger Internet service. Missy replied that she did not have a mailbox but would register and be back on the bulletin board within the hour with her particulars.

While Missy set about getting Ms. Lover one of the electronic mailboxes, I tore down to the basement, jumped in an unmarked, and headed for an adult bookstore on F Street, about eight blocks west of headquarters. There I found a photographic journal dedicated to the sublime Asian female form. By the time I returned, Missy had dug up several photographs of herself and waited with Freddie and a female computer technician armed with a scanner and an Apple laptop loaded with Adobe Photoshop.

"Choose your body double," I said, throwing the magazine on the desk.

Missy snatched up the magazine, disgust on her face. "You owe me, Sarge."

"Big-time," Freddie said, wagging a finger at me. "You'd never get me doing this. Uh. Uh. Uh."

In the end, Missy chose as Ms. Lover's body a Japanese named Hasu with gentle sloping shoulders, roseate nipples, and a love of origami. The tech scanned the centerfold's body and Missy's headshot into the computer, then went to work grafting the two together. It took nearly half an hour and several retouchings to get the pictures seamless. In the end, there was my detective, reclining demurely and buck naked on a cedar bench in a Zen garden outside Kyoto.

"Better not let Jorge or Rikko see this one," I said. "They'll never look at you the same again."

Missy punched me hard in the shoulder. "You're a shithead!"

"You get him, girl," Freddie said. "I got your back on this one."

"Calm down. I'm just kidding," I said. "Send it to Seeker. See what we get."

What we got was an all-but-drooling response begging Ms. Lover for a rendezvous, and a color Polaroid shot of a naked headless couple standing beside a sleigh bed in a dimly lit room. The man was tautly formed with an acutely small, uncircumcised penis. The woman was also in good shape, with large freckled fake boobs, a rose tattoo below her belly button, and flaming red pubic hair trimmed to a Mohawk.

"What's with the no heads?" Missy demanded. "I had to put my face out there."

"Fake body, though," I said.

"That's not the point!"

"C'mon," I said. "If they just killed their second victim, do you honestly think they'd actually send their faces around on the Web?"

Missy's lower lip grew two sizes. "I hate this case."

"Me, too, and I've only been on it one day," Freddie said. "What now?"

"Missy sets up a meeting," I replied. "We catch the killers, then drink multiple beers aboard the *Nomad's Chant* in celebration of a job well done."

TWENTY-SIX

"You reading me?" Missy asked.

"Loud and clear," I replied.

"See me?"

"All cameras functioning, you little geisha, you," I said, looking at the three glowing monitors in the back of the van we had parked in the lot outside an upscale condo complex east of I-5, south of La Jolla Town Center.

"I'm Korean-Chinese, Sarge, and you know it," Missy snarled into the tiny microphone at her neckline.

"Man, she's touchy tonight, isn't she?" I said to Rikko, who sat next to me.

"Looks pretty good, though," Rikko replied. "The robe softens her upper body. Hides the nine millimeter good too."

"You tell her that. I'm at the top of her shit list right now."

"Hell of a picture she takes," Rikko offered. "All the guys think so. Why doesn't she get more dates?"

"Why don't you ask her that while you're at it?"

It was Wednesday, April twelfth, ten past ten at night. Fog and mist had rolled in off the Pacific once again, blackening the asphalt and setting the eucalyptus trees to dripping. On the monitors, Missy was dressed in a purple kimono that hid the black gym shorts and jog bra she wore beneath. She moved around the interior of the condo's living room, past a collection of Oriental vases and carved screens, glancing up every once in a while into the corners where we'd mounted tiny fiber optic surveillance cameras, then toward the door to the bedroom where Jorge waited.

The condo belonged to a friend of Jorge's, a corporate attorney with a penchant for Oriental furniture. The lawyer was in San Francisco for a few days, so we'd arranged for Seeker, his woman, and Missy to rendezvous there. The location was challenging from a surveillance point of view: five parking lots ringed the complex. We'd chosen the obvious lot—the one facing the main drag—in which to place the command wagon.

There'd been a rash of gang killings in the city over the previous weekend, so Fraiser had balked at giving me more detectives for backup. And the SWAT team was working a hostage situation. So we were making due with off-duty patrol officers in plain clothes sitting in unmarked cars in each of the other lots. Rikko was monitoring their posts while I kept track of Missy and Jorge.

"Quarter past," Missy said, walking in circles, rapping her knuckles on her thighs. "They should have been here by now."

"Seduction is three parts anticipation," I said. "Seeker and his woman are making you wait, hoping you'll be that much more compliant when they arrive."

Rikko cocked an eyebrow at me. "Where do you come up with this stuff?"

I put my hand over the microphone. "Grew up in a house dominated by women. After a while you get a sixth sense about how they want to be treated."

"How your sister would love to hear this. How is it they want to be treated?"

"Different every time," I replied. "That's the point. Seduction's just like pitching: an ever-changing mix of skill and intuition, depending on the batter."

"Must be a jungle in that head of yours," Rikko said, then he held up a finger, pressed his headset to his right ear, and whispered to me. "We got company. Couple, late thirties, parking an Acura in the west lot."

I put on my game face and said, "No one moves till I say so."

Rikko nodded. I activated Missy's earphone. "This may be show time. I'll tell you when they're about to get to your door. Get them both inside, make sure he identifies himself as Seeker. We want him to make the connection on camera. Once he's copped to the handle, bust him. Jorge'll be right behind you. Got that, Jorge?"

"Let the games begin," Jorge said.

On the monitor, Missy shrugged her shoulders several times, then reached up to pat her weapon. "I'm ready."

I looked over at Rikko. "They out of the car yet?"

"Chubby boy," he said, nodding. "She's a platinum blonde. Skinny."

I frowned. "What'd they do, send fake body pics?"

In my headset the bell chimed at the door to the condo. Missy looked up at the camera in surprise, then hissed, "You said they were still in the parking lot."

"That couple still is. They must have come in a way we didn't think of," I said. The bell rang again. "Be cool now, Missy. Answer it. We're ready."

Missy scowled, then leaned back her head and called out, "Coming!"

"Wait for Missy, Jorge," I instructed. "She's quarterback."

"Ten-four."

Missy took a big breath, turned back the dead bolt, affected a come-hither look, and swung open the door. "Hello," she said seductively. "I've been getting wet just waiting for you."

"What a life!" Rikko roared. "Christina never says words like that to me."

"Probably because she knows you're so unstable, you'd blow a gasket," I retorted. "Now, shut up."

We still could not see the couple in the hallway, but we could hear a man's nasal voice say, "You're bigger in person, Ms. Lover."

"I've seen your picture and was kind of hoping the same thing," Missy said, not missing stride. "Why don't you come in. Seeker, is it?"

There was no reply and Missy stepped back. For a second I thought she'd gone too far again with the crack about his small penis. Then a tall man in his late thirties, stout enough to be a pro wrestler and wearing black dress pants, matching loafers, and a yellow polo shirt, walked through the door. He toted a leather suitcase the color of ox blood. He did not look at Missy, but craned his head around, as if casing the room. For a second he looked almost directly into the camera. In a way I was disappointed; it wasn't Nick Foster. Still, I had to silently applaud Mary Aboubacar: But for the set of his eyes, she had described him to a tee.

A brassy redhead entered right behind him. She wore black stirrup pants, strapless spike-heeled shoes, wide silver bracelets, and a short-sleeved silver lamé top, cut to show her silicon bust. She carried a bottle of wine wrapped in blue cellophane. She held out the bottle to Missy and said giddily, "I'm Paula. I hope we're going to be great friends..."

Her eyes were so glassy and her stance so unstable, I figured she'd been smoking pot or drinking wine—or both.

"You can call me Missy, Paula," Missy said, reaching for the bottle and looking back toward the man, who was almost directly alongside her. "Do I call you Seeker?"

She'd asked him his identity twice, and a flicker of suspicion crossed his face. Paula seemed not to notice. She stepped up to Missy, her hand reaching up toward the lapels of the robe. "Relax, baby," Paula said. "We're all gonna be friends no matter what we call ourselves."

Missy tried to step back, but the woman's fingers caught the kimono. It opened, revealing the black jog bra and the first inch of her leather shoulder harness. At the same time Jorge jumped the gun: He opened the door to the bedroom down the hall from the living room a crack. But that was enough to send a squeak through the apartment. Seeker froze, his eyes darting from the leather strap on Missy's shoulder to the still-open front door to the apartment.

"He knows!" I yelled in the microphone. "Take him. Now!"

Missy pushed Paula back and went for her gun. Seeker spun and hammered Missy so hard in the ribs with the suitcase that it burst open. Missy lurched sideways into the credenza, sending three vases crashing to the floor.

"Run!" Seeker bellowed. "It's a set-up!"

"Police!" Jorge shouted from down the darkened hallway. "Stop where you are!"

But the couple were already through the door. Missy rolled over on the floor, digging for her SIG Sauer. Jorge burst into the living room, pistol drawn.

"Seal the grounds!" Rikko bellowed into his headset. "They're running!"

I was already flying through the back doors of the van. Up the hill, through the mist, I saw the couple reach the bottom of the staircase and flee west. Paula had kicked free of her heels but was struggling to keep up with Seeker on the wet grass. Instead of following them, I circled south, racing along the rain-slickened cement walkway, my gun drawn, barking my position into my handheld radio.

"They've got to be parked to the west," I yelled. "Stop them. Big guy, yellow polo shirt. She's dressed like a hooker."

Breaching through an archway that linked two of the buildings in the complex, I saw the couple run through the far side of a central courtyard. He was forty yards from me, dragging Paula along. I angled at them. Seeker saw me coming and let her go. She stumbled after him, crying, "Dick, don't leave me!"

Missy came out of nowhere, her open kimono flapping like eagle's wings behind her, a look of grim determination on her face. She clubbed Paula in the back of the neck with her forearm and wrestled her to the ground.

Seeker took off again toward a hedge at the west end of the courtyard.

"Police: Stop!" I yelled after him. "You're surrounded!"

He did not hesitate, but rolled over the hedge as a boy might a fence rail. I tore after him, tried the same move, and felt myself falling. The hedge grew atop a six-foot retaining wall above a sidewalk. I landed hard on my side. The impact stunned me. Tires screeched. Cars honked. Seeker jigged like a fullback through the late evening traffic. Getting back to my feet, I shouted into the radio: "He's free of the complex, heading southwest."

Sirens wailed in the distance. Seeker reached the far side of the road and clawed his way up an embankment covered in ice plant. If he reached the top, he would be able to disappear into a complex of undeveloped canyons that stretched toward the ocean.

I put my head down and charged across the street. A green convertible BMW skidded to a halt, just missing my knees. "You *crazy?*" a Vietnamese teenager wearing a red bandana yelled after me. "*You wanna die or something?*"

Then he saw my gun and ducked. I reached the other side of the busy thoroughfare just as Seeker reached the top of the embankment and plunged into the bushes, heading toward the rim of the main canyon. I scrambled sideways and south along the slope on all fours. Ten yards, twenty, thirty. My breath felt like fire.

Grabbing at roots, I got myself to the mouth of the canyon and eased myself into a narrow coulee. The walls were steep and dropped away a hundred feet below me into a cinched bottom. Branches crackled. Seeker's dark form emerged fifteen yards above me and twenty feet to my left. He began to skid down the slope.

Once I knew he had committed himself to the descent, I holstered my gun, slabbed my feet into the bank, then launched myself at him. My shoulder struck him high in his powerful torso and he grunted. My arms wrapped around him, the way Rikko had taught me. Seeker cursed and clawed at me as we tumbled down the canyon side, bouncing off the trunks of manzanita and greasewood.

He pounded me in the rib cage with his elbow and we separated, each of us bouncing and cartwheeling off the arid, packed rampart. I hit the bottom and lay there dazed a second. Then I was aware of the silhouette of him up on his knees, his hands closing around a rock the size of a football. He spun, raised it above his head, then froze and looked down in shock.

I had the muzzle of my nine millimeter tight against his crotch. "One twitch, asshole, one little twitch, and your little buddy here will never go seeking again."

TWENTY-SEVEN

Brett tarentino was mistaken. Monsters could travel in pairs.

"She couldn't go another day without licking or getting licked," Dick Silver moaned the next morning around nine. "That's the bottom line. Woman's a goddamned nympho. If she coulda numbed herself down there for one month, one lousy month—"

"Oh, fuck you and the canoe you came in on," Paula Silver shot back. "You're just as much a satyr as I am a nympho. You wanted Ms. Lover much as I did."

Their lawyer, an uptight corporate attorney named Arthur Sheingold, turned ashen and put his trembling hands on their arms to calm them down. "I'm advising the both of you once again not to talk until we can get you a good criminal lawyer."

We had been trying to interrogate Paula Silver and her husband Richard, a.k.a. Seeker, separately for most of the night. But both of them refused to speak with us unless their attorney was present. We let them stew in a tank at the county jail with drunks, crack addicts, and whores while we searched for Sheingold. It took hours. He'd arrived at dawn and, after consulting with his clients, informed us they wished to talk. Against his advice. In return for leniency.

Now Dick Silver leaned back in his chair in an interrogation room inside the jail. Bits of sage and manzanita branch still clung to his soiled shirt. Up close, in the light of day, he looked like a tired, aging version of the pro wrestler The Rock.

In response to Sheingold's warning, Silver stuck out his steroidal jaw and glared at his attorney. "You don't get it, do you, Mr. Mouthpiece? Dick Silver and Silver Enterprises are boned here. Totally boned! No IPO, you can guarantee that after this comes out. Ten years of work and no payoff because of Paula's overactive pussy."

"And Dick Silver's priapic wanger!" she shouted back.

Sheingold looked ready to cry. "Please, Dick, Paula, I'm begging you to—"

Silver ignored his attorney to stare across the table at me and Rikko. "The end of the world is between a woman's legs, man."

I rolled my eyes. "You got something to say, Mr. Silver, say it."

"Yes, yes, thank you, Sergeant," Sheingold said, relieved. "But before they talk, what do they get in return? I mean, they're being forthcoming here."

"Forthcoming?" Rikko growled. "They have not said a thing, other than the pissing on each other. Only thing we know: They assaulted two police officers and they are our number-one suspects in two torture killings. How is this for forthcoming?"

"Dick Silver didn't kill no one," Silver said, reaching up to the raw skin on his left cheek-bone. "Under all this buff physique, Dick Silver's a little lamb."

"Yeah, okay, look, Bo-Peep," I said, "we've got you leaving Morgan Cook's apartment building minutes before his body was discovered. We've got transcripts of you and your wife setting up a ménage à trois with Cook the night before his body was dis-covered. And I'm betting when my team finishes going through your house and business, we're going to find snakes, a green trench coat, and a hat."

Silver scowled and shook his head. "Hate snakes. Don't own a green trench coat."

"Maybe you do. Maybe you don't."

"He doesn't," Sheingold said. "Look, Sergeant, they want to cooperate."

"Then they start talking or I'm gonna toss them back in the holding cell."

Silver blanched and looked over at his attorney, who nodded and sighed.

"All we know is about Cook," Silver said. "We don't know this guy Haines from Adam. But Cook—yeah, we were inside Cook's apartment Friday night around twelve-thirty. He'd been dead awhile. All black and swelled-up. Real nasty."

Paula nodded. Tears spilled and her mascara spidered down her cheeks as she spoke: "See, we'd been there before, to Morgan's apartment for an...intimate party. And Morgan, he liked to role-play, you know? We were supposed to, like, surprise him."

"Surprise him how?" Rikko said.

"In bed," Paula replied, fidgeting in her chair. "We weren't supposed to tell him exactly when we were coming. He liked the idea of waking up and finding us there, like we were sex burglars or something. We did it the week before and he got off on it and so did we. Everyone wanted a repeat that night."

"So you get there around half past twelve and he's already dead," Rikko said.

Paula nodded, a sickened expression spreading across her face.

"Why didn't you report it?" I demanded.

They glanced at each other across their attorney's chest, then Dick Silver crossed his pumped-up arms. "'Cause we panicked, okay? We own a chain of health clubs here in San Diego and Orange County. Silver Bodies?"

I nodded. They advertised aggressively on the local radio stations.

"Anyway, we're about to go public after a decade of building the business," Silver said. "We could smell the big payoff and the last thing we wanted to do was get dragged into a scandal."

"That's all the underwriters would have to hear," Paula chimed in. "You know, that the chief executive and chief operating officer were involved in a sex murder."

"So you were involved," Rikko said.

"No!" Silver said. "But everyone would say we were. If we'd called the cops, they'd have found the stuff we'd left at Cook's apartment."

Neither Rikko nor I said a word.

"Don't you get it?" Silver asked. "We'd been there before, okay? We left toys with Morgan, so we wouldn't have to keep toting them around."

"Like the toys you brought to Ms. Lover?" Rikko asked.

When Silver threw the suitcase at Missy, it broke open and the contents had spilled across the floor: a leather mask with chains, a cat-o'-nine tails, a strap-on dildo, and a deflated blow-up sex doll.

"Yes," Paula Silver said. "You know: lotions, a little S-and-M gear, some pot. Morgan liked to puff a little before we fucked."

"How very touching," I said. "Except we didn't find anything like that in Cook's apartment. Videos, magazines, but no toys."

"That's because we cleaned the place," Silver said.

"*You what?!*" I shouted.

"Cleaned it," Paula said, cringing. "We thought if we vacuumed and scrubbed the place down, then no one would ever be able to connect us to Cook, and the IPO on Silver Bodies could go forward as planned. I mean, we didn't have anything to do with the murder. We just cleaned the place, that's all."

Sheingold had squeezed shut his eyes and was kneading at his temple.

"I do not believe them," Rikko said. "I say go for warrants, Shay, leave them here to rot, search their home and offices. We got twenty-four hours to arraign them. Put them back in the tank until then."

"No!" Dick Silver yelled. "Please. We're telling you the truth."

"Why not just leave without cleaning the place?" I asked.

"Because Dick Silver was in the Army after high school and Paula Silver was a child-care worker in college," Sheingold said.

"Your point?" Rikko asked.

"We were both fingerprinted," Silver shot back. "And we knew our prints had to be all over that apartment from our previous rendezvous with Cook, not to mention the toys. So we cleaned it, top to bottom."

A long moment of quiet followed, then I asked, "What time did you leave?"

Silver shrugged. "Two A.M."

"Bullshit, you were seen at seven-thirty that morning," I replied.

"That's when I went back," Silver said. "I remembered something we forgot."

"What?"

"The ropes that tied him to the bed," he mumbled. "They were ours."

"You see anyone on your way out the second time?"

"Yeah, black woman. Scars on her cheeks. Carrying a bucket and a mop."

I glanced over at Rikko. I didn't know what to believe, and got up and left the room. Lieutenant

Fraiser, Captain Merriweather, and Assistant Chief Adler were outside, watching through a one-way mirror. "What do you think?" I asked.

"They're lying," The Prick said.

"I'm not so sure," Merriweather said, twirling the ends of his mustache. "But they know more than they're saying."

"Lean on them," Adler said.

I nodded and returned to the interrogation room. Sheingold said, "So we can count on leniency and your discretion in keeping the Silvers' name out of the papers?"

"You can count on nothing until I hear it all," I replied, then shifted back to the Silvers. "What did you wipe down? What did you vacuum? What did you mop? What did you throw away? Where's the vacuum now? Where's the garbage now? Where are the ropes now? And we want to know exactly what you saw when you entered that apartment, everything you can remember: where it was and where you put it."

Dick Silver blinked, then nodded to his wife, who said, "The front door was unlocked, just like before. We went into the apartment and I stripped down to my G-string and bra. Morgan liked to see me first. The play was supposed to be Dick as the jealous co-burglar who discovers us going at it and ends up getting into the act."

Rikko screwed up his face in a way that let me know that my sister was going to have a hard time explaining this one to him.

"Keep going," I said.

Paula Silver swallowed, then said, "I lit a candle, filled a pot pipe, and tiptoed down the hall toward the bedroom. I pushed open the door, took one look, and fainted."

Silver was nodding. "Hit the deck like a dropped barbell and let go the dope and the lit candle. Damn near torched the place. I got the candle, blew it out, and got Paula back to the couch, then went in and took a look myself." He stopped, stared up at the ceiling, exhaled, then said, "He, Morgan, was spread-eagle, tied to the bed, all black, with these red blisters on him."

"Where are the ropes now?" Rikko demanded.

"Burned them," Silver said.

"Jesus Christ," I grumbled in frustration. "Keep going. What else?"

"There were a couple of wineglasses on the bedstead and a half-empty bottle of Pinot Noir," Dick Silver said. "Some of our toys were on the bed and on the floor too. There was an apple on the bedstead with a couple of bites taken out of it."

"And there was that horrible message on the mirror," Paula Silver said. " 'Joy unspeakable to be holding death in your hands.' We didn't clean it off, figuring it would be important to you. We just cleaned our prints from around the message and left."

"Why would your prints be on the mirror in the first place?" I demanded.

Dick Silver blanched and did not reply.

"Answer the man," Rikko said.

Paula Silver's face and neck had turned beet red. I stared at her. "Why, Paula?"

"Because ... " she said, unwilling to look at me.

"Don't," Dick Silver begged.

Paula glanced at her husband, then back to me with resignation all over her mascara-stained face. "It's over, Dick," she said. "We cleaned the mirror because my husband sat on the credenza last time we were there. I sat on him with Morgan behind. Double penetration, you know? I was the meat in a powerful sex sandwich. I had to put my hands all over that mirror to support myself. So we cleaned as much of the mirror as we could without marring the message. Satisfied?"

Sheingold shrank down in his seat as if he could not believe what he was hearing. Dick Silver held his head in his hands. "We're ruined!"

"Nonsense," Sheingold said uncertainly. "The Silvers have cooperated with you. Surely we can come up with a deal that will keep this out of the news and spare the Silvers the embarrassment of jail time."

"Here's the best I can do," I replied. "The story checks out, we don't charge them with murder one. They'll be arraigned within the hour."

"On what charge?" the attorney cried.

"Obstruction of justice, tampering with evidence, resisting arrest, and assaulting police officers. Just to start."

There was a stunned silence in the room, then Dick Silver crumpled forward on the conference table and Paula Silver began to sob.

TWENTY-EIGHT

After the silvers' arraignment I sent everyone home to sleep. We'd been up the entire night. I stopped by the office to check my messages and found one from Professor Susan Dahoney asking me to call. But before I could punch in the number, the phone rang and I answered.

"Moynihan. Homicide."

"Where were you?" Fay demanded angrily.

"What are you talk—?" I began, then remembered. "Oh, shit. Jimmy's suspension."

"You promised, Shay. And you still didn't show."

"I was on a stakeout. We thought it was the snake guy and we ended up in interrogation all night, followed by an arraignment."

"You know what your son did last night?" she shouted, then pressed on, not waiting for an answer. "Walter tried to go in to talk with him—you know, get him prepared for the talk with the principal and the guidance counselor—and Jimmy responds to that kindness and concern by kicking him in the balls."

"No!" I said, suppressing a smile.

"I know you probably think this is real funny, but it's not, Shay," she said. "He's never been violent like this in his life, and look what's going on! I want him to talk to somebody professional. He wouldn't say a thing to the guidance counselor. Maybe your sister. He trusts her."

"Jesus, Fay. Let's not get Chrissy involved in this."

"Why not?" she demanded. "At least I know she's one person from your side of the family who will show up if I ask her to."

"That's not fair."

"You lost the right to fairness around an hour ago when I was being questioned by various school officials regarding your whereabouts!" she shouted. "Now he's coming to the game tonight because I want you to talk with him about talking to Chrissy."

"Jimmy's suspended," I reminded her. "He can't play."

"He can sit on the bench, then," she said. "Maybe it'll make him think."

The line clicked dead. I dropped the phone in its cradle and stood there shaking my head at the pressure building in and around it. The phone rang again and I almost didn't answer it, but did. "Moynihan," I yawned. "Homicide."

"Sergeant!" a woman purred. "Any updates on the investigation?"

"Huh?" I said, then recognized the voice. "Oh, sorry, Professor Dahoney. No, nothing ground-breaking, unfortunately. How about you? Any luck on our first message?"

"I spent hours today going through every concordance I could think of, looking for a reference to '*joy unspeakable*,'" she said.

"And?"

"Nothing, I'm sorry to say. But I'm going to keep looking."

"Appreciate the favor."

There was a pause, then she said, "Would you do me one in return?"

"If I can."

"Have dinner with me," she said. "I find what you do—the investigative work, I mean—fascinating. My treat, of course."

I flashed on a memory of our meeting, how she reminded me of a young Elizabeth Taylor, not to mention the intoxicating smell she had about her. And it had been six weeks for me—something of a record. I was feeling lonely.

"Sure," I said, warming to the idea. "I'd love to have dinner with you, Professor."

"Call me Susan," she corrected. "How about tonight?"

I glanced at my calendar and the Little League schedule. "It would have to be after eight-thirty. I have to coach my son's baseball team."

"Son?" she said, cooling. "I didn't know you were married."

"Divorced."

"Well, I love baseball," Susan said, the brightness returning to her voice. "My daddy was a big Pittsburgh Pirates fan. Could I come watch?"

Twenty-Nine

Seven hours later, on a Little League field in the city of Santee, east of San Diego, Jimmy played batboy, sitting on the bench alone when he wasn't organizing the gear. It was part of the terms of his suspension: He had to help his team even if he wasn't playing.

My sister thought that was a good idea. She'd listened patiently when I'd called to explain what was going on with Jimmy, then agreed to have a talk with him on neutral ground. I picked him up at home in the Green Monster to bring him to the game. He was sullen and would not look me in the eye.

I didn't say much, just told him that his aunt Chrissy wanted to know if he'd like to have ice cream with her next week sometime, depending on her schedule. He'd just shrugged. I told him I'd need an answer by the end of the game and left it at that.

As the third inning got under way, we were up three zip with no outs and two men on base. I was drinking espresso, operating on five hours of sleep, and trying to keep my head in the game. "Come on, come on," I chanted to Stetson's kid. "Rip me one now."

Fast ball low. Foul down the right-field line.

Waiting for the next pitch, I thought about what else my sister had said during our talk. I'd asked her about the fact that the Silvers had cleaned up what was obviously a much messier crime scene, then the killer had copied their tactic with Haines.

"He's probably reading and clipping everything being written about the killings," she said. "Tarentino had the cleaned scene in his first story. The killer probably realized it was a smart thing to do, then adopted the practice. Most people think these serial killers act the same exact way every time. Remember what I said about the artist painting successive panels in a larger work? The process is evolutionary, influenced by their surroundings—in this case, perhaps, his press clippings. The painting becomes a collage, more elaborate with every victim. But certain icons prevail."

Before I could give the matter further consideration, Stetson's kid dug in, then tore a double to right. When I looked back into the stands, Susan Dahoney was standing there clapping. To my pleasant surprise, the Bible expert was dressed to kill in a snug, plum-colored dress, a white sweater over her shoulders, hoop earrings, and high heels. Half the fathers in the stands were craning their heads to get a gander at her. Half the mothers, including Fay, were shooting her disapproving looks.

"Who's that?" asked my assistant coach, Don Stetson.

"That would be my date taking me to dinner after the game."

He spit out sunflower seeds. "Life is fundamentally unfair."

The next three batters flied out. As my players took the field, Fay ducked into the dugout, glanced at Jimmy at the far end of the bench, then said, "Can I talk with you?"

"Sure," I said, following her outside. "I told him about Christina wanting to take him for ice cream. He hasn't given me an answer yet."

"I'm not here to talk about that," she said, an edge in her voice. "Thought we agreed: no bimbos around Jimmy. Baseball games especially."

"No bimbo, Fayo, Ph.D.-o."

"Right."

"Believe it. Bible scholar at State."

"A Bible scholar who dresses like a Jezebel?"

"Imagine that." I grinned.

"You're a smart guy, Shay," Fay said, walking away. "You'd think you'd learn."

We won seven to two. I signaled Susan Dahoney to wait five minutes, then took Jimmy aside. "I need an answer about ice cream with your aunt and I want it now."

He looked at my knees for a long time, then nodded. "Okay."

"Okay," I sighed. "Your mother's waiting."

"Can we fish this Sunday, Dad?" he asked in a woe-is-me tone.

"Not a chance," I said. "Kicking people in the balls doesn't get you a reward."

He stared up at me with disbelief, then rising anger. "You never want us to be together, do you?"

He did not wait for an answer, but ran off through the lot toward Fay's car, leaving in his wake one more layer of frustration. I blew out a puff of regret and went into the public rest room to change into khaki dress pants, loafers, and a blue polo shirt, then met Susan Dahoney in the parking lot.

"Your boy seemed very upset," she said. "He okay?"

"Unfortunately, no," I said. "He seems downright miserable about something but won't tell anyone what it is."

"Too bad," she said, doing that neat trick again of slipping her arm inside my elbow. "He's going to turn heads someday. As you have, I imagine."

I looked at her and she grinned. She smelled fantastic. I smiled and stopped in front of the Green Monster. "You can follow me or I can bring you back here later."

"I think I'll take the ride," she said, gesturing sardonically at the Corvette. "I've never been in a phallusmobile before."

"Yeah, yeah, very funny," I said. "Where are we going?"

"Buscillachis in Hillcrest," she said. "It's Sicilian, I believe."

"My favorite restaurant."

"I know," she said, giving my arm a squeeze. "I asked around."

Thirty

We sat in the terrace room near a fountain. I ordered us a traditional Sicilian peasant meal of broccoli soup, hot sausages sautéed in olive oil and garlic, a loaf of fresh bread, and a bottle of Chianti.

"So, Shay—can I call you Shay?" Susan said, leaning forward on the table, her chin cradled across the back of her intertwined fingers, her blue eyes dazzling.

She'd found out about my favorite restaurant and my nickname. "Sure," I said, unsettled by the fact it didn't bother me. "Call me Shay."

Grinning, she took a sip of wine. "Tell me about yourself."

"Not much to tell. I'm a cop. I coach Little League baseball. Live on a boat. Drive a penismobile. Having a hell of a time with a nut who's putting snakes on people."

"I know all that. How'd you become a detective?"

"Accident. Like most things in life."

"C'mon," she pleaded. "If we're gonna be friends, you can do better."

It had been a long time since I'd narrated the disparate series of incidents that led to my joining the San Diego Police Department, but Susan was a born listener, one of those people who is adept at keeping you talking, all the while making you think you are the most interesting person in the world. Over more wine, while we waited for dinner, I laid out the skeleton of it all: playing baseball as a kid; my father's murder; our move to San Diego to live with my Uncle Anthony; playing at Stanford.

"Stanford?" she said. "That's a tough place to get into. I know: I tried."

I shrugged. "My mom was a stickler for studying, and I inherited a cannon right arm from my dad. Though not cannon enough."

Susan cocked her head, puzzled.

"I was what they call a fireballer," I explained. "My junior season I went fourteen-and-oh and averaged twelve strikeouts a game. The Boston Red Sox drafted me and made me an offer I couldn't refuse. Over the objections of my mom and uncle, I quit college to play double and triple A the rest of that summer. After two months of winter ball down in the Dominican Republic, I joined the team in spring training."

"You played major league baseball?" she cried, clapping her hands.

"Not quite one season. Just short of nineteen games, to be exact. Went fifteen and three in my first eighteen starts. They even did a story in *Sports Illustrated*, touting me as a likely candidate for rookie of the year."

"What happened?"

I hesitated, choosing my words. "It was mid-August. We were playing the Yankees. I was in the zone that night, pitching in this slow-motion world where I seemed to be the only one who understood the physics of the game. I had 'em shut down, a no-hitter through six, nine K's on the board. I was one and two on Reggie Jackson, the sort of situation where a power hitter like Mr. October thinks you're going off-speed. I decided bring it in fast, low, and inside. Went into my windup, my mechanics no different than they'd been for years.

"But when I brought my right arm whipping over and in, there was a splintering noise and god-awful pain, and it was as if the crowd sucked the air right out of Fenway—right out of my entire body, for that matter. Next thing I knew, I was lying on my left side, half on, half off the mound, quivering, in shock probably, the only one on the field who didn't understand what had just happened."

Susan covered her mouth with both hands. "What did happen, Shay?"

"Official explanation is that the force generated by my forward momentum and the strength of the muscles in my shoulder and arm simply eclipsed the integrity of my humerus bone. It exploded just above my elbow, shredding my biceps and all the ligaments in my arm."

"My God!" Susan said. "They couldn't repair it?"

"Not good enough to pitch in the majors. Career-ender before it really started."

"It must have been horrible for you."

She said it with such genuine concern that a lump formed in my throat It surprised me so much, I told her something I'd told very few people in my life: "When I woke up in the hospital, part of me had died—part of me that I'd carried in tribute to my dad all those years. Having me be a professional baseball player was his dream."

She absorbed that, then said, "But you adapted. You became a cop to honor him."

I looked at her with newfound appreciation: Susan was one of the emotionally intelligent—one of those people with a knack for saying the right thing at the right time.

"You're probably right. Took me about a year and two operations to realize that I was actually lucky. For one amazing summer I'd had what most guys only dream about when they start out playing on the sand-lots. I couldn't afford to finish Stanford without a scholarship. So I went to San Diego State and majored in criminal science. Entered the police academy two weeks after graduation. Been on the force ever since."

Susan reached across the table and put her hand on mine. "I'm sorry you didn't get to play baseball longer. But you know, Seamus, your story reinforces a theory I've had for years: Everyone faces catastrophe in life, but ultimately these upheavals are good things. They force us to reinvent ourselves to survive."

The waiter brought our dinner. After showing her how to eat the meal, putting the sausage in the bread with the garlic broccoli, I said, "You talk like you've got experience at reinvention yourself."

To my surprise, the question seemed to upset her. She laid her fork down. "Why? What do you mean?"

I shrugged. "I don't know. How'd you become a Bible scholar?"

"Oh, that," Susan said, coming up with her napkin and touching it to both sides of her mouth. Her gaze flickered off me, then returned. "A boring story, certainly, compared to your life. I mean, major league baseball. Top homicide cop."

"C'mon," I pleaded. "If we're gonna be friends, you've got to do better than that."

She hesitated, then took a drink of wine. "It's just that as a southern woman I was taught to be uncomfortable talking about myself to a handsome man." She burst out in strained laughter. "Isn't it ridiculous that none of us can get over our childhoods?"

"Oh, I don't know," I said. "You don't strike me as the demure, retiring type, Professor. You contacted me. You asked me out."

"I guess I did," she replied, laughing nervously again. "Gosh, I'm a mystery to myself sometimes."

"Aren't we all?"

She took another drink of wine, then haltingly laid out her biography in broad strokes. Born in Huntington, West Virginia, to a carpenter and his wife, devout Pentecostalists. As a girl, her favorite memories were of hearing Old Testament stories. She did well in school, graduating at the top of her class. Against her parents' wishes, she chose

189

the University of Virginia over Oral Roberts. In Charlottesville, she took a class in anthropology and her core beliefs were challenged. She learned for the first time that the Bible, the Talmud, the Koran, and all ancient religious texts could be treated just like excavation sites by scholars digging for the origins of ideas.

"I attended Chapel Hill for my masters," she said, then glanced away. "University of Tel Aviv for my doctorate. The last three years writing my thesis, then turning it into *The Second Woman*. And now I'm here."

"Happy?"

"A little lonely sometimes, but essentially yes. The book came to be in a way I didn't expect. I guess I thought it would be bought by some university press, but then several big New York houses came after it. This reinvention of myself, as you call it, was something I hadn't anticipated."

"What do you mean?"

She waved her hand at her hairdo and dress. "This is all my publisher's idea. After they accepted the manuscript and met me, they decided that I could do with a makeover. I guess I used to dress pretty frumpy: no makeup, no hairdo. But they say the book business is all about perception— who people think you are, not who you really are. Not that I'm arguing. I think I look pretty good these days."

"No argument there, Professor."

"Why, thank you, Sergeant."

We finished dinner, had gelati for dessert, then paid and got back into the Green Monster. Soon we were roaring north on the 163, the windows down. She was tipsy from the wine and giggling. "I take back the crack about phallusmobile. This is fun."

"Very," I said. "So why San Diego State?"

Susan's face darkened for an instant, then she forced a smile and picked up her chin. "To be honest, the only offers I got right out of my doctoral program were at small schools that hardly paid. I believed I was better than the offers, so instead I waitressed and worked on *The Second Woman*. When it was accepted for publication, after five long years of work, the offers to teach followed. The department here at San Diego State is quite renowned. And I liked the weather. So here I am."

"Five years writing. Long time."

"People say I'm driven," she replied. "The truth is, I want people to know my ideas, to know who I am. It's that simple."

"I have a feeling that will happen."

"I'll do just about anything to make it happen," she said. "I always play to win."

"What do your parents think about your drive to succeed? You know, carpenter's daughter becomes Ph.D...."

A pained expression crossed her face. "We don't talk much. They don't approve of my writing. Anyway, it's irrelevant. They have their way of thinking. I have mine."

She stared out the window as we drove east on the 8 back toward Santee, then spoke again. "I've got more books in me. Not just about the Bible. My publisher says I have to build my audience with this book. I work very hard at promoting it."

"Signings, things like that?" I asked.

She nodded. "And readings, symposiums, interviews with papers, radio, TV. Whatever it takes. Unfortunately, these days book publishing is a culture of celebrity. That's what my editor says, anyway. You have to build your own wall of celebrity, brick by brick. Then the books start selling."

"You really want to be a celebrity?"

"Well, I certainly don't want to be just an academic," she said. "Is that so bad?"

"Suppose not. How'd you get interested in the mystery of Cain's wife?"

She grinned craftily. "Piece of old tile."

"Huh?"

"That's how it happened," she insisted. "I was in the Tel Aviv Museum and there was a piece of tile on display, found in the ruins of an ancient Sumerian castle. It's the same tile on my book cover—the woman with the bird headdress in the crotch of a tree, stepping on the back of a dragon. I found the depiction intriguing and started digging into her as a figure in creation myths."

As we drove she went on to explain that the Lilith myth has dozens of variations throughout antiquity. The name is believed to be derived from the Babylonian-Assyrian word *lilitu,* a female demon or wind spirit. She appears as "Lilake" two thousand years before Christ on a Sumerian tablet from Ur that contained the tale of Gilgamesh and the willow tree, the oldest known story.

In that tale, Lilith is a demoness dwelling in the trunk of the willow tree, tended by the goddess Anath. In some tellings, Lilith bears the children of demons, called *lilim*. In Hebrew tales, God made her the strangler of baby boys up to the eighth day of life, the age of circumcision. She was the demoness who destroyed Job's sons. Solomon suspected her of being the Queen of Sheba. According to Isaiah, Lilith dwells among the desolate ruins in the Edomite desert, in the company of satyrs, owls, pelicans, and snakes.

"That girl gets around," I said, pulling the Monster in beside her Camry.

Susan laughed. "Yes, she does, doesn't she?" Then she looked at me. "I had a nice time. Thank you for coming to dinner."

"Pleasure was all mine. I haven't met anyone as interesting as you in a long time."

"Well, thank you," she said. Then she leaned over and I leaned over. Her lips were cushioned and moist. Her breath tasted of garlic and wine. I reached for her shoulder, to turn her fully to me, but she pulled back. "Just one for now, please."

"Why just one?" I protested.

"Because I have the feeling you're dangerous after more than one."

"Not at all," I chided. "How about getting together this weekend?"

Susan shook her head. "Sorry. Symposium at Berkeley. 'Women in the Bible'."

"I'll call you next week, then."

"You better," she said, climbing out and closing the door.

THIRTY-ONE

Early friday morning my team regrouped and plotted a new plan of action. We decided that Missy would track down as much as she could about Nick Foster. He still struck me as a complete long shot, but given the uproar Tarentino's story had caused, I felt it prudent to at least check him out. Jorge, in the meantime, returned to Haines's neighborhood on the off chance we had missed something during the initial canvas. Freddie Burnette was in rehab in the morning, not due to arrive until after noon.

I spent the early hours with Rikko, going over the reports and lab results that had piled up on my desk while we were working the Silvers' angle. The tox screen report on Haines noted a .10 blood alcohol level. Like Cook, the sonar technician was legally drunk at the time of his envenomization. He also had ingested a low dose of strychnine and that same mysterious organic compound we'd found in Cook's bloodstream.

Near the bottom of the pile of reports I found the results of an analysis performed by scientists at the University of Southern California on the venom taken from Cook's body. They found that the venom could be broken down into three distinct components called globules. These three ingredients form a poisonous mixture unique to the deadliest of American pit vipers, *Crotalus adamanteus,* the eastern diamondback rattlesnake.

"Now, why would the killer use an eastern diamondback rattler when he could have caught a sidewinder out in the desert?" I asked. "And why was the snakeskin at Cook's from a mamba and a rattlesnake when he was only killed by the venom of one?"

Rikko shrugged. "Maybe he carries the rattlesnake in a box where a mamba has been and the dead skin sticks to the rattler?"

I nodded. "Makes sense. Let's go back to the zoo, talk to Foster, find out how you'd move one of these snakes. If he is our man, we might make him nervous."

"Always a good thing," Rikko said.

We caught Nick Foster coming out of the herpetology offices with a canvas and leather duffel slung over one shoulder. He wore aviator sunglasses in addition to his usual desert boots, khaki shorts, and shirt.

"We'd like to have you take us through a snake transfer, show us the equipment and the technique," I said after introducing Rikko.

"No time to talk today, mates, sorry," he said. "My flight to Tucson leaves in fifty minutes. Off for a few days to film Gila monsters in the Sonoran

Desert. Season's premiere for next year's *Cold Blooded!* Should be a corker of a show, let me tell ya."

"When will you be back?" Rikko asked.

"Monday night. Maybe Tuesday. Depends on filming conditions."

"Travel a lot?" I asked.

"Seems like 24/7 most times," he said, glancing up at the clock.

"How about last weekend?" Rikko asked.

"No," he said, removing the glasses. "I was here in town with friends. Attended a reception at the museum."

"They can vouch for your whereabouts last Friday night?"

"What's going on here, eh?" he demanded defensively. "You thinking I'm a suspect in these snake killings?"

"Everyone who has a rattlesnake is a suspect," Rikko said.

Foster glared at us. "I was at a reception at the Museum of Natural History, like I said. Must be two hundred people saw me there."

"Okay," I said. "Have a good trip. Dr. Hood? She around?"

I must have said this with a touch more eagerness than I'd intended, because Foster set the bag down and grinned conspiratorially. "I see what's going on here," he said. "Got a hankerin' for a sniff of it, and ya needed a reason to come here, that it?"

"What's that?" I asked. Rikko frowned.

"Oh, don't bullshit an old bullshitta," he said with a lecherous wink. "She looks a keeper, don't she, with that killer figure? And in your head you can smell what she'd be like, all sexed up, legs partin' for a bit of your stingin' roger. But let old Nick Foster tell you something, Sergeant, many's the man that's tried to get in the panties of Dr. Janice Hood and failed mightily, myself included. Beneath her pleasant exterior, she's ice-hearted: no heat in the breast or between the thighs, if you know what I mean."

"I know you're a big deal on cable, pal," I said. "But I gotta tell you, you occupy a class of asshole all by yourself."

Foster's face hardened. "Suit yourself, Sergeant. Maybe you are the better man. Hood's out there beyond the snake section, working on her pet project."

He shoved his glasses back on, picked up his baggage, and pushed by me. "Good sniffing to ya, Sergeant," he called over his shoulder. "Good sniffing to ya."

The panther chameleon was three-toed, lime green, and mope-faced. He had a curlicue tail and a boney crest that ran from mid-back to brow. He crept through the branches, pausing with every careful step to peruse us with bulging eyes. The light above the tank changed from green to rose. The lizard stopped his creeping and rotated its head curiously toward the light. It was like watching paint splattered on canvas; in seconds his skin mutated to a splotchy magenta.

"Magnificent," Rikko said.

"Isn't he?" Dr. Hood replied, looking at the reptile adoringly. She had been in the sun since I'd seen her last. Her skin was the color of red clover honey. "I hand-raised him. But he isn't what you're here to see. C'mon, we'll go find Wiley. Besides Nick, he's our best snake handler. I think he's cleaning cages this afternoon."

Frank Wiley was indeed cleaning cages that afternoon. Wiley was thirty-two, a lanky, rope-muscled man who looked like he'd be better suited to cowboying in Montana than reptile rustling in San Diego. And indeed, he'd grown up near Billings and become interested in snakes after he was bitten as a child.

"Burned hard, like one of them acetylene torches been touched to me," Wiley said, plucking a large black metal box off a shelf. "I fix the memory of that burning in my head every time before I go to pick one up."

We were in the hallway behind the snake exhibits. He held the box out for Rikko and me to examine. Dr. Hood stood back a few feet, her arms crossed. The box was made of heavy-gauge steel pocked with airholes. "These are what they're carried in?" I asked.

"Most often," Dr. Hood said. "We call them shift boxes. Ordinarily we try to lure them into the boxes with food, so we don't have to touch the venomous ones."

"So you never have to handle them?"

"Oh, sure we do," Wiley said. "We just try to keep it to a minimum. No one wants to get bit if they don't have to."

"How do you move them if you're not using the shift box?" Rikko asked.

"Very carefully. Here, I'll show you how it works with the male taipan. I've got to clean out his tank and give him some medicine anyway."

Immediately, Dr. Hood lost color and knitted her brows. "The male taipan?"

"Got to be done sometime today," Wiley said.

"What is this taipan?" Rikko asked.

"Deadliest snake on earth," Dr. Hood said. "From Foster's backyard. Mean."

"Like the black mamba?" I asked.

"Much worse. Very quick. Slithers at fourteen miles an hour. Can deliver three to four bites before a man can react. Horrible venom. Neurotoxin. Goes after your brain."

THIRTY-TWO

The taipan was a six-footer, slender, rust red, thin around the neck, crème-colored about the mouth, and meaty through the middle. Its eyes were as blood orange and wide-pupiled as a stoned teenager's and set at a triangular slant, like accents on a ceremonial mask.

When Frank Wiley opened the rear of the taipan's tank, the snake was awake and agitated. The snake handler wore heavy leather gauntlets, a clear plastic face shield, and held a device called "gentle giant tongs," essentially a spring-loaded set of pincers rigged at the end with wide, soft paddles that would immobilize the taipan but not injure it. He probed after the snake with the tongs. The taipan arched away, gliding through and around stalks of cane and back on itself to create fleeting, lethal macramé.

"Careful, Wiley!" Dr. Hood warned.

"Don't worry," he replied, never taking his eyes off the snake. "He's mine now."

The taipan darted to its left, then hooked back right. The zookeeper flicked his wrist. The paddles settled two inches behind the serpent's head, pretty as a cowboy's lasso trick. Only the taipan thought he was a bucking bronco. Every muscle in the snake's body went spastic. The mid-torso and tail lashed against the vegetation and the glass. The serpent's mouth flung open and the timbre of steam filled the air.

"Step back away, Sergeant, Detective," Dr. Hood called.

Rikko was on Wiley's side. He backed up so quick you'd have thought he was working a bomb defusion. I hustled over near Dr. Hood. Wiley pivoted and brought out the snake, which kept hissing, spitting, and curling back on itself. The zookeeper used his boot to open the lid of the shift box. Then he fed the taipan's body inside, head to tail, released the tongs, and kicked shut the lid.

Wiley looked from me to Rikko. Beads of sweat ran down his forehead. "And that, gentlemen, is how it's done."

"Better you than me," Rikko said. "How many here can do that?"

Wiley shrugged. "Nick, me, two, maybe three others."

"You?" I asked Dr. Hood.

"No," she said, shivering. "I prefer to use the food lure. Much safer."

I turned to Rikko. "I'm going to talk to the doctor here a minute. Have Wiley show you where they keep the shift boxes and all those tongs. I want the names of everyone who has access to them."

Wiley hesitated, then turned when Dr. Hood nodded. He and Rikko went out through a metal door at the far end of the hallway.

"I've seen this on television," she said, shooting me a bemused look. "This is where you separate us to see if our stories jibe."

"Everyone lies to cops," I said, shrugging. "It's reflexive. The easiest way to figure out who's lying the most is to listen to two different takes on the same story."

"So you think someone from the zoo is involved in those killings?"

"It's the only place I can think of right off where I can get a rattlesnake into a box that once carried a mamba," I said.

"Come again?" she asked.

"There was both mamba and rattlesnake skin on the bed at the first murder scene," I explained. "But only eastern diamondback venom in his bloodstream."

"Diamondback?" she said, surprised. "You think the rattler picked up the mamba skin—"

"In a transfer box," I said. "Or something like it."

"Well," she said, "it makes sense. But in defense of zoo personnel, Sergeant, most collectors of hot herps have transfer boxes. Have you tried that route?"

"Not yet," I admitted, then decided to change tactics. "You see Nick Foster last Friday and the Friday before?"

Dr. Hood thought about that. "During the day, sure," she said. "He was here."

"At night?"

"Wouldn't know. Friday nights I go to the ocean, swim, then go home and work."

"And the last two Friday nights, where were you?"

"Home. Designing the display for the panther chameleon and polishing the script for the next *Cold Blooded!*"

"You write the show?"

"One of the indignities I go through around here."

"Alone those Friday nights, at home, working?"

"Very," she said, her eyes now fixing coolly on mine.

"Not married?" I asked. "No boyfriend to keep you company?"

She rolled her head to one side, shooting me a solid look of appraisal. "Personal or professional question, Sergeant?"

I tried my aw-shucks grin on her. "Little of both, Dr. Hood."

She shook her head. "Forget about it. You're not my type."

"Yeah, that's what Foster told me."

That annoyed her. "What he'd call me this time? Dragon lady? Lizard woman? Cold-blooded bitch?"

"That was the gist of it," I said. "He a violent guy?"

The question seemed to take her aback. "Nick? No...well, I've seen him kick over things when he gets pissed off, and he's one of the most abrasive personalities on earth. But murder? No. I don't think he's got it in him."

"What about sexually violent?"

She threw me a look of complete disgust. "I've never had the experience or a conversation concerning it with him, nor care to. Are we done?"

"No," I said. "Where do you ocean swim, Dr. Hood?"

"What?" she replied, taken aback.

"I'm an open-water swimmer myself. I'm curious."

Her expression eased. "La Jolla Cove, of course. Sometimes off Black's Beach."

"You swum Lion's Lagoon?"

She shook her head. "Never heard of it."

"It's a big inlet in one of the outer Coronado Islands. Very dramatic setting. Calm water. Lots of wildlife."

"You'd need a boat to get out there. I don't have one."

"I do," I said. "I'm going out there to swim on Sunday. Want to go?"

The door at the far end of the hallway opened. "Eight shift boxes," Rikko announced. "All eight are there. Clean. No record of one taken out last Friday or the Friday before." He tossed his thumb at the zookeeper. "But Wiley tells the interesting story."

"What's that?" I asked.

"The store where Haines bought his lizards does a little black-market dealing."

My attention shot to Wiley. "True?"

The zookeeper nodded. "Owner was caught selling a hot a few years back"

I checked my watch. It was three in the afternoon. I turned back to Jan Hood. "Well, Doctor, got to go," I said. "Do I swim or sink?"

She studied me up and down before shrugging and smiling. "I could go for a swim. Why not?"

THIRTY-THREE

"What was that all about back there—sink or swim—with the Richter-scale woman?" Rikko grunted as we drove into the parking lot of an aging strip mall set amid a strip of aging strip malls six blocks from the San Diego Sports Arena. More than half the signs touting the mall's businesses were in Vietnamese or Spanish.

"Just planning a get-together," I said. "We swim, I find out more about Foster. Before that, though, I'm gonna need a background check on her."

"First thing tomorrow," Rikko promised, then pointed. "There's our place."

Global Exotics occupied an old supermarket at the west end of the parking lot. It had high front windows and advertising soap-smeared on the glass. The front doors were open wide, releasing the fetid ammonia of reptile and the booming of heavy metal. Inside the store lay a maze of stacked terrariums housing red-tail boas, black and white tegu lizards, skinks, emperor scorpions, tarantulas, Indian pythons, ball pythons, and poison-dart frogs. In the bottom of a floor-to-ceiling octagonal terrarium, a monitor lizard as heavy as a beagle stalked a deformed chick that tried to run from its tongue-flickering fate. A bumper sticker had been affixed to the side of the massive terrarium. It read: TIME FLIES WHEN YOU'RE MENTALLY ILL.

Around the back of the terrarium, we came upon a twenty-something flame-haired slacker with four studs in each ear, two hoops through his nose, and murals of skulls, snakes, battle-axes, and bosomy gladiator women tattooed the length of his arms. He stood behind a cash register, using a pair of kitchen tongs to pluck white mice from a glass fish tank and drop them into a brown paper grocery bag.

"Horace's appetite still up?" he was asking his customer, a teenage boy with greasy hair and a gray T-shirt that showed a rising king cobra surrounded by the words, WATCH IT, YOU'RE IN SPITTING DISTANCE.

"Ravenous," the teen replied. "Treats the mice like popcorn. Best part about it? Watching him eat totally freaks my old lady out."

"There's a plus," the slacker laughed, walking the teen and the mice to a computerized cash register.

Rikko's nostrils flared; then he murmured, "What happened to the puppy, the kitten, the guinea pig, or the hamster?"

"Guess they're just hors d'oeuvres on the reptilian buffet these days."

The teenager paid for the mice and headed out the door.

"Help you, dudes?" the slacker said.

"You own this place?" I asked, flipping open my badge and identifying myself.

"Paul Reardon," he said, suddenly guarded. "What's this about? I been clean. Ask my probation officer."

"Uh-huh," Rikko said, glaring at the man with such malevolence that Reardon got nervous and took a step away.

I tossed photographs of Morgan Cook and Matthew Haines on the countertop. "Seen either of these guys before?"

Reardon hesitated, looked at Rikko again, then he picked up Cook's photo and shook his head. "Don't know this guy." He glanced at Haines's picture. "Sure. Dragon geek. Mealworms and crickets."

"Translation?" I said.

"This guy owns a bearded dragon. He buys mealworms and crickets from me to feed it every couple of weeks or so," he replied. "Why? What's he done?"

"He got dead," I said. "By snakebite."

Reardon's eyes widened. "That's the dude?" he said. "I read about that. Oh, man, wait till the dudes hear a dragon geek got venomized. Naked, too, right? And gay or something?"

"Or something," Rikko said, tapping Haines's photograph with one gnarled finger. "Haines, he buy snakes from you?"

At that Reardon tensed ever so slightly. "Nah, just bugs."

"He never expressed any interest in buying a poisonous snake?" I asked.

"Hey, no way. No legal trade in hot herps in California. I learned my lesson."

"That's not what we're asking."

Reardon would not look at us. "Nope. Never heard a thing."

I pulled out a copy of a receipt we'd found in Haines's file cabinet. "Says here he bought a brand-new fifty-gallon terrarium from you about two weeks ago."

Reardon blinked, then his neck muscles went taut. "So?"

"So his roommate who was away for the past month said Haines had no snake before he left. We found an Arizona coral in the terrarium he bought from you."

"Ain't illegal, selling a terrarium."

"No, but weren't you curious why he was buying a new terrarium if he wasn't buying a lizard from you?"

For a long moment Reardon said nothing; then he flushed. "Okay, okay, he asked where he might be able to buy something hot. I said I didn't want any part of it, okay? And I didn't. Like I said, I'm legit now. Squeaky clean."

"Come on, Pauly," Rikko said, sliding a little closer and twisting his face into that maniacal mask he uses to intimidate people. "Sure you don't sell the poison ones?"

"No!" Reardon protested. "Look, understand something: Used to be reptiles were just for freaks and weirdos, kind of a reverse macho thing. Now we get doctors, lawyers, shit, even soccer moms in here buying 'em for their kids. My business has quadrupled in the past two years. You think I'm gonna screw that up, selling hots under the counter?"

"But you know where to get them—the hot stuff?" I said.

"Ain't hard if you're looking," he replied. "You want something deadly, go to Vegas, go to TJ: They got them right there, five miles south of the border."

"We've heard that," I said. "But you got to learn how to handle them, right?"

"You don't, you end up in the hospital pretty damn quick."

Rikko edged closer. He made his shoulders seem a cowl and he loomed over the exotic pet owner. "I know black markets," he grunted, his eyes half-lidded. "They need communication to exist. Sellers talk to buyers. Trade information. So I figure with poisonous reptiles, there must be network, local network. I am right?"

"Never heard of no network," Reardon mumbled.

"Too bad, huh, Detective Varjjan?" I said. "Guess we're gonna have to get a subpoena, seize Mr. Reardon's books, and ask our forensic accountant to go over them while U.S. Fish and Wildlife takes an inventory of everything in the place. That should totally fuck up his quadrupled-in-five-years business for at least a month or two, don't you think?"

Rikko's eyebrows shot up. "I do think."

We turned away from Reardon and headed toward the front door. We'd gotten by a tank that held an albino python when Reardon yelled after us, "All cops are dicks. No matter what you do, how cool you run your life, they show up to fuck with you."

I said, "He's really endearing himself to us, isn't he?"

"I think of inviting him over for Sabbath dinner next week," Rikko said. "Christina's making the lasagna with the lamb sauce."

We stepped through the door, then Reardon yelled, "Word gets out I ratted out the hots, my business will be cooked. Reptile people stick together."

I turned and looked at him, then around the empty store. "Who's gonna know, Paul, except the three of us?"

THIRTY-FOUR

It was nearly six o'clock by the time we got back to the office. Freddie Burnette was working at Jorge's computer. I gave her a list of thirty-seven active underground collectors of hot herps living in San Diego County and asked her to run the names through the criminal intelligence files and every court record in the state.

"Probably won't be until late tonight, first thing tomorrow morning," she said.

"That's okay, everyone's working tomorrow. Sunday off."

"Unless we get another tonight," Rikko said, yawning. "He killed the past two Fridays."

'That's why we're all going home, getting a good night's sleep, then right back in here tomorrow. Everyone on pagers and cell phones tonight. No excuses."

I went home to the *Chant* and slept fitfully, sure that the phone would ring. My dreams were vivid and disturbing. In one, a creature with Nick Foster's upper torso and a snake's trunk and tail slithered through the roots of exotic plants, spitting and calling my name. In another, the snakes on the headdress of that painting of Lilith in Susan Dahoney's office came alive, biting at the air. Half the snakes suddenly turned into taipans. The other half became chameleons whose skin pulsated with the colors of fire.

Jimmy sat silently on the bench for our morning game at the Coronado city field. Fay said he'd hardly spoken to her since returning to school. Christina had called. She and Jimmy were going to have ice cream together after school on Wednesday. I asked Jimmy if he wanted to go fishing in the morning and he shook his head.

"Okay, Jimbo," I said sadly as he trudged off. "Suit yourself."

When I arrived downtown, Missy, Jorge, and Freddie were waiting in the cubicle. The three of them had a very specific look about them, a look hot-etched into my mind as a boy: a flushed tone to the skin, the popping and licking of the lips, the smug agitation about the eyes. It was the look that had possessed my father the last time I saw him alive: early May, the week after my tenth birthday.

My dad came home for dinner on a Wednesday, the day my mom always served spaghetti. He'd been working double shifts, and, except for my birthday trip to the amusement park at Nantasket Beach, I hadn't seen much of him in the previous month.

He'd been working a big case. At dinner he flirted with my mom and praised Christina for the A she'd gotten on a test. It had been drizzling most of the day, but not hard enough to postpone the Red Sox game with the Baltimore Orioles.

After dinner, we sat on the couch in the living room and watched the game on Channel 38. Luis Tiant threw a three-hitter. Fred Lynn went four for four and clawed his body high up the scoreboard in left center, robbing Frank Robinson of a sure triple. My mom kept insisting that it was a school night and that I go to bed. But my dad was caught up in the game and would not hear of it. He drank a Miller. I had a root beer. We ate popcorn. It was eleven when the game ended. My dad had laughed. "You won't see one like that again anytime soon, Shay. You remember what you saw tonight, okay?"

I nodded sleepily. He picked me up, hugged me to him, and carried me to my room. He helped me off with my jeans and into my pajamas. He tucked me under my Spider Man blanket and kissed me on the cheek, and I opened my eyes to see him silhouetted in my doorway. " 'Night, Shay," he said.

" 'Night, Daddy."

"Always do me proud, 'kay?"

"Okay."

I drifted off into sleep that night, enveloped in his fading smells: the tangy smoke of Pall Malls, the lime of Brut aftershave, and this singular odor I could not have identified as a child but have come to know intimately as an adult: the acid quality that adrenaline imbues in sweat; the odor that emanates off the guilty when they are caught; the scent that steams off police detectives when they know something that you don't—something that might break a case wide open.

The stench of that knowing was thick in our cubicle.

"Okay, what do you got?" I asked.

Freddie smiled, thrusting her chin at Missy and Jorge. "You two first."

Missy came off the edge of her desk, bouncing on the tips of her running shoes. "Tarentino was right. My detector was completely on the fritz. Mr. Cold Blooded *is* bisexual and has quite the temper. We contacted the Australian consulate in Los Angeles. They did an inquiry with Sidney and Cairns police. Seems when Foster was in college he was charged with statutory rape on a fifteen-year-old girl. He walked when the complainant's family refused to let her testify."

"Nothing else?"

"No, there's more—a lot more," Missy said. "He lives up north toward Poway. Sheriff's office says they've been out there three times on calls in the past year. All three times the allegations have been about sexual encounters that got out of control. One woman. Two guys. Chaco's right: Foster likes to tie people to beds. And get this—video tape them."

Rikko came around the corner of our cubicle. "Crikey."

"No kidding, huh?" Missy said.

"No formal charges?" I asked.

She and Jorge both shook their heads. "Either he gets to them and pays them off somehow or they're so embarrassed by what they've gotten themselves into, with who they've got themselves into, that they don't want it made public. Until then, no search and no possible videos."

"I want his alibi checked for the last two Friday nights. Names. Phone numbers."

"Got it."

"What about you?" I asked Freddie.

She broke into a wide grin. "You won't believe who was on that list of underground snake handlers."

"Foster?"

"We're not that lucky. Lanny Biggs, a.k.a. Tao Wu Biggs."

Neither name registered with me and I turned my palms up.

"A.k.a., Bigg Ja Moustapha," Freddie said. "Fatty Wu Marshall's heir apparent to the southland meth-amphetamine trade."

"The crazy one thinks he's gonna be a hip-hop god, cutting his own CDs?"

"That's the one," Freddie replied. "Mother's Indonesian, father's an African-American evangelical preacher. But Bigg Ja is no believer. He's got a long-standing nasty streak in him. Busted three times as a juvie. Last two were compounded by weapons charges. Never gone down as an adult, but criminal intelligence says he's a suspect in at least three gangland-style hits, all supposedly ordered by Fatty Wu."

"We know what kind of hot herps he keeps?" I asked.

Freddie shook her head. "We don't even know where he is right now. The address he gave the guy who owns the reptile store is a fake, and Narcotics says they haven't gotten a visual on him since I sent Fatty Wu to a better place six weeks ago."

"I understand your personal interest because of his link to Fatty Wu, but where's the connection to these killings?"

"Read it and weep," Freddie said, thrusting a computer printout at me. "Written and performed by Bigg Ja Moustapha on his underground CD *Chuck That Key!*"

God say so, da Scripture say so
Ain't got no use for all these homos
They stinkin' up the country
Say two daddies okay
All them dykes been rollin' in the hay
Ain't no doubt, don't you see?
Got to lock 'em in the closet and chuck that key!

Chuck that key, that's what we'll do
Send 'em back to Sodom, then we're through
With swishy little boys and bitches that're fake
Toss 'em in a hole, feed 'em to my snake
Ain't no doubt, don't you see
Got to lock 'em in the closet and chuck that key!

"The poster boy for tolerance," said Rikko, who'd been reading over my shoulder.

"Scriptures, homophobic rants, snakes, buys equipment at the same store where Haines did his reptile shopping," Freddie said. "What more do you want, Shay? We've got to bring this guy in and run a game on him."

"What about Foster?" Missy demanded.

"We go after 'em both," I said. "Foster gets off that plane Monday, I want him under twenty-four-hour surveillance. And contact the Tucson police: I want to know if they've had any murders involving snakes. Christina says these ritualistic killings can evolve, get more elaborate as they go."

"And Bigg Ja?" Freddie asked.

"We locate our meth friend, we bring him in and let Rikko sweat him."

THIRTY-FIVE

Brett tarentino made it official in an exclusive interview published in *The Sunday Daily News*' April sixteenth edition: After twenty-seven years of active duty, Chief Norman Strutt would deliver his resignation to the mayor the following afternoon.

Assistant Chief Helen Adler woke me at seven sharp to tell me about the article and looking for an update on the investigation. I shook myself awake, gave her an oral report on everything that had transpired since the Silvers' arraignment, then finished once again pressing for more detectives to help surveil Foster and for cooperation from Narcotics in the search for Bigg Ja.

"You'll get your manpower," she promised. "I want to notify Sand about Foster."

"Why?" I asked incredulously. Mayor Bob Sand was a notorious news leaker.

"Need I remind you the zoo's sacred in this town, Shay?" Adler replied. "If the mayor finds out through some back channel that we had as public a figure as Foster under surveillance on these killings and didn't tell him, there'd be a hurricane around my head."

Lying there in bed, the phone pressed to my ear, I gazed skyward, suspecting Adler of an ulterior motive. What she wanted was a reason to talk with the mayor in person, to make him feel like he was part of the investigation's inner circle. From her perspective it was a smart move. The mayor would remember her confidence when it came time to make his choice on an interim and then permanent chief.

"How about a compromise?" I said. "Tell Sand we're watching somebody at the zoo, but don't name Foster. That way the mayor's got his heads-up but can't finger the head of herpetology to anyone in the media."

Adler sniffed, and I heard her fingernails drumming on wood, a habit when she's scheming. "I want daily updates, Shay. Make that twice a day."

Since I was up so early, I took a chance and called Fay's house. Jimmy answered but hung up before I got out the words "Sure you don't want to go fishing?"

That response soured the rest of my morning, which I spent washing clothes and cleaning up the boat. I was below deck around a quarter to twelve, working with the drill to tighten down a loose porthole, when I heard Brett Tarentino bray: "And who might you be looking for?"

"Sergeant Moynihan? Do I have the right place?"

I groaned and raced up the gangway and out onto the aft deck in time to see Dr. Jan Hood standing at the back of Tarentino's boat in a tan windbreaker, blue shorts, sunglasses, visor, and running shoes. She carried a small black gym bag.

"You do indeed," Brett said, raising a tall Bloody Mary. Chaco lounged on the afterdeck, dressed in a Hawaiian shirt with a volcano motif. "And what, may I ask, is the nature of your visit, Ms.....?"

Before she could say another word, I yelled, "Don't talk to that man!" and jumped off onto the dock. I hustled to her side, turned her away from Tarentino, and murmured, "He's deranged."

"I heard that!" Tarentino snapped. "Don't believe a word of it. If anyone's a threat to society, it's Moynihan."

"Don't you have a story to write?"

"I already broke the big story this morning. My day off. Unless you've got a tip?"

"Sorry, still banging our heads against a wall."

"And you're taking a day off instead of battering your head, I see. So much for the blue knight in America's finest city."

"Even knights take off the armor once in a while," Dr. Hood said.

A smirk crossed Tarentino's lips. "She's got a brain, Seamus! Bravo! He's a tarnished knight, Ms.....?"

"Hood," she said before I could stop her. "*Doctor* Janice Hood."

"Dr. Janice Hood of the zoo," Brett said, gesturing at the tan windbreaker emblazoned with the zoo logo. "That where you two met?"

"Flee," I said, urging her toward the ladder. "Flee or he will suck you dry."

"Bye-bye, Dracula," she called over her shoulder.

I went to help her up the ladder onto the deck, but she scrambled up easily. Brett growled, then turned back toward Chaco.

"Welcome to my humble barge," I said, before giving her the grand tour.

"Some barge," she said, when we had come back up on deck. "If you don't mind me asking, how does a policeman own something like this? You crooked?"

"Hardly," I replied sobering. "The benefits of rancorous divorce."

"I'm sorry," she said, then hesitated. "Look, I don't know why I'm here exactly, Sergeant Moynihan. It makes me nervous. When I'm nervous, I say things I shouldn't."

"What are you nervous about?" I asked. "We're going for a swim. You're a swimmer, right, Jan?"

"Call me Dr. Hood, please," she said. "That's all I'm here for?"

She had large, brown, alert eyes accustomed to dissecting the behavior of creatures that crawled in dim, moist jungles, and she trained them on me.

"Far as I'm concerned," I lied, not letting my gaze waver.

The truth, of course, was more complex: I wanted to learn more about Nick Foster and more about her. Even though she doubted his ability to kill someone, I was hoping to coax her into teaching us enough about the man and his habits that we would be prepared when our surveillance began. At the same time, from a personal point of view, I was trying to figure out what made her tick.

According to the background information Rikko got from zoo administrators, Janice Hood was thirty-seven, born in Miami. Bachelor's through doctorate with honors in zoology from the University of Florida. Fieldwork in Brazil, Madagascar, and the islands of Fiji. Well respected, she published regularly and spoke at international conventions. Indeed, the following weekend she was scheduled to talk before the American Society of Ichthyologists and Herpetologists' annual meeting in Chicago.

"If you don't mind, why lizards?" I asked, leading her up onto the bridge.

"My parents were killed in a car crash when I was seven," she said. "I went to live with my aunt and uncle, who were childless and bred chameleons for the legal domestic trade. The year after my parents died, I'd sit for hours watching the chameleon families play. They were the closest things I had to friends. That's how it all started."

Then she looked over my shoulder at the *Chant*'s controls. "Twin Cats?"

"How'd you know that?"

"I used to live in Miami," she said, looking off into the distance. "Friends had these kinds of boats."

"Wealthy friends?"

"Some of them," she replied. 'They liked to marlin fish near Bimini. I'd just go along for the nightlife."

"You don't strike me as the nightlife type," I said.

"Everyone has their wild moments, don't they?" she asked.

Dr. Hood proved an able mate, at ease on the deck even when we chopped into breakwater beyond Point Loma and the swells and currents tossed and beat the hull of the *Nomad's Chant*. The open sea beyond, however, was calm and gently rolling, shimmering emerald like some vast Scottish moor in the sunshine after a spring shower. A white pelican hunted across our bow, then swooped and dove at a school of baitfish being driven to the surface by predators below.

She stood with me on the flying bridge, asking enough questions about the boat, her engine specifications, and the navigation system to convince me she could take the helm. We cruised southwest at fifteen knots and made for the hazy low islands sixteen miles distant. I stood next to her, in control of the throttle, watching as the excitement of being at the wheel on the open sea filled her head to toe. Every now and then, against the odor of brine, I caught the smell of her: musk and ripe berries.

I took the controls back as we neared the four low islands, fortresses of wind-smoothed volcanic rock and salt-stunted vegetation. The yellowtail bite was not on yet, and there were no charter fishing boats to be seen. The eastern shores of the islands were steep, flint-colored cliffs, some forty feet and higher. Three quarters of a mile north of the southern tip of the southernmost island, however, the ramparts were interrupted. Thousands of years ago, when the island was formed, the lava had run in two separate channels, leaving a sheltered lagoon that stretches deep into the island's heart.

As we came across the mouth of the inlet, a pod of dolphins breached off our starboard bow while gulls circled and screeched under the midday sun. I navigated the *Chant* into the lagoon neatly on the swell. The cliffs rose up around us forty yards to either side. Here and there along the steep shores, low and on the water, the volcano and time had left shelves and ledges covered with the scat of birds and seals. The diesels' throbs reverberated off the walls, which narrowed with every fathom passed.

At last the cliffwork turned concave and almost closed into an urn's bottom, save for a narrow slit in the western cliff wall twenty feet wide. I throttled down, then killed the motor fifty yards from the yawning crack and dropped anchor. Up close, the mouth of the opening was like two sets of rounded lips, one set within the other, before giving way to a cave without a roof. The sun came slanting and bouncing down the interior of the gash, throwing glimmering shadows on the surface of the dark water.

"We swim from here," I said.

Dr. Hood held her hand to her brow. "How far does it go?"

"A fair way until the split," I said. "There are two arms back there, which return again this way; then both dead-end. There's a head off the galley where you can change. I'll go below."

She appeared on deck ten minutes later, carrying goggles and dressed much as I was, in a thin black neoprene suit designed for ocean swimming. She was a big, lean woman and did not hesitate to follow when I plunged off the bow. The brisk salt water bit at my face, hands, and feet. Her cheeks turned cherry and she looked down the slot with anticipation. "Lead the way," she said.

I settled into a crawl, stroking and kicking my way past the lips of the entrance into the channel. Dr. Hood was a strong swimmer with sturdy mechanics, and she matched me stroke for stroke. After two hundred yards, the burn in my shoulders and legs had eased out the kinks, and I shifted to the breaststroke. She came even with me and we treaded. The sound of our rippling in the water echoed off the wet walls and mixed with the cries of gulls nesting high in the cliffs above us. "Amazing," she said.

"Isn't it?" I said. "The water's so deep in here, you couldn't touch bottom if you tried. Wait until you get to the back of this place."

After another two hundred yards the walls flared, and we swam into the broad confluence of the channel's two arms. Before us, a smooth rock shelf wrapped around the point in the Y. The ledge there ran back from the edge twenty feet at a slant before reaching the cliffwork. We swam toward it through water turned greenish-blue by the solid shaft of sunlight that bore in from above.

Yards from the shelf and fifteen feet below us, the first dark gray torpedo passed. Then another blew by, closer, undulating at what seemed impossible speed and menacing grace. I pulled up short at the sight of a third and fourth shadow bearing down on us from the right arm of the bay, reached out, grabbed Dr. Hood, and pulled her to me.

She pushed away, glaring and kicking. "What do you think you're doing?"

"Tread lightly and stay close, Doctor," I warned. "They're all around us."

THIRTY-SIX

D r. hood's head twisted about in time to see a mature bull elephant seal, fifteen hundred pounds' worth, passing at three feet, going twenty knots. She choked in alarm and threw her arms around my neck when the next seal, a young male, bumped her back.

"They're territorial," she cried. "They could kill us if they feel threatened."

"I know. Just stay cool while they check us out."

More bull seals boiled out the right arm. They came at us in a tight formation, then peeled off one by one, rolling on their sides and inspecting us as they flashed by, some barking in warning before rolling over and perusing us from another angle. Dr. Hood's face was inches from mine. Her firm body was against me, pushing and treading. Her breath came short and rapid. Her eyes were wide, excited, darting at each flash of gray shadow in the water.

"We should get out of here," she whispered tremulously. "We're wearing suits that make us look like other seals. This is very dangerous."

"More dangerous if we move right now, I think. I've seen them back in here before and they usually leave you alone once they figure out what you are."

The biggest bull breached next to the shelf. He flippered and slid his way up onto the water-smoothed rock, posturing, croaking, and soggy-barking at us, his guttural vocalizations echoing off the high walls. Soon his whole troop followed and were arrayed before us, all of them baying, yipping, growling, and tossing their heads and inflatable noses at us like tormented horses at biting flies.

"This isn't getting better," I muttered. "I've never seen them act this way."

"We surprised them," she murmured. "And they're very unhappy."

"Let's stick nice and close and we'll back our way out of here."

She hesitated a second, then her arm dropped from around my shoulder to my waist, and mine looped around hers. We flutter-kicked and used our free arms to paddle our way ever so slowly back into the main channel, our attention never leaving the threatening chorus line on the shelf.

The resonation of their fury did not stop even when we'd pulled back a hundred yards. Dr. Hood and I separated and began crawling our way toward the boat, stopping every fifty yards or so to listen. I could still hear the distant grumble of the seals when we reached the *Chant*'s ladder.

Dr. Hood climbed shakily out of the water, collapsed into the fighting chair, and tore her goggles off. She gazed at me heavy-lidded, shaking her head with a weary smile.

"Sorry about that, Doctor," I said, still gasping. "I've never had that happen, and I've been swimming back in there almost twenty years."

She got up on wobbly legs, grinning wildly at me, her cheeks flushed. "No, that was extraordinary! What an experience! To have them all around us like that and ... "

She grabbed me, pulled me close, and kissed me tightly. I was shocked at first. Then my arms came around her and I kissed her back. She lingered a moment, her eyes turning slightly unscrewed. Then she frowned and pushed against my chest, turning her head downward. "I'm sorry."

"Sorry about what, Dr. Hood?" I asked, leaning in toward her. Her hair was wet and pressed in easy curls against her face.

She hesitated, then turned toward me, her eyes more drunken, her breath as shallow and fast as it had been confronting the seals. "Sorry about ... being so cold before. And call me Jan."

When Jan climbed out of her suit below deck and stepped into the steaming shower stall with me, my breath caught in my throat. Though heavy through their bottoms, her breasts rode high on her rib cage. Her nipples, too, were upturned, pouty, and the color of Merlot. Her belly was rippled with muscle and sloped away in mid-abdomen in a taut plain toward her mons, which, to my surprise, was completely bald. I had never been with a woman who was hairless there.

She caught me staring and pressed herself against me, the hot water pounding down on us both. "It's called a Brazilian wax job," she murmured. "Do you like it?"

I pressed back against her, feeling myself grow. "I think I like it very much."

"Show me."

There are women I've known for whom sex is a chore. There are women I've known for whom sex is a tool. Other females consider sex a necessity. A handful, the ones I remember most, have treated sex as joy.

For Jan Hood, sex was both joy and escape. As she built toward orgasm, the ligature of her neck stood out like struck piano cords, her jaw jutted forward, and she gently chewed the air. Her shoulders and thighs quivered, then her whole body stiffened and I saw a part of her she kept hidden. Gone was the scientist. Gone was the orphan girl. Gone was the woman I'd seen verbally spar with Nick Foster.

She swept toward the crest, and for a split second I swore she did not know who I was or who she was. Then her face undulated through a rapid series of emotions: pleasure, fear, anger, bewilderment, and a half dozen others I could not name, but which all seemed to gather together as her base self, a self that struck me as infinite and unknowable. Then she wove her fingers through my hair and jammed herself against my mouth, trembling and bucking in total release.

After several moments her fingers and thighs relaxed and I stood to rest my forehead against the shower wall next to her. She pressed her breasts and belly against my torso and ran her lips over my cheeks and along my neck, letting her right hand trail circles along my spine.

With her other hand she shut off the hot water, then used her heel to pop open the shower door. Jan stepped out backward and got a towel from the rack and began to dry me. When she was done, she led me to my bed and pressed me down on my back.

She got up over me, so tall she had to duck her head, kept her feet under her, placed both palms open on my chest, and slowly lowered herself and began to ride, all the while gazing at me with those imploring drunken eyes.

"Go there," she whispered huskily after quickening the pace. The blood rushed to my skin so fast it throbbed. Then an indescribable wave of pleasure pulsed down through me. She rode me through it, then collapsed on top of me and we clung to each other.

"Never," she gasped. "Never like that."

"Never," I replied. "Ever. My god. Ever."

For the longest time, Jan lay there, sweaty and breathless, her weight all around me. Hot sun steamed in the open porthole. You could hear gulls calling and the ocean against the cliffs like wire brushing a cymbal. You could taste her every inch in the smell of sex stirring in the salt air. She rolled off me at last and up onto her elbow, toying her finger across my chest. "It's been a long time. You made me feel so good."

"Unbelievable."

She looked up and down my body, then ran her hand over the faint railroad-track scars that criss-crossed my right arm and then down to a ragged starfish of a scar on my left thigh. "I know about the arm. But what happened here?"

"Shot," I said. "Five years ago. I don't like to talk about it. Bad deal all around."

She frowned, then shrugged and smiled. "Everyone has the right not to dwell on bad memories. I like you, Moynihan."

"Feeling's mutual."

Then her face sobered. "But I want to be clear about something. I'm not looking for a relationship."

Another door of possibilities closed for Seamus Moynihan at that moment. But despite the sheer excellence of the pleasures we'd just shared, I did not display one dram of regret. Instead I rubbed her shoulder and gave her my standard reply to this sort of statement: "You saying we can't be pals who get together from time to time? I know it's all I'm looking for. I've got a busy life. I like to keep it as untangled as possible. But I do like my friends."

Her eyes searched my face for nearly a minute. "I don't like lying," she said. "It's the one thing in life I can't stand."

"Well, it's not high on my list either. What's your point?"

"How many other *friends* do you have?"

I flashed on my kiss with Susan Dahoney, then shook my head. "None at the moment."

"Well, then," she said, letting her hand troll down my lower belly, "if we have the understanding that we won't lie to each other, then yes, I'd like to get together time to time."

"How about now?"

She grinned slyly. "How *about* now?"

THIRTY-SEVEN

I entered the monday morning April seventeenth meeting having already met with my team. Freddie Burnette had touched base with Narcotics and Gangs. No sightings or word yet on the location of Bigg Ja's crib. At the same time, it had been almost two weeks since we'd put out the ViCAP inquiry. To date: no responses.

Christina was still convinced that the killer was modeling his method of torture on an earlier event. So I had Jorge writing a second ViCAP inquiry adding details from the Haines murder. We also decided to issue a special bulletin to law enforcement agencies in Australia and New Zealand.

But what I was really excited about was what Jan had told me after our second round of lovemaking. During the cruise back to San Diego Harbor, I had managed to slip in questions about Nick Foster, his patterns of movement, his attitudes and general behavior. Jan answered the questions but was not one to offer information if not specifically asked. She said she felt uncomfortable talking about other people. Still, she did help flesh out my understanding of the cable star.

Jan described Foster as a man of large and varied interests. He liked to wade in mucky pits, shuffling ahead with sneaker-clad feet in hopes of kicking up a ticked-off crocodile, gator, or anaconda. When the beasts attacked, he reacted with lightning speed and absolute fearlessness. Foster worked out incessantly, sometimes twice a day. He kept himself on a fanatical diet. He never drank during the week, but was often seen intoxicated at zoo functions and other public forums on the weekends. He had a nasty temper and regularly lashed out at the crew of *Cold Blooded!* Later, he'd regret it and buy the berated a gift: bottles of perfume, wine, and art.

"It's strange, but he is well thought of because of it," Jan said. "You know: the handsome, gifted sot who regrets his actions. He puts on that show for everyone but me."

"Why single you out?"

"I intimidate him. I won't sleep with him. And he's a vindictive bastard."

Jan also said that a few weeks back, during a zoo function at the Museum of Natural History at Balboa Park, Foster had gotten very drunk and involved in some kind of altercation in the men's bathroom. She said a waiter told her he'd seen Foster yelling at a young man wearing a zoo cap.

"Why didn't you tell me this before?" I asked.

She'd shrugged. "Didn't think it was relevant."

"How'd you get her to tell you all that?" Lieutenant Fraiser asked after I'd given him, Merriweather, and Assistant Chief Adler a summary of Jan's information.

I did not inform my superiors of our interlude and was not going to: When it came right down to it, at Jan's insistent definition, what had happened between us was just sex. So I shrugged at my boss and said, "Formed some common ground based on the fact she likes to ocean swim. She felt comfortable and talked."

Adler said, "We need to find whoever had the altercation with Foster."

I grinned, shoving copies of Haines's Visa statement across the table. "Look at the charges the Friday before Haines was killed. The night Cook died."

Adler, Captain Merriweather, and The Prick sat forward staring at the highlighted lines. On March thirty-first, Haines had made purchases at a gas station in Mission Valley, at a taco joint near Hillcrest, and at a souvenir kiosk—

"—at the Museum of Natural History," Adler said.

I nodded. "Same day that Foster got into the altercation."

"Wouldn't that be a coincidence?"

"Wouldn't it, though?"

It turned out that the function had been a fundraiser for Galápagos tortoise research that began at six P.M. that night. Foster had been drinking before he got to the reception and continued to drink once he arrived. That much Rikko and I were able to ascertain in interviews with zoo and museum administrators. But none of them had been witness to the tiff Foster was alleged to have had in the men's room. Nor had anyone from the catering service, the band, or the security guards. And I was wondering whether Jan had been mistaken.

Then we found Lorraine D'Angelo, a pretty Mediterranean-looking woman who had been working late that night, redesigning the window front of the museum store, directly across the lobby from a men's room. She remembered Haines.

"He wore linen pants and a blue cotton shirt and he seemed real upset," she said, "pacing and watching the hall from inside the store. It was nearly seven and I had to tell him we were closing. He bought a poster that showed the birds of the world's endangered tropical rain forests. Said he was buying it for someone special. Real specific that I shouldn't bend it putting it into the cardboard tube I gave him. Then that man from the zoo, the one who puts his face right there in front of snakes, he shows up."

"Nick Foster?" Rikko said.

"That's him," the clerk said. "Then this man—Haines?"

"Right," I said.

"He follows Foster into the bathroom. Couple of minutes later I hear yelling."

"What about?" Rikko asked.

"I couldn't tell," D'Angelo said, worrying her hands. "The sound was all garbled and muted, coming through the door and across the hall here. But anyway, next thing, Foster comes storming out and goes back into the reception. Haines left the men's room and the museum a few minutes later. He looked heartbroken."

"Heartbroken?" I said.

She nodded. "All hunched over with that poster tube dangling from his fingers. I know a broken heart when I see one."

One thing about serial killers that Christina has consistently reminded me of is the fact that many of them are charismatic, able by force of personality to lure their victims into a compromised position. The other characteristic many of them share is their unabiding belief in the superiority of their intelligence, cunning, and guile.

Foster, we theorized, believed he was simply too talented to be caught. He was using his fame and rugged looks the way a Venus flytrap secretes sweet pollen to attract prey. There was an argument to be made for pulling Foster in for interrogation the moment he stepped off his flight from Tucson that evening. He was used to handling rattlesnakes and mambas. He had a history of taking sex too far. And he'd had an emotional altercation with Haines, which implied he had a history with the sonar expert.

But before we pulled Foster in, I wanted to know more of the details of their personal history. I wanted to gather enough hard evidence so that when we did bring him in, I could break the herpetologist quickly and get him to confess. Missy and Jorge spent the evening going through nightclubs, gay and straight, circulating pictures of Haines, trying to establish where he'd first met Foster. Freddie worked it from a different angle, getting the District Attorney's Office to issue a subpoena that would allow us access to Foster's phone records at the zoo and at his home.

At seven-thirty that night, Rikko and I watched a hyper, desert-tanned Nick Foster arrive with two producers, a cameraman, and a sound technician. He bustled through the airport, intent on gathering attention to himself. He'd wink and nod to the travelers as they recognized him, like a politician, feeding on the crowd.

The plan was to keep Foster under round-the-clock surveillance. I suppose we fantasized that outside the air terminal Foster would immediately debark his crew for a nightclub, cruising for his next victim. But no such luck. He got a ride to the zoo, where he picked up his BMW SUV and drove straight to his home, a sprawling ranch-style that sat on a knob surrounded by fruit and nut trees on four lush acres in Poway, a northern and inland suburb of the city.

Foster's place had an electronic gate, a steep driveway, and a whitewashed split-rail fence that ran the perimeter of his acreage. Directly east and adjacent to the property was a forty-five-foot-wide public easement under which were buried utility and gas lines. After notifying the San Diego Sheriff's Office, which had jurisdiction in the area, I had the two new detectives Adler assigned to my team climb the hill along the easement and watch the house from within a stand of willows.

Foster's lights darkened at ten. We changed shifts at midnight. Jorge and Missy kept the watch through an uneventful night. They'd found no more evidence of contact between the herpetologist, Haines, or Cook during a tour of the city's hot pickup bars.

At precisely six-fifteen Tuesday morning, Foster left home and drove to one of Dick and Paula Silver's health clubs, the one just off the I-15 near Rancho Escondido. As predicted, the Silvers' arrest had thrown their empire into disarray. They had been freed on hefty bonds, which consumed much of their liquid assets. The business pages of the *Daily News* and the *Union Tribune* were abuzz with rumors that Silver Bodies was on the verge of bankruptcy.

The gyms were still open, however, and being used regularly by patrons like Foster. After working out with weights and climbing four hundred flights on a StairMaster, he went to work, which is where Rikko and I took over the surveillance a second time. He attended meetings with zoo administrators most of the morning. In the afternoon he did his live shows in the amphitheater with Dr. Jan Hood at his side. Both Rikko and I wore sunglasses, hats, and tourist wear. We sat in the back row, lost within a crowd of five hundred. Now that I knew so much more about her, you could see Jan's frustration at having to play second fiddle to someone like Foster. Despite her easy banter with him, not once during the entire show did the tension drop out of her shoulders. Foster left work promptly at six and returned to Silver Bodies for a yoga class. Home at nine P.M. Lights out at ten.

And so it went for two more days, with Foster sticking to a routine of rising early, exercising, then spending eight to ten hours at work before exercising again.

We took turns on the graveyard shift, which left us all cranky. To make matters worse, Fraiser and Adler were pressuring me to bring Foster in for questioning. In a tense meeting, I got them to agree to surveillance through the coming Friday night. If we were lucky and he made his move then, we had a chance to catch him red-handed with the snake and his newest prey. And if he hadn't made a move by Saturday morning, okay, we'd have him in for a friendly chat.

In the meantime, we made no progress in our search for Bigg Ja Moustapha. The entire narcotics squad had alerted their street snitches that we were looking for the new lord of the late Fatty Wu's empire, but nothing surfaced about the meth dealer with delusions of rap grandeur all that week.

On Wednesday afternoon, back at the office after watching Foster during yet another rendition of *Cold Blooded!*, I called Jan up and asked her if she felt like having a "friendly late dinner aboard the *Nomad's Chant.*"

There was a sigh, then she said, "You read my mind. I've had a rotten day. Meet you at eight?"

Before I left the office, I called Christina at home. "Hey," I said when she answered. "How'd it go with Jimmy today?"

There was a long pause. "Well, it took a little coaxing and an entire banana split, but I think I understand what's troubling him."

"And?"

"I've already talked with Fay. And we feel she should talk to you about the situation in person."

THIRTY-EIGHT

"In person? what the hell's going on, Sis?" I demanded.

"Jimmy's more than a little confused, but he'll be okay," she assured me. "Talk to Fay. She says she'll be at his game Friday night. You guys will work it out. Bye."

She hung up before I could get another word in edgewise, and I thought of going to Fay's house right then, but remembered Jan and headed toward my favorite Chinese take-out place instead.

She was already aboard the *Nomad's Chant* when I arrived, sitting on deck in her zoo windbreaker, the late day sun shining through her hair. We popped the cork on the cold bottle of Chardonnay she had brought. We ate out on the deck by candlelight. She said she'd been working long hours trying to get prepared for her speech before the American Society of Ichthyologists and Herpetologists' annual meeting in Chicago the following Saturday. I avoided talking about Foster; the last thing I wanted to do at that point was tip our hand that we were watching him and waiting. But then she asked me directly if we considered him a suspect: The zoo was abuzz at the questions we'd been asking. I gazed into her eyes, lied, and said the incident at the natural history museum turned out to be nothing. As far as we were concerned, Foster was in the clear.

The phone rang while I was cleaning dishes. "Can you grab that?" I called to Jan. "It could be my ex calling about my son. We've been having some problems with him."

Jan nodded, picked up the phone, and said hello. She paused, then said, "He's right here." She held out the phone to me and said, "Susan Dahoney?"

"Oh," I said, feeling my face flush. "Okay, sure."

Jan's expression tightened and she turned away as I said, "Hello, Professor."

"I told you to call me Susan," she purred. "Who was that?"

I cleared my throat slightly. "A friend. Jan Hood from the zoo. She's helping me out on the reptile end of this case."

There was a silence, then she said, a little cooler, "Well, it's Thursday and you promised me you'd call."

I winced. "I did, didn't I? Well, while you were up in Berkeley, all hell broke loose. We thought we had the guy and then it wasn't. And my son's been a—"

"I'm sure," she said, even cooler now. "Well, I've gone through every concordance I could think of, looking for the first message. And still nothing. I could look elsewhere if you like. Or just drop it."

"No, no," I protested. "Don't drop it. Any help you could give us would be appreciated, Susan. And I'll be back in touch tomorrow. Okay?"

Pause, then she said with more warmth, "Okay."

"Friend?" Jan asked when I'd clicked off the phone.

"Yes, uh, no … Professional acquaintance," I said, then gestured across the galley toward the table and the copy of Susan Dahoney's book I'd brought home from work earlier in the week. "That's her book there. She's a Bible expert. The killer's been leaving messages."

"I saw that in the papers," Jan said, picking up the book and studying the ancient tile on the cover. "*The Second Woman.*" Then she flipped it over and saw Susan's photograph. "My! She's beautiful."

"Yeah," I said. "In her way, I guess."

"Nice try," Jan said. "You'd have to be blind not to think she was gorgeous. She been out swimming with you?"

"No," I said firmly. "It's not like that."

She studied me. "What's the book about?"

I gave her the brief synopsis and another glass of wine. I sat beside her on the couch as she flipped through the photographs of the Lilith iconography.

"Sounds interesting," she said. "I've heard of that Lilith Fair music festival, but never understood the reference. Mind if I read it?"

"Long as it's not right now," I said, taking her into my arms.

"Oh," she said.

Jan had an amazing capacity for the erotic. At every turn that night she surprised me with her sexual creativity, a touch here, a quickening there, and amid it all her ability to become lost and wandering in the caresses we gave each other. After we made love a second time, I got up on one elbow.

"Where'd you learn all that?" I asked. "Some school for the sexual chameleon?"

"The Brazilian school," she chuckled. "Everyone's half naked there anyway."

"No, seriously," I said.

"Seriously. I was in love with a Brazilian named Tomás a long, long time ago," she said. "He was a butterfly researcher and poet who worked deep in the Amazon jungle. We lived and traveled together through the Amazon for nearly thirteen months. We talked of marriage. He was an incredible lover. Then Tomás had to take this trip to a part of the jungle we'd never been to before, a series of islands up the Del Teu tributary that supposedly held rare species of moths. I was scheduled to be in Washington, D.C., to make my annual report to my funding agencies, so I didn't make the trip with him."

She smiled wanly. "One night when Tomás was returning from the islands to his camp, his boat was attacked by river pirates. He fought. They macheted him to death."

"God," I said. "I'm sorry. That's tough."

"It was a long time ago; I've dealt with it," she said, then tapped me over my heart. "I've laid bare my soul. Now, what happened to your marriage?"

I thought a long moment, struggling for an answer, then said, "When I met Fay, I thought I was ready to break the cycle of short-term monogamies that dominated my early twenties. She was everything I thought I needed: smart, pretty, rich, ambitious."

"What happened?"

I rubbed the scar on my thigh, flashing on an image of myself standing with Rikko, holding a shotgun, getting ready behind SWAT officers swinging a battering ram at the heavy garage doors of a cement-block building. The door splintered and we were inside, running through cars, screaming at the bad guys with torches to get their hands up.

But I didn't tell Jan any of that.

"We both had demanding jobs," I replied instead. "Fay at the hospital, me as a junior detective. There were stretches where we wouldn't see each other for weeks at a time. We were both placed in a situation where weakness was a constant threat. Except, as it turned out, I was the only one without backbone."

She studied me. "Feel guilty about it?"

"More than a lot," I sighed. "More than a lot."

She got up out of bed and began dressing.

"You could stay," I offered.

"Let's keep it nice and clean and for what it is. That way no one gets hurt."

"You're right," I said. 'That way no one gets hurt."

THIRTY-NINE

The next day, thursday, April twentieth, shortly after six P.M., after a long and largely uneventful day, Lieutenant Fraiser happened by the cubicle. He grinned wolfishly at me, then threw a thumb over one shoulder.

"Adler wants to see you," he said. "Didn't take long for you to screw up, did it?"

I ignored him and went upstairs, convinced The Prick was up to no good. The assistant chief's secretary waved me through without hesitation. When I entered Adler's office, decorated in mission-style furniture, she was alone in the room, wearing a maroon suit, standing behind her desk, a look of rage all about her.

"Tell me about Susan Dahoney, Sergeant," she demanded.

"Bible expert out at State," I said. "She's noted in the reports. What's going on?"

"What's going on is, she's revealing information about the investigation on television!" Adler yelled. "She's claiming—Here, watch!"

Adler snatched up a remote control from her

desk and mashed one of the buttons. A small television on a shelf lit up, immediately showcasing a close-up of the cover of *The Second Woman.*

In voice-over, a female reporter recounted much the same story I'd heard: how Susan Dahoney saw the tile while a doctoral student in archaeology at the University of Tel Aviv, the first clue in a long trail of clues that would lead her into a full-scale investigation into the abiding mystery of the world's oldest book.

The picture cut away to show Susan Dahoney in her publicity outfit: tight-fitting jeans, jodhpurs, denim shirt, and a worn black leather jacket. She was moving about her office, showing off the Lilith art.

"Dr. Dahoney rarely calls herself a textual archaeologist, which is what she is," the reporter said. "Instead, she likes to describe herself as a detective. Lately that description has taken on new meaning. She now serves as a full-time consultant to the San Diego Police Department Homicide team working on the snake murders that have rocked the city. Published reports indicate that the killer has left biblical citations at one of the slaying sites, hence Dr. Dahoney's involvement in the investigation."

The screen cut to Susan in close-up, her face serious and intent. The reporter's voice-over again: "Now, in an exclusive Channel 4 report, Dr. Dahoney reveals new details about the messages left at the crime scenes."

She was either a natural or her publisher's makeover had included a media-skills class. However she came by it, Susan Dahoney was at ease on the tube:

photogenic, intelligent, charming, interesting to watch. Her voice was smooth and gently inflected. Every twitch in her cheek, every shift in her posture, was practiced.

"I've been over the first message—the one left at the Cook scene—in a hundred different ways, and I can tell you it is not linked to the Bible in any way," she said.

"What about the second slaying—Matthew Haines?" the reporter asked.

"That message was most definitely biblical in origin," she said, nodding. Then she leaned forward conspiratorially. "Book of Acts."

"Chapter? Verse?" the reporter demanded.

"Can't say," she replied, smiling. "My good friends in the police department would be mad if I told you any more."

Adler punched off the television's power. "It goes on. She hawks her book, using us as an endorsement of her detective skills, saying that's why we went to her. I don't like the department involved in this kind of pandering. Neither does the mayor."

"I don't, either," I said, throwing up my hands in surrender. "I should have seen that one coming and I didn't."

"She's cut off," Adler said firmly.

"No question," I replied, feeling used and growing angrier by the minute.

"And you've got two strikes against you, Shay," Adler finished. "This case is too high-profile. One more, you're out."

❧ ❧ ❧

She picked up the phone on the first ring, excited. "Susan Dahoney, Ph.D.!"

"Moynihan," I growled.

"Seamus! Did you see it? The interview?"

"We all saw it and—"

"My phone's been ringing off the hook," she interrupted. "The L.A. NBC affiliate wants to run the piece. And CNN just called. We're getting the bump we needed. My publisher's going nuts!"

"So is my boss, and that's not a good thing," I said, a hard edge in my voice.

There was a long pause. "But why?"

"'Why?'" I shouted. "You are not a full-time consultant to the San Diego PD!"

"I've consulted with you," she retorted. "You came to my office. We discussed the case at dinner that night. There've been phone calls. I have every right to that claim."

"You used me and the department. I think you probably planned this from the beginning, calling us up, ingratiating yourself."

"I resent that," she said. "I thought we were going to be friends."

"You don't get it, Susan. When we first spoke, I swore you to not to talk about the case. You've given away a vital detail we wanted held back. You've compromised this investigation to sell books. We don't work with you anymore."

"What? You can't do that," she replied in a pleading tone. "You'll ruin everything, Seamus. Don't you see? All I did was stretch the truth a bit about being full-time. Just a little lie. Everyone does it. And look what's happening! Everyone's paying attention to *The Second Woman*. Do you know how long, how hard, I worked for this?"

"Don't care."

"I'm sure you don't," she shot back, now getting angry. "No one cares about an obscure textual archaeologist. But an archaeologist who works on murder cases..."

"I know: You're marketable, Susan." Then I slammed down the phone and whipped a pencil across the room.

FORTY

I wore that pissed-off feeling all night and throughout the next day while sitting on Foster. Jan called on my cell phone around two to say she was heading to Chicago and wanted to say good-bye. At four that Friday afternoon, Rikko and I handed Foster duty to Missy and Jorge. They would follow Mr. Cold Blooded until he reached home; then Wight and Leras, the backup detectives, would take over.

I stopped by the marina on the way home, got the Green Monster, then went to pick up Jimmy. When he came through the gate and jumped in the old muscle car, there was none of the open hostility that had greeted me lately.

"Hey buddy."

"Hey, Dad," he said. "Can I play tonight?"

"Suspension's over," I said. "Your mom coming?"

Jimmy fought to maintain his smile. "She'll be there in the second inning."

"Mind clueing me in on what's going on?"

His eyes welled with tears. "Better talk to Mom. Could we go to the game?"

"Sure," I said, pulling away from the curb. "How's your arm?"

"Good," he said, looking out the window. "I've been throwing with Walter."

That opened a pit in my stomach, but I nodded. "Good. You're starting."

We played the Panthers, the best team in the intracity league. But through two, my little boy had them baffled. It occurred to me that his pitching strategy reflected life at the moment: Unable to overpower them with heat, he embraced unpredictability and threw all the junk we'd played with over the past few years. His curve had wicked movement. He actually threw a slider for a strike. His change-up was jaw-dropping. He'd set them up with a fastball outside, then ease off and lay one in slow. Kid after kid lunged at the ball and missed. Through two: six hitters up, six hitters down, four K's.

When Jimmy ran into the dugout, his teammates all around him, I flashed on myself at that age, running toward my dad behind the dugout screen the spring before he died. And right then I felt as good as I'd felt in months: grounded, connected, content.

Then I saw Fay come into the stands, and that was all gone. I had butterflies about the future.

During the bottom of the third, Missy called. After four days of spartan regimen, Foster was deviating from routine. He'd left the zoo at five-thirty and gone immediately to a singles bar in Hillcrest called Coyote. Jorge was inside, watching the scene.

"Don't lose him," I said. "And keep me in the loop."

We clung to a one-run lead through six. Stetson's kid got the last out with a tremendous leaping catch at third. It was without a doubt our best game of the year.

Gathering equipment after a team meeting, Jimmy asked, "We fishing Sunday?"

"Wouldn't miss it."

"Okay, I'll see you then," he said, then gave me a quick awkward hug around my waist, turned, and ran off by his mother, who was coming across the field at me. She wore tight jeans, sandals, and a pretty purple sweater that suited her. Stetson walked off with his son and we were alone, standing at either end of the dugout, with the last of the sun passing through the screen, throwing bars of shadow between us.

"He seems better," I said. "Christina must have really gotten through to him."

Fay smiled wanly. "Yeah, well, it's not healthy when you bottle something up inside like that. You talk about it, you immediately feel the pressure let go."

"Must be something pretty big," I said, folding my arms across my chest.

"I didn't want it to come out this way," she began. "This has all forced the issue."

"Spit it out," I said. "Let all that pressure go."

Fay gave me that same sad smile that Jimmy delivered earlier. "Remember two weeks ago when this all started? The tantrum on the mound?"

"Yeah."

"Well, it turns out, without me having one inkling, that the night before that game, an hour after his lights-out, he evidently got up to get a drink of water," she said. "And he heard me and Walter."

"If he caught you two in bed, I don't want to hear about it."

"Not that," she said. "He, uh…well, he heard Walter asking me to marry him. And he heard me say yes."

I suppose I had been expecting this for nearly a year. Still, the blow hit me with a booming sense of finality. "You happy?"

"Yes," she said, but would not look at me.

"No regrets?"

"Tons," she said, shedding tears, shuffling toward me and into my arms.

It had been so long since I'd held her that memories of our early days together flooded through me: meeting in an emergency room when I was a patrol officer; on her father's old boat, sailing beyond the breakwater, when she said she loved me; the kiss at our wedding; when she told me she was pregnant; holding Jimmy the first time. The look on her face, too many times, when she found me reeking of another woman. And worst of all: the day she told me she couldn't live like that anymore.

"Wish I'd been a better man," I said.

"I do too," she said, pushing back and wiping at her nose with her wrist.

"So you've talked to Jimmy," I said.

"And your sister," she replied. "I guess he still held dear the idea we were going to get back together someday."

I hesitated, then admitted. "I sort of clung to that idea too."

She held up her hand to my face and whispered, "I know. I just can't."

I nodded, studying her like the map of a country I once lived in. "But he's okay with it now? Jimmy?"

"I told him the truth as best I could," she said. "I told him that I've come to peace with you, even if I may never understand why you did what you did. We were so good for so long, Shay. And then you got shot and it all changed."

"Fay—"

"Shhhh," she said. "I told you I've put it behind me. I know how good you mean to be for the most part. The point is, I told Jimmy that the three of us will always be part of each other. Even if we don't all live together. We just have to make room for Walter. I care for him very much, Shay. I need him in my life."

My throat felt as if I'd swallowed a smooth stone, but I said, "Okay."

She smiled. "Jimmy's going to need to hear that from you too."

"He and I are fishing Sunday. No if's, and's, or but's."

"Good," she said. An awkward moment passed, then she pecked me on the cheek and was gone.

In the silence, I watched the last light of day bend through the screen and filter through the dust that still hung in the air from the game. The dugout turned amber and heavily shadowed. The stillness around me felt electric, like a storm coming, and I had the disturbing thought that this is what it must feel like to be out on the Kansas plains just before a tornado strikes.

FORTY-ONE

My cell phone rang. I snatched it from my pocket, anticipating Missy with an update on Foster. Instead, I got Freddie Burnette, all adrenaline: "We got Bigg Ja, Sarge."

I started toward the Green Monster. "Where?"

"Narcotics snitch puts his crib at an old ranch out in Alpine. Says he's got a bunch of snakes out there in a barn and in the house. Lights. Heaters. The whole thing."

"Who's there?"

"Just me and Rikko."

"Good enough. Let's all go pay Mr. Moustapha a visit."

Alpine lies twenty-five miles due east of the city of San Diego. As its name suggests, the topography of the area is ever rising in elevation. The landscape is broken, with steep, rock-and-brush-choked coulees scratched into the hillsides. It's the closest place to San Diego where enough grazing land can be bought to hold horses at a reasonable price, and, as a result, there are scores of five-, ten-, and twenty-acre ranchettes tucked up inside Alpine's canyons and out on the open hillsides of the community.

The moon, though only half full, was bright in the eastern sky when I drove the Monster down one of Alpine's remoter thoroughfares, a twisty creek-bottom road framed by horse fences, tawny grass meadows, and clusters of live oak. The road led into a small, sparsely populated canyon.

Around a curve and down the hill from the lane into the ranch where Bigg Ja Moustapha was said to be hanging with friends, my headlights caught a deer crossing the road and then an old barn, an unmarked squad car, and a San Diego Sheriff's cruiser.

Rikko stood beside the cruiser. Freddie leaned on a cane. Deputy Harold Champion, a tall black man who resembled Muhammad Ali in his Cassius Clay days, rested against the hood of his vehicle, his thumb tucked into his gun belt. Since we were outside our jurisdiction, we needed Champion to make our chat with Bigg Ja kosher.

"You don't look too good, my friend," Rikko said. "What has happened?"

"Nothing fatal or anything," I said. "I'll tell you later."

"Four of us?" Champion said after I'd gone over and introduced myself. "You looking to put on a show of force here, Sergeant?"

"Snitch says there's only three of them up there, but we've had dealings with these meth guys before. They can be unpredictable."

My cell phone rang before Champion could reply. I held up one finger and flipped the phone open. "Talk to me."

"Foster's got a boyfriend and a girlfriend and they're all traveling north," Missy said. "Jorge says the woman, a very busty, very pretty blonde, dressed in not much, came into the bar about an hour ago, acting like she knew Foster. He was all over her. Then another guy shows up. A hard body, Morgan Cook surfer type but younger, maybe early thirties. Well dressed. They were on the dance floor sandwiching her."

"We got an ID on either of them?" I asked.

"Not yet. They took Foster's Land Rover so we couldn't make their plates."

"You got backup?"

"Leras and Wight are right behind us," she said.

"They get to Foster's place, two of you on the fence out back. Two of you on the street. And keep me posted." I snapped the cell phone shut, then blew out a long breath, wanting to be two places at the same time. "Shall we?"

It should have been chilly this late and this far inland, but the wind blew out of the east, making the air warm and dusty. The gravel driveway to the ranch ran steeply uphill. Rikko helped Freddie with the worst of it. The moon glowed against rotting plank fences that bordered the drive and a tangled meadow. At the crest, the lane passed through a cedar hedge that shielded the ranch from the road. The dull pulse of rap music thudded in the night air, and I recognized Bigg Ja's shrill delivery from CDs Freddie had found.

Passing through the hedge, there was a tin-roofed open-front shed to our right filled with rusting farm equipment. A weak light showed off the shed's peak. About fifty yards beyond was a barn similar in construction to the one we'd parked next to on the road. A light shone inside.

"Informant says he keeps some of the hot snakes in there," Freddie whispered.

My attention, however, was on the other side of the circular driveway and, obscured by the trunk of an ancient live oak, a weathered two-story ranch house with a wraparound porch. The paint was blistered and peeling. Several pieces of clapboard had fallen away, revealing tar paper. A single naked bulb lit the porch. The window shades were drawn.

We had taken no more than five steps toward the house, caught in the glow of the shed light, when a thin Asian about twenty years old, wearing a red bandana, strolled out the barn door. He took one look at us and scrambled toward the house.

"Rabbit goes!" Champion cried, pulling out his pistol and taking off in pursuit. "I love it when they try to run on me."

"Call for backup and cover the yard!" I yelled at Freddie, and raced after Champion with Rikko right behind me.

The deputy had pro-football speed, but even he could not close the gap on the man who'd fled the barn and now scurried up onto the porch, shouldered open the door, and screamed over the thudding of the hip-hop music, "Bust! Bust! Destroy it all!"

Instantly crashes of glass and metal and the bellows of men issued from inside the house, and I skidded to a halt and yelled after Champion, "Deputy! No!"

But it was too late. He leaped up onto the porch and into the gaping front doorway with his gun loosely held before him. A shotgun blast hit the deputy square in the chest. He flipped over backward, hit the porch rail, then collapsed half on, half off the stairway. More glass and metal crashed inside. Then in the doorway a huge Samoan appeared wearing nothing but yellow swim shorts, sandals, and a shotgun. He sported tribal tattoos around his neck and up and down his arms and legs. He moved with a herky-jerky quality that told me we were in big trouble. They'd been cooking methamphetamine. The Samoan looked like he'd been sampling the goods for days.

People who have been doing meth in binges are among the most irrational and dangerous kinds of criminals. The drug worms into their brains, rotting the nerve synapses that normally control excessive behavior. Meth heads are arguably insane when you encounter them—insane with a fondness for extreme violence.

What I didn't know, however, was that Bigg Ja and his boys had taken the craziness to a whole new level that night: For every five lines of crank they snorted up their nose, they'd added a kicker, skin-pricking themselves with snake venom to create a homicidal buzz in their brains.

The Samoan ran the cha-*ching* action of the sawed-off pump shotgun, then aimed down at the sprawled deputy, wagging his tongue side to side. His eyes flickered like an old movie. "You ready to die, fucker?" he asked Champion.

"Only one dying is you!" Rikko roared. He stormed across the lawn at the Samoan like a stampeding black rhino, his Beretta up and firing.

From that point on, everything seemed to unfold in slow motion. I flanked left. Rikko's first shot went wide and splintered the front doorjamb. The Samoan rolled out across the porch planks and came to his feet blazing. Dirt exploded between Rikko and me as we went to our bellies.

My first shot hit the Samoan in the ankle. He spun around and howled, then gritted his teeth and pumped the shotgun again. Rikko's next two shots struck the Samoan high in the chest and he staggered but did not drop the gun. He swung it in my direction. Blood flecks flew from his lips. I fired a last time, catching the Samoan in the throat and blowing out the back of his neck.

Then I was up over the railing of the porch and going toward the door. Deep bass music still pumped from inside. Rikko moved at me from the opposite end of the porch. I eased up to the jamb, glancing at the deputy sprawled on the staircase.

The Kevlar vest had saved Champion's life. He bled from wounds peppered across his arms, neck, and lower face, but the majority of the shotgun's pellets had struck him in the dead center of his chest. He looked up at me, dazed and angry. "Screwed up," he whispered. "Ain't gonna die, but I sure screwed up."

"Do you think?" Rikko said in disgust.

"Forget about it now," I said, then shouted into the open doorway: "This is San Diego PD! Put your weapons down and come out with your hands up!"

Two booming shots from a large-caliber gun splintered the wooden banister right above Champion's head. "Give me cover," I mouthed to Rikko.

My brother-in-law nodded, then showed me one, two, three fingers. He stuck his pistol around the corner and sprayed three quick shots into the room. An explosion. The rap music died. I hurled myself in a low roll around the doorjamb and across a wooden floor carpeted in glass shards that crunched under my torso and cut at my hands. But there was no pain and no real understanding of the particulars of my surroundings at that moment; I had the gun up and was looking for movement—any movement—in the room.

That's why I didn't see the quick Asian with the red bandana at first. He was crouched against the wall in a little alcove just to the left of the front door. I had rolled right by him. Rikko must have shot right by him. His eyes were crimson with fear. Sweat poured off his brow and beaded up in the sparse hairs of his mustache. He braced the weight of a

Dirty Harry gun, a stainless-steel Smith & Wesson .44 Magnum, which he aimed directly at me.

My mind went mirrorlike in the understanding I was about to die. I took in every nuance of the meth lab: the folding tables upset on their sides, the broken beakers and smashed glass tubing jumbled on the floor among steaming liquids, green chemicals, and opaque powders. Smoke puffed from a boom box in the corner. A half-dozen propane gas burners flared amid the glass and the crystallized residue, which reflected the flames and made the floor appear to leap and dance with fire. The whole place could blow sky high at any moment and I wanted out. Now. But that stainless-steel barrel hovered in the air seven feet to my right.

I learned later that from his angle, Champion could see me frozen and sidewall-staring in the gun's direction. The deputy raised his pistol and blazed at the inside jamb.

The Asian cringed at each shot but never took his petrified eyes or the pistol off me. Then the bay window behind him exploded and Rikko came barreling through the curtains and landed in the glass.

Bigg Ja's man spun in his direction, fired once, the muzzle blast deafening, blowing Rikko's pistol out of his hand. Everything went ringy and dull in my ears as I crawled for cover, shooting once to empty my clip and missing him. The Asian twisted back to me, raising the gun.

Rikko came to his feet and bore down on him. In a single, devastating move, he threw his left arm parallel and on top of the gunman's outstretched hand. He caught the gunman's wrist, then twisted in his own tracks, wrenching the gun over and downward with a vicious quick movement. The sound of the wrist shattering was obliterated by the second blast of the .44 at close range. Rikko kicked out the gunman's feet and slammed him face down into the carnage of the meth lab, knocking him cold.

Rikko panted on top of the Indonesian's body. I sat there staring dumbly at my brother-in-law, my ears still ringing, finding it hard not to believe we weren't all dead.

Another crash sounded from down the dimly lit hallway that issued off the main room. I struggled to load another magazine into my pistol. I could see three doors, two on the left, one on the right. The far left door was closed. A braying, methamphetamine-fueled laugh echoed to me, and I got to my feet in time to see a stocky olive-black man with Asian features and dreadlocks dressed in a blue dashiki top and matching head net dart from the far right doorway across the hall. Bigg Ja wrenched open the closed door, leaped inside, and slammed it shut before I could get a shot off.

I started to spin to go outside, to prevent him from escaping. But my attention was captured by what followed the meth-cooker-cum-rapper out of the far right bedroom. It came swirling and coursing toward me at incredible speed. The snake, a five-footer, was copper through the body, thin behind the head, with a crème-colored mouth and devil-orange eyes.

"Taipan!" I screamed, shot, and dove to one side.

The snake rolled into the room, aggressive, head up. Rikko tried to get clear himself, moving to jump over the top of one of the downed meth lab tables. But the snake became a flash, uncoiling after him. The taipan's mouth stretched wide. Fangs glimmered in the propane light, then embedded themselves behind Rikko's knee.

He bellowed and mule-kicked. The snake jerked loose, landing with its body outstretched on the jagged carpet of broken glass. The taipan went spastic, flailed against the sharp edges before getting itself free and slithering out the front door, right by Champion, right down the porch steps, leaving a thin blood trail into the night.

I ran to Rikko, who lay against the short wall below the shattered bay window, gripping his thigh with both hands. "Like getting hit with the hammer, only sharp," he said. "It burns. It burns!"

Rikko was staring mad, sweating buckets, and I found myself praying that my brother-in-law was stronger than a water buffalo. Then I noticed the propane burners again. I had to get Rikko outside before the place exploded. I grabbed him under the armpits and dragged him toward the door. Two shots sounded behind me and I spun to find Freddie on the porch steps next to Champion, her pistol pointing at the fleeing figure of Bigg Ja plunging through the cedar hedge.

"He's headed for the road!" she shouted.

"Fuck him," I said. "Rikko's been bit by the deadliest snake on earth. He's got to get antivenin now. And there are chemicals and burners in there. This place is gonna go sky-high."

"I'll call a chopper and get them clear!" Freddie said. "You get Bigg Ja!"

Rikko nodded at me in a daze. "She's right. Get that rap bastard."

I hesitated, then sprinted across the lawn toward the hole in the cedar hedge. I burst through it just in time to catch a glimpse of Bigg Ja's shadowy form vaulting the horse fence that separated the meadow from the road, and then he disappeared. The meadow grass was high, tangled, and wet with dew. It grabbed at my ankles. Behind me, up the hill, I heard an explosion and twisted, still running, to see flames leaping above the top of the cedar hedge. I slipped and fell, and my radio went flying from its chest holster. I looked for an instant, not finding it, then raced on, going over the fence onto the road, running toward the barn where we'd parked our vehicles.

The barn doors crashed open. A maroon 1969 Pontiac GTO convertible came screaming out of the barn, spinning sideways, just missing the front fender of Champion's squad car, before peeling rubber on the road toward me. I fired and dove for the ditch, landing in weeds, hearing Bigg Ja's music come on again, this time pounding out of a 150-watt car audio system. He accelerated by me, furiously singing backup to his own CD voice. His left hand held an Uzi. He sprayed a burst into the bank above my head, then brayed with laughter again.

I got up and sprinted for the Monster, firing the old Vette to life, popping the clutch and fishtailing onto the road just as Bigg Ja's taillights disappeared around a far curve. I stomped on the accelerator. The four-twenty-seven growled. Power settled in the rear axle and in no time I had the beast going seventy-five into the big curve that led out of the canyon.

The road was potholed and strewn with pebbles. The Vette slid toward the embankment and I fought for control, aware that the first blue lights of the backup cruisers Freddie had called for were entering the canyon behind me.

FORTY-TWO

Bigg ja moustapha may not have been the most eloquent of rappers, but he had taste in cars and knew how to drive. Pontiac built the GTO to be a stylish, straight-line street dragster. But with Bigg Ja at the wheel, it might as well have been a Porsche, built to hug corners at speed. The African-Asian hip-hopper ran the GTO flat out through a descending series of switchbacks and hairpin turns that should have flung him through a guardrail and out into space before mushrooming against a canyon wall à la James Dean. But his tires never slipped, not once, and I was left even farther behind until we came down a hill doing eighty south of Alpine.

We blew past darkened trailer parks and small dilapidated homes with dirt front yards, chain-link fences, and snarling dogs. I kept cursing myself for losing the radio. No one knew where I was or what I was doing. It was dangerous and entirely against protocol. But Bigg Ja's men had tried to kill a sheriff's deputy. He'd released a taipan on my brother-in-law. And he'd just tried to decapitate me with an Uzi. There was no way I was backing off.

Bigg Ja swung the GTO onto an improved county road that ran southwest toward Bonita, a suburb with a much denser population, and I got ill thinking about what the armed meth head might do if confronted. I downshifted and ran the Monster in third to the red line, closing the gap with every second. When I shifted into fourth, less than a hundred yards separated us.

Lights of houses and apartment complexes twinkled all around us. A slow-moving delivery truck appeared in our lane and I closed the gap to forty yards. I pumped the headlights on high and put a flashing blue bubble on the roof.

Bigg Ja glanced at his rearview mirror in alarm. He threw the Uzi back over his shoulder and squeezed off a burst that blew three holes in the roof of my baby. I swerved and slowed, shouting: "Now you are seriously making me mad!"

Bigg Ja stuck the submachine gun up over the top of his windshield and fired again, this time blowing out the tires of the delivery truck, which twisted and rammed into the guardrail. The rapper aimed the GTO straight into oncoming traffic and accelerated. A silver Jeep Cherokee swerved to avoid a head-on collision, then sailed off the embankment into darkness.

Ahead, a red traffic light showed at a major intersection. Bigg Ja sped through the red light with me right behind him. A Roto-Rooter van in the east-bound lane veered, spun, and hit a light pole. A south-bound green Chevy pickup swung sideways in front of Bigg Ja's GTO, just missing him, then locked up the brakes right in front of me. I slammed on my own brakes, clawing at the wheel, my headlights passing through the cab of the pickup. Three young girls with hair big enough to choke New Jersey threw their mouths open in screams when my front left fender met their front left fender.

There was the sound of witches screeching and fiberglass crunching and the Monster was flung to the right in a 360-degree skid out the other side of the intersection. I spun the wheel and righted the beast just in time to catch sight of Bigg Ja's GTO speeding up an exit ramp to the 94 freeway, heading due west toward downtown San Diego.

I raced onto the freeway hearing the Monster's front end make barking noises. The right headlight was gone. But I kept my foot mashed on the accelerator, watching the tach needle rise and fall as I slammed through the gears. Bigg Ja had the GTO pushing one hundred as he wove in and out of traffic like a downhill skier on the edge of disaster. The Vette's steering column vibrated madly in my hands.

The cell phone on the seat beside me rang. I startled and almost lost control. I'd forgotten completely about it, then reached over, praying Freddie was on the line so I could relay my position.

"Sarge!" Missy yelled.

"Missy, call Central Dispatch!" I yelled back at her. "I'm on the 94 heading west toward downtown in high-speed pursuit of Bigg Ja. Rikko's been snakebit.

A sheriff's deputy's been shot. I've lost my radio. Ja's been spraying the countryside with an Uzi."

"We got a problem of our own out here!" she countered. "Wight and Leras are on the fence line at Foster's. They've heard a guy screaming inside."

"When?"

"Right now! What do you want us to do? We're outside our jurisdiction."

"Hell with jurisdiction! There could be someone inside making love to a rattlesnake. Go in there! Take him! And the blonde!"

I hit a pothole. The Monster's front end floated. I threw down the cell phone, grabbed the wheel with my other hand, and eased off on the accelerator until the car came back under control. Four lanes squeezed down to two. Bigg Ja slowed to eighty-five as we approached downtown, swooping away from me into the circular bypass that led to the I-5 freeway going north.

"C'mon, c'mon, be there!" I said, wanting to see the flashing lights of a blockade at the end of the freeway entrance. But the patrols had not yet responded to Missy's call. I glanced over at the cell phone, now on the passenger-side floor, and swore; I didn't dare reach for it at this speed.

Suddenly, from high overhead, a beam of light shone down, casting this way and that, searching. It passed over the GTO and the Monster. Bigg Ja swung from the far-left to the far-right lane, heading for a banked exit ramp that rose up on piers twenty stories high—the entrance to the Ocean

Beach Freeway heading west again toward the Pacific.

"You're running out of road, man," I mumbled in grim determination. "It's just a matter of time and I've got you."

Bigg Ja never decelerated going into the tightly curved ramp. The GTO came skidding into the wall like an unsettled bobsled on a rough and bumpy turn. Sparks flew into the darkness. His passenger-side mirror snapped free and came spinning by me. Smoke boiled off the sides of his burning tires. Then he wrenched the car free of the wall and sped up again, descending onto the flat heading toward the ocean.

Brine scent whistled in the window. Wisps of onshore fog hung on the surface of the damp road. Then the searchlight reappeared, accompanied by the throbbing pulse of a helicopter and a booming, amplified voice coming through a bullhorn mounted on the bird's undercarriage: "Pontiac GTO, Green Corvette, this is San Diego PD. Pull over now, turn off your vehicles, and remain inside with your hands on the dashboard!"

The freeway ended at a streetlight and a T junction. Bigg Ja ran the light, swinging sideways onto Sunset Cliff's Boulevard heading straight south into Ocean Beach, one of the funkiest neighborhoods in the city.

Robb Field, a grassy park with baseball fields and tennis courts, sits to the west of where the freeway becomes a road. With the searchlight on him, Bigg

Ja aimed the GTO at a wheelchair ramp cut into the sidewalk. He was doing fifty when he hit it. The muscle car sailed sixty feet through the air and crashed down onto the park's lawn, zigzagging, throwing turf like a rooster's tail. He wrenched the wheel sideways, missed a tree, and slid across the grass back toward the road. The GTO jumped the curb again and shot out from between two parked cars ahead of me.

Bigg Ja's dreadlocks swung in beat to the rhythm of his blasting music. To him it was all a meth-driven video game being played at his own personal gangsta party.

The hip-hop wanna-be slung the GTO right onto West Point Loma Boulevard, a narrow street lined with cars, stucco bungalows, and palm trees. As Bigg Ja veered left onto Abbott Street, heading toward the commercial center of Ocean Beach, the chopper returned, flooding the interior of his convertible with halogen light.

Bigg Ja came up with the Uzi, aimed it at the searchlight, shook his dreadlocks, chanted with his rap, then touched off a burst. *Boom!* The searchlight died. The chopper swung away, coughing. Bigg Ja held the Uzi Saddam-style and fired off a victory volley. The lights on the Ocean Beach Pier, the longest on the West Coast, shone to our south. All along the sidewalk and out onto the beach, late-night pedestrians dove for cover.

We raced toward the foot of Newport Street, the main drag in Ocean Beach, a collection of bars, restaurants, surf shops, and stores that sell drug paraphernalia. A parking lot sits at the foot of Newport, below the pier. A few years back we put a police trailer there to discourage drug dealing. I prayed it was manned.

It was almost midnight, but Newport Street would still be crowded with end-of-the-week revelers and I did not want Bigg Ja going in there. I leaned out the window with my pistol, trying to line up a shot at him left-handed. But there were too many people.

A patrol officer jumped out into the road from the parking lot, his pistol raised. Bigg Ja braked to make the hard left hand turn onto Newport. The officer fired, blowing out Ja's windshield, but it did not stop him. I downshifted and moaned at what I had to do, then did it anyway, accelerating and ramming the front end of the Monster into the rear quarter panel of the GTO.

We went skidding sideways, then parted. Bigg Ja regained control of the GTO, squeezed another burst from his Uzi at me, then slid his vehicle up an alley beside a seafood restaurant. I was right behind him.

Bigg Ja swerved right at the alley's end, heading straight onto the pier. His tires spun, hissed, and whined on the wet cement, then caught and he swerved across the middle of the wharf. Night fishermen abandoned their poles and jumped over the side.

Bigg Ja got the vehicle straight one last time, then accelerated toward the end of the pier, where it teed into two long arms. There is a shack of sorts built at the junction of the two arms, and the GTO sped straight at it. The rapper lifted the Uzi over his head like it was a flag and at the last second he cut his wheel left, barely missing the shack, then shattered through the wooden rails.

The GTO went through the fence going forty. I skidded the Monster to halt a foot away from the gaping hole in the railings, right next to a table meant for cutting bait. My front axle busted in half and my beloved '67 collapsed and smoked.

Bigg Ja's convertible flew out sixty yards, then its nose tipped down and the hip-hopper came free of the car. His legs ran in space. His arms swum against an invisible current. The Uzi fired its last rounds, throwing flames out its muzzle.

Then I lost sight of him and heard only the braying of his crank and venom laughter before the car hit the water and the music died.

FORTY-THREE

"**F**uck man, i was Johnny Too Bad, know what I'm saying?" Bigg Ja rasped.

He was soaked, squirming and twitching on a gurney in an ambulance in the parking lot at the base of the pier. There were seven patrol cars and two other ambulances parked on the pier itself. A tow truck was dragging away the carcass of the Monster. Lifeguards were trolling in Zodiac rafts.

The emergency medical technicians had Bigg Ja lashed to the gurney with nylon webbing. There were blackened tracks up his arms where he'd been skin-popping venom. He kept straining against the restraints, shaking his dreadlocks from side to side. The EMTs got an IV into his arm and added a drug designed to ease him down from his bombed state without disrupting his vitals. His eyes were open, darting; then, as the sedatives took effect, they slowed and dwelled on me. "You be straight with me, right, man?" he asked.

"Mr. Moustapha, do you understand you have the right to remain silent?" I countered. "And you have the right to have an attorney present during questioning?"

"Got myself a liar already. Man, was I on it or what? Just like in that old movie 'bout Jamaica, *The Harder They Come*? Old Jimmy Cliff starts shooting up the joint with them pearl-handled pistols."

He lay back on the pillow and started singing to himself, *"Cause as sure as the sun will shine, I'm gonna get my share what's mine, oh yeah, the harder they come the harder they fall one and all."*

I wanted to put air bubbles into Bigg Ja's IV line and put him out of his misery. Instead, I said, "Yeah, Bigg Ja. When news about this gets out, you'll be all over MTV They'll call you the killer."

He grinned, revealing a gold-capped tooth. "Yeah, Bigg Ja, killer rapper."

"That's it," I said. "Bigg Ja, killer rapper. But the cool thing? The word on the street's gonna be that Bigg Ja's the real deal. It's no image. Not like Snoop Dogg or P. Diddy. Bigg Ja's a straight-up killing motherfucker, isn't he?"

Bigg Ja nodded, smiling along, his eyes half shut as he visualized what I was saying. Then the drugs the EMTs were giving him must have achieved some sort of critical mass. He threw himself against his lashes, his rheumy eyes reminding me of the taipan's. "You up to something, man."

"Nah," I assured him. "You'll be a legend, just like Johnny Too Bad."

"Hey, man, I may be a little cranked up here, but I 'member everything went down tonight. Unidentified men 'tacked our crib."

"We identified ourselves as police officers."

"No way," Bigg Ja said, shaking his dreads. "Big black dude jumps in the front door carrying a piece. Can't help it my bodyguard got a little itchy finger and didn't see the uniform. So we defended ourselves. Righteous, like. Then I went for a little fun ride down the coast to celebrate. Popped a few caps? Yeah. Drove too fast? That too. But Bigg Ja didn't wax no one."

I grabbed him by the collar and growled, "My partner's in intensive care from a taipan bite, you fucking worm brain. We don't know if he's gonna live or die."

"Snake got its own mind," Bigg Ja said. "Can't do nothing 'bout that."

"I just got the call: We found a rattlesnake in your barn," I said. 'And a mamba."

"So what? I like hots. Ain't no crime."

"Bigg Ja, the whole world's gonna know that you killed those two white guys with that rattler. How's it feel to be tied up just like Cook and Haines right now? You hate guys who even think about having sex around other men. You rap about it. How'd it go? 'With swishy little boys and bitches that're fake. Toss 'em in a hole, feed 'em to my snake'?"

His whole face became pinched. "Them's just lyrics! Just opinion!"

"You've got the weapon that did the deeds," I said, setting up a bluff. "We're doing DNA on the rattlesnake and the mamba. We'll know, Bigg Ja. And the next fix you get will be pancuronium bromide and potassium chloride in the death chamber at San Quentin. I'll see to it. Understand me, worm brain? I'll see you in the chamber."

Bigg Ja lay there, his mouth open, his brain struggling to keep up with all I'd been saying. Then he shook his head violently. "You ain't sticking me with that freaky shit! I never killed no one with no snake, and that's a fact."

"I'll take my chances in court."

"No, Sergeant, you won't," said Helen Adler from the bumper at the back of the ambulance. The assistant chief wore a department-issue windbreaker and baseball cap. Her face was stony. I had no idea how long she had been standing there.

"Helen ... " I began, then stopped at the sight of The Prick.

"Come down out of there, Sergeant," she ordered. "Lieutenant Fraiser, will you take Mr. Moustapha's statement?"

"Glad to, Chief," Fraiser said. He climbed in and looked at me smugly. "Didn't have to wait long again, did I, smart guy?"

I ignored him and climbed out the back. "What's going on, Chief?"

"Let's get away from here," Adler said coldly, then turned and walked to the beach. It was one-thirty in the morning. The tide was going out. Clouds blew across the half moon on a stiff breeze. When Adler reached the sand, she stopped, held out her palm, and said, "Gun and badge, Sergeant."

"What?"

"You're suspended without pay," she said. 'There'll be a hearing, of course. Not to mention an Internal Affairs investigation."

"Hearing? Suspended? Investigation? For what?"

"For what?" she replied, fury building in her voice. "Where do I start? Deciding to take down a meth lab without proper backup—"

"That was—"

"Shut up! It's not your turn to talk!" Adler shouted. "A sheriff's deputy is wounded. A Samoan immigrant was shot to death. A ranch house has been destroyed by fire. One of my homicide detectives is lying in a venom-induced coma. You lost your radio, then went off half-cocked in a high-speed pursuit through five—count them, five—local and regional jurisdictions. A man was injured crashing his Jeep. The department helicopter took rounds and barely landed. Two elderly fishermen broke legs jumping off the pier. And by the way: That's not an eastern diamondback out at Bigg Ja's. It's an Arizona subspecies. He's not the guy."

"Helen—"

"I'm not done yet! Four members of your team, without warrant and without jurisdiction, raided the house of one of the county's most high-profile citizens."

"He went up there with a couple," I insisted. "We always figured the killer was using a female lure. Then we heard the guy start screaming. I acted to save a life."

"You were interrupting intercourse between two consenting adults being filmed consensually by Foster," she said. "Know who was screaming—in ecstasy, I might add?"

I had a sick feeling in my stomach and shook my head.

"Marvin Sand," she replied. "Head of the city's arts council, firstborn son of the mayor's brother. That's right, the mayor's nephew, who's also a civil trial lawyer. And the woman riding him? Anita James, his longtime girlfriend, an artist and political activist. And to top it off, Mr. Foster has quite an interesting story to tell, Sergeant. Seems you have the hots for the assistant director of herpetology at the zoo. Seems she has it in for Foster because she sees him as her intellectual inferior and has been out to get him ever since he arrived from Australia. He's alleging she put you up to this."

"Jan Hood had no idea we liked Foster for these slayings!" I shouted. "In fact, I told her the opposite. Foster's got a history of sexual violence and we have a witness who puts Haines with Mr. Fucking Cold Blooded three days before his death."

"We asked Foster about Haines!" Adler shot back. "Foster met the guy once at Coyote. They talked about coral snakes. The guy became a nuisance, a stalker, calling Foster's office all the time, showing up at events like that fund-raiser, wanting to talk about hot reptiles. The argument in the bathroom was Foster threatening Haines with a restraining order if he did not stop bothering him."

"Well, there you go. More motive."

"Not enough to break a rock-solid alibi. The mayor's nephew backs up Foster's story. Said Haines called Foster's office and house a dozen times when he was there last month. Sand and his girlfriend say they picked Foster up from the fund-raiser and spent the evening together at her house. They're all threatening to sue for invasion of privacy. Foster's adding illegal entry."

"Still doesn't give you cause to take my badge or take me off this case," I shot back. "This was legit entry all the way. My detectives came to me in a crisis and I made a call believing a life was at risk."

Adler glared at me. "The wrong call, Shay, don't you get it? The mayor's nephew and so the mayor have suffered a major embarrassment. So has the zoo. A major media personality feels his private life has been invaded. Don't you get it?"

I stood there in the sand, feeling the ocean wind bite my cheeks and hands, getting angrier by the moment. "Oh, I get it. This is not really about any of that, is it? This is about you, Helen, and the chief's office and what you'll do to get it. Doesn't anything about our past matter?"

"Not here it doesn't," she retorted. "And you've just lost another notch of respect in my book for bringing our past up like it's some get-out-of-jail-because-you-fucked-me-once card. But your sister tells me you've been having a hard time lately. Flashbacks about your father's murder or something. So I'm gonna be lenient and only give you a six-week suspension."

"Six weeks! Helen, you can't do that. I've got to work this case."

"The mayor wanted you thrown off the force. But I stuck up for you, Shay."

"Right. You sold me out to keep your shot at the top alive."

Adler's shoulders shook with ire. "Badge and gun, Sergeant," she said. "Then leave the scene. This is Lt. Fraiser's case now."

FORTY-FOUR

*O*ne more walk on the wild side, thought the naked man dying on the bed. That's all it was supposed to be, and now this. One voice and then two. The second one, the one that loathed him, dominating.

And the snake. That fucking evil thing! Where had that come from?

The naked man had long since stopped struggling against his restraints. His mind came and went, surging to memories the venom fever had not yet scorched. There were instants of perfect clarity when he saw his daughter's face like life in front of him and knew he'd never see her again. He wanted to tell her so much about the mystery of men. Why they did what they did. Why they said what they said. The wisdom of his gender.

In the end, he thought with bitter irony, it was all about his dick. During the acid divorce, his wife had predicted it would be the death of him. He'd tried so hard to be true, but then in his late thirties he had felt the uncontrollable urge to roam.

One of his friends had told him that it was all too normal, a biological thing: Facing middle age and impending decrepitude, the male feels hormonally compelled to spread *his genes one last time. And so when all the women with all the great asses walked by, he'd simply followed.*

What had it gotten him? he asked himself bitterly. He'd lost his marriage, his daughter, many of his friends. And he hadn't even spread his genes: All the women he'd fucked in that two-year frenzy had made him wear a condom.

And now this, *he thought.* My death comes with teeth.

Agony. It rent its way through his arm and testicles, canceling all thought. The venom took him and it all went to a crackling wildfire inside his body, a blaze that used his every cell as fuel, the green smoke of it flooding his lungs, robbing him of the possibility of redemption.

Now the voice was back. Where had it been? How long had it been gone? The voice stoked the fire, taunting him, taunting his desires.

"In my name," the voice said. "In my name shall they cast out devils."

FORTY-FIVE

The venom that gushes through the fang canals of an Australian taipan is a liquid firework of toxins that detonates through the blood and nervous system in intricate, delayed patterns toward death. The venoms of the black mamba and the king cobra, the reptile poisons closest in toxicity to the taipan's, have a fast-acting, bomblike component that so stuns their victims that it robs them of the sense of time. Not so the taipan. Its poison behaves more subtly, sending the victim into a slow-motion world where they suffer the brunt of the attack in prolonged, torturous stages.

After Freddie called for a medevac for Rikko and Champion, she got both men off the porch and away from the ranch house before it caught fire. It took a Life Flight chopper eight minutes to reach the meadow below Bigg Ja's crib. During the wait, doctors radioed Freddie to use Rikko's belt to jerry-rig a pressure bandage around the fang holes, standard treatment for snakebite. But by the time Freddie had the tourniquet in place around my brother-in-law's thigh, the taipan's venom had nearly nine minutes unrestricted access to his system.

Ten minutes post bite, he felt nauseated. Then he thought he had something, a twig, a bit of leaf, in his eye. At twelve minutes he complained about his vision. Everything had become a glare. He said it all with an increasingly thick tongue.

Rikko was virtually blind by the time they lifted off out of Alpine, heading for the intensive care unit at UCSD Medical Center. The taipan's venom was going straight for my brother-in-law's neuromuscular junction, where nerve fiber meets muscle and bone, guiding all motion and reception of sensory information. The doctor on board the chopper knew Rikko needed antivenin. But he also knew the wrong antivenin could kill him on the spot, so he called the zoo and workers there took taipan-specific antivenin and a treatment protocol to the hospital.

By the time the helicopter landed, Rikko had become disoriented, his speech almost unintelligible, reduced to a half-Hebrew, half-English gibberish about violent Middle East events long ago and far away. Saliva dribbled from his mouth. He had difficulty swallowing, and before they could shoot him with antivenin, a team of doctors led by Walter, of all people, had to suction his throat to keep him from gagging. Cramps racked his stomach.

By then a component of the taipan venom had launched an assault on Rikko's muscle tissue, busting it up at the cellular level and casting the scraps into his bloodstream. Each of his limbs in turn, the right arm and leg and then the left leg and arm, became paralyzed. Even with the first shot of anti-venin in him, the venom knocked out his respiratory system. My best friend stopped breathing and went into cardiac arrest.

Walter shocked Rikko's heart three times. On the fourth attempt, his heart started up again, weak but beating, and he began breathing in long, gravelly pulls.

Within minutes, however, his blood pressure dropped to eighty over sixty and once again he teetered on the brink of death. Walter shot him with another dose of taipan antivenin and he came around briefly.

Rikko recognized the voice of my sister, who had just arrived, then began vomiting. His retching was the most extreme Walter and the other doctors had ever witnessed. The liquid he threw up, Christina said, smelled rank, like stale horse urine. She was sure she was watching her husband's last moments on earth.

Right around midnight, Walter shot Rikko a third time with antivenin, and for a time he rallied. His sight came back to a blur. By one A.M., the vomiting ceased. His blood pressure stabilized at one fifty over seventy-five and stayed there for nearly an hour. At ten minutes to two, his respiration again grew erratic. At two-twenty, five minutes before I got to the hospital, Walter put him on a ventilator and he lost consciousness a third time.

"I don't know if he's going to make it," Christina said, running toward me from the intensive care unit. She looked like she'd been through a hurricane. Her sweater and blouse were misbuttoned and her long red hair, normally cared for just so, now hung askew about her shoulders. Her cheeks, always creamy, looked like dried paste. I flashed on her at eight years old, choking at the color guard carrying out our father's casket.

"Course he's gonna make it," I said, hugging her. "Rikko's the toughest man alive. Who's taking care of the girls?"

"Mom's there," she said; then she pressed into my shoulder and whispered, "What will I do if...? What will the girls do if...?"

"Shhhh," I hushed. "We're not thinking like that."

Christina pushed back from me, shaking. "I have to, Shay. I don't have a choice. I'm looking a lot like Mom right now. And that scares me half to death. It's like I'm looking at this big black hole and—"

She couldn't go on and started searching her pockets for a Kleenex. Her sense of dread only added to the frustration and anger simmering in me since I left the parking lot at the Ocean Beach pier. I felt like putting my hand through the window of the door to the ICU just to hear the sound of it breaking.

Even in the midst of personal grief, my sister is one of those people acutely tuned to emotional static. She blew her nose and looked at me. "What's wrong?"

"What's wrong? My best friend and brother-in-law's in a coma is what's wrong."

"There's something else. I can always tell with you, Shay."

"For Christ's sake, Chrissy, stop thinking about everyone else's problems for one moment. The only thing important right now is that Rikko lives."

At that, her lower lip began to quiver and she flung herself into my arms again. For the next two hours, we sat outside the ICU and told each other that there was no way the big, crazed Israeli was going the way of our dad.

But at four A.M., a pulmonary therapist had trouble finding a vein in Rikko's forearm. When she drew out the needle to try again, a thin, diluted liquid tainted with blood dribbled from the puncture. When Walter checked Rikko's mouth, he noticed the same bloody substance leaking at his gum line. Then it seeped from his nose. When they turned my brother-in-law over in bed, the bloodstains on the sheets were scarlet.

Walter came out, nodded to me, then told Christina, "He's survived the neurotoxin's assault on his respiratory system and kidneys, but the taipan venom isn't done yet, even with the antivenin in his system."

"How's that possible?" I demanded.

Walter responded calmly that although it had not been evident on the Life Flight or in the first hour in the emergency room, a stealthy component of the venom in Rikko's bloodstream must have triggered a complex biochemical response called a clotting cascade. The process is a normal body function, usually a measured reaction initiated to stem the flow of blood associated with cuts and bruising.

But the venom had triggered the clotting process on a massive scale inside Rikko's circulatory system, littering his blood stream with lumpy white blood cells that threatened thrombosis, a coagulation within the chambers of his heart. The antivenin injections, coupled with Rikko's strong constitution, had been enough to dissolve the clots and stave off thrombosis. But five and a half hours after the bite, an insidious effect of the venom was showing itself in the bloody liquid seeping out Rikko's orifices: The furious period of clotting that had almost killed him earlier in the night had ended up exhausting the blood's ability to clot at all.

"The danger to Rikko's life is now the exact opposite of thrombosis," Walter said. "His capillaries are leaking blood into his internal cavities."

"What's the bottom line, Walter?" I said. "No bullshit."

"He's facing cerebral hemorrhage," he replied, and Christina began to sob again.

I stood at the window to the ICU, watching Walter and his team pump bag after bag of blood plasma into Rikko. Christina sat at his bedside, looking so lost and frightened that I did not hear Freddie,

Missy, and Jorge come up the hallway behind me. They'd been up all night answering questions posed by a squad of Internal Affairs officers answering directly to Helen Adler.

"How is he?" Freddie asked.

I hugged her and said, "Start praying."

"We heard what happened, Sarge," Missy said softly.

"It's a raw deal," Jorge said. "We're all on record saying so."

"You should fight this," Freddie said.

"I don't give a shit right now," I said. "Rikko's dying. The rest is irrelevant."

"Leras and Wight should be taking the heat for part of it," Missy insisted. 'They were up on the fence and heard the boyfriend screaming."

"What are you saying, Missy? He wasn't screaming?"

"No, he was screaming all right," Jorge said. "They just misinterpreted it, Boss. Boy, you should have seen Wight's face when we skidded into the great room, gun drawn, expecting to face down a rattlesnake. Instead he finds the mayor's nephew banging the blonde in front of the fireplace with Foster holding a camera and acting like Cecil B. DePervo. You know what a straitlaced Lutheran Wight is, I thought he was gonna have a chest-clutcher."

I let loose a dry chortle, walked by them, sat on a bench, and held my head in my hands. "What a fiasco. What a goddamned fiasco."

Freddie sat next to me. "It's not your fault, Sarge. We'll back you up all the way. We'll go to your buddy there at the newspaper, Tarentino. We'll go public with the real reason behind this suspension."

"Stupid move," I said. "Don't fuck up your careers because of me."

"But Fraiser will be in charge of us for a month," Jorge grumbled. "Fraiser trying to catch a serial killer... the man couldn't find a psycho in Iraq."

Before I could reply, my sister came out of the ICU followed by Walter. Tears streamed down her cheeks. I felt the world tip and my stomach go horribly empty.

Christina must have seen it in my face, because she shook her head and grabbed my hand, smiling. "He's stopped losing blood, Shay. He's in and out of consciousness, but Walter thinks he's gonna be okay now. The antivenin's finally turned the tide."

I stood up and shook Walter's hand. "Thanks," I said. "He means a lot to us."

"All in a day's work," Walter said. "He's out of the woods, but he'll be ill for a couple more days."

Walter let us in to see him around nine A.M., shortly after the ventilator was removed. Rikko was gray, drawn, and slack-eyed like an old man that I'd seen almost drown once. Our shock at his appearance must have been visible on our faces, because he said, "Why so gloomy? Have you not learned we are on this earth for a good time, not a long time?"

"That how you see it, huh?" I said, grinning.

"Of course," he said. "Bigg Ja?"

"In custody. Gonna do time, but he doesn't look like our killer."

I didn't want to upset Rikko, so I didn't tell him about the suspension. I just sent the others home to sleep and stayed with Christina by his bed, ire and resentment replaced by a weary gratitude that my best friend had been spared.

Tarentino kept paging me and I kept ignoring it. Around one in the afternoon, I fell asleep in a chair next to Rikko's bed. Two hours later I woke at the buzzing of my cell phone. I answered it groggily. "Moynihan."

"You lied to me," Jan said in a low, furious voice.

"Jan, I—"

"Shut up."

"Jan, listen to me."

"No," she said. "I told you once that I would forgive anything but a lie."

"I did not lie."

"You did!" she cried. "I asked you whether Nick was a suspect and you said he was cleared. You didn't tell me you had him under surveillance. You didn't tell me you thought he was a killer! This morning, after getting bumped off a plane last night and not getting to Chicago until forty-five minutes before my presentation, I get a call from the police insinuating that I put you up to this!"

"Jan, I told them you had no idea," I said. "I told them that—"

"You lied to me," Jan said again. "And now I don't know if I even have a job when I get back to San Diego. My name's going to be all over the papers and television as some kind of vengeful bitch. I should have known better, Moynihan."

The phone clicked dead.

FORTY-SIX

I left the hospital around three that afternoon. Like a little boy seeking solace after a playground injury, I drove north in Christina's old Volvo to her house in Cardiff-by-the-Sea to talk to my mother. My nieces had left the front door ajar and I entered the bungalow without knocking. The girls' toys were spread out on the kilim rug. Their voices chattered from the kitchen, then stopped at the screen door creaking shut.

"Who's there?" my mother called in alarm from the kitchen.

"It's me, Ma."

There was silence; then "Who is this 'me'?" she said, entering the living room wearing linen shorts and a navy blouse. She'd had her hair done recently and even at sixty-seven looked beautiful.

"Your son."

"My son?" she said, squinting my way over the dining room table, then putting on her reading glasses to study me. "I admit, you look something like my son."

"I *am* your son, Ma."

"You sure? My son hasn't called or been to see me in so long, I'm not sure I'd recognize him."

"I don't know if I'd recognize myself," I said, then flopped on the couch.

"See," she said, waving a finger. "If you'd listened to me thirty years ago and kept your promise not to become a cop, you wouldn't be like this. You'd see your mother more often and Rikko would not be lying in some hospital near death from a snakebite."

"He's gonna be fine. The doctors said so."

"Christina says you've been suspended."

I nodded, then threw back my head. "It all got so crazy and turned sideways so fast. I don't know, Ma. I just don't know anymore."

She turned and went back into the kitchen without a remark. I heard her tell the girls that their dad was going to be fine and they were going to see him in the morning. She asked them to go into the family room in the meantime and watch television. A moment later she returned and sat on the couch next to me.

"I'm sorry," she said. "I know how much your job—"

"Fay's getting married, Ma."

"Your sister told me that too," she said, pained. "When?"

"Shit, I don't know. Does it matter? She's made her decision."

She looked at me with fluid mahogany eyes. "You'll find another woman, Shay."

"Not gonna happen. I seem to consistently screw up with the women in my life."

"Not with me."

"Yeah, but you're my mother."

"I am," she said. 'And you haven't always screwed up with women. You didn't with Fay until the shooting."

I winced at the memory, which refused to stay bottled. Jimmy was three at the time. Fay was a resident. I was a newly minted detective, working auto theft. I'd traced a number of cars stolen from the Lindbergh Field airport to a warehouse chop shop out in Normal Heights. We had SWAT with us when we hit the place one sweltering late Wednesday afternoon in July.

When we stormed in the front and back doors to the warehouse, every man dismantling a white Acura Integra held up their hands. But the Watson brothers, working on a second, red Integra, were not so compliant. The eldest, Clete, with two felony convictions, was facing hard time should he go down on a third count. When Clete threw himself out the chop shop's side window, his younger brother, Royalton, a mean son of a bitch with an IQ slightly above moron, decided to go desperado. He came out of nowhere with a Ruger Blackhawk .357 Magnum and pointed it at the closest person. Me.

I was quartered away from Royalton, my gun trained on one of the men working on the white Acura. Before the SWAT guys could cut Royalton down, I got hit twice. The first bullet cut through the meat of my left thigh, nicking my femoral artery. The second shot, Royalton's last action on earth, struck me square in the back as I buckled to the floor. Like Champion, the Kevlar vest saved my life. But the impact near my spine at that range knocked me cold for nearly a day.

Now I looked at my mom, not knowing what to say. She has never suffered fools lightly and I braced myself for yet another lecture on my shortcomings. Instead, her lovely face folded itself into a grimace. Her thumbnails clicked one against the other and she looked away, tears welling in her eyes. "The more I think about it, the more I think I'm to blame for Fay and all of it."

"What the hell you talking about?" I replied. "I know who's responsible here, and you're definitely way low on the list."

She shook her head. "I may be getting old, but I remember things too. I saw my influence on you when you woke up after the operation on your leg. You didn't know I was there at first. You opened your eyes and the first thing you saw was Fay holding Jimmy, both of them so frightened and alone, right on the verge of grief-stricken. I recognized your reaction: It was the same one you showed at your father's funeral."

I flashed on the image of Christina looking at me, lost, as the cortege left. Then I saw myself as if through a camera, looking up at my mother, but I could not see her face.

"That's not true … " I began.

"Yes it is," she insisted. "In Fay's face that day, you saw me dealing with your dad's murder. Those awful, awful days." The tears spilled and she dug out a handkerchief.

Again I flashed on myself watching my mother in the church. Then I caught a horrible glimmer of her face as the coffin passed. Then Fay holding Jimmy.

I shook it off. "Ma, don't do this to yourself. I'm the one responsible."

"You hear me out!" she shouted, throwing her arms about. "I've thought a lot about this. I think that deep down you couldn't stand the idea of Fay or Jimmy ever suffering like we had to, so subconsciously you pushed your wife and son away, trying to keep them from caring so much about you, keeping them at a distance so they wouldn't suffer as much should *you* die in the line of duty."

All of it laid out like that, so unexpected, was like getting shot again. "I'm leaving, Ma. With the night I've had, I just can't take any more."

I stood and made for the door.

"Rikko and Christina say you've been having flashbacks about your dad's death. You've never dealt with it, Shay. With any of it. Now you've got to or—"

The screen door slammed shut behind me.

FORTY-SEVEN

I found a saloon in Cardiff called Silver John's that was suitable enough in its squalor to match my mood. It was dim and smoky inside, with a beach-comber motif and a jukebox that played the greatest hits of the eighties. There was a baker's dozen of patrons along the bar that Saturday afternoon. I sat near the window that overlooked an alley and drank Stolichnaya with soda and lemon.

ESPN played on the television above the bar. Early-season baseball highlights. And then a feature on a kid from the University of Oklahoma who'd made the starting rotation with the Arizona Diamondbacks at the age of twenty-two. The images were of crouched batters slicing the air as the baseball dove and curled away from them. When the story ended, the camera returned to the two anchors, who yucked it up about the wonders of youth. I drank down my first Stoli and ordered a double.

Halfway through that drink, a blowsy biker chick named Sunshine, who wore a leather halter top and not much more, hit on me as Bob Seger sang "We've Got Tonight." She regaled me with stories of Sturgis,

South Dakota, then announced she wasn't wearing panties under her cutoff jeans. In another time and another place I might have taken the subtle cue and holed up with her in a cheap hotel room in an effort to fornicate my way out of mental anguish.

But I kept hearing my mother talk about Fay and Jimmy and then about the flashbacks. I ordered another double after Sunshine drifted away in search of another anonymous stud to scratch her itch. I would not allow myself to dwell on the possibility that my mother and sister were right, that all of this had to do with my dad's death. Instead I tried to convince myself that the vivid memories were all just a part of my inevitable midlife crisis.

I drained the second double as I realized that my entire life had been a midlife crisis. I'd played major league baseball, been a cop, drove a penismobile, lived on a boat. For whatever reason, my marriage had sunk under the weight of my indiscretions. My indiscretions had sunk under the weight of my indiscretions. My relationship with my son was more of an uneasy friendship than a guiding hand.

My third double Stoli found me convinced that the flashbacks were a result of overwork and my memory bank's filling with snapshots of the heinous things men do to other men, all of these violent pictures overloading and short-circuiting back to my dad's death because of some electric longing formed and buried in the heart of a ten-year-old who desperately wanted to understand the logic of why his father had been shotgunned and burned and a thousand other Boston cops had not. There was something to that theory, but still it did not get to the heart of the matter, and I tossed that one aside as well.

As I was about to order a fourth double, the central reason hit me. And it was so clear and ripping in a chainsaw sort of way that I knew I had to get out of that bar or break down and make a fool out of myself.

I stumbled out into the late-afternoon glare that hung over the coast like a sheet of foil. I got in Christina's car and drove south on Highway 1. It dawned on me coming down the hill toward Torrey Pines State Reserve that I was probably legally drunk. The last thing I needed was to get arrested on top of everything else that had happened.

So I parked and got out. The reserve, a long stretch of beach and cliff between Del Mar and La Jolla, is the closest thing to a wilderness you can find in coastal San Diego County. I took off my shoes and socks and walked south toward the remotest part of the strand, trying not to stagger. Near the point, I collapsed between two boulders, my back against the crumbling cliffs, and watched the waves crash ashore and let the heat from the waning sun gather and boil down around me like harsh truth.

In a week I would be thirty-eight, the same age my dad had been when he died. Up until then I'd always been able to gauge my accomplishments in relationship to the things he had done. But at the age of thirty-eight and two months, it had all ended for my dad with two shotgun blasts, a can of gasoline, and a legacy of unanswered questions.

The ocean of life in front of me seemed as vast, uncharted, and petrifying as it had been the day I'd left my mother sobbing at the kitchen table and gone for a ride in a '67 Corvette. The truth was that the flashbacks were caused by the fact that I simply had no idea how to live past the age of thirty-eight and two months. Until the accident during the Yankees game, my father's ghost had always been in the stands, guiding my baseball career by his love of the sport. And his spirit had always been there by my side, guiding my police career by his example. Now, in my drunken state, I felt like he was leaving me, walking away down that beach, while I prepared to set adrift in an angry sea.

And right there, the pent-up emotion of twenty-seven years became like a volcano erupting from deep in my gut, and I did something I hadn't done since the day of my father's funeral. I cried for my dad. I cried for myself. I cried for every moment in my life that we should have shared. And I cried for every moment in my son's life that I was not sharing.

It was dusk by the time I made it back to Shelter Island. I put Christina's Volvo in the garage space meant for the Monster, then trudged down the dock, wanting nothing more than deep, dark sleep for a day, maybe longer. But just as I reached the gangway to the *Nomad's Chant,* that dream was shattered by the sight of Brett Tarentino charging from his boat, a reporter's notebook in one hand, a cell phone crammed against his ear.

"Give me fifteen to get there. When's last deadline for Sunday first?" He listened, then nodded. "Cut me a twenty-inch hole. I'll fill it."

The columnist slapped the phone shut and noticed me, disheveled and coming down off the drunk. His face twisted in anger, and I steeled myself for a full frontal assault. "Go ahead, Tarentino," I said. "Take your best shot. Everyone else has."

"I take people down. I don't kick them when they're lying there," Tarentino replied. "Recent events have eclipsed your shameful exploits. You've been relegated to the slag heap of old news, a sidebar, perhaps, about the general ineptitude of the San Diego PD. Someone else will handle it. I have better things to write."

"What's going on?" I asked.

"How quickly the chosen fall out of the loop," he said, charging by me up the dock. "They found a third body about an hour ago, tied up and snakebit at a hotel in Mission Valley."

FORTY-EIGHT

Mission valley lies near the geographic center of San Diego. The lowland is a two-mile-wide cornucopia of commercial activity sandwiched between two high bluffs and bisected by four major freeways. The north and south sides of Interstate 8, west of the 163, are packed with so many places for tourists to stay while visiting San Diego's attractions that the city fathers gave the area the superimaginative name of Hotel Circle.

The Six Palms Lodge on Hotel Circle North was once the city's largest convention center. Then a gigantic commercial gathering place was built on the downtown waterfront, and The Six Palms was relegated to hosting less prestigious, less lucrative conferences like the California Association of Funeral Home Directors, gathered that weekend for two days of coffin chat and general revelry.

There had been the night before, by all accounts, the usual heavy drinking that accompanies such events. The maids were used to hungover conventioneers, so they did not think it odd that the DO NOT

311

DISTURB sign dangled from the knob of room 1157 until well past five that Saturday afternoon.

Room 1157 was in the least-used part of The Six Palms Lodge complex, in the annex building beyond the pool. John Sprouls, a thirty-nine-year-old, divorced African-American medical equipment salesman from Seattle, who had stayed at The Six Palms several times in the past year, arrived around six Friday evening and specifically requested an annex room so he could get a good night's sleep without having to endure the ravings of the conventioneers. At least, that's what he told the registration clerk.

At five-fifteen Saturday evening, forty-five minutes before maids were to go off shift, the housekeeping supervisor knocked, got no answer, then placed a call to the room with the same result. The supervisor then used his pass key and opened the door to find Sprouls naked, tied to the bed, his skin blistered. A green apple was stuck in his mouth.

In my name shall they cast out Devils! was scrawled on the mirror.

Sprouls had been the only occupant of that particular hallway Friday night. He'd been neither seen nor heard from since the time he checked in. His rental car records indicated he'd driven only twenty-four miles since leaving the airport, about nine miles more than the most direct route to The Six Palms Lodge.

Sprouls's room had been cleaned, but not with the thoroughness of the Haines crime scene, which seemed to indicate that the killer was rushed, nervous at conducting evil in such a relatively public place. The evidence technicians found fingerprints not belonging to Sprouls on a plastic cup that had been thrown in the trash basket in the bathroom. They found six additional sets of fingerprints inside Sprouls's rent-a-car and on the various surfaces within the hotel room. Like Haines, Sprouls's pubic hair had been doused with a bleaching cleanser. Semen discharge was found on the bedsheets and collected for DNA analysis.

Sprouls's Palm Pilot showed he had several meetings with doctors and hospital administrators on Monday, but made no mention of a scheduled rendezvous with anyone Friday, Saturday, or Sunday. The device contained the names, addresses, and phone numbers of the same doctors and administrators, but no one else in San Diego.

Detectives talked to a funeral director from Sacramento who had the room directly across the pool yard from the annex. He said he'd drunk too many Old Fashioneds the night before and got up around four-thirty A.M. to barf. Afterward he took a shower, then went out on his room's small terrace in hopes that the fresh air might ease his sour stomach. He noticed someone exiting the walkway on the far side of the pool, heading toward the north parking lot. He described the person as tall, wearing a floppy hat and a long, dark raincoat, which he thought strange, considering the skies were clear and the temperature was in the mid-fifties.

I did not learn these details until the following afternoon.

Of course, I went straight to the scene and stood outside the police line, trying to get Missy, Jorge, or Freddie to slip me information. Then Fraiser spotted me and all but ordered me to leave the premises. I refused at first, telling him that, as I was currently occupying public ground, he could go blow himself. Helen Adler showed up and told me I should depart or face further disciplinary action. So I left, went home, drank more Stoli, and passed out cold.

Forty-Nine

The sunday daily news, April twenty-third edition, carried banner headlines about the third murder. Tarentino's column continued to drum his theory that the killer was targeting closeted gays and bisexuals. To his credit, he quoted Sproul's ex-wife as saying that her husband had exhibited no homosexual or bisexual tendencies in the past. Their marriage had failed due to a series of heterosexual affairs.

"But," she told Tarentino, "nothing would surprise me about John these days. The way he was acting... Gay? Bi? Sure, it's one explanation."

As Tarentino had predicted, the story of my suspension and removal from the investigation was relegated to a sidebar story on page A-3. The piece focused on the fact that while I'd been chasing Bigg Ja and ordering my detectives to pick up Nick Foster, the real killer had been busy torturing John Sprouls to death with a snake.

The story identified the man shot and killed during the gunfight at Bigg Ja's as Olo Buntz, a Samoan national whose travel visa had expired nearly fourteen months earlier. Rikko's ordeal with the taipan was covered in some detail in the middle of the article. To my relief, my relationship with Jan Hood was given short shrift.

After the residuals of Russian vodka had been assaulted with enough coffee to reduce my hangover to background clanging, I picked up Jimmy from Fay's.

He was waiting by the gate with his tackle box and climbed in quickly. He did not say anything and neither did I. We drove to one of the jetties off the channel that leads into Mission Bay, parked, got our gear, and clambered far out over the rocks until we faced the open sea. I rigged us up and we each cast our jigs far out into the choppy water, then wedged the butts of our rods into gaps between the stones.

A wind had picked up, but not enough to drown my son's words: "Mom's getting married to Walter. And I was afraid of losing you."

"I know, pal," I said, taking him into my arms and rocking him while he cried.

The plan was to have dinner aboard the *Chant* before I took him home to finish schoolwork. But when we came down the dock around three that afternoon, feeling a bit better about our sorry lot in life, Jorge, Missy, and Freddie were sitting on the aft deck.

"Fraiser's an incompetent idiot," Missy said, by way of greeting.

"And you guys are jeopardizing your careers being here," I said. "Fraiser and Adler were damn clear at the crime scene. I am out."

None of them replied, and their collective silence got to me. I told Jimmy to go watch the baseball game, then plopped in a deck chair. "What do you want me to do?"

"Look at the evidence, Sarge," Jorge began. "See if we're missing something. Fraiser's horrible at this kind of thing. He's got us chasing around looking for someone who might have seen the guy in the green raincoat. Or something the guy in the green raincoat might have left behind. Talking to parking lot attendants, taxi drivers."

I shrugged. "Not bad things to do. How many times have we got lucky and solved a big case because someone remembered seeing the killer, or the killer got a traffic ticket or dropped something incriminating near the crime scene?"

"But that's the only way Fraiser's ever solved a murder!" Freddie cried. "And you've said it yourself: This killer doesn't make many mistakes. He's never been seen straight on by anyone but his victims. He's careful, sophisticated. Fraiser's best hope is to get lucky. And I don't think that's gonna happen any time soon. We need your abilities."

"My abilities are suspect these days, or haven't you noticed?"

"We liked Bigg Ja and Foster too," Missy said.

"And the Silvers," Freddie said.

"You're just in a slump," Jorge said. "C'mon, Sarge. Stay in the game."

Their eyes were on me, watching me the way coaches would in the late innings, hoping I had the strength to face another six batters. "You guys get caught feeding me insider stuff about this case, you could kiss your future good-bye too."

"We don't care," Missy said. "We want to get this guy, Boss. He's laughing at us."

I thought about it a minute, then nodded and looked over at Tarentino's boat. "I don't want to see you here again. And you're not talking to me. Right?"

They nodded as one, then told me everything they knew. When they got to the message on the mirror, I said, "Book of Acts?"

"Gospel according to Mark, chapter sixteen, verses seventeen to eighteen," Jorge said, handing me a piece of paper:

> *And these signs shall follow them that believe; In my name shall they cast out devils; they shall speak with new tongues; They shall take up serpents; and if they drink any deadly thing, it shall not hurt them…*

I read it three times, letting the words sink in. "So he's saying what? That these men, because of their sexual dispositions, did not believe in Jesus?"

"Maybe he's proving it," Freddie said. "He had them drink strychnine and take up serpents and they died."

"There's gotta be more than that," I said, shaking my head.

"Some link between the victims besides their sexuality. But I'll be damned if I can see what it is. And why's he going off his timing? He killed two Fridays in a row, then skipped a week. And Sprouls is black. Usually ritualistic killers stay within race." I looked at Jorge. "We never got anything back from ViCAP, huh?"

"Nada," Jorge said.

"Try a third time."

Freddie held up a folder. "Here's a copy of the murder book, including evidence lists, statements by his ex-wife, the hotel staff, the conventioneers and—"

Jimmy stood at the cabin door looking lonely and forgotten.

"You okay, bub?" I asked.

"Thought we were gonna have dinner, Dad. Thought you were suspended."

"I am and we are," I said. "Just give me a minute." I turned back to my team. "Why don't you leave that stuff here? I'll go over it later."

They left and Jimmy and I had a nice dinner. We played catch in the parking lot for an hour after eating. We talked a lot about the fun things we'd do in the future, and as I was driving him home it felt like he was carrying less of a load.

Walter opened the gate. When we had seen each other the night before, it had all been about Rikko. But now the altering of our relationship hung there.

When Jimmy said his good-byes and darted into the house, Walter remained behind.

"He means a lot to me," he said. "But I want you to know I'll never try to interfere between you two."

For a second I rumbled for some snide comment, then just stuck out my hand and congratulated him on his impending marriage. He seemed somewhat surprised by that, but took my hand and shook it. "Sorry about what's going on with you."

"No one to blame but myself, Walter."

"Healthy attitude, Moynihan."

"Yeah, the new me: poster child for mental well-being."

FIFTY

By the time i got back to the *Nomad's Chant*, the waxing moon cast the harbor in a pale, mellow glow. For the first time in almost twenty years, I had no purpose, no anticipation of tomorrow, no set agenda for the foreseeable future. Seamus Moynihan, nomad, or Seamus Moynihan, exile—I could not decide which. These thoughts almost sent me to the liquor cabinet in search of Mr. Stoli; then I thought hard about the various wrecks in the department I'd known who'd sailed from their troubles on the good ship Cutty Sark.

So I made coffee instead and sat at the galley table, listening to Matchbox Twenty while going over the evidence file Freddie left me. I read the notes of interviews with the maids, their supervisor, and the managers at The Six Palms. Then I went over the statements by Sprouls's ex-wife, his boss, the Sacramento funeral director, an Alaska Airlines worker who'd met the medical supply salesman at the San Diego airport, and a rental car agent.

Sprouls's boss said the dead medical equipment salesman did not have a scheduled meeting until the following Monday, but had decided to travel to San Diego early for some much-needed R&R. The Alaska Airlines gate attendant said she remembered Sprouls not only because he was such a big man—nearly six foot three and 250 pounds—but because Sprouls had asked about taking the vehicle into Mexico and was told it was against company policy.

It was nearly ten by the time I'd gone over the statements a second time, looking for any thread that might lead somewhere. But besides the possibility that The Prick was right and someone besides the funeral director from Sacramento had seen the man in the green raincoat and floppy hat, I saw no way forward. In the back of my mind, however, I heard this voice saying there had to be some common link, some reason the killer had chosen Cook, Haines, and Sprouls.

I picked up the evidence list and pored over it. The crime scene investigators cataloged more than seventy items in the hotel room, including the bottle of white wine, the green apple, and the ropes. They also took boxes of syringes, gauze pads, and IV lines—all samples of the medical supplies Sprouls sold. At the same time, they bagged Sprouls's socks, underwear, pants, shirt, tie, blue blazer, pens, and the entire contents of his suitcase, which included two changes of casual clothes, a bathing suit, and tourist guides to San Diego and Baja. Inside Sprouls's toiletry kit, they noted two Gillette razors, Edge shaving cream, Imodium tablets, Gas-X, Southern Nights men's cologne, a bottle of *Echinacea* capsules,

Claritin allergy medicine, a toothbrush, Mentadent toothpaste, three Sheik prophylactics, and a small tube of K-Y jelly. From his briefcase, they took his Palm Pilot and computer, his files, and a dog-eared paperback mystery novel.

The list went on and I scanned it, shaking my head in disappointment. Other than the man in the green raincoat who'd been spotted with Cook outside the Yellow Tail and now outside the hotel where Sprouls was killed, and the supposition that the men had reason to succumb to sexual advances, there was still nothing in the evidence list or the interrogation reports that I could see to link the three victims. I got up, stretched, and yawned, telling myself that I'd go over it all again in the morning. I went below deck, got into bed, turned off the light, and tried to sleep.

For nearly an hour I swirled in that buzzing half-awake state between consciousness and deep slumber. The images that flashed through my mind were a collage: my mother talking about Fay; Bigg Ja's GTO gliding through space as the hip-hopper swam in the night air; the taipan coursing from the hallway; Rikko on the ventilator; Nick Foster grabbing the king cobra by the neck; my fingers caressing Jan's belly; Paula Silver shouting at her husband; the ancient terra-cotta statue of the nude Lilith sitting in the tree on Susan Dahoney's book cover; the faceless man in the green raincoat shuffling out the pool gate at The Six Palms Lodge; the tank that held the coral snake in Haines's bedroom;

the faceless man in the green raincoat walking off with Cook through the mist-shrouded parking lot outside the Yellow Tail; myself inside the moon suit, looking down at Cook's black and blistered body; Dr. Marshall Solomon tearing off his hooded cowl to show me the bite marks; myself turning from Cook's body to look around the inside of the bedroom of Sea View Villas unit nine, building five…My attention drifted over the nightstand and came to rest on the dresser.

I shot up in bed. "I'll be a son of a bitch!"

FIFTY-ONE

I kicked free of the blankets and raced up to the galley. I turned on the lights, flipping through the Sprouls file, looking for the evidence list, then finding it and running my finger down through the items logged at the hotel.

"There it is," I whispered. "Imagine that."

I called Freddie at home. She answered sleepily, "Burnette."

"I think I've found something in the file you gave me," I said without preamble. "Do you have access from home to the Homicide computer?"

"What do you need, Boss?" she asked, alert now.

"Go through the list of evidence we took from the Haines crime scene. See if he had a men's cologne called Southern Nights."

"Men's cologne?"

"Sprouls had a bottle of Southern Nights in his toiletry kit," I said. "There was an open bottle of the same cologne on the dresser inside Cook's bedroom up at Sea View. See if Southern Nights comes up on the Haines evidence list."

"Give me ten minutes," she said, and hung up.

I paced up and down inside the *Chant*. I was onto something. What it was I was not sure. But every instinct I had said that this was a link between the three killings. The phone rang after only five minutes. I snatched it up.

"It's not there," Freddie said.

"It has to be there!" I shouted. "Look again."

"It's not there, Sarge," she insisted. "I ran a search on it twice. You were right about the cologne being at Cook's, but there's no mention of Southern Nights at Haines's place. Look, it's probably just a coincidence. I've seen ads for that cologne in all the magazines lately. It's new, isn't it?"

"No idea," I said, deflated. "Guess it doesn't matter. Guess I was just hoping to find something, anything that might—" I stopped in mid-sentence, staring out the windshield of the *Chant*'s cockpit toward the lights of downtown. "What about Aiken?"

"Who?"

"Lieutenant Donald Aiken, Haines's roommate. Go back into the files. We got notice from his JAG the other day that he was moving. I need his new address. Now."

Twenty-five minutes later, I pounded on the door to an apartment in Mission Hills, the establishment neighborhood of central San Diego. Lights came on inside, then a groggy voice grumbled from the other side of the door. "Who's there?"

"Sergeant Moynihan, San Diego Homicide."

The dead bolt threw. The door opened an inch to reveal a chain and Aiken, in a green plaid bathrobe, rubbing his eyes. Beard stubble showed on his chin. "You know what damned time it is?" he demanded.

"I do, Lieutenant, and I'm sorry. But it's important."

He sighed and removed the safety chain. I stepped inside the apartment. The living room was strewn with unopened moving boxes.

"Don't mind the mess," Aiken said. "You guys wouldn't let me even get at this stuff until yesterday. Do you know how hard it is to live on two suitcases of clothes for almost a month?"

"Must be tough," I agreed. "Do you use a cologne called Southern Nights?"

His face contorted and he grunted, "You woke me up to ask if I use aftershave?"

"I wouldn't be here if it wasn't crucial."

He looked at the ground and started to shake his head no, then looked up at me. "Maybe. My mother gave me some kind of cologne for Christmas, but I never used it. Could have been ... what'd you call it?"

"Southern Nights," I said.

"Could have been. But like I said, I never used it. Didn't like the smell."

"What'd you do with it?"

"Don't know," he said. "Threw it away? Stuck it in a cabinet?"

"Could it be here?" I asked, gesturing at the moving boxes.

He squinted and yawned. "Nah," he said. "At least I don't think so. I mean, I don't remember packing it with my stuff yesterday, but then again, you guys didn't give me much time. We were just grabbing everything and shoving it in boxes."

"We?"

"My girlfriend helped me move. She packed the bathroom."

"Can you take a look in the bathroom boxes?" I asked.

He yawned again. "Now? Can't this wait?"

"No."

It took Aiken fifteen minutes to locate the boxes that held the things from his bathroom at Haines's Point Loma house and the both of us another ten before I found it, buried in a shoebox filled with old prescriptions, tanning lotions, and a bag of cotton balls.

I put on rubber gloves, picked up the honey-colored bottle, and held it to the light. A quarter of the liquid inside was gone. "You figure you used that much before you decided you didn't like it?" I asked.

Aiken peered at the bottle and shook his head. "No way. I sprayed some on my hands, hated it, and must have tossed it in the medicine cabinet."

I tugged off a cap, squirted a bit on the rubber glove, and leaned in for a sniff. It was an odd gathering of odors that reminded me of the woods at night after a brief rainstorm, the smells of the forest all clean and direct, combined with some kind of

328

blossom, leather, and roasted pecans, all of it underscored by the muskiness of freshly turned soil.

"What's so important about that stuff anyway?" Aiken asked.

I smiled grimly. "If I'm right, Lieutenant, this is the scent of murder."

FIFTY-TWO

I worked the phone from the *Nomad's Chant* all day Monday and into Tuesday morning, staying in touch with Freddie Burnette, who was surreptitiously feeding me information from the team cubicle. Sophia Cook said her husband bought Southern Nights cologne in February at a Bloomingdale's in Ventura. Aiken's mother purchased his bottle before Christmas from a Fields department store in Champagne, Illinois. Sproul's oldest daughter bought Southern Nights for her father three weeks before as a birthday present at a Nordstrom in Tacoma.

"No way they're meeting the killer at the point of purchase," I told Freddie around lunch on Tuesday. "Unless he's a traveling salesman based out of San Diego."

"Thought of that," she replied. "I called Franken & Holmes Aroma Company, the makers of Southern Nights, this morning. Talked to their president, Liz Franken. She says the reps for those areas don't overlap. And to her knowledge none of our victims has ever been to Nashville, where the stuff's made. Franken said Southern Nights's been on the market since last October. Biggest seller in company history. They're coming out with an entire line of toiletries based on the scent for Christmas."

"What's it made of?"

"Formula's a proprietary, but she assured me there was no strange pheromone or anything that hasn't been on the market before."

"Great," I sighed. "So where does this get us?"

"Was gonna ask you the same thing, Sarge," Freddie replied. "It's not like we can go to Fraiser without more evidence than the fact that they all wore the same men's cologne. Maybe it *is* a coincidence."

I sat on the forward deck, pinching the bridge of my nose and watching a sailboat head out to sea. Part of me wanted to rev up the *Chant*'s engines and follow, leaving the entire mess in The Prick's lap, but I just couldn't do it.

"This is real. I can feel it, Freddie."

"Maybe so. But now you got to prove it."

Three hours later I helped Rikko into his civilian clothes and then into a wheelchair. Christina watched, looking as tired and yet as happy as I've ever seen her.

"We're going home," she said.

"Takes more than snake venom to kill a rhino."

"Rhino?" she replied, tickling Rikko's ribs. "No, he's just a big teddy-boo bear."

"Hey, hey," Rikko said, blushing. "None of this teddy-boo bear in public."

It had taken two full days for the doctors to bring my brother-in-law's system completely down from the effects of the taipan bite. Except for the massive bruising around the bite and a general weakness, however, he said he felt ready to chase bad guys.

"You're taking at least a week off," Christina said. "Adler's orders."

I stiffened. "She been here?"

"Once," Rikko said. "Been calling a couple times a day, though. See the announcement in the *Union-Tribune* this morning?"

I nodded. Mayor Sand had named Helen Adler chief of police, the first African-American woman in the country to run a major metropolitan police department. She was quoted as saying that she hoped her tenure would bring a new era to the city's law enforcement, one of regard for civil rights and an end to recent police behavior.

"I don't know why she didn't just come out and call for me to take forty lashes in front of City Hall," I griped.

An orderly came in and took control of the wheelchair. While we walked Rikko to Christina's minivan, I told them about the Southern Nights angle.

Rikko shook his head. "You are reaching. Look at the evidence found at the scenes and I bet they owned a half dozen things in common. Razors, shaving cream, ear swabs. Maybe they all squeeze that

Charmin. Why do you not just admit you are on a six-week vacation and enjoy it?"

"Can't do that," I said. "This is personal now."

Rikko's cheeks tightened. "Adler finds out you freelance, you become toast."

"So be it," I replied. "But I'm not backing away, Rikko. Neither would you."

Outside another near perfect day unfolded in my lost paradise: temps in the seventies, turquoise blue skies, a light breeze. I helped Rikko into the van and got in the backseat. Christina drove.

"What do you think, sis?" I asked once we'd gotten on the freeway, heading north. "About the cologne, I mean? Am I nuts, here, or what?"

"Could be a coincidence," she replied. "Or a trigger."

"Trigger?" Rikko grunted.

"Smell is the most primitive of the senses," she replied. "And it's the most likely to trigger vivid memories, waking dreams, déjà vu. Maybe that cologne takes your killer back to some horrible event in his life and he feels compelled to act on it."

"He smells something and then he kills," Rikko snorted. "Too simple."

"I think you're underestimating the complex mechanisms of the sense of smell," Christina shot back. "It's like taste, Rikko, a chemical sense, only much more intricate. Neurons from the nasal tract link to six different parts of the brain. Many of these structures form the limbic system, an ancient region of the mind concerned with motivation, emotion, and certain kinds of memory. Two of these brain regions—the septal nuclei and the amygdala—contain what scientists call the 'pain and pleasure centers.' Think of the first message: 'joy unspeakable.' "

"You reach," Rikko said again.

She glanced at him sourly, then looked in the rearview mirror at me. "Shay, the hippocampus, another one of the limbic structures that receives information from the nose, is deeply concerned with motivational memory. There are many documented reports of people entering dream states in the presence of certain smells. It's not a leap to believe someone could enter a nightmare with a similar trigger."

"Now what do you say? That he kills when he's asleep when he smells this cologne?" Rikko asked derisively.

"No, I'm not," Christina replied. "I'm suggesting something much more controversial. Cops hate the idea of it because defense attorneys have tried to use it to absolve their clients of responsibility for their actions. But from a purely psychiatric perspective, I happen to believe they're very real, at least in certain cases."

"Speak in complete thoughts, Sis," I said, irritated. "What are *they*?"

"Fugue states," she replied. "Some of my peers believe that ritualistic killers enter a fugue state before they act. One psychiatrist—he lives up in Montana now, I think—theorized that Richard Ramirez, the Night Stalker up in L.A. back in the early eighties, entered one of these fugue states before he went on his killing sprees."

"Define *fugue state*," I said.

We reached their exit. Christina drove to the traffic light at the end of the ramp before answering. "It's defined in different ways," she said. "In one, it's a waking nightmare, what people who suffer from post-traumatic stress disorder or battle fatigue enter when they hear a loud noise.

"In its extreme form, the fugue state can be defined as a psychological condition in which the victim, again because of some traumatic incident, completely shuts down their personality and becomes someone else—in Ramirez's case, a psychotic killer."

"Bullshit," Rikko said. "I know this case. Ramirez was the stone-cold sadist."

"I said cops hate the idea," Christina said, "but it is a real, documented condition. There are scores of case studies of ordinary people telling their wives or husbands that they're going out to get some milk and never coming back. Years later, someone they knew in their former life bumps into them thousands of miles away and they have absolutely no recall of their prior existence. Their brain makes up a new personal history and they completely disappear into it. Usually the trigger into the fugue state is caused by an abusive relationship or being witness to something brutal."

I crossed my arms. "I'm with Rikko. Sounds like defense lawyer mumbo jumbo."

"Be open to new ideas, Shay," she said, annoyed. "Or think of it in terms you might understand. Seamus Moynihan sees a woman he finds attractive, what's he do?"

"I don't know," I said, then thought of meeting Susan Dahoney. "Fantasize?"

"Right: You allow a trigger, in this case the visual trigger of the attractive woman, to cause your brain to invent the perfect unfolding for the situation. That's what people in fugue states are doing, just on a more long-term basis. They daydream themselves into a new existence with no conscious memory of their prior life."

"So what are you saying—that day to day the killer is normal, but when he smells Southern Nights, it triggers an entry into this killer fugue state? Or is he in the fugue state to begin with and reverts to his original personality when he encounters the smell?"

She pulled into her driveway. "Could go either way, I suppose," she said.

"Fraiser will never buy this," Rikko said. "Neither will Adler. They can't."

I nodded. "If they go on record saying this is what's happening, they hand the killer a defense before we even get into court."

The euphoria I'd felt the night before was quickly fading. Rikko was probably right. Despite Christina's assertion that smell could be a trigger mechanism for a homicidal maniac, I felt like I was chasing ghosts, no closer to finding the killer, no closer to proving that Helen Adler had been wrong to suspend me.

Christina pulled into the driveway of their bungalow. My nieces, Anna and Margarite, ran out the front door in their ballet tutus and dove on Rikko. He picked one up in each arm and kissed their cheeks until they both squealed with laughter. Rikko choked when he said, "I did not think I would ever get to hold them like this again."

"You are a teddy-boo bear," I said.

Rikko's glower would have scared the bejesus out of a wolf pack.

"Okay," I said. "How about a teddy-boo rhino?"

FIFTY-THREE

O'doran's ale house on Shelter Island has always struck me as somewhat out of place in San Diego. The tavern's architecture, handsome though it is, appears designed less for Southern California than some rugged fishing village on the Oregon coast. The exterior is sea-weathered shake shingles decorated with antique oars, nets, and fishing gaffs. The door has a porthole window. And the roofs are gabled.

Inside O'Doran's is all hand-rubbed teak, leather, brass, and gentle light. The west wall overlooks the harbor. The seating is in booths and the walls are covered with fishing photos and other shots of men at sea. The bar is a grand affair, built for a hotel in San Francisco in the 1920's, then bought, dismantled, and moved to San Diego after the hotel was condemned. It is a comfortable place to go when I'm not in the mood to be alone. And it's only a fifteen-minute walk from my slip.

I usually sit at the bar and watch the game or read or talk to Tommy O'Doran, the proprietor. Tommy was a buddy of my late Uncle Anthony. They served together in the Navy. He's also the man who introduced me to the joys of angling. Tommy's one of the friendliest men alive, always happy to see you, always interested, always striving to be better—one of the reasons his establishment is so popular.

It was nearly nine by the time I pushed open the front door to O'Doran's, telling myself I deserved a nightcap. There was the usual crowd in the lobby, waiting to eat the best seafood in town. Standing at the maître d's podium, a hugely grinning Tommy was shaking the hands of a woman in her mid-fifties dressed in yacht wear. He kissed the woman on the cheek, then slapped the back of her escort, a tall, silver-maned man with perfect teeth.

"Got to get down here from Santa Barbara more often, Ray," Tommy was saying. "This once-a-year stuff is for the birds."

"You should expand your horizons, Tommy," Ray replied. "We could repeat O'Doran's Ale House up in Santa Barbara. I'll bankroll you."

Tommy beamed. "A kind offer, and I'll think on it, Ray. But you know it would probably all get too big for me and I wouldn't be able to watch it the way I like."

"I'm just a phone call away if you change your mind," Ray said before departing.

The door shut, Tommy's broad florid cheeks broke into a new huge grin, and his eyes darted through the crowd, finding me on the way toward the bar. Tommy sobered, then gestured me into the hallway off the kitchen.

"Jesus, Seamus, I been hearing you've fucked up your life pretty good," he began. "That piece in the newspaper. And Rikko. There was a crew in from City Hall at lunch talking all about it."

"I hit the canvas hard, but don't count me out just yet, Tommy," I said.

"Oh, never that, lad," he said. "I've known you since you were a little boy, remember. Like a terrier: Once you bite, you don't let go. Only problem with that is that sometimes you bite into things that aren't too good for your stomach."

"Probably true," I agreed.

"And your lady friend—the one they wrote about in the papers, up at the zoo? She the one who put the finger on Nick Foster? Not that I mind. He comes in here once in a while. Real piece of work."

"He is that," I said. "But none of that stuff about her being behind it was true."

"Pissed at you, was she?"

"Ballistic pissed."

"Good-looking, I'd expect."

"Solid eight-point-oh on the Richter," I said.

"Not too many of those," Tommy said thoughtfully. "So that would have to be the same woman in the bar waiting on you the last two hours."

Taken aback, I looked at him, then down the hall to the bar. "You're kidding me."

"You don't kid about a woman like that," Tommy said, shaking his head. "She arrived in a cab around seven, turned every head in the place, and asked me if you were here. She said she'd done wrong by you, that she'd been to your boat to apologize, but you weren't there. So she came here to wait on the off chance you might show."

"Really?" I said, brightening. "The way Jan laid into me on the phone, I figured that was the last I'd ever hear from her."

"Jan?" Tommy said, puzzled. "She said her name was Susan."

FIFTY-FOUR

The barroom was crowded for a Wednesday night. Professor Susan Dahoney sat at the far end, closest to the window that overlooks the harbor. She wore black stiletto heels, tight white pedal pusher jeans, and a starched white shirt with its lapel unbuttoned to reveal a string of freshwater pearls dangling between ample bosoms cradled in violet lace. Three younger guys stood gathered around her. She was openly flirting with them.

As the name suggests, O'Doran's specializes in beers from around the world, including a fine selection from Ireland, but Tommy said she was drinking vodka martinis, five of them since arriving.

When I spied her through the crowd, she was working on her sixth martini, looking just this side of smashed and definitely on the prowl, the way she laughed throatily at any old comment, those wide glassy blue eyes gazing humidly at each of the young men in turn, her upper body leaning forward, shoulders rounding, stirring the olive in her martini glass, as if beckoning the men to let their attention wander down her shirt.

One of them whispered something in her ear. She affected a pout, shook her head, then picked up the toothpick, sucked off the olive, and laughed seductively. I took another step and she saw me. She smiled, stuck her chin my way, and eased off her stool.

"Sorry, boys, here's my date," she announced, waving aside their protests and slipping toward me, glass in hand. When she got close, she gave me an I've-been-a-naughty-girl look, then got up on her tiptoes, threw her arms around my neck, and whispered in her soft drawl, "I so hoped you'd come. I didn't want it to end like it did. Not after that kiss the other night."

Ignoring the looks I was getting from some of the men in the crowd around us, I caught her by the wrists, gently pressed them down, and released them. "I can't help with your book career anymore, Professor. I'm off the case."

A couple came behind us and we moved closer to the bar. She pouted, sipped from the martini, rolled sad drunken eyes at me again, then began talking in a low voice that forced me to lean close to hear.

"I've had enough time to think about what I've done," she said with a slight slur. "And it was wrong. All of it, Seamus. And I'm sorry. The publishing house said the book wasn't selling in the numbers they expected. I needed a bump and I stretched the truth a little and it worked. Sales were way up last week. But I hurt you and everybody else. And I apologize. I've apologized to everyone at the university and it doesn't seem to matter. *You* can forgive me, can't you?"

She was weaving on her feet, her hipbone pressed into mine.

"Sure," I said. "What the hell, life's too short to bear grudges. I forgive you."

"Good," she said, grinning. "Buy you a drink?"

"No offense, but I don't think so, Professor. Besides, you look like you've had plenty. And what happened at the university?"

She blew out a vodka-heavy breath, her attitude changing to alcohol-driven belligerence. "Oh, you'll hear about it soon enough. The bigwigs in my department saying it's unbecoming for an academic to try to promote herself. Then your chief called my boss, and then they started in on everything. You know what I say? I say I wasn't long for this town anyway. They're just jealous of what I've achieved outside their world. It isn't about the piece of paper or what people say about you, you know? It's the original work you do. That's what matters. Right?"

She had me confused. But before I could question her further, the Bible expert's eyes flared. She shook her head and flung one hand above her shoulder in defiance. "It doesn't matter. Any of it. Susan Dahoney's a survivor. Just like you, right, Seamus?"

She continued without letting me answer, her words a torrent. "I read in the paper that you'd been suspended on account of that woman at the zoo. That was her on the phone the other night, wasn't it?"

"It was, yeah."

She smiled provocatively. "She still in the picture?"

"That's none of your business." I said, then shook off the bartender, who had stopped in front of us.

The smile faltered a moment, then Susan let her fingernails pass over the back of my hand. "Maybe you're right," she said, leaning in close enough to whisper: "But even if she is in the picture, I honestly don't care. I was at home brooding about the horrible past couple of days. And I knew you must be in the same boat. And I thought it was a shame—I mean, to waste the attraction we shared the other night at the restaurant. Then I thought, you know, what would Lilith do?"

Before I could answer, she said, "I'm a good-looking woman."

"I've said it before, no argument there."

"I can have men if I want them."

"I'm sure you can."

"But I don't," she replied. "Or at least have rarely in my life. It was the way I was raised, you see. Strict Christian upbringing. So I became an expert flirt."

"I noticed."

She smiled again, then her entire attitude grew sultry and she put her palms on my chest. "But you know, deep down I'm sort of like the preacher's daughter, Seamus."

"That right?"

"Yeah. I've always wanted to be like her, to do the things she does."

"The preacher's daughter?"

Susan shook her head slowly, then put her lips to the martini glass, her eyes never leaving mine as she drained it. She set the glass down, came in close, and murmured in my ear, "No—Lilith."

I was acutely aware of her body against mine. "And what does Lilith do?"

"You know," she said. "You read the book."

"I haven't gotten to that part yet."

She eased her hand below the bar to my thigh. "Lilith rejects Adam and God. Leaves paradise. Goes to the beach. Lives by the sea. And engages in all manner of sensual pursuits with … "

Then Susan slumped and fell against me. I caught her by the elbows before she went down. "Whoa," she said, then hiccupped. "You're stronger than I thought."

I stood her up, looking across the bar to see Tommy in the doorway. I nodded to him and he started toward me. "Professor, I think you're pretty much done for the night. I'm going to get you a cab home. You need to sleep this one off."

"No," she protested, her eyes unscrewed. "I want to see your boat."

"Maybe next time," I said.

"You don't want to engage in all manner of sensual pursuits?" she asked blearily.

"Not when you're like this," I said.

"Why? Aren't I pretty enough?"

"Drop-dead gorgeous, Professor," I said. "But I'm not in the habit of taking advantage of women legally drunk. Beautiful or no."

"Oh," she said, made as if to argue, then swooned again. Tommy had arrived and caught her this time. "I don't feel good so," she told him.

"No, deary," Tommy said. "I imagine you don't."

FIFTY-FIVE

I stayed at o'doran's until Tommy had gotten enough coffee into Susan Dahoney that she was okay to take a cab home. I thought about taking her home myself, then thought better of it. Having her track me down like she had, lying in wait for me as part of some sexual fantasy, frankly made me feel strange and used somehow, so I saw her to the cab and said my good-byes there.

"I'll call you sometime," I said.

She shook her head. "Please don't. I seem to remember saying some very suggestive things to you. I'm mortified."

"It's okay," I said. "No one else heard. And I don't kiss and tell. You be safe, now."

Her face reddened. "Whatever you might hear, don't think bad of me, okay?"

I shrugged, figuring she was still fairly drunk. "Okay, Susan, I won't."

She nodded, signaled to the driver, and they left.

The next morning, Wednesday, April twenty-sixth, after a fitful night's sleep, I attended a funeral at an

348

auto salvage yard in Ocean Beach. Otis Spriggs, a tubby, bald guy with a squint and a permanent smirk on his face, bit down on a cigar stub and led me to where he kept the wrecks.

The grotesque green accordion that had been my mint '67 Corvette lay in weeds, beer cans, and gravel between a rolled Ford Explorer and a Silverado that had struck a tree head-on. I walked up to the Green Monster, flashing on myself climbing into it for the very first time. I wanted to scream, find Bigg Ja Moustapha, and wring his neck.

"Coulda been worse," Otis Spriggs offered.

"Yeah?" I said. "How's that?"

"Coulda stuck it in a crusher," he said, snickering.

"What're you bucking for, a slot on Letterman?" I said. "Is it totaled or not?"

"Up to the adjuster, course," he said. "But I'd say it's beyond totaled. Frame's bent. Front axle's gone. Trannie's ruined too. But look on the bright side."

"What bright side?"

"Engine's fairly solid. And the radio works."

"Get a lot of repeat customers with your winning personality?"

He flinched at that, then said stiffly, "What do you want me to do if they call it totaled, wise guy?"

I stood there, staring at the dead Monster for the longest time, then said, "If the engine block's not cracked, I'll take it. And anything else that's salvageable."

"And the rest?"

"Sell it for scrap," I sighed.

❖   ❖   ❖

Returning to the *Chant* to wallow in self-created misery held as much appeal as calling up Oprah and offering to confess my sins on national TV. So I went swimming at the cove instead, then ate lunch at O'Doran's.

The entire time, I kept thinking about the three victims, trying to figure out if we'd overlooked any other evidence besides Southern Nights cologne. But I couldn't come up with a single one.

Around four, I picked up Jimmy and headed for the ball field.

"I like having you on suspension, Dad," he said.

I patted him on the knee. "Being together is definitely one upside to the situation."

"Can I come sleep on the boat this weekend?" he asked. "Mom said to ask you. She and Walter want to go away for the weekend."

"Absolutely," I said, feeling even worse than I had seeing the Monster's remains. "Pick you up right after school Friday."

While running infield practice, the killer's second message—the reference to the Book of Acts and the shipwrecked Saint Paul—came back to me: *And Paul shook off the beast into the fire, and felt no harm. Howbeit they looked when he should have swollen, or fallen down dead suddenly: but after they had looked a great while, and saw no harm come to him, they changed their minds and said he was a god.*

I kept flipping it over and examining the possible meanings, but in the end saw nothing but mystery.

During the second inning, in which Jimmy made a nice stab at short, I thought about the first message: *Joy unspeakable to be holding death in your hands.*

Despite its lurid quality and the ecstatic experience suggested by the words, I could not make it bend into a key to unlock the killer's mind, either.

In the third, Jimmy got called out on three straight fastballs to end the inning. As he took to the field in the top of the fourth, I thought about the third message, the one from the Gospel of Mark and the verses that surrounded it: *And these signs shall follow them that believe; In my name shall they cast out devils; they shall speak with new tongues; They shall take up serpents; and if they drink any deadly thing, it shall not hurt them…*

After playing with that message for four batters, I was about to set it aside, too, and fully concentrate on the game. Then, perhaps because I am the son of an English teacher, I found myself concentrating not on the images the words provoked, but on the way sections of the verses of Mark had been couched: *And these signs shall follow them that believe… they shall cast out devils… they shall speak with new tongues; They shall take up serpents…*

Then I saw it. "*They,* not *he,*" I mumbled aloud, my fingers wrapped in the dugout screen. "*Them,* not *you.* The reference is to a group. We had it backwards. It's not the killer finding a singular twisted meaning in those biblical references: The references are embraced by a group that he's a part of. He believes he's a member of a chosen few. He doesn't act alone—at least not in his mind. What group, though? Who's with him?"

"You even watching the game, Shay?"

I startled and looked down at Don Stetson. He was watching me with growing concern. "You're talking to yourself."

"Sign of intelligence," I said, tossing him the score book. "I gotta go. Now."

"Go?" he replied incredulously. "We're tied up here. The kids need you."

"You can handle it," I said, tugging keys from my pocket.

"What about Jimmy?" he said.

"Take him home for me. Tell him and Fay I'll call later. I gotta go see someone."

FIFTY-SIX

A gloomy ocean fog rolled inland with me, casting the canyons around the campus in a toxic mood as I ran the walkways toward Crowley Hall. When I arrived outside Susan Dahoney's office, the book jacket of *The Second Woman* was gone. I rapped on the jamb. No answer. I knocked again.

"Susan!" I yelled. "It's Seamus Moynihan. Please, it's important!"

But no movement or sound came from inside and I hung my head, furious with myself for bailing out on Jimmy's game on impulse.

"Looking for the fallen angel?" queried a male voice behind me.

I startled, turned, and looked across the hallway to the open door of another office. A portly man in his fifties with pink skin peered out at me from behind thick eyeglasses. He wore a bad toupee, black socks, no shoes, and gray slacks held up by suspenders over a red mock turtleneck shirt. A pencil rested behind one ear and he cradled an open book in one arm.

"Professor Dahoney?" I asked him.

"Ex-Assistant Professor Dahoney has packed up and scooted," he said in a snide voice. "Good riddance, I say."

"She quit?" I said, stunned.

"More like asked to leave," he sniffed. "Seems, like so many today, Susan was caught with a great deal of fudge on her resume. All the stories being written about her and her book, it had to come out sooner or later. You a boyfriend or something?"

"No," I said, shaking my head. "Seamus Moynihan. I'm a sergeant with San Diego PD Homicide."

He studied me, then snapped his fingers. "You're one who got suspended. The one Dahoney said she worked for."

"Guilty."

He stuck out his hand. "Professor Edvard Erickson."

"Nice to meet you," I said, extending my own hand. "What happened to her?"

"I figured you would have known."

"I've been out of the loop."

"Oh, I guess," he said. "Well, after her appearance on television, boasting about being a consultant to you guys, all hell broke loose. Your chief, a woman ...?"

"Adler."

"Right. Last Friday, she called the chairman of the department and laid into him about Susan screwing up a murder investigation and claiming to be more than she was. Then on Monday the columnist there at the *Daily News*, Tarentino, he called the chairman to say he was working on a story about Susan. Not only did he know about the claim of false association, he'd done some checking on Susan's background."

"And?" I said.

"No doctorate from the University of Tel Aviv," Erickson replied. "She attended for a year, then dropped out. I always figured she padded her achievements, but never the whole shebang. Anyway, they confronted her and she swore up and down that she had the degree. They kept after her and she finally admitted that she didn't have it, but felt she deserved one because of the book. Amazing how people can delude themselves into believing their own lies."

"So they canned her?"

"Well, of course," Erickson said. "It may be different at other schools, but here it was cause for immediate termination. They gave her two days to clear her things out. I guess her publisher has gotten word of it. They're pissed because she identified herself as a Ph.D. as part of her submission and made them part of the deception."

"Jesus," I said, recalling her cryptic bitter words from the night before. "No one vetted her before she was hired?"

"She was getting rave advance reviews for her book and her publisher identified her as having a Ph.D. in biblical studies," he said. "We weren't the only ones duped. Several other universities made offers. The truth was, our chairman had the hots for her and never dug deep enough to reveal the charade. He hasn't shown his face since Friday. Rumor is, his head will roll too."

I shook my head in disbelief. "Where's she gone to?"

"She cleared the rest of her stuff out around noon today. Last I saw of her, she looked terribly hungover and then disappeared in a whirl of paper and boxes."

I shook my head at the memory of her plastered at O'Doran's. She must have felt her life was shattered, and when she came on to me, I'd rejected her. Had to have been one hell of a hangover.

"Hard to believe," I said.

"You'll evidently read about it in Tarentino's column tomorrow," he said.

"I didn't know her that well," I said. "But she had this thing about having to reinvent herself as an author. Looks like she took it too far. A shame. I was hoping she'd be here to help me."

"With what?" Erickson asked.

"I'm trying to track down a specific religion."

"Well, my field's comparative religion. Maybe I can help, Sergeant. Come in."

The religion professor's office was a veritable bazaar of books, files, framed photographs of himself—most of them younger, slimmer, and with more hair—in various far-flung locales; and artwork from those travels: ebony carvings of African women in wedding headdresses, a collection of jade Buddha statues, ceremonial pipes, bronze fertility gods from three continents, Tibetan mandalas, and three brilliantly colored canvases he said were painted by Mexican shamans during peyote hallucinations.

Erickson sat in an overstuffed chair while I paced, filling him in on the pertinent details of the killings that had not been covered in the press, especially the two biblical quotations left on the mirrors and my belief that they were somehow linked through the dogma of a specific religion or sect.

After I'd finished, I faced him. "So am I on to something or grasping at straws?"

Erickson remained silent for several moments, his chin resting on his thumbs, the rest of his fingers teepeed up around his nose. Then he looked up at me. "The first message does not support your thesis; you must suspect that, right?"

There's no reference to 'joy unspeakable,' et cetera, in the Bible that we know of. At least, that's what Susan Dahoney said."

"She wasn't making that up," Erickson agreed. "But the other two, taken in conjunction..."

He stopped in mid-sentence, got up from behind his desk, and crossed behind me to one of a dozen bookcases that lined the walls, all bulging with texts, journals, and manila file folders. He ran his hands along the exposed sheaves of an entire shelf of pregnant portfolios, then tugged one out and fished through it.

"Ah, yes," he said at last. "I think this is what you're looking for, Sergeant."

Erickson dropped a glossy black-and-white photograph in my lap. In it, a severe man with a face like rough granite stood on a wood-plank floor before a makeshift altar. A simple wooden cross hung from a wall behind him. He wore a starched white shirt buttoned to the neck, black pants, and hobnailed boots, and stared wide-eyed and lovingly at an angry rattlesnake that writhed in his hands. All around him, similarly dressed men and plain-looking women in sacklike, floral-print dresses held their hands high in the air. Many of them bore expressions I could only describe as rapture.

"Your killer probably is or was a member of one of the various Appalachian snake-handling churches," Erickson said. "The churches are all part of a loosely formed sect of Pentecostalism called the Holiness movement. Holiness people drink strychnine and handle rattlesnakes in their services. Saint Paul holds a special place in their hearts because he was bitten by the viper and did not die. They see justification for their activities in chapter sixteen of the Gospel according to Mark. Frankly, I'm surprised Dahoney didn't place any of this."

"Holiness churches…" I began, then stopped. "Why do you think she should have seen the connections?"

"She was raised a Pentecostal in West Virginia," Erickson said, sitting down again. "That's northern Appalachia. Now, Holiness laid down its strongest roots from Kentucky on south, but still, I would have thought she'd made the connection."

I thought about that, then shrugged it off and looked down at the book again. "Tell me about these Holiness people—everything you think I should know."

Erickson and I talked late into the evening. Despite his bizarre appearance, the professor was an intellectual whirlwind with a remarkable memory. If he was murky on specific details, he'd dash about his office, pulling down articles and books for me to see. The gist of it all was that ancestors of modern Holiness believers were pioneering Christian settlers who in the late 1700's pushed into the hollows of the Carolinas, southern Kentucky, eastern Tennessee, and the hills of Georgia and Alabama.

For two centuries their descendants lived isolated, hardscrabble, agrarian lives defined by physical labor, sleep, and prayer. They dressed soberly, swore off alcohol, tobacco, jewelry, and makeup, and called their culture of strict beliefs "Holiness."

But by the turn of the twentieth century, the Holiness way of life was under attack. Adherents lost their lands and had to seek work in mills and mines, on construction sites, and in the commercial areas of the larger southern cities. Not surprisingly, many of them abandoned the strict ways of their forefathers and succumbed to the odiousness of the modern world: gin and whiskey, music, dancing, cinema, cigarettes, poker, adultery, whores, and, worst of all, homosexuality.

"For many descendants of the original Holiness people, the flourishing of homosexuality among their brethren was the final proof they were living in a modern Sodom and Gomorrah," Erickson said.

In response, he went on, many of them returned to the hills and the things that had protected them for nearly two hundred years from the vulgar, wicked currents of American life: the Scriptures, the plain wooden churches, and a relatively new method of Holiness worship—the handling of serpents.

"That didn't start until roughly 1910," Erickson recalled. "Some Holiness preachers looked to the final chapter of Mark as their instruction to a new way of seeking the approval of God. From the beginning of time, in many cultures and religions, snakes have been perceived as evil. But to the Holiness preachers, the poisonous snake was more than the symbol of baseness: It was modern life given form, Satan given form. So, in their ceremonies, handling rattlesnakes or drinking strychnine is a symbolic defeat of the hellish ways of modern society."

I thought about that awhile. "So here the killer handles the snake without incident, becomes a God, as the Book of Acts puts it, but his victim dies. They're not worthy and he is. Isn't that what he's saying?"

Erickson screwed up his face in disgust, but nodded. "At some level, certainly. Horrible how religion can twist a man like that, isn't it?"

It was almost eleven by the time I got back to the *Nomad's Chant*. Fog hung over the docks like a damp curtain. In the distance, I could hear the donging of the channel buoys. I got on board, checked my machine, and found four messages.

The first was from Dick Holloway, the Internal Affairs officer assigned to review the fatal shooting of Olo Buntz, the Samoan who'd tried to shotgun Sheriff's Deputy Harold Champion to death out at Bigg Ja's meth ranch. He wanted me to know it looked like a righteous shoot, and I breathed a sigh of relief until he said he would continue to investigate the high-speed chase.

The second message was from Christina, inviting me to dinner. The third was from Don Stetson, telling me the team had lost. The fourth call was from Jorge, saying we'd gotten a hit on the ViCAP, but Fraiser had put it on the back burner.

I puffed my cheeks out, got a beer from the fridge, then dialed Jorge's number at headquarters, got no answer, then tried him at home.

"Where you been, Boss?" he asked.

"Out and about," I said. "What's this about a ViCAP response?"

"Minor blip, at least according to The Prick," he said.

"Specifics, Jorge, not Fraiser's take on them."

"We got a faxed reply this morning from an Officer Carlton Lee with the Hattiesburg,

Alabama, police force," Jorge began. "Said he had a case we might be interested in, involving...hold on a second, I got some notes somewhere. Okay, here they are. Preacher named Lucas Stark tortured and killed his wife, Ada Mae, by tying her to a bed and releasing a rattler on her, back in 1976."

"That's all the reply said?"

"That's the bones of it," Jorge said. "I can get you a copy if you need it. But anyway, I tried to call Officer Lee, looking to flesh out the details. Got the chief of police there in Hattiesburg instead. Nelson Carruthers. Nasty old cracker. Said Lee's the Barney Fife type, always looking to prove he could make it in the big leagues, and there's no way that murder is connected to our killings."

"He give you any reason for feeling that way?" I asked.

"Several," Jorge replied. "Victim's the wrong gender, first off. Second, it happened two thousand miles away, twenty-seven years ago. He said the slaying was a crime of passion, not premeditation. Seems Mrs. Stark was engaged in an adulterous relationship; her husband found out, flipped, and grabbed the closest weapon he could."

"A snake?"

"Right," Jorge said.

"Some passion," I said. "Where's this Lucas Stark now?"

"Dead. Shot trying to escape custody."

"You said Stark was a preacher," I said, thinking about everything Professor Erickson had told me. "The police chief say what denomination?"

"Some kind of Pentecostalist, I think."

I gripped the phone, closed my eyes, and prayed for luck. "He mention the word *Holiness*, Jorge?"

There was a long pause. "Yeah, he may have used that word, Sarge."

"And Fraiser thinks there's nothing to it?"

"He called up Carruthers himself, heard the same take I did, then tossed the report in a file and called it a dead end."

"We didn't have this conversation, Jorge."

"You think there's something to this?"

"Worth checking out in person."

"You going to Alabama?"

"Soon as I can get on a plane."

FIFTY-SEVEN

I caught a delta red-eye out of San Diego the following evening, changed planes in Dallas, and landed in Atlanta at seven o'clock Friday morning. Three hours later, I boarded a short-hopper bound for Chattanooga, Tennessee, the closest city I could get to Hattiesburg on such short notice.

It had rained during the night. The clouds were still gunmetal above the wings of the turbo-prop. The landscape below unfolded in spring lime pastures that gave way to ploughed fields and then to the woods and steep ridges of the Great Smoky Mountains jutting out of the racing clouds like the glistening black-olive skin of the mamba.

At that point I was still not sure exactly why I'd decided to travel all the way to Alabama on my own dime. As Jorge had said, the crime was twenty-seven years old, had been committed against a person of the wrong gender, and occurred a country away from San Diego. Moreover, the local authorities said it was a crime of passion. At best, a part of me argued, this was a fishing expedition. But the Holiness connection seemed worth checking out. At the very least, I told myself, I might come to know better the mind of the killer.

I had passed Thursday getting my affairs in order. Jimmy was crestfallen when I went to Fay's to say I had to go to Alabama on short notice and could not have him on the boat for the weekend. But surprisingly, Fay was understanding once I told her it was all in an effort to restore my tarnished reputation.

"Be careful, Shay," she said before I left. "Jimmy needs his father."

"I'm going to Alabama, not Afghanistan," I said.

"Just the same," Fay said; then she pressed into my hands a black oblong box that looked like it should carry sunglasses.

"What's this?" I said, opening it.

"Two vials of polyvalent rattlesnake antivenin and a hypodermic needle," she said. "Gift from Walter."

I picked up one of the vials and looked at it. "Smart guy, Walter."

"Yes, he is."

We touched down in Chattanooga just before noon. Light rain fell. The air was warm and sticky as honey. I retrieved my bags, including a locked metal case containing my backup nine millimeter, and rented a blue Dodge Neon from Budget.

I got coffee and drove southwest, roughly paralleling the Tennessee River toward Alabama. Swollen by the falling rain, the river ran silty, with swirling eddies that gnawed at crumbling muddy banks. North of Scottsboro, a hawk lifted off from the reedy shallows of the river and flapped across the highway over my car, clutching a bleeding white-bellied bass in its talons.

I left the main highway near Scottsboro and navigated west through Woodville and Paint Rock, then eventually north again into what looked like more heavily timbered terrain. By two that afternoon, I found myself traveling a windy, rough road through foggy hogback country: sheer-sided, shaley ridges covered in hawthorn, scrub pine, hickory, and beech.

It was thundering, lightning, and the wind howling by the time the two-lane changed to gravel on Ayer's Ridge Road, and I passed through a gap in the mountains. The foliage that hemmed the road below the crest became quilted with thorn vine and broadleaf kudzu, dense, damn near impenetrable, claustrophobic as a cave, and I had the unnerving sensation that I was spiraling into the end of something.

My wipers slapped crazily against the film of water and ragged bits of vegetation that splattered the windshield as I negotiated a series of switchbacks. Here and there, through the fog, the rain, and openings in the trees, I could make out pale gray cliffs looming over a narrow valley floor, and then the peaks of scattered farmsteads. At last the road leveled and ran west along the banks of a river called the Washoo. I crossed an arched bridge that spanned the river. Three boys stood in the rain, fishing off the bridge with cane poles. All of them turned to watch me with stony glares, and soon I emerged into the municipality of Hattiesburg, Alabama, population 665.

There were none of the common landmarks that have turned most of America into one great homogenized commercial glop: no 7-Eleven gas station, no Wal-Mart, no Osco Drug, no McDonald's or Burger King or Wendy's. Instead, I was greeted with a score of redbrick and white clapboard buildings sorely in need of repointing and repainting, all gathered around a sorry square of diseased grass, in the middle of which stood a cracked stone statue of a Confederate soldier.

The windows of roughly half the fifty storefronts were soaped over. At the north end of the square, where a civic building like a courthouse or a town hall should have stood, there were the remnants of a foundation choked by weeds. On the square's south side, there was a Laundromat, two variety stores, a used clothing shop, a Christian bookstore, the Washoo Arms Hotel, and a dimly lit diner called the Miss Hattiesburg.

I parked, peered out into the rain, and immediately felt conspicuous: The rental car was by far the newest vehicle on the square. The rest were all ten and fifteen years old, dented trucks and sedans with sagging springs and bald tires. I got out, grabbed my luggage from the trunk, and hustled up the stairs to the hotel porch. Two older men, one black, one white, both of them clad in faded canvas overalls, white T-shirts, and John Deere caps, watched me silently. I nodded. They did not nod back.

I opened the door to the Washoo Arms, entered, and found myself on a tan carpet so threadbare I could see the old floorboards through the bottom. A pinched woman in her early fifties with long brown-gray hair gathered in a bun at the back of her head sat behind a front desk and the sort of metal grille you see in old banks in black-and-white gangster films. "Hep you?" she asked.

"Need a room."

"Y'all from 'round here?" she said, rising slowly to her feet.

"No, ma'am. California."

If it was possible, she became even more pinched. "Never been there. Never want to," she said. "Land a wickedness."

"It's an acquired taste," I said agreeably. "Do you have rooms for rent or should I look elsewhere in town?"

"Washoo's only place in Hattiesburg to stay these days," she said, plucking up a white registration card. "We got singles with queens. How many nights?"

"I'll pay for two, then let you know."

She didn't seem to like that, but pushed the registration card through the portal in the grille anyway. I filled it out, putting down *San Diego Police Department* in the space labeled BUSINESS AFFILIATION.

"Come all the way to Hattiesburg on official business, did you?" she asked archly, sliding a skeleton-style key across the desk.

"Semiofficial," I said, taking the key. "Have a nice day, now."

I went up a creaking staircase to a hallway lit by a bare bulb and found the door marked 203. I set the key in the lock, twisted it, and opened the door to a clean but austere room: a queen-size bed with aged spring coils and a mushy mattress; a night table with a tarnished brass lamp, a black rotary phone, a phone book, and a Gideon Bible in the drawer; faded curtains featuring leaping trout; two ladder-back chairs and a folding table; and a bathroom with a claw-foot tub, a deep porcelain sink, and a water closet with a chain pull.

I wanted to lie down for a snooze, but it was nearly four in the afternoon by then and I wanted to get something accomplished. Besides, Hattiesburg was assuredly one of the most depressing and unfriendly villages I'd ever seen. It was one of those places that has its own pressure, which had been steadily settling in around my temples since I'd driven across the bridge into town.

I showered, shaved, changed my shirt, put on a tie and leather loafers instead of my normal running shoes, and almost donned my shoulder holster, then thought better of it and slid the pistol into the rear waistband of my slacks. From my briefcase I got out a notebook and a pen, then locked the room and went down the stairs. Miss Congeniality remained on sentry duty behind the grille, flipping through the *Weekly World News.*

"Sorry to interrupt your reading of the journal of wickedness," I said, gesturing at the tabloid. "Can you tell me where I'd find the police station?"

Miss Congeniality startled, reddened, and looked up from the tabloid just as the front door to the hotel swung open and shut behind me. Then a gruff, drawling voice said, "Won't be necessary to give him directions, Belle."

I turned to find a wild boar of a man stomping across the lobby toward me. He was in his late sixties, nearly as tall as me, with humped shoulders that disappeared into a jowly face with almost no transition of neck. His hair was silver and bristled. His angry, probing eyes were like chunks of topaz set in pools of sanguine fluid. He wore a dripping clear plastic rain slicker through which I could see a gray uniform with a star pinned to his chest. Plastic also encased his navy blue trooper-style hat.

"Chief Nelson Carruthers," he said without a trace of warmth or welcome. "Nice a you to call ahead, tell me y'all coming. That's the normal proceedure when requesting aid from a fellow law enforcement agency, is it not, sir?"

He was now inches from me. His teeth were coffee yellow. His breath smelled of Juicy Fruit gum and bourbon. He glared up at me with rheumy eyes. "But I guess y'all figured we didn't warrant that kind of consideration, seeing as how we're just the law in East Jesus, Alabama and you bein' a big shot dee-tective from Cal-eefornia."

"It's not like that at all, Chief Carruthers," I said. "Please, I should have—"

"Don't backpedal on me, boy," he said. "Show some spine. Badge and identification, if you please?"

I retrieved my wallet, got out an old laminated photo ID card that identified me as a sergeant with the SDPD, and handed it to him. That's when I noticed the backs of his hands, leathery and speckled with black, raised scars that looked like so many peppercorns spilled from a mill. Carruthers glanced at the ID, then back up at me.

"Where's your badge, Sergeant Moynihan?"

"I'm not here on an official basis, Chief."

"That so?" he replied, half closing one eye. "And why might that be?"

"Because my lieutenant doesn't seem to think there's any reason to be here."

"Smart man, sounds like, your lieutenant," Carruthers said. "A man who listens closely when a fellow law enforcement official tells him there's no reason to come all the way to Hattiesburg, Alabama, 'bout a case that's been dead and gone twenty-seven years. But you come anyway. You either stubborn or dumb, boy."

"Been called both in my time," I said, trying hard to not get angry.

"Bet you have," Carruthers said. He gave a forced laugh, then poked me high on the left side

371

of my chest, and I realized he was looking to see if I was carrying a weapon. "Y'all got a license to private investigate in the state of Alabama, Moynihan?"

"No, sir."

"Thought not," he said. Then he washed his spotted hands together. "Now, since you are not here on an offic-ee-al basis, coordinated through the correct lee-gal channels, and you don't have the requisite license to private investigate he-uh in Alabama, I suggest you go get your bags and get your great big bee-hind on out of my town."

He stood there, waiting for me to retreat, but I did not. Chief Carruthers reminded me of Lieutenant Fraiser, and I knew how to handle this type of bully. "Since I'm not here on an official basis and don't have a license to private investigate, perhaps I'll just act the tourist, take in the sights of Hattiesburg, learn a little more about the history of your fair hamlet," I said, mustering a sweet smile.

Carruthers' face turned to stone. "You don't wanna be mockin' me, boy."

"And you don't want to be threatening me for no good reason, Chief," I said. "Makes me think you got something to hide."

He crossed his arms and closed his eye halfway again. "Got nothing to hide, Moynihan. There's just no way the tragedy that happened here almost three decades ago is connected to them killings out your way."

"Says you," I said.

"Damn right, says me," he replied. "Your boy called me asking what I know about Lucas Stark, and I was helpful. Now you come sneaking in here behind my back. You're getting no help from my police force, understand? You broke the rules."

"And I apologize," I said. "I could use your help, but if I can't get it, I still believe we live in a free country, even here in Alabama. So I'll go about my business and stay out of your way. Fair?"

I stuck out my hand, but Carruthers did not take it. He just stared at me a moment, his face turning so red I thought it might erupt. Then he raised his fist toward the sky.

"Can't let it alone, can you?" he bellowed.

A choking noise sounded in his throat, and he turned even redder before stomping out the front door of the Washoo Arms, off the porch, and into the storm.

FIFTY-EIGHT

According to the scant information Officer Carlton Lee had included in the response to our ViCAP alert, Lucas Stark murdered his wife, Ada, with an eastern diamondback rattler over the course of two days, April 29 and 30, 1976. Beyond those scant facts, however, I knew little about what had occurred in Hattiesburg during those forty-eight hours almost twenty-seven years earlier. And I set out into the rain after Carruthers left to try to learn more.

My first course of action was to find the records related to the case. The Hattiesburg Municipal Court was housed in a red brick antebellum structure directly adjacent to a squat building with rusting iron bars in the windows and a sign out front that said HATTIESBURG POLICE DEPARTMENT AND JAIL.

The clerk's office occupied the end of a wooden-floored hallway in the courthouse. Parnell Jones, a nervous little man in his early forties with a ducktail haircut, black bow-tie, and suspenders, seemed to have been warned of my possible coming: He greeted me like a long-lost carrier of typhoid. When I asked how I might track down the files concerning Ada Mae Stark's death, he told me that would be "nigh to impossible." Prior to 1977, the county offices, county superior court, and city hall had all been housed in a single large wooden building that had stood at the north end of the square. In February of that year, the building burned to the ground.

"Faulty wiring?" I asked.

"Arson," Parnell Jones replied.

"So there are no records at all?" I said. "No marriage or birth records?"

"Nothing," Jones said with no trace of emotion. "Everything burned that night. I don't even have my own birth certificate."

"What about the local newspaper?" I asked.

"*Hattiesburg Herald* folded eight years ago," he said. "Everyone gets the *Scottsboro Daily Sentinel* now."

"They cover the case?"

He shrugged. "Don't exactly remember."

"Hattiesburg have a library?" I asked.

"Right across the square," he said. "Closes in half an hour."

With the notebook over my head, I jogged through the rain along the sidewalk, dodging the few pedestrians, weary people who hid under dark umbrellas. I slowed as I came to the empty lot where the county courthouse had once been. Fragments of the building's foundation showed through the weeds. It began to rain harder. I left the empty lot and sprinted toward the Hattiesburg Public Library, a white clapboard building on the northeast corner of the town square. The front door was made for someone much shorter than me. I had to duck to get through it and came into a low-ceiling room lined with bookcases set around a single long trestle table stained in dark oak. Two teenagers sat at the tables, working on homework.

Beyond the tables stood a check-out counter manned by a woman in her late forties with an angular face devoid of makeup, unplucked eyebrows, and a sparse mustache. But it was the hair you noticed first: Uncut, probably never cut, it ran all the way to the waist of her ankle-length gingham dress. The nameplate on the lapel of the dress read, DARLENE WINTERRIDGE.

"You the librarian?" I asked.

"Last time I looked," she said.

"I'm looking for microfilm of the *Hattiesburg Herald* or the *Scottsboro Daily Sentinel.*"

"Got 'em both," she said, nodding and gesturing for me to follow her through an arch at the back of the reading room into an alcove that held a microfilm reading machine and several steel cabinets. "What dates are you looking for?" she asked.

"May, 1976."

Winterridge's features turned rigid. "We've been missing April '76 through February '77 ever since I came to work here."

"The microfilm on both papers?" I asked doubtfully.

"That's right," she said. "You'll certainly be able to find the *Daily Sentinel* microfilm over in Scottsboro, but their library closes for the weekend. Try Monday. It's about sixty miles. Hour-and-a-half drive."

She made to turn as if the matter was closed, but I said, "Ms. Winterridge, why do I get the feeling no one wants to remember what happened to Ada Mae Stark?"

She hesitated, not looking at me. " 'Cause some things are best forgotten."

"Do you know what happened? No one will tell me anything."

She shrugged, though there was a hint of pain in her nonchalance. "Decent man went insane, succumbed again to calamity," she said. "He killed his wife to take her from Satan's clutches, only by doing so he took up with the Dark One himself."

"Who shot Lucas Stark when he was trying to escape?"

"Chief Carruthers," she replied. "Only he wasn't chief back then. Way I see it, the chief did Lucas Stark a favor. Put him out of his misery. That's all I'll say."

"Isn't there anybody left from that time who'll talk to me?"

"It's something we've worked hard to put out of our minds, sir," she replied coldly. "Go on over to Scottsboro Monday morning. Read what the papers said and you might get a sense of it. But no one here wants to talk about Lucas Stark anymore. Besides, there's no one alive knows the whole story, you ask me."

"Chief Carruthers must."

"Well, go talk to him, then."

"He says he won't help me."

"There you go."

She was about to walk away again, but I caught her by the elbow. "What about the house where it happened? Is that gone too?"

For an instant her eyes flickered with something you don't see very often, even in my line of work: terror. Then she composed herself and said, "No, the house still stands."

Cell phone reception was lousy in Hattiesburg and I had to return to the Washoo Arms to use the black rotary phone in my room. I called the police station first, disguising my voice in case Carruthers answered. The dispatcher, a woman, picked up the phone. I asked for Officer Carlton Lee and was told it was his day off.

Officer Lee's number was listed in the phone book and I picked up the receiver again, only to hear a hollow hiss that had not been there during the call to the police station. I flashed on the weird image of Miss Congeniality at the front desk, flipping through the *Weekly World News,* listening in on my conversation. I hung up, looked at the address, then at the map on the inside cover, and figured out the approximate location of Officer Lee's residence.

He lived northwest of Hattiesburg, on a dirt road that ran perpendicular to the Washoo River.

It was farmland mostly, with some row crops just sprouting. The rain had not relented a bit by the time I found his driveway. A thicket of pines opened into a tidy yard dominated by a small blue ranch house set behind a white picket fence. A hand-built swing-set stood in the front yard next to a sandbox. An old Ford Fairlane rested on cinder blocks in the driveway.

I got out, rushed up to the front porch, and rang the bell. I heard a child inside yell, "Mommy, they's a man at the door!"

Presently, the door opened a shade to reveal a pretty black woman in her early thirties. She held a baby who sucked on a pacifier. A lighter-skinned boy about three wearing a NASCAR T-shirt and Barney underwear clung to the hem of her yellow shift.

"Yes?" she said, looking at me with more than a trace of suspicion.

"I'm looking for Carlton Lee," I said.

"Whatchew want with Carlton?" she asked.

"I'm a detective from San Diego," I said, holding out the old identification. "He sent us a message, said he might be able to help us with a big murder case we got going."

Now her suspicion gelled. "Chief Carruthers called 'bout you," she said icily. "Told Carlton not to talk, if'n he knows what's good for him. Said you didn't play by the rules, you don't get any help."

"Figured as much," I said. "But I came a long way to see your husband. I spent my own money to come talk to him."

"We don't want no trouble," she said. "And I'm sorry for your sacrifice, but Carlton needs the job. Why don't y'all go on home, Mr. Moynihan. Leave us be."

"Two thousand miles is an awful long way to come to just go home."

"I know. But that's the way it is."

She made to shut the door. I held out my hand and stopped her. "Can you at least tell me where it happened—the house, I mean?"

Lee's wife hesitated, fear briefly passing across her face, then she pointed up toward the ridge and the limestone cliffs that loomed out of the foggy rain over the valley.

"Up there," she said. "Go a mile past the last house, up onto the plateau below the cliff out there before the church. Look for the old driveway that cuts below the mountaintop."

FIFTY-NINE

As i backed down Lee's driveway I almost decided to pack it in, to leave them all be with their secrets. And while I was at it, to say the hell with the killings back in San Diego too. Leave the whole mess and take off for sunnier climates. But Carruthers was right about one thing: I can be one dumb, stubborn man.

It took me a while to figure out which road led up to the ridge, but I found it as the rain stopped and the sun, already close to setting, filtered through the breaking clouds, turning the light in the woods the color of apricot. Here on the northern outskirts of Hattiesburg, on that tattered ribbon of switchback road, the dwellings were all busted-down trailers and shacks, their yards strewn with rusted washing machines, relic television sets, and the hulks of abandoned automobiles. Then there were no homes at all for nearly a mile as the road climbed, hugging the wall of the ridge, twisting back on itself before cresting onto a plateau two hundred yards wide and four times again as long. I almost missed the turnoff.

It was less a driveway than an overgrown two-track that disappeared into the rear of the plateau. I cursed the fact I was driving a sedan with about eight inches of clearance, then chanced it, easing the Neon up the muddy trail. Poplar branches tangled with kudzu sloughed on the hood and scratched the paint. Fifty yards off the ridge road, my oil pan whined against rock and I decided it was prudent to walk the rest of the way.

It was shadowy and dripping in the forest that late in the day. No birds called. No animals rustled in the undergrowth. There was just that steady dripping and the soft slapping of wet leaves in the breeze that carried the rain clouds northeast. My loafers slipped on the slick grass and mud, and I had to grab branches and vines to keep from falling. But the way kept bending back toward the limestone cliffs, and I followed.

My thoughts were all over the place, leaping from the annoying reality that no one in the town would talk to me, to the fact that Ada Mae and Lucas Stark had probably driven or walked this driveway hundreds of times. I found myself going slower, looking at it all, trying to understand. At last I came to an opening. A man-made opening.

The kudzu should have long ago swallowed the place. But machetes had been used recently to hack back the vines. The perimeter hedge was dappled with the cut marks. Glass bottles hung by thin wires from the branches of trees that hemmed the clearing, perhaps a hundred bottles in all, Coca-Cola and Pepsi, Dr Pepper, Fanta, and Mountain Dew. I learned later that these were called "spirit trees."

In rural Alabama, people hang colored bottles in trees to capture evil. But the people of Hattiesburg had taken the practice one step further: They hung the bottles as razor wire and hacked back the forest as a prison guard might the brush outside his walls.

The tin roof of the old house was caved in by an uprooted Osage orange tree that must have toppled in the gale of a long-ago winter storm. Slivers of tar paper clung to the flat slats of the wall. Shards of jagged glass, like the teeth of some crystalline beast, protruded from the upper sills of all that was left of the window frames. The front door hung off its lower hinge at an impossible angle. Moss grew up the baseboard of the fractured porch. Beyond the house stood a shed and then an outhouse sprawled on its side. Mushrooms grew from the flank of the outhouse, and I understood that the clearing rarely saw direct sunlight.

But at that moment, sunlight came to the clearing below the cliff. These were the last strong rays before sunset, and they shone warm and apricot down through the mist that lingered in the trees, bussed the ground, and ran out toward the shed. For some reason I followed the light out into a grove of stunted dogwoods that surrounded an old pecan tree and the shed at the back of the house.

Gardening is Fay's passion, and I was married to her long enough to learn a bit about trees and shrubs. I would have figured that most species of flowering timber this far south were done budding and showing blossoms. But to my surprise a handful of wet pink petals shone on the dogwoods, and a whiter flower on the pecan. As I walked toward the open door to the shed and looked inside, the last sun of the day hit the droplets that clung to those petals.

A jumble of soup cans, whiskey bottles, busted plates, and rusted-shut mason jars littered the floor. The top of a wire-lidded wooden box showed through moldering leaves. I squatted and picked up several of the mason jars, seeing jumbles of screws and nails, in another washers, and in a third cobwebs and mummified cocoons. I set these down and tugged out the box from the leaf pile, stood, turned, and held it out to the last light of day.

The box revealed itself as more of a cage with a rusted iron hasp that held the wire lid shut. Strips of rotting leather formed hinges at the back. Inside, on the bottom of the box, something pale showed. I squinted, turned the box at an angle, brought my head closer, then jerked back. The skeleton of a viper rattled in my trembling hands, and I sucked in so hard I almost dropped the little crate. I took another deep breath. My nostrils flared and sniffed at the air in disbelief.

I do not know how the smell did not register with me during the hike into the woods. Or even when I'd first emerged into the clearing. Perhaps it was not there in its full intensity until the late-day sun had invaded the place, striking the moist ground, heating the droplets clinging to the leaves and blossoms of the pecan and dogwood, sending the odd mélange of molecules whirling through the air that surrounded the collapsed house where Lucas Stark killed his wife twenty-seven years before.

But there it was, and its presence shook me to my core.

It was the aroma of the spring woods in the evening after a rainstorm, wet bark, pine needles, and black soil, the forest all clean and direct, combined with the subtle fragrance of dogwood and pecan blooming and the heady pungency of leather, all of it lightly underscored by the muskiness of freshly turned leaves.

"Southern Nights cologne," I said.

SIXTY

I now felt certain that whoever had tortured and slain Morgan Cook, Matthew Haines, and John Sprouls a world away in San Diego had at one time been in this Alabama clearing, on an evening just like this one, in the springtime when the rain stopped late in the afternoon and the last rays of the sun struck and warmed the droplets, releasing into the twilight a sense memory of cold-blooded killing.

But I needed to be able to prove beyond my own say-so that the clearing in the woods in Hattiesburg smelled like Southern Nights cologne, so I set the box down and scooped up leaves from the shed, bunches of grass, and pieces of kudzu leaf. Then I cut off blossoms from the dogwood and the pecan and, with my knife, dug out a chunk of wet bark from the trunk of a burly white pine. I stripped bark and leaves from the Osage orange and the magnolia too. After putting it all inside the crate with the snake bones, I started back toward the Neon.

The sky turned magenta with purple streaks. The woods darkened as the moon, a fingernail shy of full, rose and sent forth pale horizontal light. The trees threw wan red shadows that crisscrossed the clearing. The hundred spirit-catcher bottles caught the light and refracted a dull rainbow of glows. It was creepy, and I was suddenly exhausted.

I hurried toward the road, tugging my cell phone from my pocket. No service. I decided to go back down to the Washoo Arms, call Rikko and Christina, tell them about Hattiesburg and what I'd smelled in the clearing on the ridge, and also to warn them that I had to stay at least through Monday in order to get the full story out of the Scottsboro Public Library because no one here was talking.

I reached the Neon just as the sun disappeared and the woods fell fully under the moon's light. I put the box in the trunk, praying that others would smell the things I'd gathered and agree that the murders in San Diego and the slaying of Ada Mae Stark were connected. I was climbing into the car, thinking about where I would eat and if I should call Jimmy before sleeping. Then the music began and changed everything.

It came from off to my east, well beyond the clearing, amplified over a brassy electronic sound system turned up too loud, a bizarre melding of Southside Chicago blues and electronic hillbilly. It opened up with a wailing guitar, then broke over into the rattle of tambourines, the melodic wail of a Dobro, the crash of cymbals, the blare of horns, and within it all the thumping of deep electronic basses and drums.

Then singing kicked in. Several of the voices, two male, one woman, belted out their verses into microphones with hoarse delivery. But behind them came a swelling of other throats, jumping from one twangy note to the next, all of it melting into the amplified instruments, then echoing out through the forest and off the cliffs.

It was the strangest music I had ever heard, and my first thought was to get away from it. But the melody had a high-energy soulful quality that was seductive. The raw excitement in the voices, rising with the thumping of the bass and the sudden frenzied playing of the high-note instruments, drew me out into the forest again. I stumbled back to the clearing, then ducked under the spirit catchers and clawed my way into the kudzu tangle. It was a maze in the moonlight as I picked my way over downed trees and through rock piles in the shadows, tearing through the vine.

At last I came over a small knoll thick with loblolly pines and squinted at strong light shining through a matrix of branches. I eased forward to the edge of the pines, hanging in the shadows, shaken by the scene unfolding before me.

The church sat in one of the most spectacular settings I've ever seen for a place of worship. Long before man trod the earth, a massive L-shaped chunk of limestone must have broken off the ridge above Hattiesburg and been swept into the valley floor. What remained at an elevation of twelve hundred feet was a semicircular shelf of exposed rock that cut back into the ridge perhaps seventy-five yards, where it then narrowed and met an eighty foot bulwark of concave limestone that made up the back wall of a broad grotto. Well-maintained paths led out to the cliff that fell away toward Hattiesburg. Another path led off to a makeshift playground and a parking lot in the woods on the other side of the shelf. At least fifty cars were parked there.

The church itself was nestled in the grotto, its rear wall not fifteen feet from the back of the cave. The building was rather small, no bigger than twenty by sixty, built on slab. Great care, however, had gone into the church's construction. The timber frame was handcut and assembled with mortise and tenon joints fashioned by master craftsmen. Circular-cut side planking and rough flooring had been laid over the frame, sanded, then rubbed with oil so that it threw off a warm patina.

The shake shingle roof gave way to a simple wooden cross on its peak, right over the gable that shielded the front door. Below the cross, in a modified horseshoe shape, hung a sign painted in forest green lettering that read: CHURCH OF JESUS, NEW TONGUES SINGING. A second sign hung within the arc of the first. It said: *Mark 16, v. 15–18.*

I'd stumbled onto Hattiesburg's Holiness Church.

Instead of windows, the church bore wooden shutters thrown open to the night breezes that crossed the cliff face. There were three I could look through from my vantage point in the pines.

Inside, a congregation of seventy people danced and sang:

> *Pale horse, pale horse, won't you ride on by?*
> *Our hearts are on fire, our eyes to the sky.*
> *We handle your dark reins,*
> *they're here in our hands*
> *Ride on pale horse, our Lord's in command.*

The benches were filled with clapping men with ducktail haircuts, plain white shirts, and dark pants; there were as many women, all dressed like Darlene Winterridge in ankle-length, flower-print dresses, a dozen of them pregnant, their hair hanging long and free at the waist or, if they were older women, braided, gathered and pinned in gray coils on their heads. The children, eighteen of them by my count, spun and sweated barefoot in the aisles. Some in the crowd held their hands high and swayed with the music. Parnell Jones, the clerk from the municipal court, shook a tambourine. Others were stomping their feet on the heavy plank flooring, singing in wavering voices:

> *Will fire surround you and make you pay*
> *For leaving the Savior 'til Judgement Day?*
> *The pale horse is coming he gallops through night*
> *The pale horse is coming: you better be right.*

The song wound down and stopped. The whole crowd hushed and stood panting, looking expectantly toward the very front of the church, which I could not see.

"I have been pasturing you in the Holiness way nigh on to twenty-eight years," a deep, gravelly, soothing voice called over the microphone.

The congregation clapped, amened, and held their hands overhead.

"We were a young church when I came to you, a church tested by temptation. It was on a night just like this one. He toyed with us, then exposed us to unspeakable filth and depravity."

To my astonishment, several of the women in the congregation suddenly broke down and sobbed as if in rank bereavement. And then, listening to it echo in my head, I realized that their music was built on chords of grief and remorse.

Perhaps it was the fatigue brought on by a day that had begun nearly twenty hours before, but I felt like I was in a trance, commanded to get closer. I crawled out along the bank toward a copse of ash trees that overlooked the last window. The crying slowed as I bellied ten yards over slick red soil, then pulled myself up so I could see through a notch in one of the tree trunks.

I don't know what I expected. But the preacher, who I later learned was called Brother Neal, was a slight man in his late fifties, with slicked-back silver hair, long, bony hands, and shoulders that hunched and rolled when he spoke. He stood there swaying to the sounds of the crying, standing on a stage made of split and peeled pine logs, holding a microphone attached to a black cord that ran back toward a minitower of speakers and amps. At the back, on the wall, another simple cross.

"Hush, my sisters," he said. "Hush, now. I know this hurts you. But sometimes you gotta hurt a little to heal."

At Brother Neal's feet were a half dozen boxes similar to the one back in the Neon's trunk. Beyond the preacher was the band, twelve members, all hanging on every pop and gesture in his swaying. Indeed, his movement and his gentle soothings whispered into the microphone had almost every else in the room hanging with him too: their joints loose, their muscles slack, their gaze hazily focused on Brother Neal, a plain-looking man, but one whom you couldn't help but watch, the way he quivered and held each note of the crying that lingered in the hall.

"Hush, my sisters," he said. "Hush, now."

Then he raised his hand high over his head, his eyes clenched tight. "It is important that we remember that we in the Church of Jesus, New Tongues Singing were tempted, but through our faith we managed to defeat Satan and avoid his clutches."

"Amen," many in the congregation murmured.

Sweat broke out on Brother Neal's concentrated brow as he went on: "It is important to remember that for twenty-seven years we have lived on the Lord's side. We have paid our dues. Done everything to be right with the Holy Ghost."

"Praise him," the congregation said.

"Now there is one among us who suffers greatly at this time of year from the wounds that were afflicted upon him during the fight with Satan," he said. "And now when he is grieving and sure that God has given up on him most plainly, I have learned there is a policeman from California in town, looking to dig up filth about Lucas Stark."

Brother Neal opened his eyes and looked gravely about the congregation. "Make no mistake about it: This is not just a policeman, Brothers, Sisters. It is him again in a different disguise. Tempting us. Trying to lure us into evil deeds. He is not done with you and he's not done with me. Not by a long shot. We defeated him, but oh, he wants the story of that temptation told and retold. Make no mistake about it, he gets what he wants just by describing his vulgar ways. He wants his story told and we can be no part of it, for telling his story only furthers his aims."

I ducked down, suddenly free of the moment. Lying in the humid darkness outside the church of a fundamentalist Christian sect in northeast Alabama, listening to their preacher portray me as an agent of hell, I thought I'd better get my ass out of there.

I was about to slip away, when I heard Brother Neal say, "So we make a decision not to open old wounds where Lucifer can lay his maggots down. So we decide that our sufferin's over and we move on after twenty-seven years."

I could not help myself. I lifted my head up again to watch. Brother Neal had clasped both hands about the microphone and now gazed over his flock. "Did you hear me, Brothers, Sisters?" he asked. "I'm saying that the time of suffering is over."

Dead silence held in the church. Members glanced at each other nervously. Then a plump woman with a shrill voice shook a tambourine over her head and called out, "Amen. Amen!"

Brother Neal looked to her and smiled. "Thank you, Sister Rose. I say it again to all of you, but especially to one. Your suffering is over. You have been punished enough. You have washed yourself free of sin. Now I know how it is. For twenty-seven years, on a night just like this one, we have been forced to remember even if we don't want to."

Several of the women and the men glanced over their shoulders at someone deep in the church, then began to openly weep. Several more people stood, closed their eyes, raised their hands, and called "Amen" over and over.

"We remember and that becomes our burden," Brother Neal said, closing his eyes, too, and raising his fingers toward heaven. "A burden we have carried such an awful long time. Enough, Lord. Enough. Lift it from us. Lift it."

"He won't lift it for all your praying!" a bellicose voice roared. "He makes it heavier. That's what he does! He's good at making you twist on the knife."

I recognized the speaker instantly and shifted to look around the base of the ash trees. Nelson Carruthers, the chief of police, stood there tight to the wall, ten rows back. He looked nothing like the man with the hint of corn liquor on his breath who'd crisply interrogated me at the Washoo Arms. His uniform shirt was open at the collar and pulled out at the waist. His tie hung askew. Great rings of sweat showed under his armpits and across his bunched shoulders. He was drunk and carried the booze poorly.

"Hush now, Brother Nelson," Brother Neal said. "Your sufferin's over."

"Never be over," Carruthers snarled. "Damned to hell I am."

A pewter-haired woman in a blue floral print dress stood up beside Carruthers and put her hand on his elbow. "C'mon now, Nelson," she said. "Don't talk like that. There's people love you here for everything you've done for them."

Carruthers looked at her wearily, then broke into scornful laughter. "Eileen, you still think you're blessed. But all you had to do was care for his spawn." He gestured with distaste beyond the woman at a man in his late twenties who bore the unmistakable soft and droopy features of Down's syndrome. The man cringed and looked toward the floor.

"Yeah, I'm talking 'bout you, ya retard," Carruthers slurred. His attention lingered on the man, then he hauled himself upright and threw a sweeping hand toward the congregation. "For him and for you, I'm damned and there's nothing 'bout love can change that."

He pushed by Eileen, ignored the man with Down's syndrome, then stormed out the front doors of the church. Carruthers stumbled, fell on the front lawn, then got back to his feet and ran toward the parking lot as if pursued by demons.

Several men made as if to go after him. But Brother Neal called to them: "Leave him go, Brothers. He has to suffer this alone, even if he suffers for us."

Out toward the parking lot, a car door slammed.

Brother Neal waited until the hubbub caused by Carruthers's leaving had settled. Then he said, "Hard, hard thing for Brother Nelson. Terrible burden. But as I've said, Brothers, Sisters, we can make the decision not to let our suffering go on."

"Amen," many in the congregation called out.

The preacher smiled. "We of the Church of Jesus, New Tongues Singing know from the Book of Acts that with God on our side, we let our suffering go."

"Amen!" the congregation yelled.

"We let it go because we know that if we are right with God—I say, if we are right with God—then no man and no beast may hurt us!"

A half dozen women in the crowd leaped to their feet, threw up their hands, and yelled, "Hallelujah!" Miss Congeniality from the hotel was one of them. So was Darlene Winterridge.

But their presence did not startle me as much as it should have because my thoughts were on the language these people were using. References to new tongues and the Acts of Saint Paul. It was all here in some shattered form, the deep roots of the killings in San Diego.

Brother Neal held up a finger, breaking me from my thoughts. He waved it like a sword in front of him. "Do you know something, Brothers, Sisters?"

"No, Brother Neal, tell us," several in the congregation yelled.

"I already know you're right with God, beyond suffering, resisting to temptation!" he shouted out, his eyes clenched tight. *"And you know how I know!"*

"How, Brother Neal?" more yelled, others clapping. "Tell us."

The preacher's eyes danced over the congregation as he lowered himself onto one knee behind the boxes. The crates had screen for sides, so you could see the contents' shadows. Brother Neal held his free hand loosely. The church went quiet. He wiped his knuckles slow and hard along the tops of the wooden crates on the altar like someone pulling a wooden striker across a bamboo xylophone.

All around the horseshoe, behind the screen walls, shadows rose and arched. The spring night air filled with the dry chortle of many snakes rattling as one. A surge of fear and enchantment pulsed through me. I pressed my cheeks tight against the bark of the ash tree, suddenly desperate to know what Brother Neal would do next.

The preacher held his hand palm down over the top of one box, as if to feel the breeze stirred by the snake's rapid percussion. His face flushed. He rolled his head toward heaven again. "Lord, we testify to your essential goodness here in this church," he said. "For twenty-seven years, since we fought your nemesis and brought him low, we have shown you with our words and our deeds that we are right with you. And we ask your complete forgiveness and an easing to the suffering some of us feel tonight."

Brother Neal's entire body shook with passion as he roared: "We are right with you, Lord, because we show you we are righteous. We show you we are touched by your tongues of fire and immune to the diseases of Satan. We show you we are right by handling death itself!"

Sixty-One

The congregation went as painfully still as Fenway Park had the night my arm shattered. Many members were up on their tiptoes to stare at the snake boxes. Then the bass player in the band started thumbing a slow but building rhythm. The lights inside the church were dimmed until the only illumination came from candles, two dozen of them set about the rough-hewn altar.

"Feel it," Brother Neal gently exhorted.

The bass notes thudded and reverberated through my chest as the gentle hissing of a wire brush against cymbals joined the bass notes and then the steady thump of the drum in a simple, catchy rising melody accompanied by Brother Neal's words: "Feel it growing like a fire come down from heaven to loosen your tongues and bear witness to his glory."

"Hallelujah!" the congregation chanted. The lead guitar joined and then the Dobro, echoing through the windows and off the walls of the grotto, pulsing all around me.

"Feel the Holy Ghost moving on you," the preacher shouted. "Gospel of Mark says, 'In my name shall they cast out Satan. In my name you shall take up new tongues.' New Tongues Singing. Feel the fire come to your lips, Brothers, Sisters. Feel it teach you words to describe your Lord in all his mysterious ways."

"Praise his holy name!" the crowd bellowed, and the entire band came in behind the drums and the bass, the guitar, the Dobro, and the dulcimer. Within seconds the place had been whipped into a frenzy. Many in the congregation were singing in that wavering style, while others went down on their knees with hands raised high and looks of pure delight on their faces. Still others took to prophesying and speaking in tongues. I saw Miss Congeniality marching back and forth in tight drill, two fingers raised as she babbled out incomprehensible testimony to her connection with her savior.

Then, within the chaos, without any visible prompting from Brother Neal, the level of worship ebbed and with that ebbing certain men and women filtered out from the main body of the congregation. They moved silently, inexorably forward, their faces rippling with emotions I could not recognize, but which struck me as electric and primal.

A woman about twenty-three reached the boxes first and went to her knees with auburn hair cascading around her lowered face and her arms outstretched to heaven. The crowd came in around her and laid their hands about her head.

"First time, Sister Alice?" Brother Neal asked.

"Yes," she replied, her hair still in her face.

"Let this be a good thing we can remember on a warm April night," he said.

"Help me, Jesus," she said.

"May you be right with the Lord, Sister Alice."

Sister Alice raised up her head in what I can only describe as an attitude of accepting subjugation. This utter giving-in radiated through her body. Brother Neal flipped open the box on the outside right of the horseshoe. He studied the contents, then reached in and came up holding a canebrake rattlesnake with mottled green skin.

The serpent writhed back on itself, searching for Brother Neal's forearms, then found it with a dart of its tongue. It did not rear to strike his flesh, but glided up onto the back of the preacher's hand. Brother Neal brought his arm up so the rattler's tongue flickered not a quarter inch from his own lips and stared into its eyes. Then he turned toward Sister Alice, his face hard with exertion, and he whispered in a hoarse voice, in the same way I'd heard Catholic priests deliver communion as a boy, "Joy unspeakable to be holding death in your hands."

"Joy unspeakable," Sister Alice said.

"Joy unspeakable," the congregation murmured.

I jerked and my eyes went wide as the power the scene had over me was shattered. "The message at Cook's apartment!" I whispered in disbelief.

The tambourines rattled. The bass came in again, low, throbbing like a heartbeat. Brother Neal draped the snake across Sister Alice's extended arms. For a moment she became like a pillar, no movement save the viper's. Which did not bite. Then she relaxed, shook, cried joyous tears, and watched the snake in her hands with a growing smile of conviction that said she had faced temptation, faced death, and been right with the Lord.

During the course of the riveting next half hour, twelve other handlers came forward and took up snakes. I watched deadly viper after deadly viper emerge from the box. I watched the faces of the handlers as they bared their souls, their heads dancing with anticipation, their flesh rippling with surges of what looked strangely pleasurable.

At last, the twelfth person handed back the rattler to Brother Neal, retreated, and was swallowed by the congregation. The band fell silent. Brother Neal searched the crowd and got no takers. His shoulders slumped and I felt this pang of irrational disappointment pulse through me at the idea that Brother Neal was about to conclude the snake handling ceremony.

Then I heard a bench push back, adjusted my position, and saw the woman who had comforted Chief Carruthers standing again. She took the hands of the man with Down's syndrome. He had a pear-shaped body and an amiable face. Under new denim overalls he wore a starched white shirt, buttoned at the collar. He was still looking at the floor, the way he had been ever since Carruthers had cursed him.

"C'mon, Caleb," she said.

He raised his head to look at her. He had this sad smile that carried its own sense of peace. Then I saw the quality of his eyes: scarred, bloodshot eyes that said they had seen terrible things. And I had the thought: *His eyes are just like mine.*

The woman leaned close to him and spoke. I have no idea what she said. But after that and another squeeze of his hands, Caleb rose and followed her without complaint. The bass guitar began to thump again. Brother Neal raised his hands. The woman stopped and urged Caleb forward. "Go on, now," she said.

Caleb smiled that sad smile at her again, then shuffled up a few feet and knelt. Half the congregation stood on their benches, hands raised out toward him. The music picked up pace again. Caleb started to rock side to side in time with the low beats. He shut his eyes, then rolled back his head and sang in gibberish, the melody wavering deep in his throat like the chorus of voices I'd heard first out in the woods. But Caleb's singing in tongues had clear ringing accents to it, as if ball-peen hammers were being struck against the wiggling saws of his vocal cords.

The band played harder. Caleb went with it, sweating, shuddering, and singing, his lower jaw trembling, controlling the pinging of his voice. Brother Neal went to the box dead center of the horseshoe. He opened it and for the first time used a snake hook to probe the crate. He came up with a four-foot black diamondback rattlesnake with a body so thick, the hook barely fit around it. The viper's head was alert, roaming, angry, its tail flexed and a-chatter.

"Joy unspeakable to be holding death in your hands," Brother Neal said.

"Joy unspeakable," Caleb said. He was a grown man, but his voice was a boy's.

Brother Neal looked at the woman. "Who do you love more, Sister Eileen?" he asked. "Your son or God?"

The old woman did not hesitate. "God," she said.

Caleb sang slower in a glottal keening separated at intervals of five seconds, like sonar sending signals through water. Brother Neal lay the angry snake on Caleb's outstretched forearms. Caleb did not look at it but kept his eyes half shut and focused as if into a distance. The snake spun, reared up, arched back, and opened its jaws. For a moment I could see the musculature in the upper quadrant of the snake poise to strike, and I was sure Caleb was going to get bit right in the face.

If Caleb noticed, he did not show it. He just kept singing and gently rocking as the snake lunged for him. The congregation gasped. But the snake veered off, snapped its mouth shut, and arched again, thrusting and displaying its belly along the soft edge of the invisible field that seemed to guard Caleb's face.

Over the course of the next five minutes, Brother Neal brought out an even larger rattler and placed it in Caleb's hand. And then a third, fourth, and fifth.

Caleb raised the five up high, his own head tilted back. The snakes coiled and spiraled in his hands, moving in syncopation with the sound of his keening, which became labored and involuntary, like a woman wailing in the throes of childbirth.

Brother Neal went to bring out a sixth snake, but Caleb's mother shook her head.

"He's done, Brother," she said. "Caleb'll sleep peaceful tonight, knowing he's right with the Lord."

"Amen," Brother Neal said. With the snake hook he took the rattlers one by one and hustled them into their boxes. Caleb slumped as if he'd done battle with many men. Two members of the congregation helped him wobble to his feet. His mother kissed him on the forehead. Then many in the church were reaching out to touch him, to give him a smile and an amen. I had the urge to touch him myself, and I can't say exactly why. Only that what I had witnessed was extraordinary, and this man, Caleb, had been its vessel.

I shook my head as if waking from an exhausting dream, realizing that for a while there I had completely lost myself in the snake handling. I felt like I had fallen through a crack in my own identity, where there was no past and no future, a crack where I was not me but a member of the Church of New Tongues Singing. Dizzy with this sense of dislocation and the lack of sleep, I decided to rest my head in the leaves until the church cleared; then I'd slip away back through the forest to the Neon. I eased myself down from the notch of the ash.

A figure eight of steel pressed into the nape of my neck and jammed my head against the smooth bark of the tree. I twisted against the pressure and found myself staring up the rib of a double-barreled shotgun held by Chief Nelson Carruthers.

SIXTY-TWO

"Y'all enjoying the freak show, Moynihan?" Carruthers asked in a drunken voice as cold as sleet.

He looked half insane, and I sprawled on my belly from the pressure of gun steel and threw up my hands. "Chief, don't shoot," I said. "I heard the music through the woods and I came to see what was going on. I meant no disrespect. Believe me."

"You come with no disrespect, why you laying in the dirt?" he asked, reaching down and plucking my pistol from my waist. "Only one thing slithers in the dirt, boy."

Carruthers eased up on the weight the shotgun muzzle was bearing on my neck, and, despite the cruelty of his tone, for a second there I thought he was going to let me stand up. Then I felt the shotgun travel down the side of my body, as if measuring it, then reach my lower back, where it stopped and probed. At the same time, he grabbed me by my collar and hauled me to my feet, the gun jammed in my right kidney.

"Moynihan, I am your savior right now, unner-stand?" he said. "You don't do anything I don't tell you to. You listen, he-uh?"

There are men for whom restraining others is an art form. Some, like Rikko, are commando-trained. Others work big city jails, more in state prisons. The best of them toil in the hard penitentiaries like Vacaville, Attica, and Pelican Bay. I'd known several maximum-security guards over the years and been taught the art of verbal and physical control by them and gotten pretty darn good at it myself.

But I had never been handled or bull-talked to by a man like Nelson Carruthers. Drunk as he was, angry as he was, he was like this coiled force that controlled me by understanding my precise balance points and triangulating off them with the gun and the hand that held my neck. He waltzed me down the bank, my back bent limbo-like, unable to see where I was going, a fraction of an inch from falling.

The moon hung high above the cliff now and I caught glimpses of it through the treetops as he moved me out on the grass in front of the church. He spun me around down on my knees, facing the church front door and the cross above it. The shot-gun returned to my neck. Then the congregation crowded in around me, stony and judgmental.

"Couldn't just listen to me and gone on out of he-uh, could you?" Carruthers said, coming around me from the back, the gun barrel following my col-larbone, then coming to rest at my biceps. I could see him now out of my peripheral vision, watching me the way the snake handlers had watched the rattlers during the service. "Coming to dig at the bones of Lucas Stark, are you? Or you coming for me? Is that who you coming for, big-city cop?"

"Chief, I don't what you're talking about," I said.

He leaned over me, the stench of whiskey on his breath. "Don't ya?" he asked. "Ya'all come here on a night like this and you don't think I know who you really are, come to tempt and taunt me?"

Sister Eileen, Caleb's mother, now pushed her way out of the crowd. "Nelson, put that gun down," she said. "Please."

He weaved ever so slightly, looking up at her from under hooded brows. "Satan's come to torment me, woman," he said. "And I'm showing him I'm right with the Lord by handling him. Can't you see?"

"Please, Nelson," she said in desperation as tears formed in her eyes. "No more."

He pushed the gun tighter against my neck. "You never listen to sermon, do you, Eileen?" he said. "According to Brother Neal, this man is looking to profit from our misery. He could be the agent of my doom itself!"

Immediately there were confused grumblings among the congregation. I looked around wildly at the faces—Darlene Winterridge, Miss Congeniality, and Parnell Jones—that made up the wall of the crowd gathered around us.

"I'm just a cop," I told them. "I'm working on three murders in San Diego and—"

"Shut up, you," Carruthers said. Then he got this inspired look on his drunken face and his eyes searched the crowd. "Brother Moynihan says he's not here to do us any harm. Why don't he prove it?" He laughed at that, then said, "You right with the Lord, Moynihan?"

"Please, I—"

"Shut up, you," he growled. *You right with the Lord?*"

"I don't know," I confessed.

He laughed at that too. "Well, you about to find out. That's the beauty of a handling ceremony, Moynihan: You find out right quick if God is on your side or not."

Carruthers looked around the crowd, weaving, then nodded at Parnell Jones. "You—go on, you heard me—go on up there into the church and bring him a snake."

Jones hesitated. "Brother Nelson, I—"

"Not Brother Nelson!" Carruthers roared in raw fury at the court clerk. "I'm Chief Carruthers, agent of justice in Hattiesburg. Go get me a snake!"

The clerk cowered, then turned and tore up the stairs to the church. Everything seemed to go strangely muted for me then, the way it used to in the ballparks when I was behind in the count. I saw Jones race to the altar, pick up a box, and sprint back toward me as if it were happening to someone else.

"Put it down right there," Carruthers said, nodding his chin toward the rectangle of grass in front of me. Parnell Jones came up meekly and set it down not two feet from my knees. The light shone out of the church and backlit the snake box. I could see the silhouette of him in there, alive, drumming warning. The big diamondback rattler.

For an instant, reality was reduced to shadows: the shadow of the snake pivoting inside the box, the shadows of the congregation gathered around me, and the vague shadow of Brother Neal taking a step toward Carruthers.

"Please, Brother," he said. "This isn't right."

"Sure as hell isn't," I agreed.

"Shut up, you," Carruthers said, then he aimed his wrath at Brother Neal. "What ain't right? Lot a things ain't right. That's the point, ain't it? So few things are right like handling, Brother. That's what's always attracted men like you and me to it. So few things are black and white in life. Either you're running with the Holy Ghost or you're not. *You know how that is.*"

"I do," Brother Neal said. "But you and me, Nelson, we come to handling freely. No one ever forced the test on us."

Carruthers thought about that, then shook his head and made an exaggerated wink at me and then at the congregation. "Got to be wary for him," he whispered. "He's sly when he comes hunting. I know. I know."

Brother Neal made as if to take another step. Carruthers swung the gun toward him. "No, Brother," he said. "One way or another, I'm sorry, but we're gonna have us some of that old-time religion, right here, right now."

Carruthers used the toe of his muddy cowboy boot to ease open the lid of the snake box. A triangle of light from the church flooded the upper third of the crate, and I heard the rattle and felt my throat constrict.

"Get on up there, you," Carruthers ordered. "Go on. Look God in the face."

And that's when I saw my escape. I had to go somewhere deep inside myself then, to a place of peace and certainty. For some reason I flashed on myself on the beach at Torrey Pines, imagining my father walking away from me. Only now, he turned and looked back, nodding.

I shuffled forward, one knee, then the other, and reached out to the box, grabbed it, and lowered my face to the opening. For less than a heartbeat, I looked down into the black void, searching for some truth to lunge up and slash me. A sliver of moonlight shining through the side of the box revealed a diagonal slice of the viper: the rough pearl of his active rattle, the ivory scaling of his moist black back, one nickel-blue eye that turned toward me. Then the entire snake seemed to spin back into itself in a cocking motion and I bowed my back, triggering to attack as well.

I lifted the box, swinging it up and back at an angle before releasing. The mesh crate tumbled through the air, then spit out the snake, already in strike. Carruthers tried to duck, but it sank fangs through his shirt and into his shoulder, dangling there a beat before falling to the ground.

The chief dropped the shotgun, howling, "Awww!" Then his chin stiffened and he glared hell at me. "Looks like we both might be dying today."

I threw myself toward the shotgun. Carruthers's left boot slammed down on the stock. His right boot kicked me in the face. I felt the crunching slick shattering of skin splitting and teeth breaking. Rolling over on my back, dazed, I saw Carruthers draw my pistol from his belt. The chief shook, his booze-polluted bloodstream doing battle with the venom. I tasted blood and spit out several pieces of teeth. Something felt wrong with my cheekbone, which pulsed fire and threw blood. I groaned.

"Praise God, Moynihan," the chief said, thumbing off the pistol's safety. "You shall sing with new voices." He raised the gun and aimed it at my head.

SIXTY-THREE

"Put the gun down, Chief," a voice called from back toward the parking lot.

Carruthers half turned, looking for the voice, then found it. A big, lanky white man in his late thirties, wearing a hat that advertised Skeeter bass boats, held a revolver and moved right at us. "Put it down, now," he ordered.

"Go away, Carlton Lee," Carruthers growled. "You got no business here."

"I haven't been to a service in a long time, Chief," Carlton Lee agreed, moving now in an arc around the older man. "But that's not what we're talking about here. We're talking about a fellow peace officer that's wounded, and I saw you do it."

Carruthers swung my pistol toward Lee.

"That's what you wanna do, Nelson?" Lee asked. "Shoot two fellow police officers? You once told me being a cop was for honorable men."

"No honor anymore," said the chief in a bellicose grunt. "No nothing anymore."

"There's lots more," Lee replied. "You got Eileen and Caleb, who love you. What more could you want?"

"Much," Carruthers said, then he shook his fist at the sky. "Much I'm owed."

"I can understand you feeling that way," Lee said. "But you need to put the gun down now, Chief, before you do something else you regret nights in late April."

"Please, Nelson," Carruthers's wife said.

Carruthers looked away from her toward me. His eyes were clouding with tears and he raised the gun again, his hand palsied, the blind, drunken rage replaced by desperation and entrapment.

"Papa, don't hurt him."

Carruthers saw his son, Caleb, looking at him with those big trusting eyes. "You said don't hurt anyone, ever, Papa."

Carruthers stared for a long moment at his son, in some communion I did not understand. All at once it went out of him. His shoulders and chin dropped. He lowered the gun to his side and went down on his knees with his head rocked back. He tried to raise his hands toward Caleb as if he wanted to hug him, but couldn't. Sweat beaded and rolled down his face. Then his skin slackened and he pitched into the grass next to me.

Brother Neal ran toward the chief, crying, "The venom's on him. He needs to be brought inside."

Sixty-Four

I woke at ten A.M. the next morning unsure where I was or how I'd gotten there. The events of the evening before flickered against the inside of my eyelids like they had happened to someone else. My head felt thick and narcotic. My gums ached. Many of my teeth were loose. My left eye was swollen shut. They were twenty stitches in my cheek. My jaw barely opened. But the searing ache of the night before was gone. Once I realized that, I sat up and found myself in a simple hospital room at the medical clinic in Hattiesburg.

Officer Carlton Lee was standing in the doorway, grimacing at me. He held an accordion file and an old reel-to-reel tape recorder.

"You're gonna have to have permanent caps done to replace what Doc Granger did for you last night, Sergeant Moynihan," he said. "And you're pretty black and blue. Hell of a cut and a bone bruise to your cheekbone, but luckily nothing fractured. They had to dope you up pretty good. You were in a lot of pain."

"Yeah, I remember that part of it."

He brought me a glass of Sprite with a straw. "You won't be able to eat much till later, Doc said. So drink on this. Stay rehydrated."

I sipped on the tepid soda, which felt good in some parts of my mouth and not so good in others, and studied Carlton Lee in the light of day, when my head hadn't just been kicked in. He was roughly my age, with a weathered face and the callused and cunning fingers you see on people who use hand tools for a living.

"What else you do besides being a cop, Carlton?" I asked, pointing at his hands.

"Make cabinets," he said grinning. "Furniture. Hickory stuff mostly."

"What you love, huh?"

"Yeah, but it don't pay the bills," he said, sobering. "Got three kids to feed. Besides, being a cop ain't so bad. Folks here think I'm fair. Tough but fair."

"Bet you are," I said, remembering the deft way he'd handled Carruthers the night before. "What about the chief? He in here, too, somewhere?"

"Nah, they tended to him right in the church, most of the night," Carlton Lee said. "I been checking every hour just in case."

"Didn't they get antivenin to him?"

"Expect not," he shrugged. "They'll just put God to him."

"He could die."

Carlton Lee laughed and shook his head. "That angry old coot's been bit more times I can count. You could probably drain him for his own antivenin.

Hell, he almost always gets bit late April, when the blossoms are just about off and he gets to drinking, messing with snakes, and cursing at God.

"I usually keep a close eye on him this time of year, but my oldest boy wanted to go fishing over on the Tennessee my day off. That's where I was when you came by my house yesterday. Lettie said Carruthers called just before you arrived, making drunken threats about everything from my pay, to you, to my marriage and how many mulatto kids Lettie and I gonna have. Anyway, she was flustered and sends her apologies for being rude to you."

"Apologies accepted," I said, then adjusted myself in the bed. "Must be tough living as a mixed-race couple in this part of the country."

"Tougher than you might imagine," he agreed. "But we manage. Anyway, I'm sorry this all happened to you and hope you'll consider not pressing charges against the chief. He's essentially a good man when he ain't drinking. If you'd tried to contact me after all my replies to your ViCAP inquiries, I would have told you everything you need to know. I don't believe in hiding things. When you hide them, they grow."

"All your replies?" I said, puzzled. "We only got one, and Carruthers wouldn't let us talk with you about it. Called you a Barney Fife."

Carlton Lee laughed again. "Yeah, that sounds like Nelson. He must have discovered my first replies to you guys and blocked them. He don't like anyone talking 'bout the Starks."

"Why?"

"Long story."

"I got all day."

"Yeah, you do," he said, setting the accordion file and the tape recorder on the bed next to me before taking a seat in a metal folding chair. "Doc says you're not to move until evening at least."

"Carruthers gets like this every year about this time?"

"Since I was a kid, anyway," Carlton Lee said. "Way I think about him, he's like this thing I saw on the Learning Channel last week? A mud pot out there in Yellowstone Park, bubbling with steam and sulfur year round, but only erupting and splattering a day or two every three hundred and sixty-five."

"What eats him?"

Carlton Lee opened the accordion file and tugged out a folder thick with clippings and photographs. "That's an even longer story," he said, "connected to Lucas Stark. This is a picture of Lucas right here."

He handed me a photograph of a big, gangly man in a simple blue suit with no tie, clutching a microphone just as Brother Neal had the night before, holding a rattler high overhead against the glare of the flash. Stark was broad-shouldered and narrow-waisted, with wavy blond hair and soft blue pillow eyes set in a tanned face marked by the smooth rolls and deep gullies of a desert mountain.

"Guy could a been a movie star," I said.

"Everyone says that," Carlton Lee replied. "Wish I had a picture of Ada Mae for you, but they're mighty hard to come by."

He began tugging out other files. Many of the clippings, he said, had been gathered by his parents. He had amassed others since and made copies of those documents concerning the murder that survived the courthouse fire.

"Why are you so interested in a murder case that happened almost thirty years ago?" I asked.

Carlton Lee shrugged. "I'm a cop, it happened in my town, and Lucas Stark was the preacher who first handed me a snake."

For the rest of the day and on toward dusk, when I wasn't being prodded or poked by the nurse, a big black woman named Nebraska, I read the files and listened to Carlton Lee describe his personal memories of Lucas Stark and those passed on to him from other former members of the church.

The first thing that struck me was that Lucas Stark had killed within the confines of his family before. He was the first of twelve children born to a farming family in north central Kentucky, but rebelled in his teens against the strictures of the hard agrarian life. He turned to sin. Drinking. Gambling. Whoring. Fighting. And he left a trail of arrests behind him. Poaching. Several minor larceny charges. Attempted rape as a juvenile.

Stark's next youngest brother was named Caleb, a handsome, well-liked young man who enjoyed farmwork and the rhythms of the countryside. But for Caleb's twenty-first birthday, Stark lured him to Nashville for a three-day liquor and hooker bender.

On the third day, after boozing on and off for nearly fifty-five hours, Stark and Caleb were hanging out in a strip club called the Nottingham Lounge. The brothers got into a vicious argument—about what, witnesses couldn't say. But the aggression between the two quickly escalated. Caleb busted a beer bottle over his brother's head, then went at Lucas with the ragged neck, looking to cut him good. Lucas pulled a knife from his boot, tried to gut Caleb, and damn near succeeded.

"Story goes that Caleb died right there on the floor of the strip joint," Carlton Lee told me. "With his last words, he put a curse on Lucas, told him he'd live hell on earth.

"They put Stark in the penitentiary, five to ten for manslaughter," the officer went on. "He didn't blink when the judge handed down the sentence, but guards said they heard him whimpering in his cell at night his whole first year at the penitentiary, haunted by the curse his dying brother put on him."

Early in the second year of his incarceration, Carlton Lee said, Stark was put in a cell with Neal Elkins, a car thief who'd killed a pedestrian during a getaway. Elkins had been raised for a time in the ways of Holiness. Stark was first intrigued, then obsessed with the religion, especially after Elkins told him that passages in the Bible virtually guaranteed salvation through the handling of snakes. Stark found God and soon after that what he believed was his salvation: preaching. Every Friday and Saturday night for the next six years, Stark stood up in front of his fellow convicts and testified to the power of the Holy Ghost. He was pelted with food, jeered at, and beaten in the penitentiary yards, but the trials only seemed to flame his passion.

The state parole board set Lucas Stark free after seven years' hard time. He immediately got on a bus and headed south toward Scottsboro, Alabama, where Neal Elkins was living. He soon convinced Elkins to join him in the building of a Holiness congregation. Stark took to gathering rattlesnakes, buying some, catching some, given some by preachers who supported his calling. His first services outside prison walls were held in a rented hall. He and Brother Neal had no equipment to speak of, save the snakes. They made up for it with their ardor: sweating, convulsing, calling to God in tongues, prophesying, drinking strychnine, and then, as they began to draw bigger and bigger crowds, singing the electric Gospel backed by bands.

But it was Stark's way with the vipers that really brought in the people. Witnesses said he'd let Brother Neal aggravate the serpents, get them spitting mad, before he laid them on Stark's outstretched arms. The snakes would remain enraged, hissing at him, and striking at each other. But Stark himself rarely got bit.

When the Holiness preacher from Hattiesburg died, a group of locals went to Stark and asked him to be their minister full-time. Stark and Elkins moved to Hattiesburg on a muggy night in August. They were given a house in the woods beyond the church. And right away things were different in the Church of Jesus, New Tongues Singing.

"You saw it when he was up there on the altar, mostly," Clayton Lee remembered. "Lucas Stark had this diabolical way of strutting when he preached, like his body was precious as his soul. I swear, every unmarried woman who met him, black or white, had longings."

But for the first two years in Hattiesburg, Stark wanted nothing to do with women. He said for men like him women were the root of all evil and he wished to live a life of chastity.

Then, in the summer of 1967, into town walked a hippie girl in her late twenties who called herself Ada Mae Lewis. She was a large-boned, beautiful woman who went barefoot and wore simple peasant dresses. She had long, wavy blond hair, pendulous breasts, and eyes as big and turquoise as Lucas Stark's.

Ada Mae Lewis told people she was walking away from her past in West Virginia and San Francisco, looking to leave the corrupt ways of the city behind her. Sympathetic members of the church brought her to the service on a Friday night.

"My daddy was there," Clayton Lee recalled. "He said Ada Mae come right in the church wearing this thin white cotton dress, and with her lit from behind like that you could tell she was buck nude underneath. My daddy wasn't the only one shook up.

"When Brother Stark saw her coming that way down the aisle at him, it was like he got electrified and damn near collapsed. He wobbled against the lectern, then got hold of himself and called down to her from the altar in this strange booming voice, *'Are you right with the Lord, Sister?'*

"Ada Mae stood there, looking at him for the longest time, then she said, 'No, I'm not, Brother. But I sure want to be.'

"Then my daddy said she went toward Stark on her knees, like she'd known him her whole life, begging his and God's forgiveness for her sins. Sobbing, she threw her arms around him, pressed her bosoms against his thighs and her face against his belly.

" 'I want to be right with the Lord, Brother,' she said. 'I surely do.'

"Daddy said for a long time Lucas Stark stood stiff, looking down at Ada Mae's trembling body like it was a lake roughed up by thunderstorm and he was a fisherman casting for salvation.

"For a second there, Daddy thought Lucas was gonna reject her," Carlton Lee continued. "Ada Mae must have felt it, too, because she crawled up his body, whimpering, with this tortured look on her face. She was almost as tall as he was, and she looked him right in his eyes and begged, 'Please, Brother, if God can forgive you, can't he forgive me?'

"Right then, Daddy said, something in Lucas Stark gave way. He held Ada Mae's half-naked body tight to him and sobbed and babbled in a language only he understood."

SIXTY-FIVE

Lucas stark married ada Mae Lewis that same September in the Church of Jesus, New Tongues Singing. Brother Neal presided. Long before winter blew in, Ada Mae's belly was swelling. Stark told members of his congregation that it was his fervent hope that God would bless him with a son as a sign that he had been forgiven for killing his brother. He even planned to give the boy his brother's name. Ada Mae was insistent that the child be born naturally, and they brought in Carlton Lee's mother as a midwife.

"Mama said Stark was real nervous—that both of them, Ada Mae, too, were beside themselves trying to see the baby come out of her," Carlton Lee said. "It was a big girl, nine pounds, ten ounces, deep-blue eyes, blond hair, just like her parents. They named her Lil, after Ada Mae's grandmother, and my mom said you could tell Lucas was disappointed at first. But within a couple of weeks, he was telling everyone in town how much he loved the girl, how the birth of her all healthy, pink-skinned, and ten-toed made him feel, even more than snake handling, like he was right with the Lord."

Ada Mae Stark showed all the markings of a wonderful mother. She doted on Lil and told members of the congregation that the wanderlust and wicked things she'd engaged in along the road from her past were like another life, a skin of which she'd shed herself. Ada Mae taught Lil her scriptures and life according to Holiness. But she also taught her daughter to love skinny-dipping in the river and running in the forest. Lil was strong, big, and smart like her mom.

"She was a couple of years younger than me, but she didn't act it," Carlton Lee recalled. "Being out in the woods by herself was a natural thing. She'd climb all over them limestone cliffs behind her house. She could run like the wind. And that girl could handle snakes, let me tell you."

In the seven years following Lil's birth, however, Ada Mae did not bring another pregnancy to term. She had four miscarriages, and with each of them Lucas Stark became more anxious, more sullen, more given to long bouts of fulminating over wrongs that had been done to him.

But in Lil's eighth year, Ada Mae became pregnant for the sixth time. She was thirty-seven years old, and as each month passed and she became bigger and glowed more radiantly with child, Lucas Stark grew more excited. He once again told favored members of the congregation that he was sure a son would be born to him as a sign of his forgiveness from God. Carlton Lee's mother was there the night of that delivery too.

"He got his son," Carlton Lee said. "A ten-pound eleven-ounce boy afflicted with Down's syndrome. Mama said Stark 'bout had a nervous breakdown when he saw the boy's condition. He took to screeching and crying just like he did when he handled snakes, only more painful like. My mom said it was almost as if he was spitting at God when he named the boy Caleb. But Ada Mae? She loved and spoiled Caleb the same way she doted on Lil. She told my mom that she'd love any gift that the Lord thought just."

Stark's behavior, however, turned sulky and more erratic. Members of the congregation swore they smelled liquor on his breath, a practice that became more pronounced as a year passed and his son grew. Stark would not be seen in public with the boy and disappeared for ten days around Caleb's first birthday. Police records in Atlanta showed that during that absence, Stark was cited and released for trying to engage an undercover police officer in an act of prostitution.

Ada Mae had to go to the hospital twice during Caleb's second year. She claimed she fell off her bike and broke her wrist, but a doctor said it looked more like her arm had been stuck in a car door and slammed.

Two months later, Ada Mae came in spotting blood in her underwear. She said it started out of the blue and wondered if it had to do with her body aging. But the doctor suspected that Lucas Stark may have kicked his wife in her womb.

It was a different time, Alabama in the early 1970's, and the responding police officer, Nelson Carruthers, did not press charges. Carruthers admitted in several statements to the press that he should have heeded the warning signs, but when he confronted Stark, his minister and friend told him he was crushed that anyone would think he would do that to the woman he loved and always had loved.

As I suspected, Carruthers had worked as a prison bull, seven years at the Louisiana State Penitentiary at Angola, before returning to his hometown, his church, and a job as an officer in the Hattiesburg Police Department. Carruthers and his wife, Eileen, became close friends of Lucas and Ada Mae Stark.

At that time, Eileen Carruthers was a young woman, barely twenty, and she worshiped the Holy Ghost three times a week, having herself anointed with oil as she beseeched God to make her fertile. Carruthers became increasingly active in the church as well, often helping Lucas Stark and Brother Neal during services. Eventually he became a deacon.

Carruthers was in the church on the third Friday in April, 1976, when Lucas Stark arrived at the church drunk and belligerent.

"I was maybe twelve and sitting there with my parents too," Carlton Lee recalled. "Lucas come dragging them all in—Lil and Ada Mae holding Caleb—and started acting as if they were the hell on earth his brother's curse had foretold. He told the whole congregation his wife was filth and said his children were only part of his affliction. Then he got up on top of the snake boxes and started screeching at the sky, damning God. It was scary stuff."

Ada Mae tried to escape the next day with Lil and Caleb. But Stark chased her down on the Scottsboro Road and convinced her he had gotten right with the Lord again and needed her to come home and protect him.

Those who saw Lucas Stark during the following days said his skin turned sallow and waxy. When he wasn't drinking, he complained bitterly of a pain that shot from his spine diagonally through his lower guts, glancing off his testicles and weakening his left knee. On Wednesday, April 27, a local doctor diagnosed the problem as a kidney stone and prescribed a powerful narcotic to help deaden the pain until the irritant passed.

Around five that evening, Stark hobbled into the pharmacy, his arm tight around his ten-year-old daughter Lil's shoulders. The pharmacist later described the girl as "agitated and crying." Ada Mae came in, too, holding Caleb in her arms. She wore sunglasses and bought Chap Stick for a split lip. Stark took four of the narcotic tablets, twice the recommended dose, paid, and they left. The pharmacist was the last person to see the family for nearly forty-eight hours.

"So it's Friday the twenty-ninth now; service began at sundown," Carlton Lee said. "It was Lucas Stark's night to preach, only it was getting dark and he wasn't there and neither was Ada Mae or Lil to explain why. Then people got to whispering that Ada Mae missed a meeting that morning with Lil's fifth-grade teacher. And Lil had not been in school the last two days."

Brother Neal Elkins asked Carruthers to go check on the family. Carruthers got in his patrol car and drove back down the cliff road to the turnoff that led to the Stark's.

"He testified later that the place was dark," Carlton Lee said. "In his headlights he said he could see Stark's black Chevy Impala parked under the Osage orange tree. There were kids' toys strewn about the yard and up on the porch."

Carruthers knocked, got no answer, then checked the doorknob: unlocked. He entered and found the place in shambles. The shards of lamps, glasses, and cheap china carpeted the floor. What dishes had survived were piled high and moldy on the sink. The windows were all closed up tight and the heat had been turned up to ninety. The place reeked of rotting food and used diapers.

The officer looked down the hallway toward the master bedroom and saw a light glowing back there. He walked down the hall, noting that the bedroom where Lil slept with Caleb appeared empty. Carruthers entered the master bedroom and found himself in hell.

SIXTY-SIX

Ada mae stark was naked and tied spread-eagle to the four-poster bed. There were three eastern diamondback rattlers curled up on her black and blood-blistered body. A green apple had been mashed into her lifeless mouth.

From a corner of the bedroom, a naked Lucas Stark watched the corpse of his wife. His feet were drawn up against his buttocks, his elbows between his knees, his hands gripping his head, his fingernails scoring bloody scratches across his movie-star face. Then Carruthers saw the blood seeping between Stark's legs and realized he had mutilated himself. Stark was incoherent, in a drunken, narcotic stupor, and did not notice Carruthers standing there. He just kept rocking back and forth on his naked haunches, whimpering.

Carruthers vomited, then eased around the body and the snakes, grabbed Stark, cuffed him, and dragged him out to his patrol car. He called an ambulance, the county coroner, and the chief of police at the time, an ineffectual man named

Hardgraves. Then he went back into the house and looked for Lil and Caleb.

Carruthers searched the house, and when he opened the children's closet door he saw a box of Cheerios, a milk bottle, and a half dozen soiled diapers piled carefully to one side. Lil and Caleb were in the very back of the closet, hiding under piles of clothes they had pulled down from the hangers. Lil was in shock, unresponsive to Carruthers' commands, and would not let go of her brother, who slept cradled in her arms.

"Lil was near senseless, deaf and dumb for two months," Carlton Lee recalled. "They took her and Caleb to the clinic. Physically they were okay, according to the documents I've seen, except that part of Lil's hymen was recently torn, as if a finger had been rudely thrust in her. Eileen Carruthers took the children home in the morning and cared for them."

The autopsy revealed that Ada Mae Stark was bitten three times, once on the inside of her right knee, once near the angle of her jawbone, and a third time on the left outer labium of her vagina. She had lived nearly forty hours after the first snakebite. She had strychnine in her system and a blood alcohol level of .25, two and a half times the legal limit. There was evidence that Lucas Stark lay with his wife before and after death.

People who worked around him during the entire crisis said Nelson Carruthers was bewildered by the inexplicable depravity exhibited by Lucas

Stark, a man he counted as his friend and minister. But those feelings aside, they said he comported himself with integrity and levelheadedness while administering the investigation. He smartly convinced H rdgraves to call in state troopers to guard the site for fear it would be looted by ghoulish souvenir hunters. In the meantime, he kept the evidence uncontaminated by restricting access to the house and went at great pains to photograph and document the crime scene.

Carruthers left the house with Ada Mae's body at dawn and went back to the clinic where Lucas Stark was being treated: It had taken fifty stitches to the close the knife wounds to his testicles and penis. They had him on his back, his wrists and ankles lashed to the railings of the bed, a diaper around his waist. Stark was speaking in strange, out-of-context snippets of sermons he had preached over the years. The doctors said that in addition to the blood loss, Stark had overdosed on booze and painkillers. Thirty hours passed before the preacher became lucid enough to be questioned.

"Meantime, a mob gathered outside the clinic," Carlton Lee said. "Some were demanding a lynching."

Carruthers reacted well again. His experience as a prison guard allowed him to control what could have been an explosive situation. That afternoon, he convinced Chief Hardgraves to move Stark to the jail and to call in more state troopers.

The next day, Carruthers finally spoke with Lucas Stark. Carlton Lee had an old audio copy of the interrogation. The tape was crackly, and when Carlton Lee played it in my hospital room, I found it hard to hear at times. Before the interrogation, he said, Stark had been detoxed and medicated and had slept a fitful seven hours.

Given the evil he had observed and the pressures to which he'd been subjected, Carruthers sounded remarkably calm on the tape. His tone was firm but not cruel. Carlton Lee said Carruthers questioned Stark sitting up, handcuffed, and lashed to a heavy oak chair with hospital restraints.

Stark waived his Miranda rights immediately. To my surprise, he had a radio voice with the quality of Hank Williams in his later years: rich, twangy, and scarred way past its age. But during the interrogation his delivery was flat, as if in his mind he were already a dead man.

"What'd you kill Ada Mae like that for, Lucas?" Carruthers asks at one point.

"Brother Nelson, she is the beginning and end of me," Stark replies. "She was not right with God, nor am I."

"You tortured her," Carruthers says.

"Tested her," Stark replies flintily. "No more than Abraham did his son."

"Was it the boy, Lucas? That why you did this? Was it Caleb?"

Stark snorts in derision. "You want the truth, Brother Nelson?"

"We all want to understand why you'd do this," Carruthers says. "You loved Ada Mae. I know it. I seen it all the time in those early years."

Stark laughs harshly. "It was her body, Nelson, don't you understand? The unbelievable way she smelled, moved, and looked at me when we were fucking, like she could look into my soul, know I was damned, and not care."

There is a bark of sound on the tape as Carruthers slams his hand on the arm of the chair. "You make me sick, Lucas."

"Make you green with envy, is more like it," Stark shoots back. "I was able to lay up between Ada Mae's legs and give her children, you know you can't say the same."

Silence on the tape; then Carruthers says, "I sit here and look at you, Lucas Stark, and I can't believe that I considered you one of God's chosen."

"Well, now you know the truth," Stark snarls in return. "I'm not and neither was she. We were both outcasts from the Garden."

"Lucas," Carruthers says, "if you expect any chance of redemption, you have to testify before God and man to what you've done."

"There's no forgiveness—never has been!" Stark shouts. "Not since the first time I touched her after we swam naked in the river. No forgiveness, Brother Nelson. No redemption. Only God's horrible justice."

For the next twenty minutes or so on the tape, Carruthers bullies and pleads with Stark and keeps getting these oblique answers that raise more questions to which the prisoner will not respond. Then Carruthers appeals to Stark's memory. He recalls scenes from Lucas and Ada Mae's marriage before Caleb: their wedding day, a church picnic on the cliffs, the way Ada Mae carried baby Lil in a pack all over the forest. Stark eventually breaks down and tells Carruthers that he wants to confess his sins.

"But only to you, Brother Nelson," he says. "Turn off the tape recorder. Hear my sins as my deacon and my friend, not the police officer who will send me to the gallows."

SIXTY-SEVEN

Carlton lee leaned forward on my bed in the clinic and clicked off the tape recorder.

"That's all of it?" I said.

"Yup."

"What did Stark tell Carruthers?"

Carlton Lee shrugged. "No one knows. People said when Carruthers came out of the interrogation room, he was more shaken than he'd been in the first few hours after finding Ada Mae's body. But he refused to tell anyone the details of the confession. He said that once he turned off the tape recorder, he was no longer a cop but a fellow minister of God listening to a spiritual confidence.

"Carruthers emphasized, however, that what Stark told him had no real bearing on whether or not the man was guilty. The facts on that were plain: Stark had acted alone and took responsibility for murdering Ada Mae."

"But the chief wouldn't talk about the motive?"

Carlton Lee nodded. "To this day he's never said a word about why Stark did it, though I get the idea that it was almost worse than the killing itself."

I sat there, mulling that over, then asked, "When did Stark try to escape?"

"That very night," Carlton Lee replied. "By sundown the mob out in front of the jail had grown to nearly four hundred. Now, this is in an area where only two thousand people lived, Sergeant. You just can't imagine the outrage that this crime provoked. It was like the Devil himself had come in disguise to the Church of Jesus, New Tongues Singing. I was down there on my bike in the crowd. You heard all these voices calling for Stark's neck and people uttering about the 'Holy Ghost in righteous anger' and 'avenging angels with fiery swords.' I'm telling you, it was crazy."

Carlton Lee stopped, dug through his accordion file again, and emerged with an old newspaper clipping that described the escape attempt and death of Lucas Stark.

In the two hours after Carruthers heard Stark's confession, the clipping said, he watched the mob grow larger and more unruly. He later testified that he told Chief Hardgraves that Stark might be safer in the cell in the basement of the courthouse where prisoners were brought to await trial. Hardgraves disagreed.

During the next thirty minutes, Carruthers testified, he saw the situation deteriorating. The mob lit a bonfire next to the statue in the town square. A rope was hung from one of the tupelo trees. A brick was thrown at the window of the jail. Someone in the mob shot a gun in the air.

Carruthers said he acted on instinct to try to save another man's life. Without telling anyone what he was doing, he took Stark, in handcuffs, out of his cell and out the back door of the jail. He ordered the trooper guarding the alley to go help protect the main entrance. Carruthers held Stark by the nape of the neck and urged him north down the alley and then catty-corner northeast out of the trooper's sight, away from the mob, along a path through a triangle of magnolias that separated the courthouse from the jail.

Carruthers said Stark told him it was the first time he'd walked since his arrest and that he felt dizzy and thought he was going to be sick. Carruthers said he slowed down and relaxed his guard for only a second. But it was enough. Stark spun back on Carruthers, bit into his wrist, freed himself from the officer's grasp, and ran. Without thinking, Carruthers said, he drew his gun and shot twice at the fleeing murderer, striking him both times in the back of the head.

"Twenty-five yards away, running in the dark, and he gets off two headshots with a bite to his gun arm?" I said, looking up from the article.

"Chief's got the scar to prove it," Carlton Lee said. "'Cept it's kind of hard to see because of the bite speckling on his arms. Anyway, there was a bunch of investigations all the way to the state level, and no one thought Carruthers was wrong to shoot. Lucas Stark was a fiend. He might have done anything if he'd gotten free."

Several days after Carruthers shot Lucas Stark, after the coroner had gone over the body, a funeral service was held.

"Hardly anyone went," Carlton Lee remembered. "My parents wouldn't go to the church and they didn't want me there anymore, either. They said Satan had contaminated the place. But after I watched the hearse go up the mountain with only a half dozen cars behind, I got on my bike and rode up there.

"As I heard it, the plan was to bury Lucas and Ada Mae alongside each other out there in the forest between the church and the house," he went on. "But Carruthers himself shooed me away after the service. Last thing I saw, they were carrying the caskets into the woods—Brother Neal, Carruthers, a couple of the others. By the time I rode my bike back down into town, people were standing outside their houses looking up toward the cliffs. There was black smoke coming out of the trees south of the church. For almost an hour it smoked, drifted toward the cliff wall, and rose back up over the top of the ridge toward the wilderness there."

"They burned the bodies?" I said.

"Like they were unholy," Carlton Lee replied. "Even today people think the old house and the woods around it are tainted with evil."

"And Carruthers keeps his festering secret, picking the scab once a year."

"'Bout sums it up," Carlton Lee agreed.

I thought about it all in silence for nearly five minutes. "Make you a deal," I said at last. "I won't press charges against the chief. But he's got to talk to me. He's got to tell me what Lucas Stark confessed to."

"You can ask," Carlton Lee said, "but I'm betting he won't answer."

It was nearly sunset now, and out the window I could see the cliffs rising above the town, the last low rays creating their own sense of fire on the limestone. And now I was completely convinced that someone from Hattiesburg was involved in the murders in San Diego, patterning them on the torture killing of Ada Mae Stark. But who?

After all I'd been through, after all I'd learned, I felt only a little bit closer to catching the killer. My stomach cried for food. Carlton Lee must have read my mind.

"Feel like eating something more solid?" he asked.

"Milk shake might taste good," I said.

"Lettie makes a fine milk shake, and we got a guest bedroom," he said, tucking away the last of his files on Lucas Stark. "They'll give you your painkiller prescription and we can get on out of here."

Before I could agree, Nebraska, the nurse who'd been tending me all day, stuck her head in the doorway.

"Carlton?" she said, a pained expression on her face. "Just got a call from Neal Elkins up to the church. Chief Carruthers passed on twenty minutes ago. The venom finally took him."

Sixty-Eight

They buried nelson carruthers on Monday, May first, at two in the afternoon. The service was held at graveside, a crypt of sorts that had been jackhammered into the soft limestone cliff out in front of the church, not far from where the chief had handled me like a snake. It was a cloudy, humid, windless day. Mosquitoes whined at my ears. I stood back near the parking lot, the roar in my jaw dulled to an infrequent twinge.

The entire congregation of the Church of Jesus, New Tongues Singing was there. So were many non-Holiness followers from Hattiesburg, black and white, and others from Scottsboro and beyond, all of them looking on somberly as Carruthers's body was brought out of the church in a simple pine box.

Carlton Lee was one of the pallbearers. He wore his dress blues and sat with Lettie and their three children behind Eileen Carruthers and Caleb Stark, who were both dressed in black and stricken with grief.

The congregation sang "Amazing Grace," and their wavering voices echoed off the cliffs and down into the valley below. Brother Neal delivered a eulogy full of passion, pain, and, ultimately, admiration.

He said that Nelson Carruthers was the most courageous man he ever met. The chief came from the poorest family in town and took the only job he could find when he was eighteen. He became a prison guard, specializing in the most violent of criminals. Brother Neal said Carruthers came back to Hattiesburg and administered justice in the best way he knew how while trying to be the best man he could be, at church and at home.

"Nelson had his faults; everyone who knew him knew that," Brother Nelson admitted. "But a long time ago, twenty-seven years to this day, he was asked by God to perform unspeakable tasks and to shoulder burdens he carried to the minutes before he died. Few men could have taken up arms for God like he did. And he fought for the Lord right to the end. I heard him."

I flashed on an image of Carruthers battling the venom as Rikko had. Out of his mind. Babbling up the past to whoever would listen.

A gust of sudden wind blew across the cliffs just then. It came from the east, from the other side of the church, from the direction of the woods and the Starks' house. Brother Neal startled and cringed at the gust and its origin, frightened for a moment. The wind died as soon as it had come.

Brother Neal looked back at the congregation and he appeared different to me: ashen and tottering, almost like my mother the day she went into the Southern Mortuary to identify my father's body, stricken with an overload of emotional information. But what I saw in Brother Neal at that moment was more than sorrow: It was knowledge—knowledge strangling him like kudzu vine. And then his just-spoken words played in my head: *burdens he carried until minutes before he died.*

"He knows," I murmured to myself. "Brother Neal knows what Lucas Stark told Nelson Carruthers. The chief told him before he died."

Indeed, when I thought about it, the entire eulogy had been laced with veiled references that only served to steel my growing conviction that Nelson Carruthers had shot Lucas Stark not because of a spontaneous escape attempt, but with premeditation. I'd been put in choke holds and armlocks by the best physical restraint men in the business, and the way Nelson Carruthers handled me outside the church convinced me that there was no way Lucas Stark could have managed to turn, bite the chief, get free, and run.

I had explained this to Carlton Lee the night before at dinner. He said that there were a lot of other people in town who thought Carruthers had gunned down Stark in cold blood. And behind closed doors, some people applauded him for it.

"How about you?" I asked.

"No," he said. "I feel no ill will toward the people who worship in accordance with Holiness. But after Lucas Stark, my family left the church and that Old Testament way of thinking behind. Still, I can understand the sentiment."

❧   ❧   ❧

The funeral ended with a song.

When the last notes had died, Brother Neal helped a sobbing Eileen Carruthers to her feet and toward the black Cadillac parked on the lawn. Caleb Stark wandered behind them, tears dribbling down his cheeks.

I began to work my way through the departing mourners toward the black Cadillac. Brother Neal saw me coming and shrank as if I were a dark thing. Carlton Lee grabbed me. "What do you think you're doing?"

"Going to talk to Brother Neal," I said, pulling away from his grasp.

He gave me an unshakable look. "No, you're not."

"He knows what Stark said to Carruthers!" I insisted.

"I expect so," Carlton Lee replied. "Sounds like Nelson did some talking on his deathbed when he was fighting the venom; Eileen probably knows too. But you can't go asking them about none of that today."

"Why not?"

"'Cause I'm the new chief of police in Hattiesburg, and I say let them grieve in peace," he replied evenly. "These are good people, Seamus, who have struggled with difficulty beyond our imag-ining. There'll be time for *me* to talk to them later this week. I'll let you know."

The Cadillac pulled out, and as it did, the back left passenger side window rolled down. Caleb Stark looked at me with the eyes of a man who'd lost his father twice.

Part of me wanted to sprint after the car and demand to know Lucas Stark's secret. But in the end I trusted Carlton Lee's judgment. In an investigation of this sort, you rarely encounter a gatekeeper like him, someone with intimate knowledge who is able to take you quickly to the heart of the story. He'd lived in the town his whole life. Carlton Lee might not find out what Stark told Carruthers, but he certainly had a better chance of it than I would. So I reluctantly nodded and we walked after the Cadillac, out onto the potholed road, to the field where I'd parked the Neon.

"I appreciate everything you've done, Carlton," I said, shaking his hand. "Let's keep in close touch on this."

"You'll hear from me in a day or two," he promised. "And who knows what you'll find in Scottsboro."

"True," I said, opening the car door, then stopped because I realized there was one part of the Starks' story I hadn't heard.

Carlton Lee had turned to watch Lettie and the children play on an old teeter-totter board that was part of the church playground. I leaned across the roof of my car.

"Carlton, what happened to the girl—Lil?"

SIXTY-NINE

Carlton lee turned back toward me, rubbing his neck as if stricken with a spasm. "She's a tough one to explain," he said. "Just like Caleb there, the Carrutherses adopted her. And for a while she came out of the mess she was in after the killing. But it had scarred her big time—you could see it."

"How so?"

"Like I told you the other day, Lil used to be this happy thing, running in the woods and climbing on the cliffs in back of the house all the time. When her mother was alive, she was the ultimate tomboy. But after the death of her parents, she became a quiet preteen and then a surly, confused adolescent who began to act out sexually."

"Translation?"

Carlton Lee shrugged. "She became the town pump—surprising for such a good-looking gal. Smart too. But very rebellious. Drank. Smoked pot. There was this anger in her that just kept festering. The Carrutherses lost control of her. She said she hated them. In one breath she'd tell them she did not want to live. In the next, she wanted to take Caleb with her and go far away.

"Hattiesburg isn't the most forward of places, unfortunately," he continued. "They probably should have gotten her psychological help, but they didn't. Everybody in town knew what had happened. Everybody looked at her as if she was not quite right somehow. Guys talked about her as if she was running with the Devil. I figured sooner or later she'd get knocked up and be living in a trailer in one of the hollows above town with an abusive husband. I was wrong. Lil may have been a slut, but she was smart. One day, near the end of her senior year in high school, she flat out stopped talking about committing suicide. She had different ideas. She said she had figured out a way you could die and be reborn. She told people she could change herself into a completely different person."

"Who'd she tell that to?" I asked.

"My sister, for one," Carlton Lee replied; then he looked over at his wife, who was pushing their youngest girl on the swing. "Lettie too. It was right after she and I started dating and we were causing so much of a stink in town."

He paused a beat and squinted as if trying to get his facts straight. "So, two weeks after that, there was this seniors' camp-out party among the non-Holiness crowd down in a field by the Washoo River in a place they call the Rocky Narrows. I was twenty and on my second week working for Chief Carruthers as an auxiliary cop on the night patrol.

"I swung through the field around two in the morning and flashed my searchlight around a little," Carlton Lee went on. "Most of the kids had turned in. A few were drinking around a campfire and quickly tossed the bottles when they saw me. I shined my light a little more into the woods and I see this scumbag named Cricket Lorette doing Lil Stark standing up from behind. All these hoots and hollers went up from the other kids at the party. Lorette tried to hide himself, but not Lil. All these people watching her getting fucked and she didn't care. I told her to get dressed, that I was taking her home. She put on her clothes and came to the cruiser but wasn't happy about it.

"She was drunk, high, and pissed at the world. She told me on the ride to the Carrutherses that she was through going home, through going to church. She said it was time to wipe the slate clean and get a new life. I told her she'd be eighteen soon, old enough to do what she wanted. She thanked me for the ride by propositioning me. Said she'd always wanted to do it in a patrol car. I said no offense but no, thanks, dropped her off in front of her house, and that's the last anybody ever saw of her."

"Runaway?" I asked.

"Runaway in a big way," Carlton Lee replied, drumming his hands on the car roof. "I saw her go in through the Carrutherses' garage door around two-thirty that morning. Sometime after that, she went out her bedroom window, got a can of gasoline, and headed for the county building down there on the square. She kicked in the window of the court clerk's office and went inside. She poured gasoline in the file room and then went down the hall to the county recorder's office, where the birth and death records were kept, and did the same thing. Then she lit a match to all of it."

I thought of the foundation on the town square. "She was the arsonist."

"We never had a chance to save the building," Carlton Lee said. "It was four o'clock in the morning before someone noticed the flames. We have a volunteer fire department, and by the time they assembled, the place was engulfed. Total loss. Later we found out she'd stolen the microfilm for 1976 from the library and taken every photograph of her family she could find from the Carrutherses' house. Even got all the copies and negatives of her graduation picture from the high school yearbook office and got rid of those too. My theory is she burned them in the fire. Anyway, people were so focused on the courthouse that they didn't notice that the old Holiness Church was on fire, too, until it was too late."

"I get the feeling you didn't catch her," I said.

"Not like we didn't try," Carlton Lee replied. "Hattiesburg is not an easy place to get out of, Seamus. Carruthers had roadblocks on the Scottsboro Road, the only way out of town, checking all the cars. They got hounds and let 'em sniff a pair of her jeans. They tracked her from the courthouse across three farms, up the ditch beside the Ridge Road, and on to the smoldering ruins of the old church. And there the track stopped."

"She burn herself to death in there?" I asked, looking back toward the church and asking myself if it was possible for ground to be less hallow.

But Carlton Lee shook his head. "No body," he said. "We looked hard. Then a bunch of the dogs got excited about the base of the cliff over there."

"Where?" I said, moving to where I could see the ramparts behind the church.

"Left grotto wall," he said. "I've studied that cliff a hundred times. It's the only doable route."

"Gotta be almost two hundred feet," I said.

"Had to have been a hell of an ordeal, but that's what we decided happened," Carlton Lee said. "She torched the church; then, knowing we'd watch the road, she climbed that sheer cliff and disappeared into the big woods that run twenty-six miles north between here and the Tennessee line.

"Now, let me tell you something: It's a lime jungle back there—big, rugged, unforgiving," he continued. "Bears. Hogs. Snakes. Pumas. It took us hours to get up there by another route. By that time it was raining and the dogs had lost the scent. For the next three days it got downright nasty, pouring rain. We ran a half dozen search missions in there over the course of the next month, even put in some Seminole Indian tracker from Florida, but they never found her. Far as we know, she went into those woods with almost nothing: pair of jeans, running shoes, a sweatshirt, maybe. But we covered our bases. We had police on the alert in all the towns on the Tennessee side of the forest, but she was never spotted. Most people think she busted her leg, then starved to death, and the kudzu took her skeleton."

"What's the status of the file?" I asked.

"Still open," he said. "Matter of fact, Carruthers had the file on his desk the other day. Must have had it out because of your ViCAP inquiries. There's a report on top of the file that says Lilith Mae Stark is presumed dead, but charges still pend against her."

"Lilith?" I said, my face screwing up. "Why did you call her Lilith?"

Carlton shrugged again. "Lilith Mae Stark's her given name. I never knew it myself until I saw the copies of the Carrutherses' adoption papers in Scottsboro a couple years ago. No one ever called her Lilith here in Hattiesburg. It was always Lil."

Standing there in the still, sultry air below the cliff Lilith Stark had used to escape her past, I flashed on an image of an ancient terra-cotta statue of a nude woman sitting within the trunks of a tree. A dragon lay beneath the woman's feet; snakes grew atop her head. That image shredded a basic preconception we'd all had of the killer since we'd first discovered Morgan Cook.

"It's not a man using a woman as a lure," I said in complete shock. "It's a woman acting alone."

"What?" Carlton Lee demanded, confused.

"You almost never see this, so we never looked for it," I said, my mind ripping along, refiltering everything about the investigation. "She had that

Australian cowboy duster in her office. She wore it, not because it was raining, but to disguise her gender. She has her father's startling blue eyes. She probably dyes her blond hair brown at the roots. She believes you can reinvent yourself. She smelled Southern Nights Cologne, regressed to her other self, and went after those men in some twisted reenactment of her mother's death. Obsessed with the Bible. Obsessed with this apocryphal woman who rejects God and has sex with demons."

"You've lost me," Carlton Lee said.

"A woman serial killer," I said. "Lilith Stark, a.k.a. Susan Dahoney."

SEVENTY

We raided susan dahoney's rented condo in the Burlingame section of San Diego at ten o'clock the next morning, an hour after I climbed off the plane. Rikko and I went in first while Jorge and Missy covered the back and evidence technicians, my sister, and Chief Helen Adler waited outside. The front room and the kitchen were empty, save for a cracked glass aquarium on the floor and a copy of a contract for a U-Haul trailer dated Friday, April twenty-ninth, the twenty-seventh anniversary of the night her father killed her mother. She had listed her destination as "Unknown."

In the bedroom we found more compelling evidence. From the depressions in the carpet, we could tell that Dahoney had kept a desk and a filing cabinet in the room. The wall above the desk was papered with dozens of clippings of stories about her and her book intermingled with almost every article that had been written about the snake killings. My name was highlighted in many of the articles. Beside Brett Tarentino's column about the Bible message at the Haines scene, there was a notation scrawled in black ink: *See what Moynihan knows? Maybe I can help point him in the right direction! Ha-Ha!*

One of the follow-up pieces on the Haines killing jumped to an inside page, which had been torn out in its entirety and thumb-tacked to the wall. In the right-hand corner of the page, almost directly below the end of the story, was an advertisement for Southern Nights cologne.

Typed on a piece of white paper taped to the wall were the first two messages that had been left on the mirrors at the murder scenes: *Joy unspeakable to be holding death in your hands* and the Acts citation. Below them it read: *#3= St. Mark? #4 =?*

"Looks like she planned to kill again," Rikko said.

"She may yet," I replied grimly. "She's got a four-day head start on us."

While the evidence technicians combed the apartment for hair fibers, fingerprints, and anything else we might use to corroborate her involvement in the killings, we posted state, federal, and international bulletins for Dahoney's arrest. We put out watches for her at the Mexican and Canadian borders, at every airport on the West Coast, and at road blocks on the Arizona, Nevada, and Oregon state lines.

"We'll get her," Adler said outside. "It's only a matter of time now."

Lieutenant Fraiser had arrived and was glaring at us in silence. I ignored him, nodding wearily. "Yeah, but I wanted it to be over with now, Chief."

I'd driven and flown all night. It had taken a half dozen calls before I was able to sidestep Fraiser and talk directly to Adler. She was furious when I told her I was in Alabama, running a shadow investigation, but finally calmed down enough to hear me explain why I liked Dahoney for the slayings. You can say many things about Adler, but she was a great homicide detective. And at the end of my presentation, over Fraiser's protests, somewhere between Dallas and San Diego, she agreed that the Bible professor was our killer.

Now, on the street outside Dahoney's condo, Adler put her hand on my arm. "Sorry I doubted you, Seamus. Excellent work. I'm recommending you be promoted."

"Promoted!" Fraiser cried. "Chief, there's still the issue of Moynihan going off half-cocked and conducting a secret investigation."

"You knew about Hattiesburg before I did," I retorted. "You got the ViCAP response. You told Jorge to put it on the back burner. I merely looked through your trash and saw what you didn't."

"That's crap and you—"

"Lieutenant, that will be enough," Adler said. "As of today, you're being transferred out of Homicide."

"Transferred?" Fraiser said, stunned. "To where?"

"Records Division," she said. "We need someone with your management skills there to reorganize the filing system."

"Records? That's a black hole!"

"Make something of the time, Aaron," she said. "Maybe you'll get out."

Fraiser stood there sputtering, his bald head getting redder by the moment, then he stormed off.

"I don't want the promotion," I told Adler.

The chief frowned. "We wouldn't ask you to assume any new administrative duties, if that's what you're thinking. You'd be a pure investigator, Seamus, with your own team, assigned to the pressing case of the moment. The bump in rank is in recognition of all you've done."

"Let me think about it," I said. "Right now I need sleep."

"Of course," Adler said. "Go home. There's nothing you can do until we find her anyway. Keep your cell phone and pager on. We'll call the second we hear anything. And, again, I'm sorry I doubted you."

I nodded numbly and walked across the street toward Christina. She cringed once again at the swelling and stitches in my face, then threw her arms around me. "It's good to have you home," she said. "You look like you've been to hell and back."

"More than you know, Sis. More than you know."

"This is all incredible," she said. "Lil Stark would be only the second confirmed woman serial killer in history after Aileen Wuornos."

"I can see you want to talk to her."

"Me and every other criminal behaviorist in the country once this gets out," Christina replied. "Yes, as a little girl she saw her father kill her mother in a horrible way. But I'm thinking there has to be something more than that—something about Lucas Stark's secret—that planted the seeds of this monster."

"I've been thinking the same thing," I said. "And also wondering whether she planned to try to make me her fourth victim that night at O'Doran's."

My sister put her hand to her mouth. "You're probably right. She just got too drunk to carry it out."

"Either that or because I wasn't wearing Southern Nights cologne."

Christina thought about that. "Want me to take you home?"

"Nah," I said. "I'll get one of the patrols to do it. I'm going to sleep, then go see Jimmy." I kissed her on the cheek and made to walk away toward the yellow tape.

Christina grabbed me by the arm. "My God. I almost forgot!"

"What's that?"

"Happy Birthday, Big Brother. You're thirty-eight."

SEVENTY-ONE

The noon sky had an unlimited horizon when the patrol car dropped me at the gate to the marina. I had my suitcase, my briefcase, and a cardboard box containing all the things I'd taken from the Starks' yard. I figured we'd soon have more evidence than we needed to convict Susan Dahoney/ Lil Stark, certainly more than a smell I'd recognized in the Alabama woods. If the district attorney needed the box, I'd turn it over. Until then, I wanted to look at it all again.

To my relief, the dock was clear. There was no movement on board Brett Tarentino's boat. I took the chance and hustled toward my slip and eased my way up the gangway to the *Nomad's Chant* and came face-to-face with Dr. Jan Hood wearing blue shorts and a white French sailor's shirt. She looked beautiful and unsure of herself.

"I came to put a note on your door," she began in a rush. "I went away for a few days and thought about it and realized I was wrong to come down so hard on you. You probably had to withhold the fact you were watching Foster."

"I did," I said. "But it doesn't matter now. Wasn't him. We got the killer. Or at least have a pretty good idea who it is."

"Who?" she asked as I came on board.

"The Bible expert who wrote that book I gave you, *The Second Woman*," I said.

"No!" Jan said. "I read that book cover to cover. It was fascinating."

"And the reason she was killing, it appears," I said. "We raided her apartment this morning. It'll be in the papers tomorrow."

There was an awkward silence. Then I said, "I never meant to harm your career."

Jan shrugged. "Foster's got bigger plans than the zoo anyway, and I think the administrators will come to their senses when they see that."

There was another uncomfortable moment, then she said, "Well, you must be busy. I probably should be going."

"Back to the zoo?"

"No, I've got a few more days of forced vacation," she said wistfully. "I was thinking of going for a swim, actually."

"It's my birthday," I said. "Thirty-eight. I was gonna have a Bloody Mary. Care to join me?"

Jan hesitated, then smiled. "It's your birthday. How can I refuse?"

I made up a pitcher of Bloody Marys and we went outside and sat on the aft deck, watching the traffic on the bay. I told her about Alabama and Lil Stark. When I finished, she sat looking amazed by the whole thing. "So she just made up Susan Dahoney?" she asked.

"Looks that way," I said. "She knew about Bibles. They'd been around her from her first words. She cooked her identity from there."

Jan sat there, sipping the Bloody Mary, then shuddered. The thing that I find the creepiest is that smell you described in the woods."

"Me too," I said. "It was shocking, maybe more so than any of what went on in the church. And yet, it's a hauntingly beautiful scent."

"Wish I could smell it," she said.

"Unfortunately I don't have any Southern Nights."

"Don't worry, I'll find it at Nordstrom one day," she said, holding out her glass. "Pour me a little bit more?"

I leaned forward to pick up the pitcher and noticed the cardboard box near the door to the *Chant*'s main deck. "You want to smell the Starks' place?" I asked.

She looked at me, puzzled. "You said you didn't have any of that cologne."

"Maybe I got something better."

I got up, reached in my pocket for my knife, then crossed to the cardboard box and cut it open. I was aware of the sea scent around me, then Jan's smell as she came closer and watched me with growing interest. I pulled out the snake box.

"That's just an older version of the transport crates we use at the zoo," she said, admiring it. "Let me smell."

She took the box from me, sniffed, and shrugged. "Smells like grass. Is that what the cologne smells like?"

"No," I said taking it from her and sniffing, then pulling my head back, puzzled and disappointed. "That's not how it smells. It was all these different odors put together in an exotic brew. But now it's like whatever held them together isn't here anymore."

"Like what?" she asked.

"Like twilight in a hot, humid place," I said, thinking. "C'mon, I've got an idea."

We went inside, through the salon, into the galley, and I put a small pot of water on the stove. Jan sipped at her drink. "What are you doing?"

"Watch." I opened the old snake box and used scissors to cut bits off the flora I'd brought from the Starks' yard. When the water boiled and steamed, I added dead and dying grass, kudzu, dried dogwood and pecan blossoms, and bark from the old pine, the magnolia, and the Osage orange tree. Then I stirred a wooden spoon through the mix.

It took less than thirty seconds of steeping before the tea threw forth its aroma. The fragrance spilled up my nose and I was back there again, in the mute ruins of Lucas Stark's tragedy, seeing the spirit catchers and the lime jungle macheted back away from the cabin like a moat, feeling the moss underfoot, hearing the cliff owls hoot at the rising moon.

"That's it," I said. "That's the smell of Southern Nights."

Jan sniffed it and her eyes became unscrewed the way they did when she got horny. "Pretty," she said.

"Not half as pretty as you."

At that she grinned, set her drink down, took a step toward me, and pressed her body ever so slightly against mine. "How much did you miss me?" she whispered hoarsely.

My breath trembled. "More than my soul."

That seemed to please her a great deal, because she made this clicking noise in her throat, then began to kiss me along my jaw-line toward my left ear.

"I believe in birthday presents," she murmured. "My gift to you, Seamus Moynihan, is the sexual experience of your life."

Before I could take her in my arms, she broke away, crossed to the deck hatch, and locked it. She lowered the blind, then looked back at me, easing her sailor's shirt over her head and dropping it on the floor. She teased her thumbs in her belt before shucking off her shorts. "C'mere, birthday boy," she called, crooking a finger at me and then patting the tabletop. I grinned and came toward her slowly, pulling off my shirt.

She kept her hands clasped behind her back and twisted and arched toward me as I approached. Her tongue darted out and licked my nipples, one and then the other. It was one of the most strangely erotic things any woman has ever done to me, and I felt myself get hard.

Jan trailed her tongue down the centerline of my belly, then toyed along the waist of my pants. She drew them to my ankles, then pressed me back against the table. She got down on her knees and began gently brushing the inside of my thighs with her breath and her tongue. She made lazy circles, higher and higher, then suddenly stopped.

"Why don't you go downstairs?" she said. "I'll bring us some drinks."

"Okay," I croaked.

She came down the stairs nude carrying two fresh Bloody Marys, smiled at me lying there on the bed, then set the tumblers down on the end table and drew the curtains on the portholes until the light was filtered. She took a gulp of her drink, then handed me mine.

I drank and it tasted bitter. For a second I thought about spitting it out; then it numbed a bit, and I felt a rush like caffeine before coming wide, wide awake, hyperaware.

"Boy, that tastes different," I said, swallowing.

"That's my present," she said, taking another draw off her drink. "I added a little something to our drinks."

"What?" I demanded.

"Calm down, silly," she said, moving her body alongside mine. "It's extract of the distilled sap of a root only the natives of the upper Amazon know how to find. Tomás gave it to me. It's the ultimate aphrodisiac—heightens your senses of pleasure, keeps you hard for hours."

Before I could say another word, she rolled over on top of me and began to move. "Feel good?" she asked.

"Incredible," I said.

"Only gonna get better," she said, then she paused, reached between her legs, guided me far backward, then sank herself on me with a moan. With her whole body she made gentle slick spiral gyrations that swept me toward nothingness.

When Jan felt me swell, she grabbed me by the shoulders and lowered her face into mine. "This how you like it?" she demanded. Her eyes were crazy with lust and something else I couldn't place. But it didn't matter. She was giving me the fuck of my life and nothing else mattered.

"God, yes!" I groaned as it all became too much. I grabbed her cheeks and erupted into her. Jan slowed her movements, eased herself out of the squat onto her knees, and kissed me along my hairline while I panted, aware we'd broken some kind of taboo, but also aware of how mind-blowingly good it had felt.

"So good," she murmured. "So, so good to me. What shall we do next?"

"Mmmmmm," I said closing my eyes and letting my fingers trail along the small of her back. "Maybe just a nap. Then Jimmy, dinner, and I'll be ready for you again."

She ran her finger along my lower lip. "We're just getting started, birthday boy."

"You're insatiable," I said.

"Yes," she said. "I am."

Jan rolled off me and lay on her back and pulled my head onto her breasts. I went to sleep to the rhythm of her breathing like a drunk man stepping off a cliff, plunging into darkness and not understanding quite why.

SEVENTY-TWO

The *nomad's chant* swayed side to side as if God's own hand were rocking it, and, lying there, ascending toward consciousness, I thought a storm must have come up off Baja. I heard random barking, but not of dogs. Then I realized I was ill. Very ill. My gums felt raw. My stomach was sour. My head rang. And my face felt flushed and clammy. I went to bring my hand down from behind my head to wipe the sweat off my upper lip, but couldn't.

I opened my eyes, looking around wildly. There were lit candles all over the stateroom. The porthole curtains were drawn back. It was dark outside. The moon, just past full, was high in the east. The clock on the nightstand read twenty past midnight. Quarter-inch white cord wrapped my wrists and ankles and stretched out through eye bolts anchored at the four corners of my bed's head and footboards.

"Feeling right with the Lord?" a deep, velvety southern voice asked.

Waves of horror and disbelief passed through me as my eyes darted to the bathroom door. Jan stood there in a one-piece sheer black body suit. Her eyes were now a shocking emerald blue. She held one of the zoo's shift boxes under her left arm. I began to wrench against the lashes. The cord bit into my wrists and ankles. But there was no give at any of the four anchors, and I stopped struggling and lay there panting, feeling like I might vomit. This is a bad dream," I moaned.

She eased up next to me, loose-jointed like the snake handlers I'd seen in Hattiesburg. "This is no dream, Seamus Moynihan." Then she yanked on my scrotum.

"Awww!" I yelled. "That hurts. Don't do that!"

Her jaw set. Her fingers dug in around my balls and she yanked harder. I screamed. "Don't, please, Jan! Lil!"

She let me go, grinned, and rolled her head and shoulders. "So you know me now. You and I are gonna have fun before you die. Or at least I am."

For a second, as the dull ache in my groin became less nauseating, she seemed so thrilled at the thought of the fun to come that I became paralyzed with fear. Then thoughts blitzed through my mind: Jan Hood was Lil Stark. How was this possible? And then all these loose strings tied themselves together in my mind. She had worn colored contacts. She dyed her hair. She shaved her mons so we never found her pubic hair on the victims. And she was so gorgeous and sexual that no man in his right mind would have turned her down. Certainly not Sprouls, not Haines, not Cook, not me.

But where was I? How long had I been here? Did anybody see us leave the marina? What drug had she given me? Strychnine? Where was my gun? How was I going to get free of the restraints? What were my strengths? What were hers?

The implications and riddles of my predicament kept rippling and colliding, creating a chaotic din. Then I thought of Jimmy losing me as I had lost my father at age ten. I would not do that to him. My survival was paramount. I forced myself to calm down, to see not my lover standing there, but my enemy.

I took in my room again, trying to locate possible weapons should I get free. At first glance, there was nothing but the things that had always been there: my books, my stereo, the drawers where I kept my clothes. Then, on the shelf, I noticed my portable drill, covered in fresh shavings. Beside it: my cell phone and the Bloody Mary tumblers.

None of this mattered. Lil Stark had me well bound. No obvious possibility of escape. Until I could get free, as much as I wanted to struggle, I told myself to do the exact opposite. I had to reserve my energies. Time seemed my only ally. My next thought was that I had other weapons: words and information. I knew more about Lil Stark and her motivations than her other victims. Maybe I could use her past against her.

"It must have been funny, watching us go after all those suspects, and you right under my nose," I said.

She got off the bed. "I like having power over men, if that's what you mean. Jan, on the other hand, wanted you to catch the killer. Especially if it was Foster."

"You talk about her like she's another person."

"Another person? No," she replied, setting the snake box on the shelf next to the drill. "More like another skin. Or the color of a chameleon against a green leaf in a mottled light. Or think of Jan as a daydream I had one day, a daydream that took years to imagine and grow into being, like a tree before it bears fruit. Jan doesn't even admit to herself that I'm here anymore. When I take over, she tells herself she's fantasizing about a side of her she keeps deeply submerged. The naughty side."

"But you come out to kill when you smell your yard from childhood," I said.

"I didn't even know that's what made me so angry until you told me," Lil said, reaching over casually and flicking open the latch that held the snake box lid shut.

Every nerve in my body shouted at me to struggle, to flail at the lashes that held me. My stomach kept turning over, threatening to erupt. But I could see nothing physical I could do that would help matters. I had to reserve strength, keep her talking, give myself time. How long ago had she sailed us out here? Someone must have noticed the *Nomad's Chant* leaving the harbor with her at the helm.

"When did you daydream Jan first?" I asked, trying to keep the conversation going. "When you ran through the kudzu jungle toward the Tennessee state line?"

"Oh, long before that," she replied. "By the time I crawled out of that hole and headed toward Miami, I was living Jan's dreams. She was like a baby with no diapers. I gave her everything: the brain, the looks, the ambition. I got her into college and drove her to succeed. Jan's got a Ph.D., publishes in prestigious journals, talks at international conferences. Been on television."

She was smiling at that thought.

"But you needed documents to get a new identity started, to get a job, to go to school, to even get a driver's license or a place to live," I said. "How'd you do it?"

She snorted at me like I was a fool. "What money can't get, my body can."

"You were a prostitute."

"I was a whore," Lil replied coldly. "A whore for discriminating men of means interested in sexual adventure."

The index finger of her left hand found the seam of the snake box lid and eased it open. I tried not to react. "What kind of adventure?"

Lil hesitated, seeing things that tightened the skin on her face. "Whatever they could come up with," she said. "I never turned down a request."

"And how does Jan feel about that?"

"Jan doesn't know," she snapped, suddenly agitated. "Jan will never know. Jan lived a perfect life of achievement and respect."

"Was I part of that life?"

She looked at me with irony. "Your cock was, Moynihan. I liked its shape. Jan doesn't actually like to fuck. I just need to blow off steam now and then."

The box creaked when she opened it. She reached down inside without looking and came up with a rattler much bigger than any of the ones her brother, Caleb Stark Carruthers, had handled. The snake was as stout as the barrel of a bat, more than six feet long, blue-black along his spine, with ivory scales the size of fingernails set out in diamond formations all along his body. His head was big as my fist, shaped like the ace of spades, prehistoric in its construction.

"Say hello to Judgment," Lil said. She spit between his eyes, which turned him furious. Every muscle in his body flexed and popped. He rattled, then articulated spirally in her hand. "He's all-seeing. Never lies."

It was involuntary. I saw that snake coming at me, its jaws wide, fangs glistening, and I began to squirm and pull against the lashes, to jerk and flail, then squeeze with my abdomen and lower back to somehow yank the eyebolts free of their anchors. All I needed was one limb free. But nothing budged.

Her expression changed as if she were collapsing into another time and another place. She came swiftly around the bed and held the snake out over my arm.

"Joy unspeakable to be holding death in your hands."

The snake hovered there. I tried to breathe deep in hope of slowing the pulse of whatever magnetic waves of alarm I was giving off. But she spit on Judgment's head again and it was like watching the mechanism of a crisp trigger fire a weapon. One instant the snake's head was pulled back and up in a question mark curve. The next he had sunk his sharp teeth into the hollow of my elbow, driven venom through his ducts, and withdrawn. I tried to wrench away my arm, burning already, but couldn't.

"You're not right with the Lord, are you, Seamus Moynihan?" Lil said.

I howled with pain, then shouted at her, "You'll never get away with this. They'll chase you down to the ends of the earth for killing a cop."

She laughed. "Chase me down? I don't think so. I've had bloodhounds on my trail for days and beat 'em. You were after me a solid month and I was right there the whole time. Now, I know what you're thinking: Tarentino or someone will report you missing. But I saw him on the dock, just before I left, and told him that you were asleep and I was surprising you with a romantic cruise for your birthday. No one's expecting any word of you for at least another twenty-four hours. By that time I'll be finished with you and long gone into another identity."

Fire spread around the wound. Two trickles of blood mixed with venom seeped down my forearm.

"Now it's all a question of how strong your heart is," she said matter-of-factly. "Sooner or later it'll break. They always do, goin' before Judgment."

I felt a dread like no other. My pulse drummed above my Adam's apple and in my ears. She must have sensed it, for her nostrils suddenly flared. Her shiny black pupils got bigger in the liquid turquoise of her irises. She came around the bed and eased the snake back into the box, her eyes never leaving mine.

"Feeling 'em crawling through you?" she asked. "I always thought of venom like an army of fire ants marching through your tunnels, asking every cell if God was on your side. What do you think?"

Stay cool, I told myself. *She wants you to panic. Fear produces adrenaline. Adrenaline will speed the spread of the venom.*

From everything I'd read about diamondback rattlesnake bite, I knew it wasn't as devastating an attack as what Rikko had gone through with the tai-pan. It depended on the victim. Some died within hours. Others held on for days. I needed twenty-four hours at least.

"Not answering, huh?" she asked, grinning slyly. "Trying to fight it? That's good, Seamus. Go ahead. The Lord is in a bite that does not kill."

Suddenly my cell phone on the shelf rang and we both startled and looked at it. The ringing sounded five more times, then stopped. "They're looking for me," I said. "Very few people know that number, and almost all of them are cops."

She shrugged and moved toward the stateroom door.

"Where are you going?" I demanded through gritted teeth.

Lil looked at me with amusement. "To work on the new me, of course."

The door slammed shut behind her and I was left with Judgment. To keep the venom from spreading, I began taking slow, deliberate breaths, my eyes half open, trying to reduce the speed of everything, my lungs, my heart, my thoughts. Then, without warning, my head spun and pounded as if I'd drunk a half bottle of whiskey. I tasted aluminum, leaned my head left, and vomited off the side of the bed.

When the retching had stopped, I heard the barking outside the porthole again, listened closely, and realized it was coming from seals. We had to be on the outer Coronado Islands, at the cove of the elephant seals. Then everything started to spin. My last thought before I passed out was that I was only sixteen nautical miles from home.

SEVENTY-THREE

I felt a stabbing in my left arm. Then I began to come to, feeling less nauseated, with more energy. My eyes half opened and I saw Lil had used one of my ties as a tourniquet around my left biceps, which looked darkly bruised. A hypodermic needle sat on the bedstead next to one of the vials of antivenin Walter had given me. She must have found it in my luggage. The needle still had a few cc of the liquid and bubbles of air in it.

The moon was coming in through the opposite porthole. The alarm clock read three-forty-five A.M. Lil sat cross-legged between my spread legs at the foot of the bed, watching me. She had dyed her hair a flaxen blond, cut it closer to her scalp, and moussed and teased it up. Her lipstick was different, darker. And mascara and eyeliner had been applied generously. If she walked down the street, I never would have recognized her as Jan.

"Feeling better?" she asked. "You puked a bunch. Pain to clean up, but I couldn't stand the smell."

"Need water," I croaked.

"Course you do," she said agreeably, unfolding herself and getting off the bed. She took the Bloody Mary glass off the shelf and walked to the head. "You must have been very weakened by your visit to my hometown, Seamus. You almost died on the first bite, not putting up much of a fight at all. I guess I expected more of you than the others. I think I deserve more, don't you?"

Terrible understanding razored through me. She had shot me up with antivenin just so she could prolong my torture. But I didn't care, because with every moment I was feeling stronger, more alert. She brought the water out, then held it six inches above my face and dribbled it around, but not in, my mouth, so that I had to use my tongue to find the moisture.

"That's it," she taunted. "Work for it."

I did just that. I was in survival mode now. Nothing else mattered. When she'd finished pouring the water on me, she turned and moved around the bed, back toward Judgment's box. I wanted her to stay away from him as long as possible. So I took a chance on a suspicion I had developed, based on the description of how Nelson Carruthers had found her in her bedroom closet with her brother, Caleb.

"Where were you hiding when your father tortured your mother to death?" I asked. "Were you in the closet, Lil? The closet in your parents' room, watching your father rape your mother as she died?"

She stopped and stared at me as if no one else had ever known that about her. Then she whipped the glass at my head. It missed, but shattered against the wall to my right, shards landing all around me. "You shut up about all of that now," she said, in a voice that reminded me of Carruthers.

"You saw it, didn't you?" I asked. "You watched your father releasing the snakes on your mother. You watched him fuck her while she battled against the venom. And you, a little ten-year-old girl, had to save your defenseless brother, Caleb, from that nightmare. I saw him just the day before yesterday, your brother. He's alive because of you, Lil."

Lil took two quick steps, then backhanded me across the mouth. Blood spurted from my lips. She got down right in my face, breathing hatred. "Shut up about Caleb and all of that, or I'll bring Judgment out right now."

I gambled again, trying to push her over the edge, trying to get her to make a mistake. "That's what this is all about, isn't it? You going through the same ritual as your father did with your mother? Getting even with him and every other guy you had to fuck to create Jan."

Lil grabbed a handful of chest hair and tore it out of me. I bucked at the pain.

"Keep it up," she snarled. "You don't know what you're dealing with."

"Sure I do," I replied shakily. "Pussing anger and horror and your warped way of dealing with it. Because deep down you don't understand it—why your father, your own father, would lay snakes on his wife, then mutilate himself. Do you?"

She reached back her hand and I was sure she would strike me again. But she hesitated, then her attack posture slackened, her eyes glazed over, and her hand slowly fell. She was back in that room again. "Oh, I know," Lil murmured. "I know what haunted my dad and my stepdad their whole lives."

"You do, don't you?" I said. "Why'd he do it? Was your mom having an affair?"

Lil twisted her head from side to side, still seeing the terror play in her head. "The affair had ended years earlier, long before she and Daddy were married in the church, sticking it right in God's face."

"Sticking what in God's face?" I asked. "What did your father tell Carruthers? Why did you burn down half the town to get rid of all traces of yourself?"

Lil continued to stare off into space with that glazed expression, lingering over scenes only she could see. Then her skin tautened and her eyes widened in dismay that gave way to rage. "You think you have some right to the truth?"

"It's my judgment day, isn't it?"

Lil grimaced, but she nodded. "You're right."

Then she got the snake box off the shelf and set it down right next to my head. "The truth is that my parents were damned to hell. And me and Caleb with them. That's what my dad told Carruthers."

"Why?" I demanded. "Why were they damned, Lil?"

She smiled ironically through her anger; then, to my surprise, she climbed back on top of me. She put her hands on the round of my shoulders, then spread her legs wide, and I saw that the bodysuit was slit at the crotch. She rubbed her naked, hairless sex against mine, and to my disgust I felt myself stir.

Lil's laugh at my response was acidic. "They were damned for the same reason you are, Seamus," she said. "Damned because they loved doing this. Damned because they loved their bodies more than their souls."

An involuntary shudder passed through me. "What are you talking about?"

"It was all there in that woman Dahoney's book, *The Second Woman*," she replied. "What did she call it—the oldest unsolved mystery? Let me tell you something: My parents knew the solution to that puzzle all along."

"Cain's wife?" I said, bewildered. "What does that have to do with your mother and father?"

"Everything," Lil said, sitting upright on me like a cobra before it spits. "The Bible says Cain killed Abel because he was jealous that his brother held God's favor. But Pa knew better. So did Ma. And Carruthers. And I do too."

I flashed on the fact that Lucas Stark had killed his brother, Caleb, during an argument no one understood, then saw a connection. "Your father and his brother both loved the same woman as young men," I said. "The affair Ada Mae had all those years ago was with your uncle Caleb. That's what caused the fight."

Lil shook her head scornfully. "It's much, much worse than that. C'mon, I know you can figure it out. Big detective like you? Didn't you read Dahoney's book?"

I ignored the look of superiority she was giving me and churned the facts again and again, but I still could not make them organize and cohere in another way.

"What did your father tell Carruthers?" I demanded.

Lil leaned over me and whispered: "I don't know exactly, but I know what he should have told him. Pa should have said that the second oldest story in the Bible had been written down wrong. Cain killed Abel, not because he felt slighted by God, but because he found out that he and his brother both loved fucking the second woman: Adam and Eve's daughter, their own sister."

For a heartbeat I felt suspended in a darkness worse than any I'd ever imagined. Then my mind reeled with the implications of it all. Lucas Stark stabbing himself in the crotch. His bitter rage against God for giving him a retarded son. And then Carlton Lee's description of Ada Mae entering the Church of Jesus, New Tongues Singing for the first time, naked beneath her dress. And Lucas calling down to her from the altar: *Are you right with the Lord, Sister?* And Ada Mae answering: *No, Brother, but I want to be.*

"They were speaking literally," I mumbled in revulsion, then startled as Lil popped open the lid to Judgment's cage, reached in, and pulled the beast out.

"Know what my stepdad used to say my name means?" she asked stonily, letting the snake course its body across her breasts. "Lilith?"

"No," I admitted, watching Judgment's head pass out across her open palm and turn toward me.

"He said Lilith is the child of incest, the incubus, the sexual demon born of her parents' sin," she said, the fury building once again in her voice.

With that, she got herself off me and wiggled backward until she knelt between my splayed knees. Her teeth grinded. "Gonna be right with the Lord this time?"

"Don't do this, Lil," I said, squirming at the sight of Judgment's tongue flickering in the air, inches from my shriveling penis.

She laid the snake on the sheets between my legs, then gazed up at me with a look of loathing. "I'm a demon aroused by smells in the night. What else would I do?"

I stared bullets at the snake, twisting my hips left to get away from him. Lil leaned forward and spit down on the serpent's head. Judgment yanked sideways and back, then whipped forward and bit me in the balls. It was like taking a punch there, followed by razors cutting and a blowtorch flaring.

I screamed and Lil smiled grimly. "Don't take it so hard, Seamus," she said. "My mother didn't pass God's test there, either."

While I bellowed in agony, she returned Judgment to the box. "Only a couple of hours until dawn, now," she said. "Soon you'll begin to fall back into the venom. Before long, it will take away all sense of who you are for a while before you die and are reborn. Then your real judgment will begin."

"They'll judge you too," I gasped. "Don't you care?"

"Why should I? I already know where I'm going when I leave this life. That was decided even before I got here."

SEVENTY-FOUR

Whoever said time slows when you are dying had it backward. The things that mattered came clattering at me from all sides, a circular bombardment of thoughts and feelings: the satisfied look on Lil Stark's face as the door shut; the lava sensation in my testicles; the racing of my heart; the sudden shortness of my breath; the odd spots that appeared before my eyes, burst, and became Jimmy on the mound; my sister wishing me happy birthday; Fay telling me she was marrying Walter; my mother crying; then each of them bursting again, leaving ragged patterns of black, like ink blotted over my memory.

Between four and five that morning I struggled for air and fought against the darkness. Gradually, Jimmy's face returned, and I kept it there like a lifeline in a night sea. I could not die. Not now. I coughed and spit up phlegm, trying not to panic at the memories of Cook's autopsy and the understanding that the venom would take me as it had taken him, Sprouls, Haines, Car-ruthers, and Ada Mae Stark: by drowning.

Chills oscillated through me. I gazed all around, feeling like a man trapped in a flooding cave, mad with the desire to be free of his confinement. I rocked my head left and then right, fighting to stay clear of the darkness that threatened again.

Then, out of my peripheral vision, I saw the shard of glass, a curved jagged piece about two inches long that looked like a mini-saber. When Lil shattered the Bloody Mary tumbler against the wall, the shard had landed on the corner of the mattress between my head and my right hand. It was big and sharp enough to cut me free.

If only I could get hold of it.

I strained to turn my head more, then focused what remained of my alertness on the shard. I tried to angle my hand this way and that to reach it, but couldn't; the jagged piece was at least three inches from my outstretched thumb.

"Damn it!" I whispered, then stopped straining, raised my head, and slammed it back against the mattress in frustration.

The piece of glass hopped into the air and landed closer to my hand. I blinked, then raised my head again and slammed it back down. The glass jumped a second time, landing on the lip of a gap that separated the headboard from the mattress. It teetered there, ready to spill over and take my hopes of survival with it.

I had no choice. I had to try. I looked up toward the ceiling and did something I hadn't done since before my father died: I prayed. For real.

"I am not a perfect man, God. I know that," I began. "But I'm not an evil one, either, and I need your help right now."

Then I gazed at the shard one last time, raised my head, and slammed it down sideways. The piece of glass bounced up, glanced off the headboard, then arced to the right and disappeared on the other side of my hand.

For a moment I lay there suspended, caught in the not-knowing, waiting to hear the glass strike the bedstead or land on the floor. But I heard no sound save the hum in my breath. I strained upward again, arching, looking, and finding the piece of glass there on the long edge of the mattress, just to the right of my pinkie.

I eased myself back down, feeling soddenness in the bottom of my lungs, as if a wet towel had been pushed in there. The venom was on me again. I glanced at the door, trying to hear above the rush of blood at my temples, trying to hear if Lil had heard my thrashing and was coming.

Nothing. I stretched my hand as wide as it would go, then arched it backward. My pinkie struck the shard's razor edge and was cut. A droplet of blood formed. I ignored it and reached again. Slowly, over the course of perhaps a minute, I prodded the piece of glass until it lay below my ring and index fingers. Then I got it between my knuckles, elated, possessed by something beyond myself.

Shaking now, babbling silent words of direction and encouragement, I maneuvered the shard between my fingertips, then bent my hand toward my wrist and the rope that held me. The tip of the shard caught the topmost loop of the cord, and I sawed at it. A fray appeared on the surface of the thin rope. And then another.

I worked at my bonds for nearly fifteen minutes. All that time, the venom worked on me. Blood trickled from my pinkie onto the cord, changing it from white to rust. But even the staining could not hide the fact that the frays were becoming a cut, and before long the binding was half parted. My forearm and bloody, sweated hand cramped from the effort. I eased the tension on the blade and let it come away from the cord.

The venom swelled hard on me right then, like a rogue wave breaking over the reef of my sternum, gathering speed, weight, and height. I swooned. My vision turned hazy and yellow. The room spun. I retched again. I looked over at the bedstead to my left, at the hypodermic needle and the half-empty vial of antivenin. I needed it. Now.

My cell phone began to ring again.

I startled and stared at it on the shelf, ten feet from my reach. It rang again, and a third time. Lil came banging down the gangway. I fumbled with the shard, trying to hide it the way a magician might a coin from an audience.

She threw open the door as the phone rang a fifth time and then stopped. We both watched the silent phone and I prayed she wouldn't look at my hand. A half inch of the blade, including the keen tip, was still visible between my middle and index finger, but only if you looked closely.

She gave the phone one last glance, then hurried toward the snake box. She had changed again. Gone was the sheer, crotchless bodysuit, replaced now by her open-water swim gear. She held a green apple in her hand.

"They're going to catch you," I rasped. "They're gonna put you in the chamber."

"No they won't," she said. "You'll be gone in a matter of minutes. You're already laboring hard. 'Fighting the fire,' as my daddy used to say. Wrestling with death, there, aren't you, lover?"

"I'm not your lover," I said, hearing the slur in my voice and telling myself to keep her talking, keep her away from the box. "It was just sex."

"But it was the best you ever had, wasn't it?" she said. "I bet somewhere in the back of your mind, you thought Jan was your salvation. Pretty, smart, unbelievable fuck. But that doesn't matter now, does it? You got other things to think about. And so do I."

"Going for a swim?" I asked, thrusting my chin at the suit.

She looked at me, tossing and catching the apple. "Soon enough. After Judgment renders his verdict, I'll head up the coast and hug the beach somewhere between La Jolla and Del Mar, then I'll turn the bow out to sea and hit the throttle. I'll jump into the waves and be washed away forever. They'll find the boat and your body in a week or so."

"You can't erase your past, Lil," I said. "You're a prisoner of it—always have been, always will be."

"You got it wrong. Your past is something you can crawl out of. I know. I've done it once. I can do it again."

"You may shed your skin, but it'll always be there in your soul," I countered. "That's what happened to Carruthers. It ate at him that he had to kill your father. You're going to feel that same self-inflicted torture. Every late April, the terror of your parents' bedroom is gonna come back no matter what you do, whether Southern Nights cologne is there to bring you out of hibernation or not. The curse your Uncle Caleb left on your family will always be there to chew on your insides. What your father was. What your mother was. What you have become. None of this'll help you get away from that."

"You shut up," she said, flustered, and she came alongside of me and crammed the apple in my mouth. I spit out the chunks even as I began to pull at the rope binding my right wrist. At the same time, at some level I knew I should keep quiet now, but I could feel the venom surging through me, accelerating my heart rate, and I imagine it was like speaking in tongues; I began to spout off whatever erupted in my mind.

"What's the matter, Lil?" I asked. "Feeling something there in your heart? Maybe like you did when you were a girl? So ashamed of what your parents were that you burned down the courthouse? So ashamed of what was running through your blood

that you ran and spent a whole life inventing someone else?"

"Shut up!" she ordered, then held the snake box
toward me. "Had enough of you."

The phone began to ring a third time, ring after
ring after ring, ten in all.

Meanwhile, I was tugging so hard on my right
arm, I thought my shoulder might dislocate. The
whole time I kept babbling at her: "What did you
call yourself back then before you left Hattiesburg?
Not Jan. Not Lil. How about an abomination? A sin
against God? That what old man Carruthers called
you? What'd it make you feel like back then? What'd
it make you feel like when the boys jeered at you
after you had sex with them?"

At that, Lil began to shake with unbridled rage.
"You shut up!" she shouted. "You're the one's facing
his sins right now!"

She drew Judgment from the box, and I
flashed on the fact that all four of the previous
victims had ultimately died from their third bite,
the one administered at the throat. Solomon
had said rattlesnake venom entering the carotid
arteries would go directly to the brain, death to
swiftly ensue.

As Lil came at me, the room went concentric and
spun, and I felt like I was falling into a whirlpool.
Judgment rattled in the glimmering depths of the
vortex. Lil's hand came free of the snake and she
picked up my limp, blackened penis and laughed
bitterly, even as she spit down on Judgment's head.

His casket mouth came open with a hiss, revealing its tufted white lining.

I jerked away and, with every last ounce of my strength, yanked and pulled at the partially cut cord. Lil did not notice. She moved the enraged snake toward my neck with the same sort of entranced, vacant look she displayed when approaching orgasm.

"Right with the Lord this time, Seamus?" she asked.

Judgment struck. With a loud snap, the cord that held my right wrist broke. My hand came whistling forward, the cord whining and unwinding through the eye hook that had held me to the headboard.

Before his fangs could reach my neck, I slapped him across the throat with the shard, slicing it wide open.

The snake went spastic, flailing and bucking in Lil's hands, gouts of his blood spraying over all of us. The serpent whipped backward. His head found Lil's forearm and his jaws clamped reflexively. She screeched and tried to fling the viper from her. It held tight. She spun and beat the snake against the wall of my stateroom, but it clung to her like a snapping turtle, the muscles in its cheeks flexing, delivering a final liquid decree.

I reached over with my free right hand and, in a gathering venom fog, hacked at the cord that held my left wrist, desperate to get the antivenin on the table. The cord cut through. I dropped the shard and reached for the vial just as Judgment bled out, went limp, and dropped from Lil's arm.

I got the vial in my hand, then inserted the needle and drew the liquid, bubbled with air, into the syringe. Lil was bent over the dead snake, spattered with its blood, sweating, panting, examining the wounds to her arm. She turned toward me. Her eyes were half up in their sockets, her lips pulled back to show her teeth. She saw my intention as I popped the needle free of the antivenin vial, then attempted to clear the air bubbles from the syringe's barrel. She looked around insanely, then plucked the portable drill off the shelf and went after my legs with it.

I dropped the needle, threw myself toward her in a diagonal sit-up, my feet still bound to the footboard, and slashed at her with my open hands, trying to grab the drill. But she nimbly dodged out of my reach, triggered the device, and set the whirling bit to my ankle with a sound that reminded me of her brother singing.

The pain was beyond excruciating, a stunning, searing vibration that seemed to amplify through my body until I was convulsing head to toe. She stopped about an inch into my fibula, then backed out the bit. I flopped, gasping, moaning, unable to truly comprehend what had been done to me. My left hand fell on the hypodermic needle.

Then I was aware of Lil sitting on me, grinning at the drill now six inches above my sternum. "I'm gonna fuck with your heart," she said.

"Not before I do," I grunted, coming up and over with the syringe, driving it between her third and fourth rib, deep into her chest.

A sound like the plumping of a pillow spilled from Lil's lips. She peered stupidly down at the needle and the trickle of bright blood showing under it. For a second you could tell she thought she was going to be okay, that it was only a pinprick, nothing more than a nuisance, really.

She triggered the drill alive and smiled that depraved smile at me again. I gazed into her mad eyes, strangely calm and outside myself as she moved the whirling bit toward my flesh again. But everything in my being was concentrated on my thumb settling on the plunger of the syringe, then pressing the antivenin and all the air bubbles through the needle directly into the blood vessels that led to her brain.

One moment Lil was preparing to press the drill into my chest, and in the next the language of her shoulders, neck, and head stammered. The drill stopped spinning, dropped from her hands, and fell to the mattress and then to the floor.

The veins about Lil's temples and out across her forehead bulged hideously; then one toward the center seemed to pop. A ragged purple welt appeared. Her mouth voiced silent words of hatred at me even as her eyes bugged, then went flat, dull, and vacant.

Her entire carriage collapsed into itself like a dynamited skyscraper. Then she fell over onto me, her slack lips trailing over my own before she crashed off the bed.

SEVENTY-FIVE

I laid there, barely breathing, shaking as if afflicted with Parkinson's, my mind feeling scalded. Dawn came with the roaring and barking of elephant seals out my porthole window.

Got to get free, I told myself. *Got to get the needle out of her and shoot myself with the last of the antivenin, then get to the cell phone or my radio and call the Coast Guard.* Blood and bits of bone flowed out of my splintered right ankle, and I knew I was going to die soon if I didn't act. With my last bit of energy, I willed myself upright and untied the cord that had held my left wrist and cinched it around my calf as a tourniquet.

Then I reached toward the knot in the cord above the grisly hole in my ankle, but never made it. I swooned and fell backward, overpowered by the venom and shock of all that had been done to me. Ragged black spots appeared before my eyes. Within seconds, the blotches had blackened all memory of who I was and what I had been. All that was left of me were these terrifying blips of the now: the sound of air bubbling in my lungs; the sweat beading and rolling on my blackening skin like rain against a night window; the pounding of blood trying to find its way past the tourniquet into my leg; and then a dim, hallucinatory awareness of the crown of a pecan tree wafting in a twilight breeze against the backdrop of chalk-colored cliffs.

Heat lightning flashed. Cicadas called in the night. And there was a smell on the breeze, an intoxicating smell that summoned images of a naked woman with no discernible features. An invisible animal rustled in the undergrowth between us, and I knew it was Death. Low, menacing clouds appeared before a crescent moon.

Lightning flashed again. The featureless naked woman waited at the edge of the cliff. Rain fell, then hail. The pattern of the hail took the shape of a tornado that struck the woman, knocking her from the cliff perch as if she were no more than empty skin.

Then the trees, the cliff, the moon in the hail, the call of the cicadas, the hoot of owls, the smell on the breeze, the ringing of a phone, the last inkling of myself, all of it was sucked up by the typhoon and blown outward, like liquid gushing through a bony, hollow canal, spraying forth into an aluminum radiance in which I saw my father waiting.

SEVENTY-SIX

"**D**ad?"

I looked back over my shoulder and saw Jimmy. He was hanging out the front window of Fay's Range Rover, which was parked on the south side of Broadway, across from the county courthouse in downtown San Diego. The traffic at nine A.M. was bumper to bumper. He looked worried. My ex's expression was more complex and disturbing.

"Why the long faces?" I asked.

"Want me to go with you?" Jimmy offered. "I could skip school."

"No, Jimbo. This is something I have to do alone. Don't worry. I'll be okay."

"See you tonight?"

"Six o'clock, right?" I asked Fay.

She nodded awkwardly. "My flight leaves at seven-thirty."

I did my best to smile. "Six, then."

"We'll go fishing?" Jimmy asked.

"We'll go fishing," I promised.

"And play catch?"

"And play catch."

Fay waved, and my hand came weakly off the crutch in return. Then I heard the beeping of the crosswalk signal, turned from them, and swung the soft walking cast that encased my right ankle out over the curb.

It was a beautiful August morning, with a sky like a deep blue sea and dry air shimmering in the low eighties. Despite the fact that my ex-wife was leaving that night to marry Walter in Las Vegas, I was feeling physically okay. I was tanned, rested, and prepared. But for the limp, the crutches, the livid depression in my ankle, and the fang scars on my arm and scrotum, you'd swear as I made my way across the intersection toward the courthouse that I hadn't been cored out by a drill bit or bitten twice by a rattlesnake. As I reached the other side of the busy city street and made for the entrance at the courthouse, I made my daily thanks to God for the miracle of my survival.

It turned out that shortly after midnight, May third, while I lay groggy and ill from the strychnine and the Amazon plant concoction Lil had put in my Bloody Mary, a Wyoming state trooper who had seen our bulletin came upon Susan Dahoney's car and U-Haul trailer parked outside a motel off Interstate 80. Over her vehement protests, he placed her in custody, impounded her vehicle, and brought her into the barracks at Wamsutter.

There she continued to proclaim her innocence, saying she'd left San Diego, not because she was on the run, but because she was too embarrassed to stay once Tarentino's column came out and all the reporters she'd misled turned angry and began hounding her at home. Her publisher wasn't returning her phone calls and she was depressed and frightened, so she'd headed toward the only sanctuary she could think of—her parents' home in West Virginia.

Word of Dahoney's arrest did not reach the San Diego Police Department until nearly three A.M. Lieutenant Anna Cleary took the call and immediately notified Chief Helen Adler. Helen, in turn, tried to raise me on my cell phone. When no one answered, she called Rikko, Missy, Freddie, and Jorge and told them to get downtown to prepare to fly to Casper, Wyoming, at dawn.

It took ninety minutes for them all to reach downtown headquarters. When Rikko arrived and found out I'd not been contacted, he immediately tried to call me and got no answer. He and Missy decided to drive to the marina in case my phone was off the hook.

While they were gone, Jorge made backups to all the electronic files we'd gathered on the case so they could be brought to Wyoming for the interrogation of Susan Dahoney. While doing so, he noticed in the San Diego Homicide general E-mail box a message with two JPEG attachments addressed to me from Chief Carlton Lee of the Hattiesburg, Alabama, Police Department.

Since I had been anticipating the arrival of any correspondence from Hattiesburg, Jorge opened the message. Carlton Lee wrote that he had spoken at length with Brother Neal Elkins and the widow Carruthers. Informed of the fact that we were operating on the assumption that Lil Stark was responsible for the killings in San Diego, they admitted that the late Nelson Carruthers had told them his secret the night he died: that Lucas and Ada Mae Stark were siblings; that Lucas killed his brother Caleb out of jealousy over the fact that they were both sleeping with their sister, Ada Mae; and, finally, that Lilith and Caleb were the progeny of incest.

The two JPEG attachments turned out to be scanned photographs of Lil and Ada Mae Stark. The picture of Lil was fuzzy, taken from the side during a picnic with the Carrutherses sometime shortly after the deaths of her parents, about the time she turned eleven years old. She seemed unaware of the camera and was staring off into space.

The photograph of Ada Mae was a close-up taken shortly after she gave birth to Caleb. She was a beautiful woman with long blond hair parted in the middle and tumbling about her shoulders. Jorge said he noticed the sadness in her eyes right away.

Rikko and Missy returned, announcing that the *Nomad's Chant* was gone. They'd woken up Brett Tarentino, who told them that Jan Hood had taken me on a birthday cruise and we weren't planning on returning until late afternoon.

Missy happened to glance over at the photograph of Ada Mae Stark on Jorge's screen and got a puzzled expression on her face. "When did she go blond and grow her hair out?"

"Who?" Jorge asked.

"Her," Missy replied, pointing at the photograph. "Janice Hood."

Four Coast Guard helicopters lifted off in the predawn, split up, and began a grid search of the ocean beyond San Diego. In each chopper was a member of my team and a pair of paramedics carrying polyvalent antivenin. At a quarter to six, just about the time I lost all sense of who I was and traveled into that aluminum radiance, the helicopter in which Rikko flew came swooping in over the southernmost island of the Coronado atoll, over the *Nomad's Chant,* scaring the elephant seals and sending them splashing into the water and out to sea.

Ten minutes later I was being lifted off the deck in a rescue basket. Flying east, the paramedics shot me with several doses of antivenin and managed to stem the flow of blood from my ankle. But as the helicopter passed over the Coronado Bay Bridge, bound for UCSD medical center, my heart stopped beating. The venom had triggered a massive coronary. Rikko said he figured I was a goner.

To this day I don't know how to explain what happened. I'd heard about other people who'd had near-death experiences, but never believed them. But I swear I saw my father in that aluminum radiance. He motioned me forward and I emerged into a brilliant sunshine, squinting from far down the left-field line out onto the glinting emerald field where my last life's hopes had been exploded. It was early morning, the sprinklers were turned on. Fenway Park was empty. The Green Monster was cast in shadow.

My father took a seat, pulled off the cap he always wore to the park, and smiled. "Welcome to my heaven, Shay," he said.

He wasn't the blown-apart, charred thing in death I'd always imagined. Indeed, my dad seemed whole and content in a way I'd always associated with him after one of those rare games when the Red Sox drubbed the Yankees.

"Is it mine too?" I asked, looking around.

He shrugged. "Heaven or hell, son, it's your invention."

"I've been to hell here already, Dad," I said, gazing toward the mound.

"Bullshit. I was here that summer. Watched every game you pitched. You had heaven here. And when it ended, you became a good cop."

"Now that's over, right?" I said. "Probably a good thing. Haven't been a very good cop lately. Botched this investigation at every turn."

"Yeah, you fucked up. Pretty royally, as a matter of fact. But it's not your time. You still have a lot to do."

"But I don't know how to keep going forward," I said.

"You don't have to," he replied. "Jimmy will show you. I'll still be around. But don't expect me to be out front. You'll have to look over your shoulder to see your way."

The next thing I knew, it was two days later and I was waking up in an ICU. When my vision cleared, the first thing I saw was Jimmy sitting beside my bed with Fay. And I felt like I'd been given another chance at life.

SEVENTY-SEVEN

"**D**on't go that way," Rikko said, startling me. He had seen me crossing Broadway toward the courthouse and hurried to meet me before I could turn the corner to the main entrance. "Tarentino and the other vultures are circling. We go in the jury entrance."

He hustled me around the side of the building, through security, and up the elevator usually reserved for judges. When we reached the third floor, we got out and walked down the narrow hallway that separates the courtrooms from the judges' chambers inside San Diego Superior Court. Across from a door marked Judge Nina Allen, we took a right down a short passage and emerged beside the bench of courtroom number five.

The jury box was empty, but the public seats were packed. Brett Tarentino noticed me first. Then others did and the courtroom fell into a nervous silence. Rikko and I took seats on the aisle, first row, next to my sister. Jorge, Missy, and Freddie took up the next three seats. At the end of the row sat

Hattiesburg Police Chief Carlton Lee. I managed a smile and shook his hand.

Brett slipped up behind me. "Have you been reading my series?" he crooned.

The investigative reporter had been writing about the case ever since my rescue. In that morning's *Daily News* he took his readers to Lost Hollow, Kentucky, where he discovered the birth records of Lucas, Ada Mae, and the first Caleb. And then their family. He described the Starks of Lost Hollow as a sullen, reclusive clan, living a self-imposed banishment in an Eden of their own design: a pig farm on three hundred acres of bottomland.

Brett got several of the Starks remaining from Lucas and Ada Mae's generation to talk. They said Lucas Stark loved Ada Mae from the moment he set eyes on her. She was the second child, born four years after him. He doted on her even as a baby. When she was a toddler, he proudly pulled her in a red wagon everywhere he went. When Caleb was born, he put the baby in Ada Mae's lap and pulled the both of them around the farmyard. Until the murder, the three were virtually inseparable.

In the wake of Caleb's murder and Lucas's incarceration, they said, Ada Mae suffered a nervous breakdown. She ran away and became a hippie, "someone else," as one of her younger sisters described her. They claimed they never heard from her or Lucas again.

One of Brett's earlier articles had described how Lil Stark met her victims. He found witnesses who saw her at the Yellow Tail talking with Morgan Cook the week before he was found murdered. Zoo officials said they believed Matthew Haines must have encountered her after one of Nick Foster's shows. Airport workers said her plane to Chicago to speak at the Society of Ichthyologists and Herpetologists had been canceled about the time John Sprouls's jet from Seattle arrived. Brett speculated that Lil Stark had smelled the Southern Nights cologne on the medical equipment salesman as he waited for a shuttle to take him to his rental car, then stalked him. A sidebar noted that the national sales of Southern Nights cologne had collapsed in the wake of the story's dissemination. There were rumors the company was about to pull it from the market.

"Impressive reporting," I told him. "Fills in a lot of the blanks."

"Thanks, Moynihan," he said, then his face tightened. "Can you believe she ends up walking to the bank on this?"

I turned and followed his gaze to Susan Dahoney, who was sitting near the back on the other side of the courtroom, wearing her leather jacket, and scribbling in a notebook. Proving the old adage that bad publicity is as profitable as good, when word spread nationally that the serial killer Lil Stark had explained her father's secret to me by solving the mystery of *The Second Woman*, sales of Dahoney's book skyrocketed onto bestseller lists. The rumor was that she was in San Diego researching a chapter on the killings to be included in the paperback edition.

Her eyes flickered my way. She smiled awkwardly and I nodded. The bailiff came into the courtroom. Brett hurried back to his seat and I turned toward the bench.

"You ready?" Christina murmured.

"As I'll ever be, I suppose. You?"

She shrugged. "God took it out of our hands, didn't he?"

"He did at that."

"How's the ankle?"

"No sign of infection in almost three weeks," I said. "They say if I keep at the exercises I'll be back to work and normal in two months. But I'm not sure either of those things is going to happen."

"People heal, Shay," Christina said.

"No, Sis," I replied sadly. "If I've learned anything from this case, it's that people don't heal. They just scab over."

Before she could reply, a hush came over the room again as a marshal came in the back way, pushing a wheelchair. It was the first time I'd seen Lil Stark in person since my rescue, and despite the descriptions I'd heard of her condition, her appearance came as more than a shock.

She wore a blue prison-issue hospital gown, robe, and slippers. Her hair had grown out thick and blond like her mother's and father's. But she had lost twenty pounds. Her muscles looked flaccid, her skin pale.

Her head listed toward her left shoulder. There was a visible tremor in her right hand. Her mouth hung agape, and she showed no sign of being aware of her circumstances. But for that general slackness and lack of affect and grooming, however, she remained beautiful. It was like looking at the face of an exquisite porcelain doll that you know is cracked and destined to disintegrate, but that you can't help but admire.

The marshal pushed Lil Stark in beside Chris Whelton, her young public defender. He put his hand on her forearm, then leaned over and whispered something in Lil's ear. But she did not respond in any way. She just sat there, her eyes unfocused at some distance only she could see.

The bailiff called the court to rise. Judge Marcia Allen entered. A pixie of a woman in her early fifties with a keen intellect and a no-nonsense, sometimes imperious style, Allen banged her gavel and called the court to order.

"The State of California versus Lilith Mae Stark," the judge said. "Charged with three counts of murder in the first degree, one count each kidnapping and attempted murder. This hearing of mental competence is called to order."

I took the stand first. Both Whelton and Ruth Harris, the district attorney, peppered me with questions concerning the battle Lil Stark and I fought aboard the *Nomad's Chant*.

"What happened after you stabbed her and filled her bloodstream with air?" Whelton asked near the end of my testimony.

I glanced at her. "She fell over off the bed. I thought she was dead."

"What do the doctors say happened to her?" Whelton pressed.

"You'd have to ask them," I said. "I'm no expert."

Christina was called next. In her capacity as a neuropsychiatrist, she testified that from all the descriptions I'd been able to give her about Lil Stark's words and deeds, she believed that the pain and shame of her childhood had been great enough to allow her to create and wrap herself in a fugue state for years, a state in which she'd become Jan Hood, a functioning, contributing member of society, except when events turned sexual.

"In a way Lil Stark's method of coping was not that unusual," Christina said. "Each of us invents him or herself anew almost every day, adapting to meet the circumstances of living both present and past. For some this daily invention is an act of creativity and good. For others, like Lil Stark, I'm afraid it is a way of masking themselves from the true darkness of their beings.

"Of course, this discussion of Lil Stark's prior mental state is largely moot," she went on. "When Lieutenant Moynihan drove the needle into her chest, it passed through the intercostal area between her third and fourth rib and entered her aorta a half inch above where it leaves the heart. The antivenin and air bubbles formed an embolism that went directly from the aorta into her carotid artery and on up through the matrix of vessels into her brain.

MRI shows she suffered four or five minor strokes and one significant stroke in her frontal lobe."

"What does the frontal lobe control, Dr. Varjjan?" Whelton asked.

"Identity," she replied. "Personality."

"And whose personality and identity does she now exhibit?" the public defender pressed. "Lil Stark's or Jan Hood's?"

Christina shook her head. "Neither," she said. "Both are gone."

"Replaced by what?"

"By nothing," she replied. "Everything she was or invented for herself has been erased. She can't even follow rudimentary commands. She can't feed herself or use the bathroom unassisted. For all intents and purposes, Lil Stark is a vegetable."

Seventy-Eight

Shortly after noon, judge Allen issued her ruling: Lil Stark was unfit to stand trial and participate in her own defense. Allen ordered her moved to the prison unit at the new state psychiatric hospital north of Lone Pine in the eastern Sierras.

Within minutes of the ruling, Christina and the rest of my team returned to work. Rikko and I went down to the courthouse basement to watch the deputies move Lil Stark from her holding cell into the transfer van, a white utility vehicle with a mechanical lift on the side. It was parked tight to a column supporting the roof of the underground parking lot, about twenty yards from the elevator. Two transfer specialists from the state, both trained as prison guards and as emergency medical technicians, lounged against the side of the van, waiting.

When they wheeled Lil Stark out of the elevator, her head listed even more to the left, and I had the thought that she had at last become the person she'd always wanted to be: a person without a past, a person without a God, an exile wandering in the land of Nod.

To my dismay, that realization only served to amplify my own sense of punishment. Yes, I had been given another chance and I had forged peace with my father. But I felt also that in a way I had inherited the curse that the dying Caleb Stark had invoked upon his brother, Lucas, so many years ago. I had deleted Jan Hood and Lil Stark, backspaced both personalities like a troubling sentence on a computer screen.

I told myself that if the skin that had once held her soul had died aboard the *Nomad's Chant,* I might be able to let the wound of her scab over in my mind the way my father's death had for decades.

But alive like this, a shell of her two beings, I knew that as long as her body lived, she would be this laceration that would ulcerate and fester from time to time, most likely when it was late April and sunset after a rain and the last blossoms of flowering trees perfumed the gloaming woods.

The deputies wheeled Lil Stark toward the open side door of the van. I could barely look at her as she approached. Then she was right there, parked beside me while they adjusted the mechanical lift. One of the deputies wheeled her onto the platform. I found myself studying the slack side of her face and her useless left arm, which, like the other, was strapped to the wheelchair. Our fingers were barely an inch apart.

The transfer guard, a burly Latino named Romero, pressed a button on the side of the van and her wheelchair began to rise. I made to step back away. Lil Stark's index finger stretched out and stroked me along the back of my hand.

Then she was inside. Romero strapped the wheels to special rings mounted in the van floor. His partner, a heavyset white guy named Gunnerson, held the chair. Lil Stark exhibited that flat, slack expression and nothing more. Romero nodded, then stood. Gunnerson jumped out and made to close the door.

"Wait," I said. "She touched me."

"What?" Rikko said.

"She touched me," I insisted.

"Nah," said Romero. "I saw that. That was just a muscular twitch. Stroke victims get these involuntary spasms all the time. See?"

He clapped his hands right next to her ear, then again in front of her eyes. She showed no startle sign whatsoever. "Man, you could do anything you want to this bitch and I don't think she'd blink," Gunnerson said, leering at her.

"Got that right," Romero said.

I turned, dropped my crutches, and threw Gunnerson against the van. "One more crack like that and I'll break the both of you in two."

Rikko jumped between us. "Knock it off, Shay."

"Hey, calm down, man," Romero said from inside. "He was just joking about a bitch who tried to kill you."

"No jokes," Rikko said. "Do your job. Get her to Lone Pine. Lock her away."

Gunnerson shot me a last glare, then climbed into the cab. Romero shut the side door. They pulled away with a squeal of tires. The last I saw of Lil Stark was her listing silhouette through the tinted rear window as the parking garage's stainless-steel gate rose and they drove up the ramp into the late-afternoon sun.

EPILOGUE

Around ten that night, I put Jimmy to bed after a happy evening of fishing for bonito with our fly rods. Before he turned off the lights, he told me that he was happy Lil Stark had been put away and that he loved me. I looked at my framed jersey over the bed and saw myself in the reflection looking very much like my old man.

"I love you, too, sport," I said, then clicked off the light. "Get a good sleep."

I went up the gangway to the main deck, feeling that my father's prediction was coming true: My son would be the legend to a map I would explore and draw myself. I decided that after a certain point in everyone's life—for some, sooner, for some, later—there are no clear paths and no guides; and each of us is forced to hack our way forward into the wilderness of our remaining days, leaving cartography for the loved ones who follow us.

I got a beer from the fridge, turned on some Bob Marley, and went up on the flying deck of the *Nomad's Chant*. The night was warm and the San Diego skyline was lit up like an ocean liner bound for exotic climates. And slowly as the beer cooled the burn in my stomach and the reggae slowed the pace of my thoughts, I tried to will myself above the stark Southern California reality that always needles me in the late hours after I've toiled among the dead.

But before I could fully escape, my cell phone rang. It was Helen Adler.

"Lil Stark escaped," she said. "One of the transfer guards is dead. The other's in critical condition."

"*What!?*" I shouted. "How? Where? That's impossible."

"Not according to California Highway Patrol," she replied. "From what they've put together, those two idiot guards decided that even as a zombie she was too fine to pass up. They pulled off the highway about eighty miles south of Lone Pine and took her to a secluded spot. They untied her, undressed her, and were raping her, one in her vagina, one in her mouth, when she came out of her stupor and went berserk.

"She bit half the penis off the Latino guard, Romero. But Gunnerson got the worst of it. She got his gun, stuck it in his mouth, and blew his head off. She shot Romero in the ass as he tried to run away. They've got dogs on her. She's heading southeast toward Death Valley. It's been hitting a hundred and twenty in there. She's in slippers and a robe. She won't get far. Get your gear together. You and Rikko are going up to help in the search."

That was nearly a year ago. Despite a massive manhunt that covered more than a thousand square miles, there has not been a single sighting of Lil Stark. Many believe that she died in the hellish August heat, somewhere on the salt flats leading into Death Valley, and they expect that a winter hiker will someday find her remains.

But I live day to day with the feel of her finger trailing along the back of my hand, the smell of her body during sex, the taste of her serpent kiss, and the look of deep nothingness that lay in her eyes when she set Judgment on me.

In the files of Seamus Michael Moynihan, Lil Stark remains at large.

ACKNOWLEDGMENTS

I am indebted to many individuals who helped me in the research of this novel. Thanks first to Executive Assistant Chief Barbara Harrison of the San Diego Police Department, who graciously talked me through the intricacies of homicide crime scenes, and to retired Homicide Captain Ron Newman for teaching me the framework of death investigations. My appreciation also goes out to Sergeant Terry McManus, who helped me to understand the dynamics of detective teams and offered critiques on the manuscript. Any errors in the depiction of police procedure, however, are my own.

Thanks to Brian Blackbourne, San Diego Medical Examiner, who gave freely of his time and case reports of snakebite victims.

John Kinkaid, animal care manager with the San Diego Zoo's amazing department of herpetology, helped immensely by taking the time to instruct me in the proper handling of deadly snakes. The works of Laurence M. Klauber, the late great San Diego herpetologist and rattlesnake expert, were invaluable resources. Also of great help were *Snake Venom*

Poisoning by Findley E. Russell, *Clinical Toxicology of Animal Venoms,* edited by Jurg Meier, and *The Anatomy of Motive,* by former FBI behaviorist John Douglas.

For insight into the culture of Holiness, I relied on Dennis Covington's exceptional book *Salvation on Sand Mountain,* on Jeremy Seal's equally fascinating work, *The Snakebite Survivors' Club,* and on Thomas Burton's *Snake-Handling Believers* and Weston LaBarre's *They Shall Take Up Serpents.* Again, any misrepresentation of the intricacies of the Holiness religion are solely my responsibility.

I am likewise indebted to Jonathan Kirsch, attorney and Bible expert, for explaining to me the history of the mystery of the second woman. Thanks, too, to wilderness medicine authority Dr. Bill Robinson for coaching me through the physiological intricacies of snakebite and the anatomy of the circulatory system. And to Dr. Kenneth Olson for teaching me the theories behind fugue states.

One of the most important things a writer can have is a sounding board, a panel of peers who read and critique the work in progress. Thanks to all of you who patiently read and reread the early drafts: David Hasemyer, Wenda Morrone, Robert Rice, Damian Slattery, Matthew Sullivan, Kitty Donich, Barbara Daniels, Randle Robinson Bitnar, and Louie Rodd. Your advice was invaluable.

This narrative would not have achieved texture and form without the skillful attention and proddings of Mitchell Ivers, my editor, who seemed to understand the story better than I did. David Chesanow did a masterful job copy-editing. Thanks also to Judith Curr, Karen Mender, and Louise Burke for believing in the book when it was just an idea about the oldest mystery in the Bible.

77567474R00326

Made in the USA
San Bernardino, CA
25 May 2018